Everlasting, Us
Book One

A.J. Hughes

Asicaic Publishing

Anicale Publishing—Madison, WI
Paperback ISBN: 978-0-9998967-1-6
eBook ISBN: 978-0-9998967-6-1
Library of Congress Control Number: 2022914181
Title: Everlasting, Us
Author: A.J. Hughes
Digital distribution | 2022
Paperback | 2022

This is a work of fiction. The characters, names, incidents, places, and dialogue are products of the author's imagination, and are not to be construed as real.

Illustrations by Junior's Digital Designs

Also by A.J. Hughes

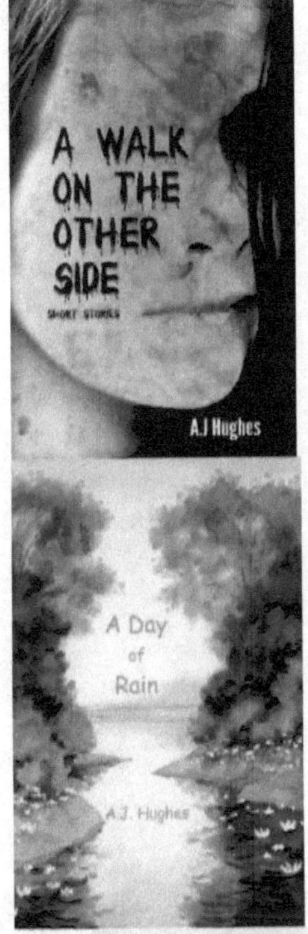

A Walk on the Other Side

Are you ready to take a walk on the other side? Be prepared for the supernatural, thrillers, fantasies, and tales of ghosts, fairies, and even death. These creepy stories are surely to die for. But not before getting weird or just weirded out.

Release Date: 01/31/2018

A Day of Rain

A Day of Rain is a collection of LGBT short stories about romance, heartbreak, loss, rejection and acceptance on rainy days and nights.

Release Date: 12/03/2020

A Life: Worth Living

Recently aged out of the foster care system, Maya moves to New York City for a new start on life. After little success, loneliness and depression, Maya decides to commit suicide when a fateful meeting with Daniel changes her outlook on life.

Release Date: 05/11/2022

Coming Soon

The Beauties and Her Beasts
The Kingdom of Encleadious

Dedication

To my mom for all her support and being my inspiration.

To my family for their support.

To my Grandma Renee, love you.

Chapter One
Lyour

The field was dark and dry. Very little light was seen through the burnt orange sky and gray clouds. The wind was strong, throwing the tall grass around the barren wasteland. The sound of galloping mixed with the sound of thunder as Jae searched his surroundings. He wanted to evade the storm as soon as possible. He didn't want Galland, his horse, to become sick. She ran nonstop for over 6 miles and her steps faltered. In the distance, Jae spotted a rundown town. No different from the others, empty and dirty.

"Another abandoned town?" Jae grumbled. "Looks like there's a place we can get shelter. Just a little more."

He whipped the reins and Galland picked up speed. Once in the town, he tied Galland to a pole for water.

"There you go," he said, petting her. Jae sat beside her.

"Well, well, well, look what we have here, a foreigner," a man said, with a heavy southern accent. A trio of bandits surrounded him. Each carried a makeshift weapon and their clothes were dirty.

"You've come to the wrong town," another bandit said.

"No, this is where I'm supposed to be," Jae said.

Jae tried to walk off before one of the bandits stopped him by moving a steel pipe to his chest. "That's a mighty nice sword ya got there. Must be expensive huh Dan?"

"Why yuhs it is Lin." Dan smirked.

"Well, how 'bout we gon head an' check't," the third said.

The bandit lunged at Jae and swung a large wooden block. Jae ducked, the wooden block missed by inches. Jae turned over his sheath and jabbed the bandit in the stomach with the end of it. He groaned and fell. Dan and Lin hesitated.

"Anyone else wanna take a spin on this 'expensive' sword?" Jae asked.

Dan growled and ran toward Jae. Jae stepped to the left and swung the sword around to hit Dan on the back of his neck and he fell to the ground. Jae looked at Lin, who stepped backwards.

"Well?" Jae said.

Lin turned around and ran away.

Jae looked down at the two bandits and sighed. "It's not as valuable as you think."

Jae stepped over the men and untied Galland's reins. "I guess it's not abandoned. I'll look around for something you can eat. Stay put until then."

Jae turned around and looked at the buildings. He spotted people peering through the boarded-up windows and doors. On the other side of the town, Jae saw an open door and decided to check it out.

The building was burgundy and designed like a tower. It was shaped like an oval. Its circumference was large and 5 stories high. There were spiral stairs that led to the backside of the third floor from the front side of the building. The building extended into smaller structures. Attached to the right side of the building and one to the backside. That room was long and attached to a home. It was the only building in the town so far, that looked nice.

As he walked through the streets, he could sense the stares from all around. He had a bad feeling but continued, making sure to not let his guard down. When he reached the doorway, he was greeted to a young woman storming out. She had mocha skin and her hair was long and curly with a rose clipped to the side. She was skinny and wore a black slim fitted dress, and black flats.

"I will not! You can't force me," the young woman shouted.

"Yes, you will," an older man said. He had grey hair, green eyes, aside from crow's feet and a few wrinkles around his mouth, he looked younger than Jae would have guessed from his quivering voice and southern accent. "If that's what he wants then it's your job to make it happen!"

"Yes, but my *job* isn't to marry anyone."

The man rushed over to her and grabbed her arm. "What you would do is delay the world's demise."

"How would marrying that creature stop the world from being destroyed? He already destroyed it."

"But the rest of us will survive."

"At the cost of my freedom."

The man paused. "Your freedom was given up a long time ago. Now get inside, you're already dark as is."

The man threw the woman toward the building. She looked at Jae and went back inside.

"Sorry for that little display. What can I do for ya?"

"I need a place to rest for me and my horse and food."

"You've come to the right place. I can send one of my women to tend to your horse, you can come inside and rest."

"How much?"

"Since you're new, and had to see such an unpleasant display, I'll give ya the first night free. Afterwards, 10 cluorgs a night. How does that sound?"

"That works," Jae said.

"Right this way." The man led Jae inside.

The inside was nothing like Jae had imagined. It was extravagant, the wallpaper was maroon and looked dated but nice. There were stairs that went from the left side of the hall and curved its way up to the 4th floor. It leveled for a long stretch to accommodate the rooms. There were 6 rooms on each floor. A large chandelier hung from the ceiling. The room that extended into another building was next to the front door. On the opposite side of the door was a long hall. At the end, were two double doors. Jae assumed that was where the house was attached. The building was musty with perfume and incense. The man called a woman over and told her to care for Galland.

"I never introduced myself. I'm Frank Johnson, I own this here bordello," Johnson said, extending his hand.

"Jae," he said, grabbing his hand.

"Pleasure, but let me say this, the women are a separate fee than our lodge fee. Just let me know before ya go for one."

"Don't worry, I'm here on business. I don't need a woman."

"Whatever ya say." Johnson smirked.

Johnson continued to lead Jae to a room on the third floor. The woman from earlier was inside cleaning it.

"Bianca, when you're done, call Sasha to bring him some food. She'll be his servant until he leaves."

"Okay."

Bianca finished making the bed and bowed to Jae and Johnson then left.

"That one I tell ya, quite the handful." Johnson shook his head as he turned around. "If ya need anything, Sasha will take care of you. Remember, these women come with a price, don't touch any of them."

Jae nodded and Johnson left the room. Jae sat by the window and looked outside. A woman fed Galland while another groomed her. She seemed to be fine, so Jae flopped in bed onto his back, resting his hands on the back of his head. He gazed at the ceiling. The warmth and silence in the room enveloped him and coaxed him into sleep. A loud knock on the door jarred him awake.

"Come in," he shouted.

In came a woman with tawny skin, blonde hair with orange and light brown highlights, her roots were black, and she wore blue contacts, the outer edges exposed her black eyes. She was beautiful. She wore a white slip and no shoes. She looked significantly younger than Bianca. There was no way she was an adult. She carried a tray with different foods, a pitcher, and a tall glass cup.

"You must be Sasha."

"Yes," she answered, her sleeve falling off her shoulder as she placed the tray on the nightstand. "Would you like me to feed you?"

"I can feed myself thanks."

Sasha sat on the bed. She placed her hand on his leg. "Are you sure?"

"Yes, now please leave, I have a lot to do tomorrow and need sleep."

"What about the dishes?"

"I'll being them down in the morning. Now will you please?" Jae motioned towards the door.

Sasha stood, shrugging nonchalantly as she turned and walked out. The door quietly closed behind her.

Jae rolled over, reaching for the tray. He grabbed a piece of bread and dipped it into his soup, the kid deserved a much needed break. He rolled over again onto his back and took a bite.

The next morning, Jae woke to the sound of screaming. He stumbled to the window, looking out. The townsfolk ran frantically around town. Sasha came bursting into Jae's room.

"Please stay here, we're having another storm and it's unsafe to leave."

"Where's Galland?"

"…"

"My horse, where is she?!"

"Oh, she is still tied up outside."

Jae looked back outside, Galland was jumping about, avoiding the objects hurtling by. She couldn't move fast enough. The women that cared for her the night before, tied her too close to the pole. Part of a wooden fence flew and hit Galland. She screamed as she fell to the ground. Jae opened the window and jumped out. He ran to Galland, who lay partially on the ground, her neck straining from the reins.

"Are you okay?"

Galland groaned.

"You'll be fine."

Jae untied the reins and lifted Galland, he dragged her to a nearby stable.

"I don't know why they didn't have you here to begin with."

Jae examined Galland's leg. It was broken.

Jae sighed. "Guess we'll have to prolong our stay. Only until you're able to stand."

Jae petted Galland who rested her head on his lap.

"You really care about her huh?" Bianca said, coming from one of the stalls. She dried herself with a towel.

"Of course, she's all I have in the world. She's been with me for a long time. She's been my rock for years."

"Wow, how old is she?" Bianca asked, sitting next to her. "Don't animals have a short lifespan?"

"They did, but after most humans died off, animals began to have longer lifespans. Maybe it was the pandemic, or just the fact that humans were a hindrance to their evolution, but I'm glad she's still here."

"That's nice," Bianca said, studying Galland's coat pattern. She ran her hands along the brown part of Galland's side, to the white leading to her back. "I've never seen a horse with this coat, she's so pretty."

"Thanks," Jae said. "She's called a varnish roan."

"Wow," Bianca said, smiling.

"Have you had any pets?" Jae asked.

"No, I've been here since I was little. You don't get those kinds of luxuries at a brothel."

Jae didn't know what to say. He looked back to Galland's leg.

Changing the subject Bianca asked, "So, where are you from?"

"South Korea," he replied. "I started traveling when I was 16. What about you? I know you said you were here since you were young, but do you remember where you're from?"

"I don't. I was sold here when I was 6. I don't really remember where."

"I'm sorry."

"Don't be, you didn't sell me for money."

"It's still sad regardless."

"It was tough times," Bianca said. "I don't really blame my parents. They had many mouths to feed and did what they thought best. I remember having two older brothers and a baby sibling."

The Yulogna region had just lost a war. Everyone was in a panic wondering how they were going to survive. They'd lost their homes, families, and were thrown into a second wave of poverty. Johnson put out ads, offering 10,000 cluorgs for girls.

Although many parents didn't want to lose their daughters, they chose the survival of their family. Johnson promised the girls would be well taken care of and that reassured most of them.

She continued, "But Johnson treated us, the children at least, well. We had a good education and were well fed…"

Bianca frowned, her eyes falling to the ground. Her head lowered too, as if the weight of her eyes were a ton. Jae studied her as she stared into space.

"But you don't like it," Jae said.

"No." Bianca shook her head, she gazed at Jae. "Who would?"

Jae smiled. "Sorry, that was a stupid question."

"Not at all. You'd be surprised the number of men that believe we want to be here."

"Wasn't it illegal back then?"

"It was, but what do laws matter when there's no government to enforce it?"

"That's right. I remember something about the Yulogna region collapsing again."

"Yeah, no one was prepared for it. And after the first few deaths, people still weren't taking it seriously."

"You know a lot for someone that doesn't remember her hometown."

"I read all of Johnson's books and newspapers that were published from the fall until now. I'm well versed in the day of ruin."

Jae's eyes widened.

"Is something wrong?" she asked.

"Uh…no. I…didn't know there were documents about it. No one speaks of it, and the people old enough to remember died off years ago," Jae spoke quickly. "How much do you know about it?"

"Just that—"

"Bianca!" Johnson shouted, his voice muddled by the thunder.

"I have to go." Bianca scrambled to her feet. "Hope she feels better soon."

Jae watched her run toward the Lyour town gate as the stable door slammed shut. "She's pretty interesting, isn't she?"

Jae softly caressed Galland's mane. She stared into Jae's eyes as she slowly fell asleep. Rain pitter pattered on the roof, filling the once silent stable with the sound of rain.

Jae glanced around, searching for a safe place for her to rest. Carefully, he slid from underneath her, making sure she wasn't uncomfortable. He looked in each stall. There weren't many animals inside. He found a dark stall in the corner far from the doors. It was perfect for her. It wasn't taken care of, which meant no one went that far inside. He walked back to Galland.

"Sorry, this is going to be a little uncomfortable."

He lifted her upper half. Galland whined in complaint as he dragged her across the stable and into the stall. Jae placed her down gently and lay beside her.

"Not the best morning, is it?" he said. He nuzzled closer and placed his forehead on hers. "You'll be okay. I love you Galland."

Jae came out of the stable an hour later. The storm was still raging but calmed down tremendously. He jogged back to the bordello, shielding his eyes from the debris with his arm. Waiting inside was Johnson.

"You're crazy," he greeted Jae.

"Not when your horse's leg is broken because she wasn't put in the stable."

"Oh no," Johnson gasped, his reaction exaggerated and insincere. "You're telling me *my* women didn't do a good enough job caring for *your* horse?"

"Not so much that, but rather leaving her tied to the pole all night and not in the stable."

"Surely there's some way I can make it up to you?"

"No, nothing can be done. But I'll need to extend my stay. Just until her leg is healed."

"What happened to her leg?"

"It's broken. Some debris hit her leg."

"Oh dear," he said, his tone was phony. "It's all my fault. I should have directed my women better than that."

"It's not your fault or theirs. They, I assume, don't know how to take care of a horse."

"Yeah, but the consequences are grave…"

"How so?"

"Well, you had to put her down, right?"

"No." Jae shook his head offended.

"But it's damn near impossible for her leg to heal. It'd be too hard."

"Not anymore," Jae replied, quickly. "Animals have evolved. She will heal just fine."

"If you say so," Johnson mumbled, finally turning around. "Your horse, not mine. I couldn't handle the hassle."

"Well, I best be going," Johnson continued, walking away. "Guests to attend to. You have another night on me as an apology."

"Thank you," Jae said, walking to his room.

When he entered, Bianca was cleaning up his dishes from the night before. Sasha was also inside placing his breakfast in the same spot Bianca cleaned.

"Sorry," he said. "I didn't take out the plates like I said I would."

"Told you," Sasha whispered, hitting Bianca's arm. "It's fine, really. Here's your breakfast. We'll be on our way."

Sasha rushed out the room. Bianca took her time, she looked annoyed, but didn't say much.

"I'm sorry you have to clean up after me," Jae said, sitting on the bed next to where she knelt.

"It's fine, it's my job," she said, standing up. "Well, if you don't need anything else—"

"Would you like to join me," Jae interrupted. He needed to know how much she knew about the day of ruin. Any information, including the location of the documents were needed.

"I can't," Bianca said. "Johnson would need to know in advance and…"

"Then I'll pay for you to talk to me," he interrupted again.

"I'm not allowed to be 'booked' by anyone."

"Why not?"

"It's nothing really."

"Is it because of what you said yesterday?"

"What did I say?"

"I overheard your argument with Johnson, remember? Is it because of your arranged marriage?"

"Yeah," she said, quietly looking dejected. "It's obvious I'm not a virgin, but Johnson promised no one would touch me until our wedding."

"Why do you hate it?"

"I want my freedom," she said, softly smiling. "When you turn 30, you have the choice to leave. Women I've admired found happiness in different ways and left. I was so close. 5 years away. *5.*"

"But won't you have your freedom with him?"

"How so?" she asked. "I was bought, permanently. I don't get to choose who I marry. And he'll be just as controlling if not more than Johnson."

"I'm sure…" Jae paused. "You've been with him before. There must be something appealing about him."

"He's a monster," she responded, quickly and harshly. "He's been with every woman here, yet I'm the one he chooses."

"Well, you're beautiful. From just the few conversations we've had, I can tell you're insightful, intelligent, you have a charming personality, and you're not afraid to speak up for yourself."

"I appreciate your compliments, but if that's the reason I have to go through this, then I wish I hadn't been so outspoken."

"Then you wouldn't be who you are today."

She shook her head. "I just wish there was something I could do to change their minds."

"Maybe there is," Jae said. "But you might have to volunteer another woman."

"I wouldn't wish that on my worst enemy."

"Is he that bad?"

"He's—"

Before she could finish, Sasha knocked on the door. "Bianca, Johnson is calling for you."

"Thank you," she replied. "Well, in the end I guess you did get to talk to me."

Bianca walked out of the room. Jae heard her down the hall asking, "You didn't tell him where I was right?"

Jae stood up and closed the door. Something seemed off. What was Bianca going to say about her future husband? It seemed like every time she mentioned something important, someone would interrupt. Jae needed to know more. How he was gonna get it out of her, he didn't know. But he had a feeling it had something to do with his journey.

Jae sat on his bed, bored out of his mind. He wasn't used to being indoors and he never stayed in one place for so long. He stared at a bug trapped in a spider's web. Watching as the spider crawled up the web and wrapped the bug in its thick strands. Just as the spider consumed the bug, someone knocked on his door. It was probably Sasha. Jae didn't know how old she was, she was a pretty young lady, but after knowing how old Bianca started there, he didn't trust what age Sasha was. He could tell in her body language and her awkwardness she wasn't comfortable "tending" to her guests.

Rolling his eyes he said, "Come in Sasha."

"Sasha?" the voiced asked as the door opened. It was Bianca. "If you prefer her, I can have her come and tell you."

Shocked and a little delighted he replied, "No, no, not at all. Sorry. She's been checking on me all day, I assumed it was her again. What can I help you with?"

"There's an event happening downstairs. You're welcome to stand in the foyer free of charge."

"I might just join you," he said, leaping off the bed. "It's pretty boring sitting in this room."

"You can always have the women you want entertain you."

"No, I don't need that kind of entertainment."

"You don't have to have sex with them. We do other things too. Storytelling, singing, plays and skits, we even just sit and talk if that's what you like."

"I tried that, but you rejected my request."

"I told you, I'm not available. But there are plenty of other women you can have the same kind of conversations with."

"No conversation is the same."

"That's a very wise statement," Bianca replied, stopping on the stairs. "But it doesn't make one person's conversation with you any less important."

"Maybe." Jae shrugged. "If you want to talk with one person, there won't be a good 'replacement.'"

"You're right, but when that person is unavailable, it's best to give up."

"Never knew how." He smirked.

Bianca couldn't hold back her smile and turned away. She continued down the stairs.

They reached the auditorium, referred to as the main room and Bianca stopped Jae. "Johnson said you're free to watch no charge, but you have to watch from here."

"I'll take it," he said, leaning in the doorway.

The women were talented. Each one spent no more than 10 minutes dancing, storytelling, performing skits, playing instruments and even games that involved the guests. It was fun, but Jae was growing impatient. He knew at some point Bianca would get a turn on the stage. He rested his head on the door, his legs were getting tired. He didn't mind. It surely beat staring at a wall in his room or having to pay just to see them perform.

It was Bianca's turn, the room erupted in hoots and hollers. Men shouted from everywhere things like, "She's back."

"I missed her."

"Come to my room!"

But she stayed composed.

She took a deep breath, and the room went silent. She strummed her guitar. It was soft but loud enough for everyone to hear.

"Deep in the woods, sings a sparrow.
No one hears her, no one sees her
She flies from forest to forest
Free as the leaves, blowing in the wind
Caged is the canary
Her song heard by many
No one sees her, No one hears her
Her longing to fly free
The wind carrying her, To the woods
In the cage, Lies the canary
No one hears her, No one sees her
Her spirit trapped in a cage…"

The room was dead silent, everyone was in awe, even Jae. As she sung, sadness filled the room and her listeners. When it was all over, no one clapped, no one spoke. Bianca bowed and turned to leave the stage. Jae snapped out of whatever trance her song placed them in and started applauding. Soon everyone joined in, and she took one more bow before leaving.

Everyone stood up and grabbed their belongings. Jae noticed and stood up straight. He wanted to see if he could find Bianca again. He stepped into the main room and moved to the side so the other guests could leave.

"Man, she really knows how to entertain," one said.

"Right, she was also very good at service." The other guest laughed.

"Too bad she ain't for sale no more."

"Yeah, I heard Hellim bought her."

"Hellim?! No way, not that monster," a man shouted. He wasn't in the original conversation but that set him off and many other guests.

"Yeah, I don't know all the details, but I heard from Tina that he made some sort of proposition with Johnson."

"This is outrageous. Her talents and beauty are going to waste on that beast!"

Jae listened silently wondering who Hellim was. The men left the room and Jae weaved through the crowd. He watched carefully making sure Johnson didn't see him.

Soon, he reached the stage. He moved quietly up the stairs and into the room Bianca entered. He looked around and saw Bianca by herself folding the clothing the women wore.

He took a quick glance around the room before approaching her. "Quite the work load you have."

Bianca flinched and asked, "What are you doing here? Guests aren't allowed back here."

"I wanted to see you," he replied.

"Yeah well, now that you have you can leave."

Bianca dropped the last piece of clothing in a hamper and stormed off.

"Wait," Jae said, chasing after her. "Can't we just talk a bit?"

"We did."

"That was hardly a conversation."

"Yeah well, you're not supposed to be here. So that's all you're getting. I'm not getting punished because of you."

"But I can help you clean up. You have to put all of this away. It'll go faster with me."

"It's my job, now will you please?"

"Only if you promise to see me tonight."

"Wha—? Are you crazy? You know I can't do that."

"That's why I want to talk to you now. At least it's not behind a closed door. If Johnson comes, I'll tell him I wanted to help because I watched for free."

Bianca stayed silent. She sighed and said, "Fine. This is a lot anyways. It'd take me hours to do."

"Great." He grabbed a box labelled "props" and put things inside. "I wanted to ask you something."

"What is it?"

"Who's Hellim?"

"My 'fiancé,'" she mumbled.

"Yeah, but WHO is he? I heard the guests talking shit about him. Is he that evil?"

"He's a monster. He terrorizes our town as well as this region. But he's taken a liking to Lyour because of the bordello. We're the only reason he hasn't destroyed it."

"Is he really that big a deal? All the dangerous people I saw in this town, and no one wants to stand up to him?"

"It's not that. People have tried, we even had a war years ago. But as you can see, we failed. No one's brave enough to fight back now."

"Man, this guy must be something."

"And I'm the one forced to marry him."

"Does it have to be you?"

"Yes, he only wants me."

"And what proposition did he give to Johnson?"

"Man, people really love to gossip don't they," she complained.

"You don't have to tell me if you don't want to."

"It's fine. As you can see, I'm very outspoken despite my situation. I didn't acquiesce to his power like the other women did. So to spite me, he made a deal with Johnson. If Johnson gave me to him, he would leave and never come back. I doubt he'll do as he says, but even if he was serious, I just can't stand the fact that I have to spend the rest of my life with him."

"I can see the predicament you're in. Lyour is riding on your marriage."

"Exactly. This region is."

"That's unfortunate. That's what your argument was about right?"

Bianca nodded. "I told him I didn't want to do it, but he accepted behind my back. I'm sick of it. I lived my entire life trapped."

"19 years," Bianca continued. Her voiced quivered as she spoke. "I've been trapped here my entire life."

"There must be some way out of it."

Bianca didn't say anything, her back turned to Jae. She cleaned the makeup off the floor and counter. Jae walked closer. Her hair covered her face, as tears dropped onto her hand and the counter.

Jae took the rag out of her hand and pulled her to him. He embraced her tightly, his face buried in her neck.

"I'm sorry," Jae repeated over and over.

Minutes passed before Bianca pushed him away. "I need to get this done."

"When do you get married?"

"Five months."

"I just…I don't think it's fair."

"Doesn't matter what you think. Won't change a thing."

"I know. I just wish there was something I could do." Jae started cleaning again. "Maybe, since you're leaving anyways, this might be a bad idea but, do whatever you want."

"What do you mean?"

"You know, don't do what Johnson says. Shit, he sold you anyways. Least he could do is not work you to death."

"That's not going to happen."

"Why not?"

"It just won't."

"Can you tell me why it won't? What's he going to do, kick you out?"

"Look…I appreciate you trying to help, I really do, but it's not that simple."

"It's not, there's a lot riding on you. And that's why Johnson can't do anything *to* you. Use the last of the time that you do have, doing what makes *you* happy."

"I ca—"

"Don't say you can't. Just do what you want. He owes you that much."

Bianca stayed silent.

Jae finished cleaning. He walked up to Bianca. Seeing her upset made him want to erase all of her problems. If he could take her away from there he would in an instant. But it wasn't possible. A lot rode on her back.

He cleared his throat and said softly, "Just think about what I said. Nothing worse than what you already have to do *can* happen. Good night."

Bianca still didn't say anything. Jae left the room back to the stage. He looked out at the empty chairs and sighed. He left the main room and headed to his own. He put on his cloak and grabbed a banket from his bag and the fruit left from his breakfast. He headed outside. The storm from earlier was gone, but it was still dark, and the faint smell of rain filled the air. The street was disheveled. People picked up debris and the boarded-up windows were gone.

Jae pulled his hood over his head and walked to the stable. He saw a pile of hay sitting to the side. He grabbed bundles of it.

"Galland," he said, sighing as he entered her stall. "You shouldn't be standing."

He had her lie down again. He wasn't too worried though. It was also unhealthy for horses to lie down for too long.

"Here," he said, sitting the fruits and hay on the ground in front of her. "Sorry, this is all I could get for now. I'll make sure the women taking care of you, get you your favorite foods."

He stared at her while she ate and sighed. "You're a girl, right? Maybe you could give me advice on women."

He laughed at his terrible joke and placed the blanket on Galland. "There's just something about her that draws me in. I don't know how to describe it. She's beautiful yes, but so are the other women. Maybe because she knows so much about the day of ruin for her age. It's odd but intriguing. Could be her intelligence. I don't know. But what I do know, is that I need to find out about that husband of hers. What kind of monster they're talking about—"

Jae stopped talking. He sat in silence, fiddling with a knot on Galland's mane. He was overthinking. Her fiancé was probably just an asshole with power. Nothing like who and what he was looking for. And there was nothing he could do anyways. He was a skilled fighter, but he couldn't take on an entire army.

"It's cold in here. Sorry I can't give you more warmth than this," he said, standing up. "I better get back inside. I'll see you later tonight or tomorrow."

Galland continued to eat as he left.

Jae composed himself as he walked back to the bordello. If he could search Johnson's belongings, he could find those documents and destroy them. How could Johnson even get them? He looked around 50 years old.

The day before ruin happened 135 years ago. It was an alien attack. Aliens, referred to as gods, once ruled earth with dignity and respect for humans. After 5 years of harmony, they were angered and wiped out 95% of the earth's population. No one knew what happened and why they did it. There were no documentations… or so Jae thought.

He needed to see what was written and how factual it was. But where could it have been? He looked at the back hall that led to a house. That was probably where Johnson lived. But it couldn't have been there. Bianca said she studied them, no way Johnson let her and the others in his home…right?

He pulled a woman to the side and asked where Bianca was. She said she was in the kitchen. He wasn't allowed back there, but she would grab her.

Bianca emerged from the back. When she saw Jae, she sighed. "What now?"

"Nothing. Just wondering if there's a library."

"You don't look like the reading type," she said, eyeing him up and down.

"I like to read." Jae smiled.

Bianca smiled. "The library is for employees only."

"Damn. No way you can convince Johnson to let me in?"

"You're already staying here for free. I doubt he'll be more accommodating."

"Only for today. Starting tomorrow, I'm a paying customer."

"Ooh," she teased. "I'll see what I can do. Maybe you could ask Sasha, she might have a better chance at a yes than I do."

"Hm, nah, I don't want to bother the kid."

Bianca scoffed. "Well, I have work to do. If you'll excuse me."

Jae waved as she went into the kitchen. He knew it wouldn't work, but it was worth a shot. Maybe Johnson would offer some time in the library, for a fee of course. And if push came to shove, Jae could always sneak in. Like he cared if he got caught. What was an elderly man like Johnson going to do? From the looks of it, only women worked at the bordello. No male servants, no male cooks, no security, who would stop him? He was stronger than everyone in town, but he hoped fighting was the last option. Despite the… aesthetic of the town, it was a nice place to live. One of the nicest he'd seen during his travels. He didn't want to be barred from there.

He waited for word from Bianca, naturally it was a no go. Jae had to resort to plan b, sneaking in. He didn't know where the library was, but if Jae had to guess, seeing as it was forbidden, the library was in Johnson's home. The next problem was how to get there? Entering through the Bordello seemed slightly easier, but how could he find time to sneak in? The main hallway was always packed with guests and women. Someone would surely see him.

Jae stood in the main hallway. He leaned on the wall by the passageway to Johnson's home for hours each day. He hoped to see a pattern or a small chance to slip in. He couldn't just barge in there and he didn't trust other guests to not snitch. He did take time to ask a worker to make sure Galland was fed. He needed his undivided attention on this mission. Jae had to shoo away Sasha on numerous occasions. She was confused as to why he wasn't partaking in any of their events. She knew and was grateful, that Jae did not want to sleep with them, but they offered other activities, so why wasn't he doing anything else but standing in the main hall watching everyone?

After a few days, Jae felt like he understood the dynamic of the bordello. At 10 PM the guests retired to their rooms, some with women, the workers went to bed or whatever it was they did, once most of the guests were gone. He was confident in his investigative skills. When the time hit 10 PM, Jae went down to the main hall. He started to walk into the passageway when Johnson emerged from the foyer.

"You need somethin'?" Johnson asked.

"No…Just bored…." Jae walked towards the stairs.

"Hmm, seein' as you're a man of your word and been paying rent, I'll give you some suggestions. You could buy a woman for the night. Join us at 7:30 PM tomorrow for the showcase, you can take a tour around our lovely little town, it ain't much, but it's the best in the area, you could buy some souvenirs to help our wealth, anything you want to do. But standing in my hallway, scaring my guests, won't do. Utilize your time elsewhere. As a matter of fact, go to bed."

"Gotcha," Jae said. He didn't like Johnson's tone, but he put up with it solely because he planned to destroy his property. Jae could call it even. He walked up the stairs and said, "Goodnight."

"Hmm," Johnson grumbled. He stared at Jae until he was out of sight.

Jae plopped on his bed and kicked off his shoes. The showcase was a great chance to sneak into his home. At the last event, every woman participated and the main room was packed, not a soul was in the foyer or main hall. It was the perfect plan, he wouldn't have to fight, it would be a quick execution and back to the event. Johnson wouldn't know who did it, assuming he ever checked his library.

The next afternoon, Jae walked into the stable. He felt guilty for not visiting Galland enough. After what happened the first day he stayed in Lyour, he shouldn't have been as trusting with the women.

"Hi Galland," he said, walking into her stall.

Jae froze. Bianca sat next to her and brushed her blonde mane. She looked at Jae and said, "So much for saying you care about her. You haven't visited her in a week. I think the Bordello is getting to you."

"Maybe," he said, sitting down on the other side of Galland. "Have you been the one taking care of her?"

"Who else?" Bianca replied. "Did you think she would feed herself?"

"I thought there were women assigned to her."

"Nope, Johnson told them to stop. Said he wasn't gonna be held accountable for any more problems."

Jae scoffed. "I guess having her taken care of is something I need to pay for."

"Basically, but I don't think that should be the case. She's a living being with a beating heart, just like us. Johnson is from an older generation that doesn't view animals as anything more than objects. That's why I care for her in my spare time. Even her partner didn't visit her all this time," she said, playfully.

"Thank you," he said, taking her hands. "Really. I can't thank you enough for looking out for her. How's her leg?"

"Oh thanks for reminding me. You thought her leg was broken right?"

"Yeah. It is."

"No, it's not… She has a sprain but nothing in her leg is fractured. You're not well-informed on horses, are you?"

"I'm pretty sure I told you Galland has been with me a long time? I know about horses."

"Doubtful. Just because you've been with her for years doesn't mean you know how to properly take care of her. When was the last time you brushed her mane? It was matted down until I started brushing her. What do you feed her? How often does she get cleaned? You're a traveler, so how long are her breaks in-between your departures and destinations? Those are things you have to think about with a horse… or any pet."

"Well, we had more important things to do." Jae cleared his throat. "Hair isn't that important."

"It's uncomfortable. Being busy doesn't excuse not taking care of her. I'm sure if she could communicate with you, she'd ask for a bath."

Jae rolled his eyes. He gazed at Galland while Bianca continued to rant. He wasn't really paying attention to what she said.

"Hellooo, Jae, are you listening?"

"Sorry, I heard what you said. I'm just surprised you know so much."

"Well at one point, I wanted to be a vet."

"A vet?"

"Yeah, a veterinarian. They were really common decades ago. They're basically animal doctors."

"I know what a veterinarian is…. I thought you couldn't remember anything from your past?"

"I don't. It was during my studies here. I read a lot of books about animals. I wanted to be a vet so badly I—" Bianca paused and looked down. She continued to brush Galland's mane. She exhaled, "I'm sorry, it's stupid, me dreaming about that kind of thing here."

"There's nothing wrong with dreaming. What were you going to say?"

Bianca laughed. "It was pretty silly. I went around Lyour giving rats band-aids and when we had a lot of animals, I pretended like I knew how to take care of them. I would wrap their legs in bandages."

"That's cute, but seems like a bad thing to do."

"It was. I was a menace. I realized how horrible that must have been for them. I treated them like dolls. I stopped like a month later."

Before Jae could respond, Johnson called out for Bianca. "Bianca, your breaks been over. Get in here!"

"Yes master," she said mockingly, rolling her eyes. "I forgot the time. It was nice speaking with you."

"Same here."

Bianca sat the brush on the ground, stood up and walked out of the stall. Jae looked at Galland. "Do you really need a bath?"

He examined her. She was definitely filthy, but so was Jae. He'd only recently bathed because Johnson said he smelled "worse than hot garbage." Bathing was a luxury. Jae credited the decent hygiene in Lyour to the bordello. Most of the townsfolk were still dirty, but they weren't as bad as other places. Johnson built a public bath and charged 30 cluorgs for 30 minutes. And the bordello had a bath service for guests. Thinking on it, Jae actually understood why Bianca thought hygiene was so important and easily accessible. It was a requirement for her and the others, they didn't understand how privileged a bath was. The best Jae could do prior to Lyour was a quick rinse if he ever found a source of water.

Jae promised Galland he would visit her more often, and left the stable. He spent the rest of his afternoon planning.

At approximately 7:30 PM, Jae arrived at the showcase. He paid Johnson 50 cluorgs and asked for a seat in the last row. When the lights dimmed and Johnson took his seat, Jae slid out of his chair and out of the main room.

He stealthily walked through the building to the foyer. So far, no one was there. He jogged down the passageway and attempted to open the doors. Locked. He came prepared however. He took out a long needle and lockpicked the door. After 5 minutes, he managed to open it. He crept in and carefully closed the door behind him. An alert silently hit Johnson's watch but ignored it, assuming it was one of the women.

The house was well lit. It looked like a home from the 1960's. The furniture was antique, it looked worn but was still nicely preserved, the wall print was yellow with floral print, the carpet and the furnishing was maroon. He had an entryway with three openings. The opening facing the doors had a small hall and to the right of the hall led upstairs. To the right of the entryway was the living room, and to the left was the dining room and a door to the right of that room was the kitchen. Jae guessed the small hallway would be for the women.

He lowered his head and walked down the hall. There were two closed doors at the end of the hall and underneath the stairs, was a sliding door. Jae checked both rooms, there was a bathroom, and a small room that had a child's bed and dresser. He turned around and slowly slid the door open. On the other side, were stairs that led to the basement. Jae cautiously walked down. The basement was large. There was another set of doors, two by the steps and 6 more down the hall.

How many doors does this man have?! Jae thought.

He checked the room closest to the stairs. Inside was a playroom. It had dusty toys strewn across the floor, 4 school desks lined in front of a chalkboard, and in the back of the room, was a small bookcase.

Is this the "library" Bianca talked about? Jae thought. He scoffed and walked to it. He bent down and grabbed all 7 books on the shelves. All children's books.

He placed them back on the shelf and closed the room door. He walked to the next door. Inside was a small bed with hot pink bedding. He cringed and closed the door. He couldn't stomach searching the room. He turned to another door, this one was further down, deeper into the basement. He walked down the hall and placed his hand on the doorknob. He took a deep breath, hoping he didn't waste his time, and opened the door.

There were 10 rows of bookshelves, 2 to a row. Closer to the door, were elegant tables, the tables and bookshelves had the most beautiful, darkest brown wood, and carvings along the edges. The carpet was emerald green, chandeliers hung above each aisle. The wallpaper was dark brown, it looked almost like wood. Jae whistled as he stepped inside. He tripped over something, he assumed his own feet, and continued to look through the aisles for anything on the day of ruin.

Another silent alarm pinged Johnson's watch. He looked down and a message ran along the screen. "Library." He rolled his eyes and went backstage.

"Who isn't here?" Johnson asked, harshly in a hushed tone.

"Everyone's here," a young woman said, as Sasha brushed her hair.

"Where's Bianca?" he asked.

"Folding clothes," Bianca sarcastically said.

Johnson counted the women, everyone was there. He quickly looked at his watch and typed something. A holographic screen turned on and displayed the rooms in his home. He searched the cameras until he found the library. He scanned each one and saw Jae walking through the rows and grabbing a book from one of the shelves.

"That son of a bitch," Johnson raged. He turned the off screen and stormed out of the backstage area.

Jae found a book of documents labeled 2037. He skimmed the pages looking for anything that said day of ruin, the cause or about the gods. He put it down. Nothing in that one. He grabbed the next book. As he skimmed, he found an article about the first mind uploading and brain transplant. Jae remembered something about it. It was a cancelled process. In the article read:

> After trial and error, the first mind transfer was completed. Although illegal, testing was still in progress. A man (identity unknown) underwent the process. He was the only one out of 10 subjects to survive the transfer. We have yet to hear from S.T.R.I.N.G (Scientific Trials, Research, Industrial, Non-human, and Gambles) who held the transfers about who this new android is, or the lawsuits they are facing over the experiment.

Jae shook his head. All that research and the world was destroyed. He wondered if the robot survived. He shrugged and put the book down.

He went to the next book labelled 2039-40. Laminated on the first page was a news article about the day of ruin. It was dated November 15, 2040.

What the hell happened?!

> If you're as scared and confused as I am about why the gods killed 95% of humanity, you're in the right place. In this article, I am going to give a day to day synopsis of what might have been the answer for their rage….

Jae couldn't finish it, there was no point. He skimmed the rest of the book. It was full of articles before and after the day of ruin. Theories and photos of events newspapers believed was the cause. He checked the last page and saw a photo of a man in a yellow mask and black cloak. The picture was of terrible quality, but he could see enough that the mask had the face of a smiling god on it. Jae took the photo out of the album and crumpled it into a ball.

He grabbed all the books labeled from 2035-2045 and dropped them in a metal trashcan. He took out a lighter and dropped it inside. The trashcan lit up in flames as Johnson entered the library.

"What the hell're you doing?" Johnson exclaimed.

Jae glanced back at him. "Reading."

"You're lightin' my library on fire."

"So..." Jae walked around the corner.

Johnson walked up to the blazing trash can and peeked inside. He could see part of the covers and slammed it in the trashcan.

"Hold it!" he yelled. He ran in front of Jae. "You destroyed valuable documentation! One of a kind!"

"I hate anything that involves the gods. Nothing personal."

"You need to pay for them!"

"How much?"

"1,000 cluorgs."

Jae scoffed. "For trash? I'm not paying that."

"You ain't leaving 'til you do."

"Who's going to stop me?"

"Me."

"You?" Jae burst into laughter. "Please, one push and you'll lose a hip. Just take the loss old man."

Jae stepped forward and Johnson stepped in front of him again. Jae unsheathed his sword. A low flute sound resonated in the room. He continued, "I don't want to hurt you. Get out of the way."

"Put that sword away boy. I'll teach you a lesson about threatenin' me."

"Step aside."

"Pay me."

Jae sighed and swung his sword at Johnson, but Johnson propelled towards him, grabbed Jae's neck, and slammed him against the wall. The force of Jae smashing into the wall cracked it and rubble dropped to the ground.

"You'll pay for that too," Johnson said.

Jae struggled to speak. "I ain't paying shit."

"Then you die..." Johnson said.

Jae grabbed Johnson's arm. Jae grunted. Johnson's grip was so strong, if he tightened it even an inch, he would snap Jae's neck. Johnson opened his mouth, a whirling sound pierced the air and a large barrel of a gun came out.

Jae let go of Johnson's hand, raised his hands in the air, and said, "I give up. I can't pay you because I don't have 1,000 cluorgs."

Johnson released Jae's throat and he fell limply to the ground. "Don't think about running either. I'll kill you and that horse."

The gun in Johnson's mouth retracted, and he said, "You're going to work here to pay me back."

"Got it," Jae said, standing up. "Does that mean you're the man in that article about the robot transfer thing?"

"Or just a regula' old man with a gun in his mouth."

Shit, Jae thought. He rubbed his neck. *If I'd known that, I wouldn't have pissed him off. Fuck, at least the documents are gone.*

"So what do I have to do?" Jae asked.

"I'll figure that out later. For now, you can start by cleaning up the shit in that trashcan. After that, go to your room."

"Can't watch the show I paid 50 cluorgs for?" Jae asked. Johnson glared at him, and Jae put up his hands defensively. He went to the trashcan that still burned and said, "Can you at least give me something to put the fire out with?"

Johnson walked to the trashcan and his wrist opened up. A large tube shifted out and foam sprayed the can. "Clean it up… and while you're at it, clean the rest of the library, then retire to your room."

"Yes sir," Jae grumbled. He waited until Johnson closed the library door and kicked the trashcan. He tsked. "I could have easily beaten him. Stupid old geezer."

After he finished cleaning the library, he did as Johnson ordered and went to his room. He stared at the ceiling deep in thought. He wasn't all that pissed over the outcome. He'd gotten what he needed and making it up to Johnson for ruining his property wasn't a bad idea. He was stuck until Galland healed anyways. Maybe temporary work would satiate his boredom. But until then, his boredom was at an all-time high. Stuck in his room until who knows when Johnson assigned work. For all he knew, this could have been a ploy for imprisonment.

"Damn it," he complained. He closed his eyes. A knock on the door broke the silence and Jae opened his eyes. "Come in."

"Man, you are something else," Bianca said, entering. She carried a tray of food. It was significantly less than what he received prior.

"Where's Sasha? And why is there so little on the plate?"

"You're not a customer anymore, therefore I'll be the one taking care of you, no different from the women. And you have no right to complain about food rations." She sat the tray on his nightstand… or rather just short of the definition of slamming it. "Of all the places to destroy in Lyour, you chose Johnson's library?"

"I wasn't trying to destroy it," Jae said, sitting up.

"That's not what I heard." Bianca crossed her arms.

"I'm telling the truth. I just wanted to read about the day of ruin, it angered me, and I set it on fire."

"Why?"

"It just did. None of it was factual anyways."

"What do you mean? How do you know that?"

"I just do. Everything in there was a speculation or an opinion. Why keep something that's spreading lies?"

"How is it spreading lies? It was in his personal library."

"You read it didn't you?" Jae grabbed the tray and sat it beside him on the bed. "And you believed every theory, right?"

Bianca was stumped, she knew he was wrong, but she didn't know what to say. He would have reversed whatever she said.

"Regardless." Bianca cleared her throat. "It was wrong to destroy someone else's property."

"I agree. But what's done is done. I'm making it up to him by working right? Free labor is in these days."

"It's not free when you owe money." Bianca slammed the door behind her.

Jae whistled. He thought, *Man, she's pissed.*

He scarfed his food down, and went to bed.

⋅————⦿⦾————⋅

Chapter Two
Unexpected Friendship

The next morning, Johnson woke Jae up at 5 AM. He dragged him to the main hallway. "You're working security today. Don't leave this spot until I say so."

"Yes sir," Jae grumbled, sarcastically.

Jae leaned on the wall as men came and went. There wasn't much of a fuss during his shift. Only one man caused a scene, and with a flash of Jae's sword, the man calmed down. Johnson dismissed Jae for his lunch around 2 PM.

Jae walked into the kitchen. There were better meals lining the employee table than what the guests were served. Jae grabbed one of everything and sat at the kitchen table. Bianca entered not long after.

Jae smiled and said, "Care to join me?"

"Can't, still working." Bianca rushed past him and put food on multiple plates.

"Why not?" Jae asked. "I mean, I'm not a customer."

"And?" she said.

"And that makes it appropriate for coworkers to converse."

"In theory, yes, however, I have a lot of work to do."

"Doesn't have to be now. We can talk another time."

"Can I ask why you're so fixated on speaking to *me* specifically?"

"Hmm, well," Jae paused for a moment. Originally it was because he needed information on what she knew about the day of ruin, but seeing how that was all crap, why did he want to speak with her? "Well, we had some nice conversations, I'd like to know more about your stance on things, like the world."

"It's trash. Happy?"

"But why do you think it's trash?"

"Why?" Bianca stopped preparing the plates and turned to him. "Hello, welcome to the 22nd century. You know, where the world's a shithole. No safe, governing laws, people dying to tyrants, and to survive, people have to do what us women do. What's great about it?"

"You're right." Jae nodded. "It's definitely not ideal. But I think it's what we make of it."

"'What we make of it?'" Bianca scoffed. "Easy to say for a man carrying a sword around."

"I'll have you know this sword was a gift from an old friend of mine. He called it, 'Magord.' Of course I'm not going to get rid of it," Jae said. "Does it help? Obviously. We have to deal with bandits and crooks, so it's safe to carry around protection. Prior to the day of ruin, there were criminals. The world wasn't all that safe."

"You're wrong," Bianca said. "The gods ended all conflicts. It really was a safe world."

"No, it wasn't. They ended wars but people were still terrible. They still murdered each other. They still committed crimes. The 'gods' did nothing that didn't benefit themselves."

"That's your opinion," Bianca said. "Reality and the documents you destroyed said otherwise."

"Those documents were only opinions."

"So is yours," Bianca said. "I'm more inclined to believe people from that time period than I am listening to a 19 year old."

"I'm 26," Jae said.

"Oh wow, a whole 7 years closer to an event from 135 years ago."

"There's more to it than articles from people who worshipped them. It's up to you whether you want to believe why they killed over 6 billion people. It's hard to believe good aliens would kill people they supposedly helped."

"To each their own," Bianca replied.

Before she could continue, Johnson rushed into to the kitchen yelling, "Bianca! How long does it take to add food to a plate?! Quit slacking off and get back to work. You can do that much right?"

"Sorry…" Bianca mumbled. "I'm finishing up now."

"It's my fault. Don't be so harsh on her," Jae said.

"So not only are you destroyin' my property, you're distractin' my employees."

"I wouldn't say distracting. Just having a conversation while she works. Nothing wrong with that right?"

"When it's interfering with her work, yes."

"Sorry," Jae said. "I'll refrain from talking on the job…unnecessarily…"

Johnson glared at Jae. "You know what, you're gonna help Bianca with lunch orders."

"Pfft," Jae scoffed. "I'm working security."

"Not if I say you aren't," Johnson snapped. "Your break's over, help her fill plates and bring them to guests. You made her late, you can help her catch up."

Jae rolled his eyes and walked over to Bianca. "What a stick in the mud…"

"Well, that's what happens when you don't follow his rules." Bianca didn't look a Jae.

"Less talking, more working," Johnson demanded. "Bianca, you're in charge of him. If he gets out of line, call me."

"Okay." Bianca smirked.

Jae eyed her suspiciously. Seemed like she had some nefarious ideas about ordering him around. Johnson left the room and Bianca showed Jae what to do.

Seeing how Bianca's day went, made Jae uncomfortable. The hopeful and flirtatious men trying their luck with Bianca and losing any arousal after Jae entered the room, the occasional man that made a move on Jae, and Bianca holding him back from hitting customers. He didn't understand how the women at the Bordello did it. He commended what they did.

When his shift was over at 10 PM, he was exhausted. He had traveled around the world, fought bandits, endured the harshest climates, but a few hours of work at the Bordello was the hardest. How long did he need to work off his debt?

The next morning, he sluggishly walked down to the main hallway. He positioned himself at the doorway when Johnson emerged from the passageway to his home. He looked at Jae, the bags under his eyes worse than ever.

"I don't know what you're doin' there," Johnson grumbled. "But you're helpin' Bianca."

"That was a one-time thing," he complained. "I'm not doing it."

"What did I tell you yesterday," Johnson said, approaching him. "If I say you're doin' somethin', you're doin' it. Now get in the kitchen."

Jae wanted to hit him, badly, but the last thing he needed was an unnecessary brawl. Now, when it was time to leave, he'd gladly punch the old man.

Jae walked into the kitchen. Bianca was already there making breakfast.

"Do you do all the cooking?" he asked.

She glanced at him. "Most of the time. The girls, on their days off, help me when they can."

"Well, show me what to do," Jae said. "I'll gladly do this than deal with yesterday's fiasco."

Bianca laughed. "You have to admit that was a little funny."

"No," Jae said, unamused. "I don't need any perverted men touching me."

"Why not?" Bianca asked. "I'm sure Johnson'll clear your debt faster if you do sex work."

"Absolutely not," Jae said. "Besides, I get to talk to you, right?"

"Something you've been pestering me about since your arrival," Bianca said, scoffing. "Of course you'd love this."

"You asked me yesterday," he said. "I think it's my turn. Why are you so reluctant to talk to me?"

Bianca couldn't answer him. She didn't know what to say. At first, it was because he was a guest. She figured it was nothing more than him trying to weasel his way into sex, then once he became an employee, it was like his drive to speak to her intensified. Maybe she couldn't because she never spoke to men outside of the trivial conversations before and after sleeping with them. It was an easy script for her. Then you had this guy show up out of nowhere forcing her to improvise. And he couldn't even give a logical reason as to why he was so hooked on speaking to her.

"I…" Bianca started. "I don't know how to speak to you."

Jae scoffed. "What do you mean you don't know how to? You're doing it now."

"I mean," she said, emphasizing her words, "I don't speak to men like I speak to you, and it's new to me. Conversations with you versus the women and on occasion Johnson, are different. We were taught not to converse with men, something about it being difficult to not grow attached."

Walking away from him, she continued, "I just don't know what your intentions are."

"I can assure you, my 'intentions' are nothing perverse," Jae said, in an amused tone. "It's rare that I can have conversations with someone. I'm a traveler. It's been so long since I willingly spoke to someone. The only time I did speak to anyone was when they were trying to rob me, or if I desperately needed something. I have Galland but it gets lonely sometimes. If I'm honest, in the beginning, I was set on speaking to you because you knew about the Day of Ruin, and I was curious as to what you knew. But as we talked, I started to enjoy it. I won't be here for long. I just figured before going back to my old ways, while I'm on this little 'vacation,' I could borrow a bit of your time."

Bianca sighed. She thought, *Why did he say that? Now I feel bad.*

"Look, I'm sorry for the way I treated you," she said. "I shouldn't have been so hard on you."

"Don't apologize," Jae said, walking towards her. "I did have a motive and I was pestering you. Maybe now that we've cleared the air, we could get to know each other?"

"Only if we both have time," Bianca said. "You seem to annoy Johnson."

"I don't care about that old fart."

"I do," Bianca said. "I hate hearing him scream. It's annoying."

Jae smiled. "I understand. How about you and I speak during our breaks in the main room. Johnson won't bother you there."

"Hmm…I can do that," Bianca said.

Johnson entered the kitchen and stared at them.

"You're a magnet," Bianca whispered, walking away from Jae.

She continued to cook while Jae brought the guests food. He was slightly better at handling his discomfort. With Jae's help, Bianca's workload dropped significantly. There were certain things she couldn't trust him to do properly, like the laundry and cooking, but handling the guests for her, made everything much easier.

By their lunch break, they were exhausted. They met in the main room and talked about their day. They spent most of it together but it was hilarious listening to Jae's rants about the perverts. Bianca had one cheesy and awkward love confession in front of Jae. He couldn't explain why, but it pissed him off. He scared away the guy and tried changing the subject. Even remembering it, made him angry.

In only a few days, their bond had grown stronger. Bianca felt comfortable talking to Jae and soon, they were talking outside of the main room. She didn't care where she was at the time, whether Johnson was around or not. They developed a friendship on a level deeper than she had with the other women. On the exception of Sasha and one other woman.

Jae was glad he had spoken to her. She made his time there tolerable. He couldn't imagine what it would've been like if she wasn't there. And there certainly would not be anyone there to stop him from murdering guests.

During Bianca's morning and evening breaks, she went to the stable to take care of Galland, and soon Jae was going there with her. They had so many intellectually stimulating conversations, it was like a drug to Jae. Traveling as many years as he had, it had been a long time since he encountered someone with a brain. Jae understood that education was considered a luxury, but that didn't excuse the level of stupidity society became. Jae knew in the olden days, humans were somewhat smarter.

Johnson was the only exception, aside from Bianca, and that was only because he was from an older time…pre-apocalypse. He learned to adapt and scam. Easiest way to make money was to keep everyone else stupid. Johnson was one of the wealthiest men in the Yulogna Region. He had the resources to better their society, create schools, jobs, etc. but he enjoyed having money, and didn't want to ruin that. He only gave the women at the bordello an education solely because he didn't want idiots working for him and because he felt it was only right as most of them didn't choose to be there. He didn't require them to study, and many declined his offer. Only Bianca, Sasha, and a few others wanted to learn. Each took on different responsibilities in their education. Johnson taught them only the basics and from there, they helped each other. Bianca's strong suit was history and medicine, so she taught the ones who were interested how to provide medical treatment to humans, animals, and aliens who had a similar makeup to humans. She also excelled in the arts, and dedicated her time to teaching a select few including Sasha, to learn them. Once the women "graduated," they were moved to the bordello to start their sex work.

Bianca refused to go. She couldn't fathom letting disgusting perverts touch her. She told every lie in the book to avoid joining the bordello. Johnson knew they were lies, but he liked how crafty she was and wanted to reward her for it. When she turned 18, he stopped giving her passes and forced Bianca to sleep with guests.

Bianca could only find solace in his library and with Sasha. She didn't want her to go through what she went through. It was nearing Sasha's 15th birthday and graduation, and Bianca taught her every possible lie she could. Unfortunately, Johnson didn't fall for it and he didn't care about Sasha's potential. He forced her to dye her hair blonde and wear blue contacts. She was "unique" compared to the other women, and men were asking for her preceding her graduation. He couldn't risk stalling such a "money maker." Seeing how crushed Sasha's spirit was, Bianca spiraled into a deeper depression.

Johnson noticed the decline in her passions and interests, but didn't think much of it. Whether she dreamed or not was her decision, and in the end, she wouldn't be able to live any of it out anyways. And seeing that lack of interest was the only reason Johnson condoned her relationship with Jae. So long as it was platonic and it didn't interfere with his income, he was fine with it.

As for how he handled Sasha's depression, he lessened her visiting days and increased her costs. Most men couldn't afford her, leaving her only to the rare rich men that showed up or the pooled funds of a desperate man. She still worked as a servant, but it was no longer easily obtainable to pay for her.

And while he was heartless when it came to them not wanting to live that kind of life, he still wanted them to be happy…sort of.

Johnson brainstormed better ways to use Jae. He could definitely do more than the women, and Jae, no matter how many times Johnson offered, refused to sleep with the guests. He had another set of hands to make money off of, but he couldn't think of what to do with him.

Then the idea hit him, a delivery service for the bordello. Johnson realized he could make more money having Jae make deliveries. Johnson had a lot of mooching townsfolk entering his establishment, stinking up the place, and taking up space for higher paying customers. He thought about hiking up his food prices, but he wasn't *that* horrible to starve humans. He thought about a delivery service many times, but he couldn't trust anyone. He wasn't afraid that the women would run away, it was the Lyourian men who were the problem. He didn't need something happening to his women. He knew Jae could hold his own, and didn't need protection. It was so safe a plan, Johnson advertised all over town and Jae was almost as swamped with work as Bianca was. Johnson was ecstatic hanging the sign, *Lodging and sex service guests only.*

Jae did an okay job at first, he didn't want to talk to the Lyourians but if it helped lower his debt quicker, he could tolerate it. A lot of customers were disappointed it was him and not a woman, but they continued to order. They had no choice.

The current customer insisted on a woman handing him his food instead of Jae. Johnson gave up, ordering Bianca to go with. Bianca complained like usual, saying Jae had to work some of her tasks so she could finish on time. Bianca and Jae walked out of the kitchen. Jae carried bags of food.

They left the bordello as two people on a horse stopped in front of the doors. The man's black and red attire looked familiar to Jae but he couldn't figure out where he knew it from. The man hopped off the horse and helped a woman with a short brown afro off. She wore sunglasses, a black sunhat, a black and red romance dress, and red heels. She thanked the man and walked around the horse. She looked from Jae to Bianca with a smile plastered across her face.

"Bianca!" she shouted, running and hugging her.

"Serenity!" Bianca smiled, hugging her back. "It's so nice to see you!"

"I missed you." Serenity buried her face in Bianca's chest.

"Me too," Bianca said. "Why are you back so early?"

"Ah!" Serenity jumped back. "You just reminded me! You won't believe what happened to me!"

"What?" Bianca asked.

"So Winfred and I were on our way to Myetorp, and…" Serenity burst into laughter. She struggled to say, "He was…he was trying to be roman…romantic but we were attacked by bandits.—"

"Oh my gosh," Bianca interrupted. "Are you okay?"

"I'm fine," Serenity said, finally calming down. "They didn't go after me. They only wanted to embarrass and steal from Winfred. I felt so bad for him. Winfred was so humiliated he kicked me out of the wagon and sped off. The bandits offered me a ride home."

"You took a ride from bandits?" Bianca asked. "Why would you do that?"

"I was screwed either way," Serenity shrugged. "I mean, I was stranded. Why not?"

Jae nudged Bianca's arm with his elbow and moved his head sideways for her to keep moving.

"Follow us," Bianca said to Serenity.

"Oh no, it's fine," she said. She turned to Jae and said, "I'm sorry sir, I don't mean to take up your time…"

Jae smirked.

"Noo," Bianca said. "He works here."

"Since when?"

"A few weeks ago," Bianca said. "He tried to burn down the library, and destroyed most of Johnson's old newspapers."

"I didn't try to burn it down," Jae said. "I only wanted to destroy those binders."

"Whatever you say," Bianca said, giving Serenity a look. "He owes Johnson 1,000 cluorgs."

"Ah okay," Serenity said. "I still won't join you 'cause I'm tired and I wanna see Sasha, but it's nice meeting you."

Jae smiled and nodded.

Bianca hugged Serenity once more before Serenity went inside.

"You're awfully quiet," Bianca said.

"No, just don't want to interrupt your reunion," Jae said. "I'll see her later anyways, right?"

"You'll love her, she's so sweet and thoughtful."

"Like you?" Jae grinned.

Bianca rolled her eyes. "No, she's actually a sweetheart."

Jae shrugged and they continued the delivery. The guy was larger than Jae imagined him to be. He attempted to woo Bianca but Jae nipped it in the bud. Bianca had to defuse the situation before Jae got his ass beat.

On the way back, they discussed Galland. They both agreed that she was probably healed. Of course, Bianca didn't want her traveling just yet. She knew Jae would somehow injure her leg again. She wanted Galland fully healed, bathed, and healthy before they left.

Secretly, she also didn't want him to leave. She was enjoying their time together. He brought up amazing topics, posed interesting questions and gave her the chance to rant about everything. She also didn't want to lose the only person that helped her with her work. Jae thought numerous times the moment Galland healed he would skip out on his debt, but he also didn't want to leave yet. Once he did, it was back to his lonely life. Galland was good company, but not in the same way as human interactions were. His policy was to never return to the same place. Maybe Lyour could have been his exception, but who knew how long it would take him to complete his mission. There was no guarantee any of them would be alive by the time he came back. The gods were brutal, and at the drop of hat would murder entire cities. He felt bad for saying this, but he hoped Galland's leg wasn't healed. He even wondered if he could lie about it if she recovered.

Jae watched Bianca hand Johnson the money, then separated themselves. He told her to meet him in the stable once her daily tasks were finished. Jae still had work to do himself, but there was no rush, nor any specifications on when Johnson wanted them finished. Galland came first no matter what the situation was.

When he arrived at the stable, Jae examined Galland. Her ankle looked healed. He thought about taking her on a ride. He thought it was safe enough for her to leave the stable. He put on her headstall. "Ready?"

Galland snorted in excitement, barely staying still.

Jae clicked his tongue and they rode out of the stable. Galland galloped through the open field, happy to finally run around. They rode for miles. Jae remembered Bianca's scolding over not giving her a break, so he hopped off and let her do whatever. She ran around a pool of mud neighing and running at intense speeds.

Jae smiled. He loved seeing her happy. She must have been depressed while stuck in that stable. Soon his smiling face turned into incredulity. Galland wasn't planning on just running around the mud, she drove headfirst into the mud and rolled around.

"G-Galland," he stuttered, scrambling to his feet. "Don't do that."

Of all the places, he thought. It was natural for horses to roll on the ground for many health reasons, he understood that. But with all the dry grass and dirt surrounding them, she chose to flop into the messiest spot. Jae couldn't go in after her, he just stood by the side, his arms folded until she got out.

"You done," Jae asked.

She snorted.

Jae shook his head. He couldn't stay mad at her. She was adorable, muddy and all. He didn't want to get dirty himself, so he grabbed her reins and walked beside her. Thankfully they hadn't gone too far from Lyour. When they were roughly a mile and a half away from the stable, Jae felt the mud had dried enough for him to ride her. He mounted her. Just a small bit of her back was still wet, but he was content with that. They rode back with ease.

When they arrived at the stable, Bianca was just leaving. Her eyes widened and her mouth dropped when she saw them. "What the hell happened to her?"

"She was a little too happy and rolled around in mud," Jae said, jumping off her. He took the headstall off and said, "Go in your stall."

Galland brayed and did as told.

"Ah ah ah," Bianca said. "You're not leaving her like that, are you?"

"Well, yeah," Jae said, as if Bianca was the weird one. "I doubt anyone would be okay with me bringing a horse into the public bath. It's fine, if she cared about being dirty, she wouldn't have gone into the mud."

Jae started for Lyour when Bianca stopped him. "There are other ways to clean her. She's a horse, animals don't think like we do. Of course she's going to get dirty, but it's up to us to clean her."

"Then what am I supposed to do?" Jae complained. "There aren't any rivers or anything over here. I'm not travelling a long way just to come back. If I leave, I'm not coming back. She can wait until we're ready to leave Lyour."

"Good thing you don't have to go far." Bianca smirked. "Grab your wallet."

Jae grumbled as Bianca pulled him to a store at the edge of the town. It supplied travel necessities from horse gear to wagon accessories. She forced him to buy bathing supplies, two buckets, and other travel accessories, like a saddle. She was shocked he had been riding bareback. He was so cheap.

They carried the supplies to the stable, and took Galland out with them. Jae followed Bianca west of the town. There was a small stream flowing north. There was also a poorly dug trough that flowed into the town. Jae knew it was probably Johnson's shitty bathing service. They followed the river until they reached a small lake. It was gorgeous and serene. How could such a beautiful place exist? And by Lyour no less.

"Why didn't you tell me this was here?" he complained. "I could've saved so much money."

"Well now you know," Bianca said. She smiled. "I guess this means you'll bathe more."

"Honestly, yeah," Jae said. "I don't have to waste money."

"Good," Bianca said. "Have you ever bathed her before?"

Jae nodded. "Years ago, before I started traveling."

"Oh so this should be easy for you?"

"Yeah, for the most part." Jae stepped in front of Galland and said, "It's bath time, *behave.*"

Galland turned away from him and walked to Bianca.

She laughed. "I guess she prefers I do it."

Bianca grabbed a bucket and scooped it into the water. She poured soap into it and swished the water until suds appeared. She looked at Galland and sighed. She pulled out a dandy brush and started brushing her coat, knocking off clumps of dried mud. She shouted to Jae, "Don't just stand there, grab the other brush and help me get this off."

Jae didn't say anything. He stared at Bianca. He knew she was different from the other women, but he hadn't truly realized how amazing a person she was. His heart was racing again. He hadn't felt that way about a woman in years. He watched her as she gently brushed Galland, a soft, loving look on her face. He watched her lips moving, he couldn't hear a word she said. He wanted to kiss her.

"Jae," she said. "Come on."

He snapped out of it, grabbed a random brush, and wiped the mud. Jae couldn't wrap his head around what had come over him. Maybe it was the setting sun reflecting off the lake that created a romantic atmosphere? He focused on brushing Galland.

Once they were finished, Bianca tossed a sponge to Jae and they lathered her mane and coat. She tossed water from the river onto Galland's legs so she wouldn't get startled by the water. She accidentally splashed Jae as well and he complained. She laughed and ignored him as she gently used the other bucket to rinse off the soap. They dried her with towels.

"See?" Bianca said, wiping water off her arms. "Wasn't so hard."

"Except you splashing me with water."

"You're still whining over that?" Bianca laughed. "It was an accident."

"Oh yeah?" Jae said. "So's this."

He lifted Bianca and threw her in the lake. She rose to the surface shocked, makeup running down her face. Jae laughed.

"Jae!"

"Now we're even," he said, through labored breaths.

"Help me out," she demanded.

Jae grabbed her hand and she pulled him into the lake. She laughed and tried running to land, but Jae grabbed her and dunked them both under water. They splashed each other before finally getting out of the water. Jae had no idea when it happened, he had fallen in love with Bianca. He couldn't take his eyes off her. Bianca used the extra towel they had for Galland to dry her hair and wipe the remaining makeup off her face. Maybe it was because he was in love with her, but she looked even more stunning to him.

"Johnson's gonna be pissed when he sees I'm soaked," Bianca said.

"He'll be alright," Jae said. "Just tell 'em you were washing something and fell in. He's dumb enough to believe it."

"Yeah right," she said, rolling her eyes. "He doesn't believe a word I say, even if it was happening in front of him."

"Ask Sasha or something to distract him." Jae held out his hand.

Bianca stared at it and said, "What?"

"Get on Galland," he said.

"No. You didn't bring her saddle."

"Who cares?"

"I told you I don't support you riding bareback," she said. "It's stressful for her back."

"No it's not," he said. "Guess what, hundreds of years ago, they didn't have saddles. Galland doesn't mind."

"Still," Bianca said. "I don't like it."

Jae sighed. "Fine."

He pulled on Galland's reins for her to follow them.

"You can ride her if you want," she said.

"Nah, if you're walking, I have to as well."

Bianca smiled. "You're so weird at times."

Jae smiled. He was nervous. They walked in silence until they reached the stable. Bianca was fairly dry. She only needed to explain her lack of makeup if Johnson caught her. Bianca asked if Jae was heading back with her but he declined. He needed to make sure Galland was situated before retiring for the night. He watched as she walked into the town gates.

He found Galland lying down in the stable. With her leg healed, Jae wondered why she still lay on the ground. He sat beside her, leaned back, and looked at her. She stared at him.

"I know," he said, as if reading her mind. He leaned against Galland's back, rested his head on hers and petted her. "I love her. You like her too, right? Too bad she's engaged huh? We could have brought her with us. And you would have an owner greater than me. I know it never seemed possible, but..."

Galland snorted.

Jae looked at her. "What's that supposed to mean? I know I apparently missed a few steps, but it's not like you'll die anyways."

He sighed. "Would be nice, right? If I remember correctly, she said you were 8. Yeah, you're really past your time. I'm sorry I dragged you into this."

Jae turned to his side, looked her in the eyes, and smiled. "Don't worry. I'll fix everything. It's apparently in this region. After we find it, hopefully we'll go back to normal. Just hold on a little longer."

Jae closed his eyes and fell asleep.

Jae woke up. His neck was hurting. *Shit,* he thought. Johnson was probably freaking out. He didn't care all that much though, he just hoped there wasn't any backlash aimed at Bianca. He patted the dirt and hay off his clothes and rubbed Galland one last time before heading back to the bordello.

"Where the hell have you been?" Johnson snapped, when Jae entered the foyer.

"My bad, I was taking care of Galland," he replied.

"Who?"

"My horse, the one your women ended up hurting..."

Johnson rolled his eyes. "And I compensated that. Your *debt* is more important than that horse. Don't let it interfere with paying me back."

Jae didn't respond, he shook his head and left the foyer. He went to his room and flopped on the bed. Deep in thought, he wondered when he fell for Bianca. He thought about how they acted the past week or so and believed Bianca might have felt the same for him. The chemistry was there, the only real obstacle was her engagement, but what did that matter? He wanted to tell her how he felt. There was no need to hide it, her arranged marriage meant nothing to Jae, he loved her and if she felt the same way, he was going to have her. Jae rose from his bed and went to Bianca's room. He tapped on the door… no response. Was she asleep? Jae sighed and returned to his room.

It was better he told her at night. There were no prying customers or Johnson in his way. Jae decided, when the time was right, he would tell her the next day. He valued their newfound friendship, but a romantic relationship would be treasured.

The next morning, Jae woke up bright and early. He paced the halls and the foyer hoping to run into Bianca before the guests woke, but there was no sign of her all morning. As the day went by, Jae grew more and more impatient. Why wasn't she working? Johnson made sure she had something to do all day. So where was she?

During his evening break, he searched for Sasha. She might have known something about Bianca's whereabouts. He found her in the kitchen cooking with Serenity.

"Oh…" Sasha said. She glanced at Serenity. "She's uh, been sent away."

"Sent away where?" Jae asked.

"His attic…" Serenity said.

"Why?"

"Because she came back soaking wet," Sasha said. "Johnson thinks she's sneaking around."

"No, she just—" Jae shook his head and stormed out of the kitchen. He couldn't believe Johnson would do something like that.

When Johnson suspected women of sneaking around with men, he locked them in his attic. It was a punishment and a hopeful attempt at ending the alleged affairs. He knew the women had genuine feelings for their lovers, but their lovers didn't care about them. It only happened because they wanted "free service" and Johnson wasn't letting that happen. The women were forced to stay inside for a week, give or take if they were able to lose their dream of a relationship. The room wasn't bad, it had a soft bed, sofa, coffee table, bookshelf, desk, and a small window just big enough to look out of. There was a door to a bathroom. Inside was a small shower head and a toilet. That bathroom was only used for lock down. It was never cleaned and parts of the shower were rusted and falling off. Most of the women didn't like being there. It was boring and lonely, however, they started playing the game when they needed a break. They would sneak off every night doing nothing in particular, for a little vacation.

Bianca was angry at first about being locked away. She intentionally did her best to not end up in that situation. However, after a few hours, she realized it was a break. She had already read all of the books, but just lying down and relaxing was perfect for her. She felt bad because everyone else was busy as is, and now had to do her work. But she would make up for it another time. She worried about Jae. If Johnson put two and two together, what if he thought something was happening between them, and killed Jae? That to her was worse than staying locked in the attic for years.

Jae searched the bordello for Johnson, when he found him, he shouted, "Why the hell did you lock Bianca up?"

"Watch your mouth, boy," Johnson said. He excused himself from a group of guests and pulled Jae to the side. "Don't be talkin' to me like that in front of customers. Now what's the problem?"

"You locking Bianca up," Jae repeated.

"She came home soaking wet," Johnson said. "It ain't rain, she was sneaking in. I know she was up to something, and I ain't risking shit with her fiancé."

"Nothing happened," Jae said. "She was helping me wash my horse and fell in the lake. She isn't sneaking around with anyone."

"I know you're tryin' to cover for her." Johnson shook his head and turned to leave.

Jae grabbed his hand. "We can go to the travel store to prove she was with me buying bathing items."

"You got receipts?"

Jae nodded. He jogged to his room and grabbed his wallet. He thankfully kept one of the receipts. He handed it to Johnson.

"An' these ain't forged?" Johnson questioned, glancing at Jae.

"How would I even be able to do that?" he answered.

Johnson thought for a minute then said, "Well she's still staying in there for lyin' to me."

"When's she getting out?"

"Whenever I decide," Johnson said, waving him off.

Before Jae could press him to let her go, he stormed out of the hall and into his own home. Jae flipped him off and went back to the kitchen. Serenity and Sasha were still there. Jae grabbed a plate and slopped

…whatever they made…on his plate. He definitely wished Bianca was back. He sloshed the mysterious specimen around with a spoon, then cautiously raised it to his lips. He paused and set the spoon down.

Serenity noticed his displeasure and said, "Gonna have to deal with it until Bianca's back."

"You think Johnson's going to be cool with you serving disgusting food?" Jae asked.

"The guests don't care. They'll eat whatever we make." Sasha shrugged. "I could bring a boot and they'd smile and say it was delicious."

Serenity nodded in agreement.

And they weren't wrong. The bordello women could get away with anything when it came to the guests, as well as the citizens of Lyour…aside from the envious women. It could even be said, Johnson and now Jae, could get away with anything. The world wasn't as bright as it was a century ago. As the years went by, the need for an education dwindled. Subjects like math, history, reading, and writing were considered irrelevant. Humanity's biggest priority was survival. With the gods rampaging daily, the full seizure of the planet to aliens, and the raise of bandits, there was little point to taking up an education. Only the rich could afford something as luxurious as an education. All the Yulogna Region survivors needed to do was learn the gods' currency system, minimal counting, and staying on the gods' good sides.

And because of the Lyourians' illiteracy and lack of intelligence, Johnson was able to swindle whoever he wanted. When charging fees, he would say the amount of cluorgs given were lower than what was intended, or shortchange guests. When buying things, he could give a lesser amount and convince them it was right. Johnson loved how stupid the world had become. The dumber they were, the more money he made, the more power he created. Soon, he was the unspoken mayor of Lyour.

The exception to the world's unintelligence was some of the women at the bordello. Johnson was able to provide them educations *if* they wanted it. It was never offered, never enforced. Again, what better a way to make money than through the uneducated? Bianca was a clear example of how difficult Johnson's life would be if everyone strived to learn.

It also helped Johnson's cause that the world didn't have easily accessible paper. Another luxury only the rich could afford. With the lack of trees, infertile and toxic soil, planting more was virtually impossible. Cutting the remaining trees down was dangerous. The rich didn't care about the potential aftermath of losing all trees, and paid thousands of cluorgs to receive it. Not for use, but for show. Some places within the Yulogna Region had an abundance of trees and lived worry free, capitalizing off of the trade. Johnson bought bundles of paper to resell in Lyour. Some traded goods, others paid full price. Of course, Johnson was smart enough to not give them full sheets, he sliced them in strips and sold them as preprinted receipts. The receipts had words none of the townsfolk could read. But a few underlines on the end of each line they understood was where the price went and that was good enough for them.

Jae had only been in the Yulogna Region for 9 years. He noticed instantly upon arrival the differences between other regions and that one. There wasn't any sign of development, towns were dirty and poverty stricken, and the sheer stupidity of many. While they were considered street smart without the smart part, it was astounding to him how they managed to survive as long as they had.

"Well," Jae said, standing up. "I'm not a guest. No offense, but I'll eat out for the time being."

Jae tossed his plate in the trash. Neither Serenity nor Sasha were offended. They knew they couldn't cook and understood Jae refusing to indulge in that disaster called a meal.

Jae searched the streets for a decent looking restaurant. He remembered Johnson's "scamming technique" lessons but didn't have the heart to cheat others. He ordered his meal, and paid the correct amount. If he cared more, he most likely would've given extra, knowing Johnson at one point, probably scammed them. But…he didn't. He returned to his room and ate.

He was feeling down for missing the chance to tell Bianca he loved her. He planned to tell her the moment she left Johnson's house. But his most pressing concern was freeing Bianca.

~Bianca~

Bianca relaxed on the sofa. It had been 5 days since she was locked up. While she was bored out of her mind, she enjoyed having a break. She thought about causing more problems if it meant she could lounge the days away until her marriage.

Only three months left until she had to leave. She felt silly letting it consume her. This marriage tortured her to the point of wishing she'd never wake up. She thought back to when Hellim first became her client.

It was two years ago. It wasn't the first time that she had seen him. He stormed around Lyour like he owned it. He discovered the bordello when she was 16. He was notorious for switching women every few months. Bianca knew sooner or later Johnson would stick him with her. So she made sure to check with everyone who previously serviced him. Bianca heard horror stories about the weird kinks he had, the things they had to do, what he did, etc. Just the thought of him doing those things to her, made her stomach churn.

The world felt like it moved in slow motion when Johnson called Bianca to Hellim's bedchambers. A cold sweat ran down her back as she made her way down the hall. The women around her, watched in terror. Bianca was one of the last people who should have been requested. What was Johnson doing?

Bianca slowly opened his door.

Shrouded in the shadows of his canopy bed, Hellim called out to her, "You're just as beautiful as I imagined."

"I-if you don't mind me asking, where did you hear about me?" she asked, trying her best to not sound frightened. She did everything in her power to *not* be seen by him.

He chuckled sinisterly. "Where haven't I heard of you? It seems you've upped the ranks of best pleaser."

"Uh, not to be frank, but…whatever rumors you heard were wrong."

"Don't be shy, come closer," he whispered, the funkiness in his voice as he beckoned for her, ignoring her comment completely.

Bianca hadn't left the doorway. Her back pressed firmly against the door. She hesitated and he commanded her to come again, that time in a forceful tone. She approached cautiously.

Once she was close enough to the bed, she could see him patting the spot next to him. She sat down, her heart pounding against her chest. He towered over her. And not only was he taller, he also had a muscular build. Just one squeeze could crush her into a pancake. She wondered how he was even able to comfortably have sex with women almost half his size. He reached his large hand out to caress her cheek. She shivered at his long fingers. He slid his fingers down to her neck, then her shoulders, and back to her face.

As he slid a finger in her mouth, he said, "I'm sure you've heard this by now, but I like a little foreplay before I begin."

Bianca did her best not to bite his finger. The revolting taste of his finger as it awkwardly brushed against her teeth, tongue, and inside cheeks made her nauseous.

He continued, already out of breath, "I want, you to suck my toes."

Hellim moved slightly and the moonlight shined on his face. He licked his lips as if he hadn't eaten in weeks, ready to devour the little lamb in front of him.

Bianca snapped out of it. She pushed his arm away and swallowed her vomit. "Absolutely not!"

Hellim flinched. For a second, he thought he misheard her or maybe she didn't quite hear what he said. He scoffed and cleared his throat. "I said, I want you to suck my toes."

He moved his long, thick legs between them. He curled his toes upwards. They were almost as long as his fingers and the same putrid smell from his fingers was also on his toes, but with an even worse smell.

Bianca moved back. "I heard you the first time. I will *not* suck your toes. That's disgusting. I don't even know where your feet have been!"

Hellim let out an amused breath. "You must not know who I am."

"I know very well who you are."

"And you choose to defy me?"

"I have my standards."

"You're a whore. What standards do you have?"

"Many." She clenched her fists. No one had ever referred to her in such a derogatory way. "We may have to sleep with you creeps, but we're human nonetheless. We can say no to whatever we want. Be grateful we're even humoring you!"

"You lost me at human. Do you think I care about whether or not you're human? This place could be filled with women from Ngberfta, and I would still expect a slut to do what a slut does. This is your last chance."

"Or what?"

Hellim burst into laughter. "I see why that fool Johnson advised me against requesting you. Do as I say…or I'll crush your head."

He laughed for minutes. And while it seemed like his laughter was full of hilarity, it was the opposite. He was laughing away his urge to kill her.

"Do it." Bianca was bluffing, but if it came down to it, she would gladly die rather than put those things he called toes in her mouth. Hellim shifted slightly and her heart raced. She thought, *Is this where I die? Over this man's stupid smelly toes?*

She closed her eyes as Hellim's large hand stroked the back of her head. He snatched her by the hair and shoved her face close to his, only a breath away.

"Let's see how long your stubbornness lasts." He pulled on her hair, the force alone almost snapping her neck, and threw her towards the door.

She gasped from the impact. Her body trembled, but she stayed firm. She rose to her feet, ignoring the spikes of pain from her head, back, and legs, and raised her chin. The moonlight cast her way, and her skin glistened. Hellim was enthralled. She was an ultimate beauty, even with blood dripping from the top of her head. It almost made her look more beautiful.

"Leave me," he finally said. "Call Hannah in."

Bianca struggled to stand. She didn't want to look weak in front of him. Her muscles tensed as she turned around to leave. Once the door was closed, she let out a sigh of relief. She stumbled as she made her way down the steps and into the main hall. Women crowded the halls, waiting to hear about her experience. Their mouths dropped as she turned the corner. The women rushed to her aid, taking off their clothing to stop the bleeding from her head.

Johnson waited on the stairs. He screamed, "What the hell happened!?"

Bianca's lips trembled as she mustered the strength to say, "He wants Hannah."

Everyone turned to her, frightened about what he was going to do to her. Hannah however, looked unfazed. She was his escort prior to Bianca. She was the only person who didn't speak ill of him. Bianca thought it was a little weird, but everyone knew Hannah grew attached to anyone she slept with. When it came to servicing Hellim, he was the only man his current escort could see. So in that time, 1 year to be exact, Hannah felt a connection. Everyone doubted he shared the same feelings but never said anything. She brushed past Bianca and ran into his bedroom.

Everyone shook their heads. Disgusted by how loyal Hannah was, even after what happened to Bianca. After Bianca calmed down, she gave them a quick run-through of what happened. They tried their best to suppress their laughter. The situation for Bianca was stressful, but reenacting what possibly went down in there about sucking toes was hilarious. Half the women agreed with Bianca, that was going too far, the other half disagreed, stating he had made them do worse. Johnon was practically foaming at the mouth. He didn't want to disturb Hellim, so he pulled Bianca into his home and screamed at her. Things along the lines of how foolish could she be? Why would she risk everyone's safety over something so childish? And, was she crazy, she could've died. Johnson was terrified thinking about it. Not only would he lose his best money-maker, he also didn't want any of the girls he raised dying. He promised to find a way out it for her and demanded she never see Hellim again.

Hellim unfortunately, had a different plan. A few days after Bianca healed, he requested her again. Everyone was sure she was dying that night. When she arrived in his room, she spotted a large makeshift plastic pool filled with Grateyian noodles, an alien pasta dish that originated on the planet Grateyap. She covered her nose and bile crept up her esophagus. It smelled worse than sauerkraut mixed with vinegar and dog shit.

Hellim sat at the edge of his bed. He smiled watching her reaction. "You have two choices—"

"What? Gonna make me eat that shit?"

"No," Hellim said. He stood up and walked around the room. "It seems you've awakened a different side of me. You have two choices. You can get naked and swim in the noodles or we can continue what would've happened the other night."

Bianca sighed. She stripped and stepped into the pool. The noodles smushing beneath her feet. It wasn't the first time she had to do something naked in a tub or pen filled with random liquids. And the noodles in spite of that, smelled better than his toes.

He commanded her to sit and cover herself in the noodles. He rested his lips on the back of his hand as he watched her sit. Why was she so stubborn? He was sure she would shrink back from the assault on her senses. While this was a newly developed kink he would try on others, he was pissed nonetheless. He wanted her specifically to suck his toes. All the other woman had a defined kink they had to explore with him. He hated how defiant Bianca was. He let women slide on a lot of things, but she was pushing it. He had an entire strategy wasted. After she did a few kinks with him, including his toes of course, he planned to rip her head off. It was a humiliating death that turned him on.

Bianca finished bathing when Hellim told her to. He called Hannah again to finish him off.

The next day, he called her outside. "Clean my ship."

"That's not part of my services."

"It is now," Johnson said on the side of the building, counting a large wad of cash.

"What?" Bianca exclaimed. She bit her lip, so as not to entertain Hellim's sadistic nature. She rushed to Johnson and whispered, "Why are you on his side?"

"I'm not on any side, especially yours. Whatever he wants, he gets. And he paid 2,000 cluorgs to have you do it. So get to working."

"Crooked sell-out," Bianca mumbled, as she walked to his ship.

Hellim's ship was magnificent. The ship was large, inside had almost 30 rooms. Many for his own recreation, the rest for research and his soldiers. There was only one room Bianca wasn't allowed in. And in that room, she could hear bloodcurdling screams. She gladly listened to that command.

It took her 9 hours to properly clean his ship. It was filled with weird goo and fluids. His ship came close to his stench, yet it wasn't enough. She notified him when it was finished, and waited inside. Not even 5 minutes later, Hellim arrived. He carried a takeout bag from the bordello and opened it in front of her.

"You know what," he said, smirking. "I don't want this anymore."

He poured the contents on the ground and smeared it with his boots. Bianca scoffed. That tiny mess wasn't going to annoy her. Observing how relaxed she was, he grabbed the whistle around his neck and blew it. His soldiers came marching in with mud, dirt, and blood on their feet and bodies. The soldiers flopped on the ground spreading the mess everywhere. Bianca tried her best to seem unperturbed but her eyes gave her away. Hellim grinned viciously, extending his original proposition or having to reclean the ship all night. Bianca grabbed the mop and cleaned the floor.

This mistreatment from Hellim went on for months. The more he waited to kill her, the crueler his fantasies of murdering her strengthened. However Bianca was too damn stubborn, and no matter how horrid the things he made her do were, she continued to resist him. His urge for her to suck his toes died down and now it was a matter of getting her to submit. For her to get on her knees and beg for his forgiveness.

A year later, Bianca commented that she would never bow down to him, not even in a million years. And that statement inspired Hellim's idea to ditch killing her, and making her suffer until her death bed.

Bianca sneered. "I'm not marrying you."

"Too late. I've already bought you." Hellim grinned devilishly.

Bianca didn't dignify him with a reaction. She stormed out of his room and searched for Johnson. When she found him, he sat at a desk counting stacks of money. Her heart sank at the sight of it. He really sold her. "How could you?"

Johnson's head remained down, but he glimpsed at her. "Didn't have a choice."

"You had a choice." Bianca's eyes reddened. Her throat constricted as she held back her tears.

"It was you or the world." Johnson stopped counting his money and looked her in the eyes. "And I chose the world."

"You're nothing but a coward!" she screamed, as she left the room. She would never forgive him.

***

Bianca couldn't help but laugh through her tearstained face. Did all of her torment really stem from that one kink of his? She wondered if she had lowered her pride that one time, would she still have been tortured by him?

Honestly, she thought. *He would have found another reason to harass me. He can't handle being told no.*

Bianca cupped her face and silently cried. Regret possessed her, betrayal wounded her, and heartbreak killed her.

She curled into a ball on the bed, remembering all of her emotions that day.

Tink...tink, tink.

Bianca looked up, and towards the small window. A rock smacked the glass harder that time. She sat up and stared. Another rock followed immediately after and she peeked out the window. She locked eyes with Jae. Bianca smiled widely. He waved, gesturing for her to open the window.

"Cinderella, Cinderella, let down your hair," he shouted.

"Wrong princess."

"Same difference."

"What do you want prince charming?"

"I'm breaking you out."

"You know that's impossible."

"How so?"

"Well, I don't know, maybe the locked door."

"Jump out the window, I'll catch you."

"Now I know you're joking."

"I'm totally serious. I won't let you fall."

"Even if I could squeeze through this window, I doubt you can catch me from this height."

Jae reached out his hands. "Try me."

Just as he spoke, Johnson appeared from the back door of the bordello carrying trash bags. He spotted Jae and hassled him until he walked away. Johnson turned to the window and pointed to Bianca. She couldn't hear him and he stormed into the house.

Since Jae's arrival, her depressing thoughts diminished significantly, and she was having the time of her life. Of course, she loved and enjoyed her time with the women at the bordello, but something about him gave her hope. Although he wasn't the best influence on her, and constantly got her yelled at, he was a new and fun friend that spiced up her life. He opened her eyes to the impossible. She imagined spending her days with him and the girls until she was thirty. And afterwards, she would leave with Jae on adventures.

The lock on the door clicked and Johnson walked in. He carried a tray with soup and crackers. "What did I tell you? No socializing."

"I can't control what Jae does," Bianca said, taking the tray and sitting at the coffee table.

"You could've kept the window closed."

"And what? Have Jae continue to throw rocks until it breaks? Then who would you blame? I'm not Jae's mother, I can't tell him what to do."

"Yeah, I'm seein' a problem with Jae."

"What 'problem'?"

"He's nothing but trouble. Since he's been here, you've been slackin', sneakin' out…" Johnson walked fully into the room and leaned against the door. "What's up with you?"

Bianca lifted her eyebrow quizzically.

"You used to be my best girl. You had a mouth on ya, but you ain't never lied to me before."

"That changed when you chose to marry me off to a monster."

"I didn't have a choice. I told you back then, and I'm telling you now, the survival of humans is more important."

"How much?"

"Excuse me?"

"How much did he pay for me?"

"That has nothin'—"

"How…much."

"90,000 cluorgs."

Bianca scoffed and shook her head. *Unbelievable…*

"Sure seems like you did it for the money. As if you care about the human race. The stacks of money prove otherwise."

Johnson face turned red. He stepped close to Bianca's face and said through gritted teeth, "That had nothing to do with my decision."

Bianca stood, almost spilling her soup. "Stop pretending like it didn't! You're the biggest crook in Lyour…possibly the world. You scam old women and steal from children. *You run a business selling women*! If you cared about the human race, you would have done something to better it. Now that it's my life on the line, you suddenly care about others? That's bullshit!"

"I may be crooked, but I have my limits. I care because *we* shouldn't be involved in *your* problems. You caused this, not us. I'm not dying for you."

"And I'm not saying you have to. But cut the lies."

"I ain't talkin' 'bout this." Johnson threw his hands in the air and left the room. He shouted from the hall, "Get outta my house."

Bianca packed up her things and left. She grew angrier as she walked through the passageway. She hated how much of a coward Johnson was but she hated his lies even more. Why did he even care about how she thought of the situation? He forced women to do everything against their will. But he couldn't just say, "Yes I sold you for 90 thousand cluorgs."

She walked out of the bordello. Deep in thought, she hadn't realized she was in the stable until she made eye contact with Jae. He was cleaning Galland's hooves. He smiled and stood up. He fought the urge to hug her. He inquired as to why she looked so glum but she brushed it off. There was no point in explaining anything. It would change nothing and she didn't want it to appear like her engagement was all she thought about. She apologized and left.

Bianca was embarrassed. It was weird that the first place she went to was the stable. Jae must have thought she was a loon. She should have gone to Serenity or Sasha first, but her legs brought her to him.

She sighed, thinking about Jae's encouraging words. Johnson would kill Jae if she ever did decide to do whatever she wanted. It didn't matter to Bianca what she did. It meant nothing if the end result was her demise.

Conveniently, she saw Sasha and Serenity walking around a corner, past the bordello. She was curious as to where they were going unaccompanied by Johnson. She quickened her pace to trail them.

When she caught up, she realized it was nothing secretive. They were accepting an order from Johnson's merchant, Malarian Goods. It was a popular service from Malarik that supplied everything their customers needed. Their slogan was, *If we don't got it, then the earth must have been destroyed.* They were a fairly confident business. Their services were limited to certain areas. Not really needed to explain why, but there were *certain* places they didn't want to go due to safety concerns. Lyour would have been on that list if not for Johnson being one of their highest spenders and the deals they got at the bordello.

As Bianca walked closer, the merchant's eyes brightened and his cheeks turned a dark purple. "Bianca!"

"Hey Oplytuo." Bianca waved and stood between Sasha and Serenity.

"I...if I had known you were coming, I would have brought a...souvenir..." he said, shyly handing her the clipboard to sign. Oplytuo had blue skin, large black eyes, and hair dyed blonde. He was soft spoken and had a gentle nature. He was the main deliverer for the Bordello's orders. It was also commonly known that he was in love with Bianca. Whenever he arrived with a delivery, he would always make sure to book Bianca in advance. Sometimes for a day, other times, a week. It was rare they did anything physical, he just wanted to talk to her. Spend as much time as he could with her. Some would argue her engagement hit him the hardest. For a while after, Oplytuo didn't deliver to Lyour. It was only after a few months that he appeared again.

"I do miss your gifts," Bianca said, courteously.

Before Oplytuo could give a shy response, Serenity butted in. "Oh so you're still only giving her gifts? I thought we were friends too?"

"W-we are, it's just—"

"Just that his honey gets all the sweets." Sasha winked.

"Cut it out." Bianca elbowed Sasha.

"Oh it's alright," Oplytuo said. *She isn't wrong....*

He gasped and turned to his wagon. He searched through the pile of items, each time he moved, the pile wobbled and Serenity backed up. He handed Bianca a can of sweetened peaches. "I know it's not much, but please take this. I'll say it's coming on another delivery."

"I love peaches," Bianca said, smiling as she reached to grab it. "You know me so well."

Their hands brushed each other and he instinctively pulled his hand back. The can dropped to the ground and rolled under the wagon. Oplytuo apologized profusely as he got down on his knees to grab it.

Jae tsked and kicked the stable wall. He'd already failed once, but this time was despicable. Even if Bianca was in a rush to leave, he should have been more assertive in confessing his feelings. It was as simple as blurting out his favorite color. While he waited for Bianca, he had already blabbed it to Sasha and Serenity. He kept his distance from Sasha but on occasion of her being with Serenity, he had befriended both of them. Gushing about Bianca was the only real conversation they had together, but it was better than nothing. Jae desperately needed to let out his emotions and he didn't know *when* Bianca was leaving lock down. So he had no other choice but to rely on them.

Thinking on it, Jae felt even more of a failure. How could he so easily express himself to them and not the one meant to hear it? Did being single and basically a hermit for years really mess up his game? Or was it *her* that kept him from speaking to Bianca?

The thought of his prior relationship stung his heart. He swore to never love again, but there he was throwing hay around a stable and camping with smelly animals because of his inability to say 3 words.

Jae kicked pebbles as he left the stable. He needed to clear his head before he saw Bianca again. He walked down the main street of Lyour. Ever so often a Lyourian would greet him. Since his "best friend" had been locked away, out of sheer boredom, he became more familiar with the townsfolk. And even though they were crooks and he couldn't trust them as far as he could spit, he enjoyed the occasional conversation with them. He disliked bandits, but the Lyour bandits were tolerable. They were shady but they still had some ounce of morals left.

As Jae walked, a loud sound as if two cars collided into each other, filled the air. He looked around, cars were a luxury, he didn't think anyone, besides Johnson, was able to afford one. A scream followed the noise. Jae ran in the direction of the scream. When he turned the corner, people crowded a large pile of junk on top of the bed of a collapsed wagon, another expensive item no one in Lyour could afford, there were large back wheels, both on the ground beside the wagon, and smaller wheels in the front, just barely hanging on.

Jae pushed through the crowd. He saw Bianca, Serenity, and Sasha at the front, they stood in horror, as pale as ghosts.

"What happened?" he exclaimed, running to them.

"O-Oplyt—he—" Serenity stuttered. She cried and hugged Bianca, Sasha followed her lead.

Bianca held both young women and said, "Our merchant from Malarik i-is under there."

Jae looked from Bianca to the wagon. It was stacked high, if the weight from the wagon wasn't enough, the added weight of the items stacked on top of it was sure to crush him like a bug.

"Step aside," Jae said. He squatted and clasped the tongue of the wagon. "Move!"

Everyone glanced at each other, wondering why someone as skinny as Jae thought he was strong enough to do something.

"*Move*!" Jae commanded again, this time louder.

Bianca snapped out of it and ushered everyone back. She looked at Jae and nodded.

Jae smiled and grunted as he lifted the wagon up. The onlookers' mouths dropped. How was Jae able to lift it by himself? He held the wagon at waist height, struggling to balance the items on top as they wobbled.

"Do you see the merchant?" Jae asked, glimpsing at Bianca.

"U-uh…" Bianca stuttered. "Y-yeah, he's f-fine…."

Jae sighed. "If you can move, get from under this, it's heavy as hell."

Oplytuo whimpered as he scrambled from under the wagon. Jae dropped the wagon and the items fell. The glass shattered and food spilled all over the ground. Oplytuo thanked Jae. He was thankful the bottom of the wagon was curved. He had moved to the center of the wagon to grab the canned peaches that fell and the wheels finally collapsed from the weight. He thought he was going to be stuck there forever. Possibly requesting for one of the gods to help him, but he would have rather died there than face whatever consequences arose from bothering them.

The crowd cheered for Jae, they shouted praises like, "Johnson's dog is amazing."

"You're not as weak as you look!"

"Twig boy isn't actually a twig!"

Jae rolled his eyes. He didn't want to stand out. He didn't want to catch the interest of the gods. Who knew what would happen? And he certainly didn't want Bianca and the other women…and somewhat Johnson, roped into it. He waved at Oplytuo who still thanked him and rushed away from the crowd.

Oplytuo apologized again to Bianca and handed her the peaches and a message for Johnson. He scurried off with what remained on the cart. Bianca, Serenity, and Sasha followed Jae, almost running to catch up.

"You're amazing," Sasha said. "How long did you exercise to get that strong?"

"Years," Jae quickly responded.

"You should lift Bianca up," Serenity teased. "Oh wait, Oplytuo's peaches might get in the way."

"Shut up," Bianca said, rolling her eyes.

"I don't mind picking you up." Jae smirked.

Bianca shook her head. "Y'all are so annoying."

"You should do the heavy lifting at the bordello," Sasha said. "Maybe you can use that to lower your debt."

Jae stopped and turned to them. "No, you can't tell anyone about this."

"It's too late for that," Serenity said.

"Half the town knows," Bianca joined in. "You can't silence all of them."

Jae tsked. They were right. Maybe once his debt was paid, he could leave forever. If any gods sparked interest in him, they would only arrive to a weak town, maybe, it wouldn't punish Lyour either. He could only hope.

Jae separated from the women and went back to the stable. News had already reached the other side of town and Lyourians were asking him for help lifting boxes. Jae helped a few and declined others.

He sat beside Galland and exhaled. She rested her head on his lap and he petted her. He closed his eyes, enjoying the silence on the small occasion of one of the animals calling out or Galland.

"Jae!" Johnson shouted, busting through the stable doors.

Jae rolled his eyes and stayed silent. Johnson stormed into the last stall and glared at Jae.

"You just goin' to ignore me?" Johnson sneered.

"What is it?"

"When were you gonna tell me about that strength of yours?"

"Never."

"Well, we're gonna make a business out of it." Johnson grabbed Jae by his collar and lifted him up. Galland whined and stood up.

"I'm not doing that," Jae said.

"Why not? You could make big money off this."

"Because we don't need any gods coming here. They'll try to kill me."

Johnson paused. His face scrunched deep in thought. "Well how 'bout this, we make sure to keep it between us Lyourians. No one outside needs to know."

"I don't want to," Jae declined. He removed Johnson's hand from his collar.

"It'll pay off your debt faster." Johnson smiled. "50 cluorgs a pound."

Jae sighed. "Fine. But it's on my terms. *I'll* choose which jobs I do."

"Deal," Johnson said, grabbing Jae's hand. "I get all the money until you reach 1k."

"What?" Jae said. "I've worked every day. How did I not make anything?"

Johnson shrugged. "Should've checked how much you were 'earnin'.'"

"Crooked bastard," Jae grumbled. He faintly regretted loving Bianca as much as he did. If not for her, he would have packed up and fled with Galland long ago.

"You act as if there's any morals in today's world." Johnson smirked. "Grow up kid, get with the times or suffer in poverty."

Johnson patted Jae's back and left the stable. Jae tsked and followed him.

"So when are we doing this?" Jae asked.

"How 'bout now?" Johnson pointed at an elderly woman struggling to carry three large boxes. "I'd say 50 cluorgs."

"No," Jae said. "I'll just help her."

"Again boy, you can't make a livin' bein' a gentleman. How're you gonna pay me back if you can't even sc—charge an old lady?"

Jae rolled his eyes.

"Follow me, I'll show you how to do it." Johnson approached the woman and said, "Excuse me ma'am, need some assistance with those?"

"Oh! How sweet, please, my back is killing me."

"We'd be much obliged," Johnson said, his tone like a southern gentleman. "But I'm much too old, and my boy, well, he can do it for 50 cluorgs."

"50?" The woman shook her head. "That's too expensive, I can just move these myself."

"You don't think my boy should carry all this for free do ya? You can do this yourself, but what'll that cost ya? A week off whatever you're workin' on?" Johnson leaned on the stack of boxes. "Come now, you're worth the money. I don't want to see you 'round here hurtin' 'cause you didn't take our offer. We charge almost triple what we're offerin' you."

"Hmm." The woman looked from Johnson to Jae. "Well, I could always charge extra for these…."

"Exactly," Johnson said. "How 'bout it? Need my boy ta carry these? …Payment upfront of course."

"Alright," the woman said. She reached in her pocket and took out five 10 cluorg coins and dropped it in Johnson's hands. "There best not be a scratch on any of these bottles."

"Of course not. What do you take us for?" Johnson grinned. "We'll get this there safe and sound."

The woman moved so Jae could pick up the boxes. She pointed to a tavern on the other side of the bordello. Jae and Johnson walked faster than her. Once they were a good distance away Johnson said, "That's how ya make money. 50 down, 950 cluorgs to go."

The rest of the week, Jae spent more time working his lifting job than he did deliveries at the bordello. He was only 400 cluorgs away from paying his debt. He walked inside the bordello, even though lifting boxes and crates weren't a problem for him, moving all day without a break was. He waved at the regular guests and headed towards his room.

"Jae," Johnson called, emerging from the passageway to his home. He motioned for Jae to come with him. "I need your help."

"What now?" Jae rolled his eyes.

"Don't 'what now' me." He looked behind him to make sure none of the guests were within earshot. "Bianca's fiancé, Hellim, is comin' in two day—"

"What?" Jae exclaimed. The guests in the hall turned to them.
Johnson shushed him.

"What do you mean he's coming? Doesn't she still have two months?"

"Yes, but he still likes to come to the bordello. Now, stop interruptin' me," Johnson said. "I need your help to clear out the bordello."

"Why?"

"Because he don't like men, if he sees y'all, he's gonna kill ya. He's nice enough to give us a warnin'."

"I doubt he can kill me, but I'll help you get these guys out of here."

"Jae... you lost to me…. You can't be here either."

"I wanna see what her 'man' looks like."

"No!" Johnson shouted. The guests once again looked at them. "Look, we may have our differences, but I don't want ta see ya hurt…. Just do me a favor and stay in hidin'."

"I'll get the guests out of here." Jae walked away from Johnson.

He shouted through the halls for everyone to evacuate. Hellim was arriving and didn't want to see any of their ugly faces. The men complied easily. The color draining from their faces as they left. Johnson asked Jae to deliver the message around town as well. Stay hidden until he gave word. Jae offered to for a cut off his debt, an agreed 70 cluorgs. He walked around town telling the men. They complained and headed for the lumber mill not too far from Lyour. Jae caught the end of a conversation between a group of men. They complained about how unfair it was. Only women were free to move around while Hellim was there. The men had to board up their homes, Hellim apparently destroyed everything in sight upon arrival as well. Jae remembered Bianca mentioning they had a war with Hellim and failed. Was he really that strong? Jae definitely needed to see the guy. Not only was he tormenting Bianca, but he had the entire town in his grasps. Jae was going to size him up. He would deal with his little army after the fact, but he needed to know if this guy was just another rich asshole that cowered at the sight of a sword.

Over the next two days, the women grumbled about, Bianca more than the others. They prepared the main room. They, with the help of Jae, moved a large stone throne onto the stage. It was larger than what the average sized male needed. How could he even sit? What man would find pleasure in his feet dangling off a chair? Jae was disgusted, what was he, a child? Johnson kept begging Jae to seek refuge with one of the Lyourian men. He said he didn't want to see Jae killed. He couldn't live with himself if he could've stopped it. Jae denied of course, he reassured Johnson he wasn't going to die and just wanted a sneak peek at him. He would take one look and go in his room.

~Bianca~

"This is such bullshit," Bianca complained. She aggressively neatened the room. She slammed the pillows on the bed, whipped the covers of any dust and tucked the corners in, she dusted and vacuumed.

Bianca glanced around the "royal suite." A room meant only for Hellim. It was attached to the other side of the main room, just behind the stage. It had 2 Alaskan king-sized beds combined, turned sideways so the wide side became the long side of the bed, it had black and gold covers, and 8 matching pillowcases, and stretched across the middle of the covers was an embroidered ℋ. There was a gold painted vanity mirror and dresser, the carpet was black with golden specks across it, the walls were painted black, and a golden ℋ was painted on one wall with a white circle behind it. His room was tacky and ridiculously large, but Bianca couldn't say anything, or at least not anymore, if Hellim was a man of his word, he wouldn't be back in that room ever again, and they could demolish it or use it for something more useful.

It was utter bullshit to have her clean the room. Bianca felt like Johnson had slapped her in the face. Not only was he ruining the rest of her life, but he also had her prepare his room? The room he was going to use to mentally torture her into submitting to him. Once Bianca was finished, she stormed out of the room. She ignored everyone that said hello to her and went into the stable. She smiled when she saw Galland.

"Hey pretty girl," she said, petting her. "Has Jae visited you? Your mane is matted again. What are you doing?"

Bianca laughed and grabbed her brush. She brushed her mane and said, "I wish I could just run away. If I had an amazing horse like you, I could do it. Would you ditch Jae to go with me?"

Galland neighed as if she was saying yes.

Bianca smiled. "You're such a sweetheart. I really wish we could leave. I guess I was never meant to be happy. Maybe I did something in a past life and cursed myself."

She continued, "Honestly, maybe Hellim will find something better to do with his time. That'd be nice, him focusing his attention on anything but me. He can't be this petty over something as little as defying him.... I sure hope so..."

~Jae~

The day arrived, and Johnson begged Jae to leave. He followed him every minute of the day. Eventually he gave up.

"I can't help you if you want to die." Johnson threw his hands in the air. "What is with the youth wanting to die? What? So you can show my women how much of a 'man' you are? Trust me boy, you don't know the definition of being a man. Throwing your life away to prove what? That you can't be told what to do?"

"Calm down," Jae said, rolling his eyes. "I'm not trying to prove anything. I just want to see what he looks like."

"Even dumber." Johnson shook his head. He headed for his home. "If you want to die, that's on you. But come help me carry a few things into the main room, least you can do before you die."

Jae followed him. "Glad you understand you can't stop me. This'll cost ya 100 cluorgs."

Johnson didn't respond. He continued to walk into his home and to the back hall. "There's metal boxes in the basement, bring 'em up for me. It's in the room to the right of the library."

"Got it," Jae said, walking down the steps. He smirked. *Johnson is such a pushover.*

He heard the door slam shut, lock, a metal clanking sound, followed by a large bang, and another lock.

"Shit!" Jae ran up the stairs and jiggled the doorknob. "Damnit Johnson!"

"It's for your own good," Johnson shouted. Johnson looked at his watch and turned on the camera. He flipped through the cams until he reached the camera at the bottom of the basement stairs. Jae ran up and down the stairs slamming into the door. "Break my door, and you're gonna owe me another 500 cluorgs."

Jae stopped just in front of the door. The last thing he needed was to owe him more money.

"Look, I'll take off another 200 from your debt if you stay there for the next few days. It's for your own good, as well as the safety of everyone in town."

"Fine! You better not con me again!"

"You have my word."

Jae grumbled as he walked down the steps. Where was he going to sleep? What would he eat? How many days did Johnson expect him to stay down there? There was no entertainment, did he think Jae was going to pick up a book? He opened each door, shuddered when he opened the little girl's room, and continued past it. There was a cheap couch in the library. Jae plopped on it, rested his head in his arms and closed his eyes.

Johnson better remember to bring me food.

~Bianca~

Johnson leaned on the wall outside of the bordello. He bit his fingernails as he waited for Hellim to arrive. Johnson called Bianca outside to greet him as well. It was getting late. The sun had set and it was chilly. They heard a loud engine and looked up. They watched as a large spaceship flew over Lyour and landed sloppily by the main gate. The ground rumbled like an earthquake as a large shadow appeared between the gate entrance. Hellim had arrived, he was 8 ft and muscular. His red skin was covered by a large brown cloth.

He walked slowly through the street, looking at each building. He was intentionally searching for men outside. When he reached the bordello, Johnson's facial expression changed from anxious and annoyed to all smiles, his eyes like crescent moons.

"Hello sir," he said, hunching over. "We've been waiting for you."

Hellim looked from Johnson to Bianca and to the bordello. "I see you haven't done any renovations like I asked."

"Uh, not yet," Johnson said, awkwardly. "It costs a lot of money to extend the building. We still don't have enough to cover it."

"If I donate, you'll do it?" Hellim asked.

"Of course, of couurse," Johnson said, as cheerfully as possible. "Anything for you."

Binaca was disgusted with how Johnson behaved around Hellim. He was such a coward. Hellim continued to walk towards the bordello's back entrance, Johnson followed close behind him, urging Bianca to move faster.

Hellim sat on his throne on the main room stage. Two women, Rachel and Hannah were waiting for him with a tray of food and the bordello's finest wine.

"Are there other guests?" Hellim asked.

"Of course not," Johnson said. "You have the women's undivided attention. We will be closed to others until your departure."

"Good," Hellim said, drinking. He exhaled loudly after taking one last sip. "I need to speak to Bianca alone."

"Right away." Johnson bowed. He grabbed Bianca's arm and threw her towards Hellim.

Hellim thanked Hannah and Rachel then commanded both women and Johnson to wait outside the room until he was done.

"How have things been?" he asked.

She didn't respond. She picked at her nails, avoiding eye contact.

"What's with the cold treatment?" He laughed. In a mocking tone, he said, "We *are* soon to marry."

"So you think," Bianca finally said. "I didn't agree to marry you."

"Doesn't matter what you say. It's a decision between me and Johnson."

"I'm not marrying you," Bianca said, harshly. "I'd rather die."

Hellim scoffed. "Are you ready to submit to me then?"

"Never," Bianca said.

"I don't want to marry you no more than you want to marry me," Hellim stated. "This can all be avoided if you just bow down to me."

"Not in a million years," she said. She knew it wasn't that simple. It was never just doing one thing he ordered. Anything could have happened if she did submit to him.

Hellim sighed. He wasn't going to let her get under his skin. He fought back the urge to kill her. He knew that would be giving her the easy way out. "Fine then, I'll enjoy tormenting you until the day you die."

Hellim called Johnson back into the room. "Lock her up. I don't want to see nor hear her while I'm here. Send the other two in."

"Y-yes sir," Johnson said, still smiling. Johnson grabbed Bianca's arm and pulled her out of the room. Once far out of earshot of Hellim, Johnson turned to Bianca and whispered forcefully, "What the hell're you doin'?"

"I don't know what you're talking about," Bianca said, turning her face away from him.

"What the hell did you do to piss him off?" Johnson asked. "You're risking everyone's safety with your childish tantrums."

"I'm not throwing a 'tantrum.' He's pissed for the same reason he's always been since he became a client of mine."

"Stop antagonizing him," he said. "I don't care what he says to you. You don't always have to have the last word. Let him say what he wants. If you care about the other women here, you won't put them in harm's way."

"I would never do anything to put them in danger," Bianca said. "Hellim may hate me, but he would never kill them. "

"You don't know that," Johnson said. "His mood could change at the drop of a hat. Don't risk their safety over whatever petty fights you two have."

Johnson continued, "I can't risk you being in the bordello. You'll need to stay in my house. Come on."

Johnson led Bianca to his home and into the kitchen. He had Bianca prep a few meals and carry them to the basement doors.

"Jae is also down there," Johnson said. "You might as well keep him company. Make sure he doesn't destroy anything else. When Hellim leaves, I'll let the two of you out."

"Okay," Bianca said.

Johnson lifted the metal door and unlocked the basement door. Bianca stepped on the stairs and Johnson slammed the doors shut. Bianca heard the locks click and continued down the stairs. It had been a while since she was down there. She liked going to the library, but flashbacks of her childhood invaded her mind to no end.

She walked through the hall, running her hand along the doors. She opened the library to make sure Jae didn't set it on fire. She walked inside and saw Jae asleep on the couch.

How nice to be that carefree, she thought. She crouched in front of him. He was surprisingly handsome. Maybe it was his attitude and snide remarks that kept her blind to his attractiveness. She ran her hand through his hair. Out loud, she said, "Hey, wake up."

Jae groaned and turned away from her. She sighed. "Jae, come on. Your food's going to get cold."

Jae opened his eyes and looked behind him. He smiled tiredly. He caressed her face, and said, "You're so beautiful."

Bianca's face grew hot and she moved his hand away from her. "You're incoherent. Wake up Jae."

Jae smirked. He yawned and stretched then sat up.

Bianca handed him a plate, and dug through the foods she brought down. She spooned mashed potatoes and a sandwich onto his plate.

"I love your cooking," Jae said.

Bianca scoffed. "It's just a sandwich. Nothing special about it."

"It's special because you made it." Jae smiled.

"Why are you getting so cheesy?" she asked, uncomfortably.

"Why not?"

"I don't know," Bianca said. She looked down at her food.

"Why are you down here?" he asked. He wanted to change the subject. She was clearly uncomfortable and he didn't know how much more his ego could handle.

"Hellim didn't want to see me anymore," Bianca said. "Johnson figured I keep you company and watch you. Don't need this place burning down.

"I wouldn't do that with me trapped inside. Besides, I told you I only did that because I hate the gods."

"Who's to say you don't get mad at another book?" Bianca stated.

"I won't," Jae said. "So why didn't he want to see you?"

"I refused to bow down to him," she said. "He admitted to only marrying me out of spite. Said he'd call it off once I submit to him."

"Why don't you just get it over with?" Jae asked.

"It's not that simple," she said. "I won't give him the satisfaction."

"If all you have to do is submit and he'll leave you alone, why not just throw away your pride? Better than marrying him right?"

"I doubt he'll just let me slide." Bianca shook her head. "I know the moment I do he'll kill me. There's no way out of this for me."

"Is he really that shitty of a person?"

"Thing. And yes, he is. He's killed people over sneezing in front of him. The only reason he's kept me alive for so long, is because he wants the gratification of me giving in."

"Want me to kill him?" Jae asked.

Bianca laughed. "You can't. He's too strong."

"I bet I'm stronger." Jae grinned.

"He took down half of Lyour's men, you don't stand a chance alone."

Jae shook his head. "The men here are weak. The only one strong enough to stand a chance against me is Johnson."

"You lost to Johnson, don't act like he's weaker than you."

"He is," Jae insisted. "I only backed down because he had a gun in my face."

"Whether it's in your face, or halfway across Lyour, you can't dodge a bullet."

Jae didn't respond. He just smiled at her. She was so wrong, but he didn't want to argue with her, especially when she was already upset. "Fine, I won't try to kill him."

"Good," Bianca said. "I don't need you dying after I started to like you."

Jae looked down to hide his smile. He knew she meant it as friends, but he couldn't help not thinking it was meant romantically. Bianca yawned.

Jae slid off the couch and said, "If you're tired, you can have the couch."

"I'm fine," she declined. "There's a bedroom next door."

Jae shivered. "I'm aware of it…it's just not my cup of tea."

"Why? Because it's designed for little girls?"

"Honestly, yeah. I keep thinking about how weird it was, raising young girls into prost—" Jae bit his lip.

"'Prostitutes?' No need to bite your tongue. That's what we are."

"It's still rude to say. I'm sorry."

"You're more polite than others. It's alright." Bianca stood and stretched. "Wanna join me in the other room?"

"I'll stay here," he said. "There's only one bed anyways."

"Are you sure?" Bianca asked. "It's only one bed, but it's the only room with heat and blankets. We can move the couch in there."

Jae thought about it. While the room made him uncomfortable, he could still speak with her until she fell asleep. He could even just return to the library afterwards.

"Sure," he said.

He followed Bianca into the room. The vibe was creepy, like a room out of a horror story. Any moment, a little demonic girl would pop out and steal their souls. Bianca went into one of the wardrobes and pulled out a blanket. They both sat on the floor and looked at each other.

"You can sleep on the bed," Bianca offered.

"Absolutely not," he said.

"Just take the bed," she demanded. "There's nothing wrong with sleeping on it."

"No can do. It's more than just that. One, I would never let a woman sleep on the floor, two, the bed is ridiculously small, I couldn't fit if I tried, and three, I want you to sleep on the bed."

Bianca rolled her eyes. "I'm only doing it, because you said you're too tall for it."

Jae chuckled. She was too proud to let him be a gentleman. He watched her climb into the bed. It was small for her as well, but she was able to fit comfortably, at least more than Jae would have.

Jae went under his blanket and turned to her. He wanted more info about Hellim and what he looked like, but Bianca was out cold. He thought about how cute she was. He closed his eyes, and fell asleep.

They spent the next 2 days chatting about everything. Jae still tried to work up the courage to tell her how he felt, but he could never find the right moment. He couldn't get over Bianca's marriage. He wondered if he would have accepted the marriage if "Hellim" did love her. The more he thought about it, the angrier he became. He was losing someone he loved simply over a petty argument.

It felt weird to Bianca to not be worked to death by Johnson. It was a nice little vacation, if, of course, she forgot about the monster that stomped throughout the town, rattling everything around them.

She didn't answer Jae's questions about what that was. She didn't want to scare him. It was better to keep him oblivious during his stay than worry about the welfare of the bordello's women.

They were sitting in the library. Bianca was reading while Jae played with his sword.

"You know what pisses me off even more," Jae said.

"What are you talking about?" she asked, peeking from her book.

"Your marriage," Jae said.

Before he could continue, Bianca interrupted him, "I don't want to talk about it."

"I know, but it just pisses me off that he's doing this. Maybe I could get over it if he wasn't such a prick and actually loved you."

"Love doesn't exist," Bianca said. "If he weren't a tyrant, and a genuinely nice guy, his 'love' would have been nothing but infatuation."

"Love does exist," Jae corrected her. "With how amazing you are, I'm sure you've had a lot of guys confessing to you."

"It doesn't." She shook her head. "They weren't in love with me, all they wanted was to sleep with me. There wasn't one conversation between us that surmounted to anything intellectual."

"Like our conversations?" Jae asked.

"Yeah, kind of. But that has nothing to do with this."

"It does. I can tell you love exists, because I'm in love with you."

"You don't love me. You're only confusing lust with love. It's no different than the others who've said they 'loved' me."

"Have I *ever* asked to sleep with you?"

"No…"

"Have I talked to you about anything sexual?"

"No."

"So how am I confusing lust for love? I've *never* flirted with you sexually. Sex was never in any of our discussions."

"Still, you don't love me because love doesn't exist."

"I've been in love before. It's real."

"If it was real, you would still be with her," Bianca said, smiling smugly.

"I'm not with her," Jae said, sadness in his voice, "because she died."

"I—I'm so sorry. I…I didn't mean to bring up anything hurtful."

Jae shook his head. "I know you didn't mean to. But what she and I experienced years ago was real. And I know what I'm feeling now is love."

Bianca shook her head. She didn't want to press Jae anymore about love, but she just couldn't accept that love was real. "Love" was sucking the soul out of another until there was nothing left to give. It was nothing more than a fantasy. There was no such thing as love in their society. Bianca had no reason to believe in it. Hearing "soothing" words from older women about her family still loving her when they sold her, the words of wiser women telling her a man couldn't love them. Bianca believed she was in the group of wise women. Not falling into that fake fantasy the world still tried to push on the tormented.

"How about this," Jae said, breaking the silence. "Why don't you let me prove to you love is real?"

"What would be the point?" she asked. "I leave soon."

"Well, you'd get to enjoy your last moments on earth experiencing true love, and I'd get to express my feelings for you. It's a win-win."

Bianca looked down and said, "What if Johnson finds out?"

"Who cares if he does?" Jae grabbed Bianca's hands. "What's he going to do? He can't do anything to you, and he can't hurt me. Take the next month or so to do what *you* want to do. Why spend it miserable?"

"And what happens if you don't convince me in time?"

"I don't know," Jae said. "It's up to you."

"Let me think about that."

"So does that mean you accept the challenge?" he asked.

"…Why not."

Jae smiled widely. While he didn't like how his confession went, he still got the message somewhat across and could use the time to love her before she was gone forever.

Chapter Three
Malarik

The next morning Jae woke up to an empty room. He searched the library and the study for Bianca. Her "fiancé" certainly wouldn't have stayed only a couple nights so she had to be somewhere. "Yo, Bianca," Jae called.

Bianca emerged from a room further down the hall. It was the part of the basement he never had reason to venture to.

"Good morning," she said, as they met halfway in the hall.

"Morning," Jae said. "You think Johnson's gonna remember to bring us food?"

"Doubtful," Bianca said. "But we don't need him. Follow me."

Bianca led Jae to the room she was in. Inside was a kitchen that resembled a small cafeteria. Johnson during the majority of the day, would not let the girls out of the basement. His belief was, if they wanted to study, they had to live in the basement. It was only during what he referred to as "gym class," which consisted of forcing them to run laps around his house to avoid them gaining "too much weight." Some of the women from the bordello, all gone now, volunteered to cook for them.

Bianca continued, "This is where we ate…obviously. There should still be food down here. Let's just hope it's fresh."

Bianca searched the cabinets and Jae searched the pantry. Most of the food was still good, with only a few months left before its expiration. She pulled out a box of cookies and powdered mash potatoes. While she prepared the meals, Jae found bowls and they set the table.

They sat across from each other at a table and Bianca asked, "Were you serious about last night?"

"I meant every word."

"So what are you doing to 'make me love you?'"

"I can't tell. Defeats the purpose if you know in advance."

Pointless, Bianca thought. She didn't bother responding to him. She just knew he was wasting his time, and hers, if she played along with his debates.

Jae was glad Bianca dropped the subject. It had been so long since he did anything romantic, it was like he was inexperienced again. He had no idea what he was doing, and being in that mildew smelling basement wasn't romantic.

After breakfast, Bianca went to the library and Jae went into the classroom. He sat down on the floor with a sheet of paper. He needed to plan out what to do. He wrote:

Operation Love Bianca

He tapped the paper and rested his head in his hand. He continued to write. He wrote whatever came to mind. His plan was horrible, but it was better than nothing.

He leaned against the wall. Maybe he was in over his head. How could he prove to someone as hurt as Bianca that love was real, when he couldn't even express it?

Jae stayed in the classroom most of the day. He couldn't face her. Not until he found something romantic to do.

Bianca wondered where he was. She was confident he'd lose. And the fact that he was nowhere to be found after declaring that, meant he had given up. She selected a random book off the shelf and reclined on the couch. When she finished reading, she went to return it. She looked at the time, it was late in the evening. Being in the basement had warped her sense of time and she slept later. It was a nice vacation if she erased the memory of her 'fiancé' storming about upstairs.

The ground shook once and simultaneously Bianca and Jae paused. They had gotten used to it, but that one was stronger. Bianca hurried to put her book away and speed-walked through the aisles. Jae stood to make sure nothing fell on him. The ground shook again.

Its rumbles intensified, violently shaking everything around him. Jae rushed to the library to check on Bianca. She stumbled around the library holding onto the bookshelves. Jae ran to her and grabbed her arms before she fell over. She felt butterflies as he pulled her to her feet and held her close. She looked up at him and he smiled. After 10 minutes, the rumbles stopped.

"Feel the spark?" he asked.

"Thanks for catching me, but you're wrong." Bianca stepped away from him and left the room.

Jae smirked. *Guess that's a point for me.*

Bianca walked to the steps to sit down when she heard the lock click. A light shined down as she turned around.

"He's gone," Johnson said, and left the doorway.

Bianca couldn't be any happier. She jumped up and ran up the stairs. She stopped in the doorway remembering Jae. She sighed and went back down. She peeked in the library. Jae sat on the couch twirling a pen in his hand.

"Hellim left."

Before Jae could respond, Bianca left again and ran up the stairs. For a second Bianca thought she had lost the bet, but she remembered from one of her textbooks that scary situations can make a person believe they're in love. She brushed it off and retired to her room. She missed her bed.

Bianca heard a knock on her door and looked up. A note was slipped under the door. She read the note:

Meet me at the lake tomorrow on your lunch break.

She sighed. He was really committing to it. She lay back in bed and stared at the wall. *Was it right to agree?*

The next afternoon, Bianca snuck out of the bordello and went to the lake. On the right side of the river, Jae waved at her. On the ground was a blanket and a basket.

"What is this?" she asked.

"Exactly what it looks like."

"And that is?"

"You don't know what a lunch outing is?"

Bianca shook her head. "Not the kind of things you see in Lyour."

"Or anywhere today. It's something that was done regularly before the Day of Ruin. They'd go out on a perfect day like today, sit in the best spot, and eat lunch."

"How do you know so much about the past?"

"Research…" Jae sat on the blanket, twisted a small timer beside him to 30 minutes, and tapped a spot next to him. The timer obviously for their break. It was more so for Bianca than Jae. He didn't care if he returned on time.

"But how accurate is that?" Bianca asked, as she sat down.

Jae laughed quietly as he poured water into a cup he stole from the bordello. In fact, everything he had with him was bordello property. Bianca was amused. How romantic could something be if it was stolen? She thought about questioning him on how he acquired them but she didn't want to embarrass him.

Jae, on the other hand, didn't necessarily care if she knew. He had to make do with his surroundings. He loved to blame his actions on the state of the world. It wasn't his fault no one besides the wealthy could afford lunch baskets and tableware. Johnson wouldn't even notice Jae had the belongings. Jae "borrowed" the items from a box Johnson had stored in the basement. It was covered in cobwebs and partially wet. Jae showed no remorse for taking them.

Though the start of the lunchbreak was a bit rough, they eventually settled in and talked away. While it was nothing more than simple banter on whether love was real or not, they still held each other's interests. Jae was positive Bianca loved him. He couldn't quite put his finger on it, but something in her body language gave him all he needed to know. Every time the timer went off, Jae restarted it for 30 minutes. After a while, they lost track of how many times it went off.

The sun was setting, and the stars slowly peeked onto earth. Jae pulled out a bottle of wine and popped the cork out. "I saved the best for last."

Bianca's mouth dropped. She knew everything was from the bordello, but she didn't think he would actually steal one of Johnson's most expensive wines. "He's gonna kill you."

"That old geezer isn't going to do shit. Besides, this is our little secret." Jae handed her a glass and asked, "This may not be the best thing to talk about, but I'm curious. I know Johnson requires you all to have some talent, but do you get to choose what it is?"

"Sort of. It's not necessarily required, it's just a good way to focus our minds on other things besides…you know."

"So you chose to play guitar?"

"Yeah, that among other things."

"Like what?"

"Storytelling, poetry, piano, and violin."

"Wow, multitalented." Jae clapped. "I never got the chance to tell you, but that performance my second day here was amazing."

"Thanks, glad someone paid attention to it."

"I think everyone was listening."

"No, I've been here long enough to know they don't." Bianca smiled awkwardly. "That song was meant to be said as poetry, but after I realized no one would actually listen to what I said, I had someone compose it into a song."

"I thought it was pretty."

"Yeah? What do you remember about it?"

"…It's been a while. I don't remember everything but it was about birds."

Bianca smirked. "I'll give you an A for effort."

"How about later this evening, or tomorrow, you redo that performance for me in the stable?"

"I don't know about that."

"Why not? I'm sure Galland would love to hear it too. You can bring your guitar. We'll call it round two of courting you."

Bianca rolled her eyes, suppressing her oncoming smile. "'Courting me?' You know what, fine, let's do it."

Jae extended his hand and they shook on it. It was getting late, and they both knew Johnson was probably throwing a fit searching for them. They packed up agreeing to meet tomorrow at whenever their lunch break would be. Bianca headed back earlier than Jae, making sure her breath didn't reek of alcohol.

Jae stashed the rest of the bottle in the stable. He sat down and leaned against the wall. The date didn't go as great as he thought. They had a blast, but it came off more as friends hanging out than lovers. He didn't want to shove his feelings in her face or make her feel pressured, but he had to do something and quick.

Easier said than done, he thought. He seemed cool and composed… at least he hoped he did, but on the inside, he was a complete wreck. He spent the prior night wracking his brain for romantic gestures and activities he could do, yet nothing came to mind. In the end, he banked on Bianca's "hidden feelings" to set the motion. Once he was done wallowing in his self-pity, he headed back to the bordello.

Bianca rushed to the stable. She hoped Jae was still there. Her lunch break was pushed back due to an accident with a guest. She peeked inside. Jae was packing up.

"Sorry, a customer made a mess in the dining hall…"

"That's alright. Better than you standing me up." Jae sat back down and set up again. He laid a blanket in the middle of the stable walkway and opened the lunch basket from the day before. Inside were leftovers from yesterday with the breakfast Bianca made that morning. Jae wasn't a cook and he was barely getting paid for his work. He was shameless about using her own cooking to woo her, but it was always the gesture that counted.

Bianca shook her head and accepted the plate of food. "I decided on what your penalty will be."

"Oh? And that is?"

"I want you to leave Lyour two weeks before my marriage."

Jae smiled uneasily. "You want me to leave that badly?"

"It'll make things easier."

She couldn't guarantee Jae wouldn't do anything when it was time for her to leave. The last thing she wanted was for him to attack Hellim and die. Having that on her conscience would drive her insane.

Jae nodded and agreed to her terms. It just meant he had to fight harder for her. The air was awkward and it took them a while to get the mood back up. Bianca rattled off a few poems and Jae did his best to seem interested and understanding of the meaning behind her words. It was obvious he knew nothing about the art of spoken word. So Bianca switched to teaching him guitar. It was hilarious watching him struggle. They practiced until late in the evening and Bianca hurried off again 10 minutes before Jae could leave. This time telling Johnson she wanted to refine her guitar skills distraction free. That was the only time Johnson ever believed her. Bianca, before Jae's arrival, was obsessed with playing guitar. Johnson was glad everything was slowly going back to normal.

From that moment on, they met in the stable. Whenever Jae came up with a new idea or just wanted to talk, he left a note under her bedroom door or in the kitchen cabinet above the stove. After a week, Jae stepped it up a notch. He, with Bianca's consent, was more physically affectionate. He used every opportunity to hug her or hold her hand. He made sure she wasn't suffocated from it.

Time was of the essence and it seemed like he made no progress. He just needed the right moment. He believed from the bottom of his heart that Bianca loved him. The time at the lake with Galland must have been when they both felt the spark.

Bianca said she was going to be busy that day, but Jae knew the perfect distraction. Galland's bath times. Bianca couldn't resist cleaning her. Jae was lazy when he cleaned her, so Bianca felt she needed to step up for Galland's sake.

He searched the bordello for her and asked if she wanted to join him that evening to wash her. Bianca agreed and later that evening they met to clean her. Galland was as difficult as bathing a cat and even threw herself into mud after they cleaned her. It was around 8 PM when they completed her bath. Bianca sluggishly dropped to the ground and pulled her knees close. She admired her work, proud Galland finally accepted being clean.

Before Bianca could speak, they heard a loud shriek ring through the air and ran to the stable doors. As they peered outside, a blue light burst into the air. Bianca's eyes lit up.

"I forgot Johnson planned to do these!"

Bianca started to run but Jae pulled her back. "Why the rush? Watch with me."

"I can't. I have to help Johnson."

"Says who?"

"…Johnson…."

"You didn't even know it was happening. Doubt he cares."

"He does, for years he had *only* me discard used fireworks. He cares."

"Well," Jae said, pulling Bianca close and wrapping his arms around her waist. "Can this year be an exception?"

Bianca smiled. "Fine. You win, but you better take the brunt of his nagging."

They stared into each other's eyes before turning their gaze back to the night sky. Jae raised his left arm to her upper back and arm. He questioned how Johnson could get fireworks. What couldn't he obtain? Jae wouldn't be surprised if Johnson possessed a star.

The warm night breeze blew, gently brushing their faces. The sky illuminated in bright colors. Red, blue, pink, there were different shapes like stars, smiley faces, dolphins, but hearts exploded the air the majority of the time. Jae was feeling confident. He didn't care about piggybacking off Johnson. He turned to Bianca and gazed lovingly into her eyes. He tilted his head and kissed her. Bianca felt a strange murmur in her heart and she pulled away.

"I—I have to go…" Bianca walked briskly to Lyour's gates.

"I'm sorry."

Bianca didn't respond. She continued to walk, folding her arms. She walked past Johnson who complained about having other women do her job. She apologized, not really paying attention to what he said, nor what she said herself.

She flopped on her bed and covered her cheeks. They had been burning since she left Jae. Why was she so flustered? She kissed many men, so it wasn't her first. Not even her first kiss made her feel the way she felt.

What the hell is happening to me? she groaned. She couldn't continue with the bet. Anxiety possessed her. What was she doing swooning over someone? It was pointless feeling anything for him. All it did was guarantee heartbreak. She was stupid and overconfident to take his offer. She had to stay away from him until her feelings subsided.

For days, she ignored his notes and avoided him in the halls. Jae knew what was up but left her alone. Seeing that he got the hint resulted in the wrong emotion than what Bianca hoped for. Although she would never admit it, she was disappointed he gave up so easily. He proved her point. He never loved her. It was nothing more than infatuation.

A week passed since Bianca and Jae last spoke to each other. It was strange not interacting with each other. Jae's patience was dwindling. He was convinced Bianca was avoiding him because she lost.

He thought she was at least honorable and would keep her word. He pulled out his final note to her. When he finished writing he slipped it under her door and went to the stable.

Bianca stared at his note, a cold sweat rolled down her spine. In the letter read:

Dear Bianca,

I want to apologize for what happened the other night. I should have never kissed you. If you want nothing to do with me, I understand. But avoiding me is heartbreaking. If we can't be lovers, then I am fine being just friends. So long as you're in my life. Please meet me at the stables tonight at 10. I'll be waiting.

Bianca sighed. She wanted to see him, but what awaited her when she arrived? Could she hold back the bizarre feelings she held for him? She thought about it throughout the day. A storm raged by the late afternoon, limiting her work.

10 PM came and Bianca paced the main hall. She stopped at the door every so often, twisting the doorknob and backing out. 30 minutes passed and she finally had enough courage to leave. She rushed to get out of the still raging thunderstorm.

Bianca walked into the stable. Jae stood on the other side of the room, his back facing her, his hair still wet from the rain. "You're late."

Lightning streaked across the sky, thunder loudly clapping behind her. "I got here as fast as I could."

"Not fast enough." Jae turned, slowly facing her. "I couldn't wait to see you."

She lowered her eyes unsure of what to say. "You missed me huh?"

Jae stalked towards her, backing her into the wall. "Always."

His eyes locked into hers. And with one swift magical motion, a rose blossomed in the palm of his hand.

She looked up, gazing at him through her lashes. "Magic?"

"I got a few tricks up my sleeve."

"It's beautiful."

He caressed her cheek with the back of his hand. "Not as beautiful as you."

She looked away turning her head. "Jae—don't."

"I love you."

"But I don't love anyone."

"If you don't love me, tell me and I'll leave. And I'll never come back."

Bianca looked away. Her heart pained with the thought of never seeing him again. She closed her eyes.

"I love you too," Jae whispered. He leaned in, kissing her breathlessly.

Bianca wrapped her arms around Jae's neck. Even if it was for just this moment, she would let herself be whisked away.

Their lips slowly parted and touched their foreheads. Bianca couldn't deny it any longer. She loved Jae. And no matter how much she wished she didn't, her heart couldn't push him away.

"Let's meet in secret."

"But Hellim..."

"I don't give a damn about Hellim," he said. "Leave him."

"I can't."

"Why?" he asked.

"You proved to me love was real, you win. But we can't be together."

Bianca looked away, her heart wrenching with pain. The thought of losing him driving her to the edge. She thought, tears swimming to the corner of her eyes, *I just can't.*

Jae swept her into his arms, pulling her close to his chest. "I'm not walking away without you. I'll be here at dawn."

Jae walked away, his silhouette retreating into the mists of rain.

Bianca's knees gave way, and she collapsed to the floor in defeat. Her heart giving into her selfish desires, at dawn they would meet.

~Jae~

Jae's heart raced as he walked into Lyour's gates. He questioned if it was a good idea to pursue her beyond their agreement. He had already lost the person he loved once, he didn't know if he could handle it a second time. Not when he could stop it.

He promised himself that he would walk away when it was time. Jae walked into the bordello and Johnson stood by the stairs.

He glanced at Jae. "You seen Bianca?"

"Yeah, she's at the stable."

Johnson tsked and shook his head. "You're gonna need to take care of your own horse. We got more important things to worry about."

"As a matter of fact," Johnson continued. "Why are you still in Lyour?"

Jae shrugged. "I'll leave soon."

"Can't have you stayin' here rent free."

"I'll continue to work, how about that?"

"I don't know…"

"Business has been running smoother since I showed up, you need me." Jae walked past Johnson and went up the stairs. "You can pay me in a room and Bianca tending to Galland."

"You don't call the shots."

Jae waved and went to his room. Johnson knew it was a good deal. He even thought about charging him double for food and anything else he needed.

Bianca entered the bordello, twirling the rose Jae gave her as Johnson left the bottom step.

"Where'd you get that?"

"Huh?" She hid the rose behind her.

"I already saw it. Where'd you get it? And don't lie."

"Uh, Jae showed me a magic trick."

"Is it real?" Johnson reached for the rose.

"Yeah." Bianca handed it to him.

"How in the world—" Johnson started. Flowers were rare and to get one, especially a rose, cost an arm and a leg. How in the world did Jae get one? "And it just…appeared?"

"Yeah."

"Huh." Johnson tossed the rose back at Bianca. She'd given him a new business idea. If Jae wanted to be a freeloader, he could put his little "magic" to use.

The next morning, at dawn, Bianca snuck out of the bordello. The wintry morning air kissed her cheeks as she walked through Lyour. She still couldn't wrap her head around what she was doing. Everything up until yesterday was just a game, a bet, how did it end up like this? Bianca was scared, but on the other hand, it was thrilling.

She pulled open the stable door and peered inside. Sitting on a wall by Galland, was Jae. He looked at her and smiled. He hopped off the wall and approached her.

Jae brushed her hair behind her ear. "Good morning."

"What does this entail?" she asked.

"Whatever you want. It's not a business deal."

"Well, you know this is new to me…"

"We'll take it slow." Jae kissed Bianca and led her to the stall.

They talked for an hour before they had to run back into the bordello. When they arrived, Johnson was just leaving his home. His eyebrows furrowed when he saw them.

"Bianca, get breakfast ready. Jae, come with me."

Bianca and Jae exchanged glances and she went to the kitchen. Johnson wrapped his arm around Jae's shoulder and said, "Ain't you just full of surprises? I heard about your little magic trick. How many flowers can ya make appear?"

"As many as I want." Jae wondered how he found out. Did Bianca tell him? That couldn't have been the case, if there was any sign of them flirting, Bianca would've been locked in the attic and he would have tried to kill Jae.

"Look, I'll let ya stay if you make me a bunch of flowers."

"'A bunch'…it takes a lot of energy to do it, if—"

"That's fine, you're free of your other duties if you produce 'em."

"I'll still help Bianca but I'm not doing anything else."

"Yeah sure, come on."

Johnson led Jae to a room in his home. He pulled out 5 open wooden crates and told Jae to make as many as possible. If he could make more than 5 crates worth, he could grab more crates from under the counter and he would pay him a profit of 10% for the extra crates. Johnson sat at the other side of the table. Jae asked him to leave, he had to keep his magic tricks a secret. Johnson ridiculed him before giving up and leaving. He had "other important things to do anyways."

Jae stared at the crates. What kind of flowers did he want? Jae knew roses were valuable, but were other kinds as rare? He decided to start with making the roses, and think about the rest later. He held his palm downwards over the crate. A faint light appeared in his palm and a red rose grew from his palm and dropped into the crate. He thought, *One down, shit ton more to go.*

To increase production, he stuck out his left hand and grew roses in the second crate. He grew two crates worth of red roses, one crate of miscellaneous colors like pink, blue, black, yellow, orange and many others. By the fourth crate, his nose bled and he stopped growing with his left hand and plugged his nose. He knew he was over doing it, but he needed this reason to stay. The last two crates were filled with daisies, carnations, cherry blossoms, and lilies.

He hoped it was enough, he couldn't make any more for a couple of days. He looked around the kitchen for a towel to clean his nose. The kitchen door opened and Jae looked back. He saw it was Bianca and faced away from her.

"Oh my gosh." Bianca rushed to Jae and turned his face to her. She pulled out a handkerchief and wiped his nose. "What happened?!"

"I'm fine." Jae took the handkerchief from Bianca and held it to his nose. "It's just a little drawback of magic."

"When you say magic, you don't mean like a magician do you?"

"I do mean like a magician. This is how they were before the day of ruin."

"Really? I never saw that in my books."

"It's a hidden talent." Jae walked to the crate and pulled out a blue rose. He handed it to Bianca. "The 'gods' wouldn't be happy with us knowing it."

"I…guess that makes sense…" Bianca lied. He was speaking absolute nonsense. But at the same time, he was doing something enigmatic. So maybe it was better to believe him. Even if the story itself was garbage. "If it's causing this much damage, don't use it."

"I'll be fine."

"Promise me, please."

"I need to do this to stay at the bordello. This should last him a few days. When he needs the next batch, I'll do it."

"You don't have to stay at the bordello. You could live in the stable with Galland."

"Never."

Jae leaned to kiss Bianca when the kitchen door flung open. He rolled his eyes and looked to the door. Johnson entered, a look of greed smeared across his face.

"I don't know why you're bleeding, nor do I care, but you just made me even richer!"

Johnson stacked the crates and exited. He stopped a bit from the door and called for Bianca to come with him. She said goodbye and left.

Jae rinsed off her handkerchief and left Johnson's house.

Over the week, Bianca and Jae met in the stable at dawn. They spent the hour they had talking, and sometimes would sneak out at night to see each other. They sat in the stable pampering Galland. Jae combed her coat while Bianca brushed her mane. Jae glanced at Bianca every so often. Their relationship was pure, the most they did was hug and kiss. Jae thought about making a move, but with how Bianca grew up, he wasn't sure if she wanted to go further.

He didn't want her to think that was all he wanted from her. Maybe if the moment was ever right, something could happen. Even if he waited until their last day together. But until the topic ever arised, he would respect her comfortability.

There was an event happening in the evening, Bianca and Jae had to cut their meeting short. They rushed back to the bordello. Jae went to his room and Bianca into the kitchen.

Jae fell back asleep and didn't wake until the afternoon.

Johnson paced around the hall. "The hell am I supposed to do now?"

"What's wrong?" Jae asked, stretching as he came down the stairs.

"The merchant I order from had an accident and can't bring my supplies. We're fucked without it."

"Want me to go?" Jae asked.

"You would do that?" Johnson paused.

Jae nodded. "Yes…for a price of course."

"What are you looking for?"

"Hmm, 500 cluorgs."

"5 hun—" Johnson exclaimed. "I could get anyone in this town to go for a third of that price."

"But would you trust them to bring you everything you ordered?" Bianca joined in, appearing from the kitchen.

Johnson didn't respond. He needed to think it through. Bianca made a good point, that town was full of crooked people. They would go for a cheaper price but would take half his stock.

"Shit," Johnson finally said. "Alright, but you get paid after you bring the supplies. You'll be deducted pay for anything damaged, missin', or if you take longer than 2 weeks. Deal?"

"Deal," Jae said. As he left the bordello he said, "Bianca can you bring Galland's saddle supplies to the stable? I'll leave tomorrow."

"Johnson, I should go with him," Bianca said.

"Absolutely not," Johnson yelled. "Hellim is comin' next month. I ain't riskin' anything happenin' to you or this deal."

"I know where Malarik is. Jae's new to the region and will take a long time to get there. Not to mention, the merchant won't know who he is and probably won't give him the supplies."

"I can have someone else go with him. Doesn't have to be you."

"You can't. Everyone here is booked. I'm literally the only person who has free time," Bianca said. She grabbed Johnson's hand. "Please let me go. In 3 weeks, I'll have to go with Hellim to who knows where, he might even lock me away forever. Let me see someplace other than Lyour as my last place."

Johnson snatched his hand away from Bianca and sighed. Even though he was harsh on her and the others, there was still a soft spot. And he knew the deal was unfair. But what was one person's freedom to the rest of the world's? It was a cruel decision but one Bianca should've accepted, understood. "Fine. But Jae, you better get her there and back safely. And don't you *dare* lay a finger on her."

"I know, I know." Jae waved him off and left.

"Thanks Johnson." Bianca smiled.

As Bianca turned to leave, Johnson grabbed her arm forcefully and pulled her towards him.

"I'm not done. There are rules you need to follow. This isn't a vacation for you. We'll have a serious conversation on this tomorrow before you leave. I have things to do. Get whatever equipment he needs for his horse and come back inside right away." Johnson let go of Bianca and went to another room.

"Asshole," Bianca scoffed.

Jae waited for Bianca in the stable. When she entered Galland's stall, Jae pulled her towards him and kissed her passionately.

Bianca pulled away. "We can't. I need to get her ready and head back inside."

"You can take your time." Jae leaned in for another kiss.

"No." Bianca moved to the side. "I don't want to risk Johnson seeing us. I really want to go to Malarik."

Jae frowned. "Fine. Most of her stuff is already in here. The rest is in my room. Nothing has to be done today unless you wanna give her a bath. It'll be the last one she gets until we come back."

"I can do that. It'll be easier if you grab the things from your room and bring them here. Less trips later, right?"

"Yeah. Well…I'll leave you to it. I'll be right back."

"Okay." Bianca watched as Jae left the stall then said, "Don't worry, we won't have to worry about Johnson once we're in Malarik."

Jae smiled and shook his head as he left.

Once Bianca finished bathing Galland and all of her travel necessities were gathered, Bianca went back into the bordello. She did her best to stay on Johnson's good side. One wrong move and she would be sitting in her room after Jae left. She avoided Jae as well. If Johnson suspected any flirting, she had to stay. Bianca hoped Jae understood what she was doing.

The next day arrived and Bianca helped Jae saddle Galland. And by help, she really just watched to learn how. But every so often handing him what he needed. They exited the stable and met Johnson by the bordello.

"Alright, this is what you're expecting," Johnson said, handing Jae a sheet of paper. "Make sure he doesn't try to cheat me. He's dishonest, especially with newcomers."

"Got it," Jae said, folding the paper and putting it in his pocket.

"Here's the money. Don't lose it. It's 1,000 cluorgs. Make sure to count it out to him, because again, he's dishonest."

"Alright."

"Everything on there is valuable. Make sure none of it is damaged." Johnson handed him a card. "Here's my pass into Malarik. Say you're there on behalf of J Bordello, and they'll let you in."

"Got it."

Johnson leaned in close to Jae and whispered, "Don't you dare lay a hand on Bianca. This isn't a fun little getaway. You're there to get my merchandise, she's there to speak to my supplier. And protect her with your life."

"All things I know," Jae said, turning around. "If there isn't anything else I should know, I need to finish getting ready."

Jae walked away before Johnson could confirm. He didn't want to hear anything else from him. He was annoyed with how he spoke about Bianca, as if she were an object. Johnson didn't respect her, that was obvious. But Jae held his tongue, not because he was afraid of Johnson, but because he didn't want to jeopardize Bianca's chances of going. They were treading on thin ice as is.

Johnson waited until Jae was out of ear shot before yanking Bianca by the arm. "Get over here. There are *rules* you need to follow. 1. You only have to speak with the merchant. Don't have sex with him. I don't care if he offers to pay or not. 2. Like I told Jae, you are not allowed to sleep with him. Don't think that I don't know what's been going on between you two. I wasn't born yesterday. I let it slide, but it better not get in the way of your marriage. 3. Don't even *think* about running away. I will hunt you down myself and kill Jae. Get there, get the stuff, and come back *immediately*. 4. I'll give you spending money. This is only for necessities. I better not see any souvenirs for yourself or any of the girls. Go."

Johnson threw Bianca's arm as he let go. He reached into his pocket and took out 400 cluorgs. He softened his tone and said, "I know it's difficult but what you're doing is for the greater good. Don't forget that."

Bianca didn't respond. She took the money and walked away.

For the greater good my ass, Biance thought.

Who could even trust what her fiancé was saying? He was an evil man. Once he had her, what reason did he have to spare the people in Lyour? Or anyone in their region of the world for that matter? How could Johnson trust him so easily?

When she made it to Jae and Galland her expression relaxed and she smiled. He was the light in her darkness. Even if it was only until she was married, this meant everything to her. Something that would last past her marriage with Hellim. Jae wrapped his hands around her waist and lifted her onto Galland then mounted Galland himself. Bianca placed her arms around him.

Johnson walked over once again. He couldn't shake the feeling they were up to something. What, he wasn't sure. Who knew what they were planning to get away with on this trip? He was second guessing whether he should let her go, but he knew the merchant wouldn't trust Jae. "Remember what I said you two. This ain't a vacation."

They both nodded, not really acknowledging him. Jae clicked his tongue for Galland to start walking. Bianca's excitement picked up the moment Galland moved. She tightened her arms around Jae.

Once they were out of Lyour, Jae asked, "How far is Malarik from here?"

"It's east of here. I've only gone to the outskirts of Malarik twice. Once it took 3 days, the other 1 week. It all depends on how fast you want to get there I guess."

"Well if it's not that far, I won't rush. We can enjoy the scenery."

Bianca laughed. "What scenery? You mean the dead grass or burnt, leafless trees?"

Jae shrugged. "You can find beauty in anything."

Bianca smiled. As cheesy as it was, he was right. Even the desolate land around them had some appeal to it. While it looked similar to what surrounded Lyour, everything looked new. She hugged Jae tightly, mesmerized by the scenery. "Maybe you're right. The outside world is beautiful."

"Hm…" Jae started. "I wouldn't say the outside world itself is beautiful. The environment is stunning, but it's just as crooked and evil as Lyour. I would even say worse."

"How?"

"Bandits for one, Lyour may have tough men, but after being there so long, they're soft compared to the people I've encountered." Jae glanced back at Bianca. "Not just because of how cowardice they are towards your 'fiancé,' I've seen some terrible things. Vile beings plague the earth."

"Did you not just say that 'you can find beauty in anything?' How can you say that, then do a complete 180°?"

"Because meeting you gave me some hope. However, I don't want you to see anything that shatters yours. It's better to tell you the truth."

"I mean, I've seen some ghastly things. I'm not oblivious to how dangerous some places are, but I doubt the entire world is that bad."

"You're right," Jae said. He disagreed with her completely. He had been travelling for most of his life, across the world to many different regions, and had yet to come across a town that was pure bliss. Everything was the same, bandit ran cities, poverty, and gods that killed on whim. But he didn't have the heart to convince her there wasn't a safe place.

They rode for hours, Bianca stopping Jae to give Galland a break more times than Jae would have. They set up camp once the sun set. Jae was upset they didn't make as much progress as he wanted to, but there was no point harping over it. He dug through his pocket and pulled out a mini suitcase smaller than his palm.

"Aw," Bianca gushed. "That's so cute. Is it a good luck charm?"

"Not at all," Jae said. He smirked and grabbed the tiny handle. He held it by the handle with his right hand and with immense force, moved his arm down. The suitcase expanded into a large suitcase.

"Whoa!" Bianca shouted. She studied it. "How did you do that?"

"It's an antique device," Jae answered. "It's a high tech travel case. I found it in the trash, not many know the value of it. These were introduced by the gods…before they annihilated humans of course."

"Wow. How much can it hold?"

"Infinite," Jae said, pulling out a blanket and spreading it on the ground. "I can change the size to anything and I have yet to fill it."

"If you can change the size, why not make it large enough for us to use as a bed?"

"Well, if you mean sleeping inside, I wouldn't trust it, while I can grab what I'm looking for, I doubt living creatures can go in and come out unscathed. I can try to make it large enough for us to sleep on, but why not use the ground?"

"We can…" Bianca said. "It's just…"

"That you're used to sleeping on soft luxurious beds, and sleeping on the ground seems meager?"

"No, it looks uncomfortable. I am used to luxurious things, doesn't make me snobby."

Jae smiled. "I wasn't saying you were. Try it first, if it doesn't work out, I'll expand the suitcase."

"Okay…" Bianca said. She wasn't going to keep asking. It was his and it was valuable. So she understood why he was reluctant to use it.

She sat down on the blanket and Jae joined her.

"See not so bad," he said. He unfastened his cloak, laid it on top of her lap and lay down himself.

"Uh, yeah…it's nice in the sense of camping or something…." she said, lying on his chest. She pulled the cloak up and pushed some onto Jae.

"I don't need it," he declined.

"Why not?"

"I can't sleep. There could be bandits at any point."

"I mean, we're not that far from Lyour, so obviously there are going to be bandits and I doubt they'll rob me."

"They might not, but you never know who's going to pass. It's safer if I stay alert. Last thing we need is Johnson blasting my head off for you getting kidnapped."

"Is that the only reason you'd protect me?"

Jae smirked. "Of course not, I'd murder every bandit that touched you. And *not* because of Johnson."

"Crazy, but somewhat…sweet."

Jae smiled. "Go to sleep. I'll wake you at dawn."

"Alright, goodnight," Bianca said, resting her head on his shoulder and closing her eyes.

The rest of the trip to Malarik was pleasant. Jae hated how much time was wasted for Galland's breaks, and the potential threat of bandits and mentioned many times to rush Bianca. Bianca wanted to have a nice vacation as much as Jae did, once they were in Malarik, they could relax and enjoy it to their hearts content. But she respected Galland's health, she came first. Overworking her wasn't worth it. They traveled for 4 days total, and on the 4th day, they could see the Wall of Malarik in the distance. Bianca smiled with anticipation.

They arrived in the outskirts of Malarik 5 hours later. The area was a slum. It was dirty, the wood on buildings were rotting, feces, human and animal laid everywhere in the road, the people were disheveled and dirty, and the stench was foul. Jae knew it. The smell of rotting flesh. He couldn't see where the bodies were placed, but the smell filled the streets. In the distance, deeper into the outskirts, was a large cement wall 40 feet high. The shadow cast over the outskirts making it look even worse. Jae guessed that was where the actual city was. But why was the wall there? As they made their way through the slums, they were given dirty looks. Jae stayed on guard. Who knew what they were capable of?

When they reached the wall, an opening blocked by a gate was not too far off. The opening was at the top of a small hill. Two guards stood in front of the gate. A long line of people, some from the slums and others looked like travelers.

"Is this normal?" Jae asked.

Bianca nodded. "From what I remember yes. Johnson always complained about the line but I've never been this far."

"Guess we have a long wait ahead of us," Jae sighed. "Of all the things Johnson repeated to us, the least he could have done was warned us about this."

"It's not that bad. There's what? 20 people ahead of us. It shouldn't take that long."

"I hope you're right," Jae said. Then he whispered, "The last thing I want to do is spend the night in this place."

"Oh relax. It's not dangerous."

"Coming from a person that lives in Lyour. I think your sense of danger is warped."

"What's that supposed to mean?" Bianca crossed her arms.

"Exactly what you think it means. I don't know how much Johnson normalized this kind of living, but it's not healthy nor is it great. The people living here can attest to that. The smell, the dead bodies…that's not normal."

Bianca didn't respond. He was a traveler. He knew more than she did. She was embarrassed. Did she really have childish thoughts about reality? When did this become normal to her?

"I didn't mean to offend you," Jae said, breaking the silence.

"You didn't. You're right."

"Maybe once we're in Malarik, you'll see something different."

"What do you mean?"

"If Malarik was as beaten down as the outskirts, this wall wouldn't be placed here. So there must be something of value in there."

"I wonder what." Bianca looked up at the wall. The sun slowly peeked from the wall as she stared and she looked down.

Ahead at the gate they heard screaming.

"Please!" a woman begged. She clung onto the guard. "I need to see my husband!"

"Get back!" the guard shouted. Throwing the woman onto the ground. "No proof, no entry."

Bianca gasped and cupped her mouth and Jae moved out of the line to see what was happening. The second guard dragged the woman out of the way by her hair and threw her down the hill back into the slums.

"Next," the guard shouted.

The people in line murmured to each other. Unsure what just happened and why.

"Come on!" the guard yelled, motioning impatiently for them to keep moving.

The line slowly proceeded to the gate. Checking in one by one. Travelers were allowed in, but most of the locals were rejected without Malarik citizenship.

When it was Jae and Bianca's turn, the guard stopped them. "She can't ride in on the horse."

"Why? Are horses not allowed inside?"

"They are. But you can't ride them. It's for safety reasons. You can check her in one of the stables."

"Alright," Jae said. He helped Bianca off Galland and showed the guard the bordello pass.

The guard motioned for them to enter. Jae grabbed the reins and guided Galland through the gates. Once they passed the second gate, their mouths dropped. They were greeted with a bright blue sky, glistening blue sea, and a large city that looked like New York City prior to the Day of Ruin. Malarik was by far the most gorgeous city Jae had visited. The Malarians' skin was blue, different shades, and their hair color ranged from white, black, red, and brown.

Bianca and Jae walked through the city side of Malarik. Johnson gave them a map of where the merchant would be. When they found his shop, they tied Galland's reins to a pole and entered.

At the front counter was Oplytuo, the merchant Jae saved in Lyour. His face turned purple when he saw Bianca.

"Bianca!" he shouted. Taking a chance, he opened his arms for a hug.

"How are you doing?" Bianca asked, reciprocating his hug.

"Great," he said, he scratched the back of his head. "I…take it you're here for Johnson's merch?"

"Yes sir," she said. "And you remember Jae?"

"Of course!" Oplytuo exclaimed. "If not for him, I'd be stuck under that wagon forever. I could never forget him! It's a pleasure to see you."

Jae nodded in acknowledgement, shaking his hand. "The stuff?"

"Right," Oplytuo said, scampering to the back. He returned a moment later with a cart full of different items. "Here you go."

"All of this?" Jae asked.

Oplytuo nodded. "That's why my boss declined delivering it. Johnson refused to pay us extra for its weight."

"Typical," Jae said.

"Yeah, I'm sorry," he said. "After what happened to me last time…we have a weight limit."

"That's fine," Jae said. He reached for the cart.

"Ah," Oplytuo said, jumping in front of the cart. "Uh, sorry. This is our property. You have to pay first, then find another way to carry it."

Jae rolled his eyes. He counted out the cluorgs and handed it to Oplytuo.

"Jae," Bianca said. "You can just use that suitcase, right?"

"Yeah but…" Jae started.

"So let's do that. Is it heavier with it?" she asked.

"No, not really. I just didn't want it mixed with my things. You know as well as I do, Johnson'll claim some of it is his."

"True." She looked at the items and said, "We just need something to pack it in. Oplytuo, do you guys have any boxes?"

"No, but there's a shipping company not far from here. They sell everything package related. Just take a left and continue down, you'll see it."

"I'll stay with the stuff," Bianca offered.

"Okay, I'll go," Jae said. He didn't like the idea of Bianca staying with Oplytuo. He didn't know what their relationship was, but it was a little to handsy for him. It was clear as day, he had a crush on her. Who didn't? Jae left to the shipping company, checking on Galland on the way.

When he arrived, there was a small shop, only 6 people fit inside. Jae sighed and entered. He asked for 10 boxes and paid 60 cluorgs. He returned to the merchant shop and they packed the items into boxes. Jae took out his suitcase and loaded the boxes inside.

"I still don't understand how you know where everything is," Bianca commented.

"Took some time," Jae said. "Let's go."

"Thanks Oplytuo," Bianca said. "Is there an inn nearby? Best Malarik's got."

"Oh yes…right by the ocean," he answered. "It's really pretty."

"What do you think?" Bianca asked Jae.

Jae shrugged. "Doesn't matter to me."

Bianca said goodbye to Oplytuo after he finished giving them directions to the inn. It was a straight shot from a boardwalk.

They arrived at "Jwambulo's Hostel" 2 hours later and the sun was setting. After navigating through the busy, overcrowded streets, it was an easy find on the boardwalk. It was extravagant. Larger than the bordello in both height and width. Jae asked Bianca to watch Galland while he got a room. The manager was a stout older gentleman, his skin looked like midnight and his hair was silver. He kept his conversation with Jae brief. A stable check in on the far right side of the inn, and their room was on the first floor, in the back. The price was 20 cluorgs a day, 50 after a week. Jae had no concerns over the price, they didn't plan on staying that long, and if they did, he'd find a way to scam…. negotiate the price down.

He met Bianca outside and they searched for the inn stable. It provided food, water, and baths to horses so their owners didn't have to worry about them. That decision came about after many careless guests forgot about their horses and starved them, only to sue Jwambulo for negligence. They said their goodbyes to Galland and headed towards their room.

Bianca gasped when they opened the door. The room was beautifully decorated. The walls and floor were tan, there was a couch in front of a holographic TV, and a queen sized bed with a bamboo bedframe, and white sheets and blankets. There was a large bathroom with a black glass steam shower and jetted tub. They walked to the patio door and were greeted with a breathtaking view of the ocean, the sun peeked over the horizon, its orange and red light reflected off the water. They stepped out onto the veranda. The warm breeze caressed their skin.

"It's beautiful," Bianca said, she leaned on Jae's shoulder.

"I can't believe it exists," Jae said, wrapping an arm around her.

"Guess there *are* places in the world that are beautiful."

"Well they certainly proved me partially wrong."

"Partially?"

"Well, look at all of this. Malarik has so much space and resources, yet it has a slum right outside its walls," Jae said. "And the people here live as if they don't exist. Nothing more than a fake utopia."

"That kinda ruins our vacation for me…" Bianca said.

"Don't let it," he said. "That's just how the world is. What you saw outside is how things are. Inside is the exception."

"Still…"

Jae lifted Bianca's chin, and kissed her. Their lips parted slowly and Jae said, "Don't think about it. Focus only on me."

Bianca lowered her head and nodded.

Jae smiled. "Wanna try the inn's restaurant?"

"Sure," Bianca said.

They headed to the restaurant and ordered a Malarian specialty comprised of dried space squid, kalamata olives, and linguine, beef meatballs and kmnuye cheese, kmnuye was a space cow, but it had a unique taste and color when milked that made it more desirable than earth cows, and they finished with an earth delicacy from "ancient" times called castella cake.

Bianca offered to pay that time. It wasn't her money anyways. They headed back to their room and discussed sleeping arrangements. Jae insisted on sleeping on the couch and Bianca stayed on the bed, but she wanted them to share it. After arguing for 30 minutes, Bianca gave up. If he didn't want to share with her, then it was whatever. Jae on the other hand, didn't want to share, because he felt it was inappropriate to do so. And as much as he didn't respect Johnson and his "don't try anything" warnings, making sure he didn't sleep with her was the only thing he agreed with. Not for the same reasons of course.

The next morning, Bianca and Jae went to a tourist shop. Initially they were leaving in the morning, however since they arrived earlier than expected, they could spend an extra day relaxing on the beach. Johnson couldn't guess if they were slacking, even if he tried.

They walked around the shop until they found a swimsuit section. Jae leaned towards Bianca and said, "Those are swimsuits. They were used a lot before the day of ruin."

Bianca laughed and said, "I'm well aware of what a swimsuit is. Johnson makes us wear them during summer months."

Bianca looked through the racks. She eyed a blue and white striped bikini. "What do you think about this?"

"It's nice," Jae said. "But anything you choose will look amazing on you."

"Then I'll go with this," she said, walking to a section for beach accessories, like a towel, parasol, a yellow off-the-shoulder coverup dress, etc. She noticed Jae following her and asked, "Aren't you getting a bathing suit?"

He shook his head. "I'll just wear shorts."

"You sure?" she asked.

"Yeah, the prices here aren't worth it. I have a lot of worn out clothing in my suitcase."

"Well, I'll get something for the both of us to use," she said, grabbing two towels, sandals, buckets, and shovels. "This should be everything right? I want my first time on a beach to be fun for both of us."

"I'm not letting you pay for everything," Jae said. He reached for the items.

Bianca moved away and said, "I'm not paying. Johnson is."

Jae scoffed and shook his head. She had a point. Bianca was set on using all of the money he gave her. Whatever wasn't used for them, she was definitely going to spend on the women at the bordello. Malarik was a city for the rich, almost everything was expensive. So long as she hid the souvenirs, Johnson would hopefully assume she only ate at luxurious restaurants. After paying, they went back to their hotel room to change.

Bianca ran off their veranda and into the warm sand. Her eyes sparkled with jubilation. She turned to Jae and shouted, "Come on slowpoke!"

Jae smiled as he walked down the steps. Her excitement was endearing. In the weeks that he spent with her, he had never seen such a look of happiness from her. He held Bianca's hand and they walked to the shore.

"It's beautiful." Bianca wrapped her arm around Jae's and rested her head on his shoulder. Being by the water erased all of her troubles, even if it was temporary. It was like a weight was lifted off her shoulders and she could just exist. Her past didn't define her and her obligation to the world was absolved. The waves crashed against their feet and Bianca jumped, letting out a small "eep," from how cold the water was.

Jae laughed and said, "Let's go to the boardwalk."

Embarrassed, Bianca replied, "Okay…"

They walked slowly to the boardwalk. Bianca kicked the sand through her sandals with each step. Jae, on the way to the inn, noticed a part of the boardwalk had games and stalls. He led Bianca to that location. It was crowded, it smelled of booze and cigarettes. Music played loudly, it was a mix of Malarian traditional music, from when they referred to themselves as Luna before moving to earth, and a traditional earth music called hip-hop. The sound was unusual but catchy.

Bianca and Jae spent an hour playing the booth games. They were listed as Malarian games, but Jae knew they were rip-offs of carnival games from before the day of ruin. Bianca wanted to try a skewered dish called, "drunghun" at one of the food stalls but Jae begged her not to, refusing to answer why. They settled on corndogs and cotton candy. Jae wondered how Malarik was able to have antique earth foods but just brushed it off as "rich people privilege."

They made their way back to the beach. It was surprisingly less crowded than the boardwalk. They stabbed the umbrella into the ground and laid the towels underneath it. Bianca braced herself for the chilly water and ran to it, Jae jogged behind her.

Bianca splashed Jae and said, "Rematch."

"Oh yeah?" Jae said. He cupped his hands, and pulled them far behind him to the side and flung a pool of water at Bianca.

In one swing, she was drenched. She'd forgotten about his strength. Playfully, she said, "Cheater."

"I can't help that," he said, approaching her slowly.

Jae lifted her up and carried her farther into the ocean. He feigned he was going to toss her in the water. Instinctively, Bianca wrapped her arms around Jae's neck. Jae laughed and let her down. Before her feet could reach the sand, a large wave crashed against her and pushed her to Jae. He clasped her arms to steady her. They paused, Bianca looked down at the water and Jae looked at her.

Jae sensually moved her hair out of her face and caressed her cheek. Bianca glanced up at him. He slid his arms around her waist and embraced her. They stared into each other's eyes and she closed her eyes. He tilted his head and kissed her. The waves softly swayed them.

As their lips slowly separated, Bianca buried her head in the crook of his neck and sighed. Jae tightened his hug, pulling her as close to his chest as possible, and rested his head on hers.

It felt like time was moving too fast, and this moment would be their last. Johnson stated he knew about their affair, who knew what awaited them when they went back? There was nothing tying him to the bordello. Would Johnson let Jae stay until Bianca left?

They promised themselves they would say goodbye when the time came, but the thought of that moment arriving, pained them. Bianca promised herself, when she and Hellim were off earth, she would take her own life. If she couldn't be with Jae, what was her point in living? He showed her a world she never thought she would experience. A freedom she could never have. With no purpose but to rot on some planet far away, she was better off dead.

Jae gently let go of Bianca. He grabbed her hand and they went back to the shore. They didn't speak as they walked back. Both tried to erase the pain in their chest. When they made it back to shore, most of the beach was empty.

"What next?" Jae asked, breaking the silence.

"How about we build a sandcastle?" Bianca smiled.

"You sound so excited," Jae teased.

"Well yeah," she replied. She squatted and filled a bucket with sand. "I've never done it before, and it looked like so much fun in books."

"All the sand around Lyour and you didn't try it?" he asked, crouching beside her, and taking the other bucket.

"Absolutely not," she said, shaking her head. "That's dirt for one, secondly, it's filled with who knows what kind of filth. This is way better."

"I guess," Jae said. "I can't lie, I haven't built one either."

"Oh wow," Bianca said, sarcastically. "The first thing you aren't more experienced with than me."

"I excel quickly." He winked.

Bianca held back her smile and continued building her side of the castle. The sandcastle was simple, just three bucket shaped towers, and a few "windows."

Proud of their work, Jae sat down under their umbrella and motioned for Bianca to join him. She sat down and tucked her knees towards her chest. Jae gazed lovingly at her. Her curly hair flowed gently in the wind, the glow of her brown skin glistened from the sun, and her round black eyes that stared at the ocean. The more he loved her, the more beautiful she became. Each time he laid eyes on her he fell more in love. And his love for her was unbearable. At heart, he regretted falling in love with her. He should have never pursued her. In only a few weeks, she would be gone from his life and there was nothing he could do but face his heart's demise head-on.

"I wish we could stay like this forever," Bianca said. "Just you and me."

"Why don't we?" Jae asked.

Bianca looked at him and asked, "What do you mean?"

"Run away with me," Jae said, sitting up. He grabbed Bianca's hands and said, "Let's escape everything. You deserve your freedom and happiness. He isn't going to provide that for you. Let's just leave, you, me, and Galland."

"I—" Bianca started. "I don't think I can…"

"Who's going to stop you?" Jae asked.

"Jae," Bianca said, tears filled her eyes. "You know this was only short-term. Please don't do this."

"I know," he said, cupping her face. "And I shouldn't have asked for you to love me. But now… I can't let you go. And I know you feel the same."

"It doesn't matter what we think," she cried, lowering her head.

"You're wrong," Jae said. "Only your feelings matter. Not your 'fiancé's', not Johnson's and honestly, not even mine. It's your life, you get to choose what happens."

"I—" she said, "I don't want to marry him."

"Then let's go," he said.

"We can't leave the bordello without food," she said.

"We can drop off the bordello's merchandise in the night and run away." Jae gave her a reassuring smile. "Let's enjoy Malarik for a few more days then go. Everything will be okay."

"What if Hellim really does try to destroy the region?" she asked.

"Focus on what's happening in the now, not the later and the what ifs," Jae said.

"How can I tell him?" she asked. "I don't want him going to Lyour and killing them."

"Well, there's a shipping service here," Jae said. "Why not send a letter?"

"I can't believe I'm doing this," Bianca said.

"You don't have to, it's your choice," Jae responded.

"No, you're right," she said. "I should take a stand for once. And if Hellim comes after me, then I'll die there. I won't lie down and take his abuse. I'll die fighting for my freedom."

Jae stood and extended a hand to Bianca. "Let's go then."

They dried themselves off and headed towards the boardwalk. They searched the city for the shipping service. When they found it, Bianca picked the ugliest stationary they had. She wrote intensely then showed it to Jae. She didn't know if what she wrote was too harsh, but Jae didn't think it was as mean as it should have been. Jae wasn't scared of the guy. He was nothing more than a coward that tormented the weak. If Jae had the chance, he would slice his head off.

Bianca paid for expedited mail, and their guarantee was that it would arrive by morning. They did however charge extra for shipping to Hellim. Even though most of the company's deliveries were through drones, they couldn't risk any damage Hellim could inflict on the drones or their business. Jae rolled his eyes. He couldn't understand why everyone was so afraid of the guy. Was he that powerful of a tyrant?

"Well, this is it," Bianca said, exhaling.

Jae gently placed a hand on her lower back. "Welcome to your new life."

Bianca smiled widely.

They walked back to the beach to pack up their things and noticed their sandcastle still intact.

Bianca smiled, and quickened her pace. "It's still here!"

"Maybe it's another Malarik technological thing," Jae said. "As close as it is to the water, there's no way it could've survived."

"Guess it's a strong foundation," Bianca said. She pulled her towel close to the castle and sat down. Jae sat next to her and wrapped his arm around her. Bianca leaned on him and asked, "Do you think we could have a home like this castle?"

Jae laughed. "Sure, we'll build a castle big enough for just the two of us."

"And children," she corrected him.

"And children," he repeated. "We'll have as many as you want."

Bianca bent forward and wrote in the sand, "Bianca and Jae's home."

Jae smiled tenderly at her hope. It moved him. Sadness enveloped his heart as he thought about having to leave her. Although it would be temporary, he hated that he had to do it. But he couldn't let her freedom be snatched from her. He would do everything he could to make her happiness a reality. He just hoped when the time came, she would understand.

He second guessed going through with his journey. He hadn't seen what he was searching for in all of the years he traveled. Was it okay for him to stop looking? Was it alright for him to live his own happy-ending? His first goal was to get her somewhere safe. If by that time, he still felt an obligation to what brought him to the Yulogna region, he would leave.

Bianca and Jae relaxed on the beach until it was dark out. They walked slowly back to their hotel room, hand in hand. Bianca managed to convince Jae to lie in bed with her. Bianca lay on his chest, and fiddled with his shirt.

"Do you think we're doing the right thing?" Bianca asked.

"Of course," Jae said. "You have a right to decide what happens to your life. You deserve your freedom."

"I hope the women understand," she said.

"They will," he said. "If they love you, they'll understand why you had to leave. Besides, in a few years, we can always go back to visit them."

"Mmhmm," she said, dozing off.

Jae kissed her forehead.

~Welmn Village~
~Hellim Territory~

The Malarik Shipping Service drone hoovered through the morning twilight sky to a large ship that belonged to Hellim. It lowered itself and entered an open window. It flew through the halls until it found Hellim's living quarter. The buzzing sound from the drone woke Hellim. Pissed off, he grabbed his nightstand lamp and threw it at the drone, smashing it into pieces. He reached over to his other lamp and turned it on.

On the ground, he spotted the letter from Bianca. He swung his hand and the letter floated towards him. He ripped the letter open.

In the letter read:

Dear Hellim,

Sorry to say but I am turning down your marriage proposal. I've had time to think, and there are more important things I want to do with my life. If you need a reason to fully grasp why I'm rejecting you, then it's simple. I love someone else. It's obvious you don't really want to marry me. Your petty, childish tantrums over me not bowing down need to stop. I can say for a fact, that you would only be torturing yourself whisking me away to some place forever, which by the way, I know you're full of shit. Someone like you will never honor your agreements. Don't bother showing up to the bordello, I'm not there.

Hellim growled and crumpled the paper. "Who the *hell* does she think she is?!"

No one disobeyed him and lived to speak about it. Bianca not only disobeyed him, but she'd also disrespected him far too many times. He was bloodthirsty. He wanted desperately to kill her, but someone like her needed to be brought to her knees first. And the prick who wooed her was his next target. He fantasized killing him brutally and watching Bianca's distraught. He even imagined killing her in her most fragile state.

Hellim stormed into the cockpit, waking up his soldiers. "Prepare two fleets, we're going to Lyour."

Chapter Four
Hellim

The town was in shambles. The residents trembled as Hellim's troops entered the town, destroying everything in sight. The ground rumbled as Hellim stormed into Lyour.

"I've come for my bride," he shouted.

Johnson emerged from the bordello slowly, his head lowered he said, "Bianca is not here right now, please wait a bit longer. We were not expecting you for another two weeks."

"Where is she?"

"Our merchant experienced an unexpected delay, Bianca volunteered to retrieve our goods from the next town over. She went by horse and should be back within the week."

"What town?"

"Ma—Malarik…"

"Then I'll go there. Do not expect her to return."

"Why not wait," Johnson asked quickly. "She may be on her way back as we speak. We need our merchandise anywa—"

Johnson stopped talking as Hellim turned around and glared. Johnson bowed and rushed inside the bordello.

Bianca rolled over and placed her arm on the empty spot beside her. Bianca sat up and looked around the room. Jae slept peacefully on the couch. She sighed. She told Jae it was okay to lay next to her, yet he still chose the couch. What was his hesitation? She got out of bed and got dressed.

Bianca walked out onto their veranda. The warm breeze caressed her cheek. The faint smell of the ocean filled her nose. She enjoyed her newfound freedom.

I wish we could stay like this forever, she thought. *I wonder what life will be like now. Is Hellim really going to be okay with me saying no? I don't want to run away for the rest of my life.*

Deep in thought, Bianca hadn't noticed Jae standing next to her.

"The weather's really nice here," he finally said.

Bianca flinched. "Oh! I didn't know you came out. Yeah, it's luxury compared to Lyour."

"To any city. This is one of the only cities I've seen that still looks like before the ruin. Clean, safe, and wealthy."

"How many places have you been to?"

"Too many to count."

"Well, name the ones that left the best impression."

"Hmm, that left an impression." Jae paused for a bit as if he were thinking hard. Continuing, he said, "I've been to Yurik, Posolum, Hrayrp, Utewz. I've been to the Myetorp region, Relife region, Jtrepo region, Trwqoy region… I've been to every region but this one."

"Wow, it must be great to travel so far. What I would do to travel like you."

Jae stayed silent.

"I wonder how many oceans are left in the world."

"Not many," Jae laughed.

"What are you laughing at?" Bianca said frustrated.

"Originally, there was one body of water that covered the entire planet. But they were named in 5 different areas."

"Not in the books I read. There were 117 million before the ruin."

"Do you mean lakes? They're different from oceans."

"They're both bodies of water, right?"

"Yes, but they're completely different. A lake has freshwater, and the ocean is the largest body of water and contains saltwater. Different fishes and life forms in the ocean too."

"So how do we know this is the ocean and not a lake?"

"Um…Well, I have traveled a lot. I know the difference."

"Why do you know so much about the land before the ruin?"

"It was something I was interested in for a long time. I also needed to know these things so I could figure out where I needed to go."

"Is that why you called your region, 'South Korea?'"

"Yes. It's the original name for it."

"What's the current name?"

"I…don't really know," Jae awkwardly said. "It's been a while since I went home. I just call it by its old name."

"Ah. We can visit sometime. It's not very far, right?"

"It is far. But there's no body of water separating it from the Yulogna region. From Malarik it would take a year on foot."

"Then let's do it. Let's go there next."

"I…can't…"

"Why not?"

Jae stared into the distance, a serious look on his face, yet sadness in his eyes. "I still have unfinished business in Yulogna. Once you're somewhere safe, I'll continue with my journey."

"But why can't I go with you?"

"It's too dangerous." Jae turned to Bianca. "I couldn't bear it if something happened to you."

"I'm tougher than you think." She winked.

Jae smiled and looked back to the sea. "I believe you. I just don't want to risk you getting hurt."

"So how long do we have together?"

"Hm, I don't know. Maybe until we find the best place for you."

Bianca placed her arms on the railing and rested her head. She watched Jae silently before saying, "I hope it takes a long time to find it."

"Me too." Jae smiled.

"Let's go to the beach," Bianca exclaimed.

"Now?"

"Of course, when else?"

Bianca took Jae's hand and ran down the steps. She let go of his hand and ran as quickly as she could to the shore.

"Slow down," Jae yelled.

When she reached the water, her face lit up. Something about the ocean and the sand between her toes always made her feel better. It was magical. She hoped playing in the sand would ease the pain she felt in her chest. Jae finally caught up to her.

"Doesn't the water seem more beautiful today?"

"Yeah," Jae said looking at Bianca. "Very beautiful."

Bianca smiled and took Jae's hand. They walked slowly along the shore.

"I hate that we have to leave."

"Me too." Jae held her hand tighter.

"Say, let's find a safe place with an ocean."

"Huh?"

"You know, we could continue what happened here but in a better place. Once you're done with your journey, of course."

"Yeah, let's do that." Jae softly smiled.

Bianca smiled and leaned her head on his shoulder. Something in Jae's eyes told Bianca differently, but she wasn't going to pressure him to say what he really thought. They walked until they saw the boardwalk.

"We went pretty far." Bianca let go of Jae and shielded her eyes from the sun as she looked at the boardwalk.

"Yeah. Well since we're here, how about a little food?" Jae asked.

"I'd like that."

They slowly parted from the shore. Halfway across the beach, a loud bang filled the air, the shockwave threw Bianca off balance. Jae lunged for Bianca's hand, and they fell over.

"What was that?" Bianca asked.

"An explosion, but from where?"

Bianca looked up at the smoke rising from beside the boardwalk. "There."

They could hear faint screams in the distance, and Malarians ran away from the area. The buildings crumbled, and another explosion set off. Jae told Bianca to run by the shore while he checked out what was happening, Bianca of course, didn't listen and followed after Jae. They were a short distance away from where the commotion was and saw Hellim's soldiers shooting down everyone.

Hellim roared in anger, "Where is she?!"

The soldiers stopped and everyone was silent. No one knew who he was referring to, but they didn't want to be anywhere in the crossfire. Bianca took Jae's hand and ran into a shack. There was a small circle window, just big enough for them to see through.

"What the *hell* is *that* thing doing here?" Jae asked.

"That's Hellim," Bianca whispered.

Jae's head snapped in Bianca's direction. "Your fiancé?!"

"Yeah."

"You couldn't tell me he was a god?"

"I told you he was a monster. Look at him, he is one."

"Yes, but something along the lines of he's one of the gods that destroyed earth *would* have been a better way to refer to him as."

"Are you having second thoughts about running away with me?"

"No, not at all. We're in this together," Jae said, holding Bianca's hands. "I just wished you would have given me more details than 'he's a monster.'"

"I didn't know how to. I don't refer to him as a god. He's just an alien freak that people decided to call that."

Hellim walked down the sand. Looking everywhere he said, "I know you're here! Johnson told me where you were."

"That snake," Bianca whispered harshly.

"If you don't come out, I'll kill everyone on this boardwalk."

The Malarians screamed and began clearing the boardwalk and stores. No one remained.

"Come out!"

"Bianca," Jae called out softly. "I think we should go out."

"Are you kidding me? He'll kill you and take me away."

"You need to be direct with him. Tell him to his face you won't marry him. He won't kill me. He can't."

"What do you mean he can't?!"

"Don't worry about it," Jae brushed her question off. "I have a feeling he won't harm you either. It's better than these people dying."

"I will destroy this city. You have to the count of three," Hellim yelled. "1…"

"Bianca." Jae touched her arm delicately. "Trust me."

"2…"

Bianca stayed quiet.

"3…" he said slowly. "Fine then, have it your way. Every day I wait, I'll destroy another city. Until there's nothing left in this world. If you care about the lives of others, I suggest you give up this fairy tale of yours and come out."

Jae watched Bianca. He could see in her movements that she wanted to leave the shack. But it meant everything would be wasted. Bianca took a deep breath and began to stand when Jae grabbed her arm. He shook his head and pulled her towards him. He hugged her tightly. "Don't go."

"Jae," she said. She buried her face in his shirt and sobbed.

"We'll find a way," he whispered.

"But the world…" she said, before Jae shushed her.

"I'll figure something out. No lives will be lost. Just trust me."

Jae lifted Bianca's head and wiped her tears. He held her close and kissed her passionately. It was like Hellim disappeared. It was just them in the world. Bianca rested her head back on his chest and closed her eyes. She trusted him and knew she was safe with him.

"I love you," she said.

"I love you too."

They could feel Hellim's footsteps walking away in the distance. They didn't hear anything else he said. They were just thankful he was giving up today. They waited a little longer and stepped out of the shack.

"He's really gone," Bianca said.

"Yeah."

"I'm sorry I dragged you into this."

"You didn't 'drag' me into anything," Jae responded. "If anything, this is my fault for pursuing you, and making you fall in love with me."

"Let's not play the blame game." Bianca shook her head. "We're both at fault."

Jae sighed. He noticed people once again fill the boardwalk. They lifted the bodies of dead Malarians and dragged them out towards the slums.

"Come on," he said, taking Bianca's hand.

"Where?"

"We need to see what else he said."

They walked to a man and asked what the last part of his speech was.

"The god said he'd wait a week."

"Did he say where?" Jae asked.

"L—" the first Malarian said, before being interrupted.

"He'll be in Parahae awaiting her arrival," another Malarian chimed in.

"He's going to the Timeless city?" Bianca asked. "How is he going to tell a week has passed?"

"Who knows, maybe it doesn't affect him. I just hope, whoever she is, goes to him. I'm not dying over their little dispute," the second Malarian said.

"She needs to see the rain prophet," the first Malarian said.

"Rain prophet?" Jae asked.

"Yes, she's never wrong. She could tell her the right thing to do. And if he'll really destroy the world."

"Where is she?"

"In Kwtamg." The first Malarian pointed westward.

Jae rolled his eyes at the mention of the city.

"Why the city of Rain?" Bianca asked.

The Malarian shrugged. "Beats me. But if you follow the boardwalk to the end, you'll come across a trail that leads to a small gate. That gate of course is for us Malarians and rich folk—just a tip if you've actually been waiting in the slum line. Once out that gate, travel west. It's a long journey. There aren't any cities to my knowledge in between here and there, so if you actually go, I suggest stocking up. Once in the city, there will be a path that leads to the edge. There's only one house."

"Thank you," Jae said. "Let's go."

"Wait," the second Malarian asked. "I-is she who he's referring to?"

"No," Jae replied. "I think I know who he's talking about. She left town long ago. I think she said she was going to Gravick."

"Gravick? That's in the other direction of Parahae."

"Yeah, so she's lucky, I guess. If you'll excuse us."

"Are you going to tell her?"

"Yeah sure," Jae said, grabbing Bianca's hand and walking away quickly.

"Was it okay to lie to them?" she whispered.

"Smartest thing to do. If they knew he was talking about you...let's just say it wouldn't turn out pretty."

"You're right, they wouldn't understand the problem we're facing because it's not their lives."

"Exactly," Jae said. "We need to see this prophet as soon as possible."

"We need to get the food back to the Bordello."

"We'll figure that out later. Who knows what's waiting for us if we go back now."

They rushed back to their hostel. They wasted no time packing their things. Bianca was still worried about the bordello's foods. They wouldn't survive without any of the merchandise. She remembered the shipping service in the city and asked Jae if they could send it via them. With how advanced Malarik was, the business could condense everything into small packages and have it there in 1 week. Faster than they would have brought it back.

Bianca disguised herself before they left the inn. She wore blue sunglasses, and Jae's clothing. A black shirt and pants, and she wore his black cloak. How her disguise would actually hide her, was another thing. She looked more suspicious than she would have if she dressed normal. But they didn't care, so long as the Malarians from earlier and Hellim didn't recognize her.

When they reached the shipping service, they placed all the items in bags. Jae didn't mind paying more for it to arrive in 2 days, if it meant Bianca would stop worrying. After the payment, the clerk thanked them and confirmed the date of arrival.

"Wait," Bianca said. "There's one more thing I would like to add. I can pay for it, Jae."

Jae nodded and watched her. She grabbed a Malarik beaches stationery paper and wrote something down. After writing for 5 minutes, she handed the 3 pages to the clerk and 20 cluorgs.

"Okay, I'm ready," Bianca said, nodding to Jae.

Jae reached around her and rested his hand on her back as they left. They checked Galland out of the hotel's stable. They were stopped on the boardwalk numerous times about how she wasn't allowed to be there, and every time they were let go because they mentioned they were heading to the secret gate. They picked up a lot of groceries, foods that didn't need refrigeration, a tent, and stored them in Jae's luggage.

Bianca and Jae walked until they reached the end of the boardwalk. By the time they arrived, it was already dark. And just like the Malarian described, there was a trail that led off the main street. The area was densely covered in trees and bushes. You wouldn't expect a large city like Malarik to have a forest area. The trail leading to the gate was dimly lit, and they could see in the distance how far the lights went.

"Let's go," Jae said. He pulled down on Galland's reins. The path was low, and Galland needed to walk with her head lowered. Bianca held onto Jae tightly and followed his lead.

An hour passed, and Bianca stopped moving. She sat down on the trail and said, "We should rest here for tonight. Who knows how long this goes."

"Okay," he said. He tied Galland to the root of a tree and sat beside Bianca. "You can rest. I'll stand guard."

"Why? There aren't any animals around that would attack us."

"You never know. Besides bandits could appear."

"You need your rest too."

"I know. I'll go to sleep after you."

Bianca wanted to protest more, but her eyelids could barely stay open. She rested her head on Jae's shoulder and fell asleep.

"You must have been really tired." Jae laughed.

He stayed awake for another hour. Not many people passed. The ones who did, kept to themselves. Or rather they were afraid Jae was going to rob them. Seeing as it seemed there wasn't a motive with how rich Malarians were, there was no chance of a bandit or anyone poor finding the trail. Soon he dozed off.

The next morning, they continued on the path. Jae underestimated how big a city Malarik was. By late afternoon, they finally reached the end of the trail. And there it was, a small wicket gate. Or rather a small hole in the middle of the wall. The doors were poorly latched on. But compared to the "slum line" as the Malarian put it, the walls and surrounding area were clean. The color of the wall around the gate was practically a different color than the rest of the wall.

The guards by the gate opened it for them as they approached. After they were outside the city, the guards slammed the gate behind them. A loud crack filled the air. It sounded like they had broken the doors.

Bianca tsked. There was no reason to close it so forceful. They should have been treated like the Malarians.

The Malarian wasn't lying. The gate was just on the edge of Malarik. Literally. The gate was built just inches away from the edge of a cliff.

Nothingness stretched passed the edge. Only a wooden bridge suspended by ropes, and in the far, far distance, the other half of the cliff. On the other side, was a desert.

"I would worry about landslides," Bianca mumbled in awe.

She walked to the edge and looked down, they were so high up, she couldn't see the bottom. Even though the sun shined into the valley, it was pitch black. Bianca slowly looked up as Jae came over.

"It's a bottomless pit," he said. "No matter how far you look, you won't see anything."

"That's scary," she said taking a step back.

Jae laughed.

"But the view is amazing," she said holding him.

"It is, if the circumstances were any different, this would be perfect."

"Yeah," she mumbled. "I just want to sit out here forever."

"I wish we could," he said. "Come on, not scared of heights, are you?"

"Not even," she said. She stepped on the bridge, and it wobbled. She cringed and continued, "See, not that bad. If you aren't that scared, go first."

"Pfft, I've been to higher places than this," he said stepping forward. The bridge shook again and Bianca squatted just a bit. Jae grabbed her hand. "Don't be scared, we won't fall. Just focus on me, okay?"

"Wait, what about Galland?" she asked.

"I'll have her come after we cross. The bridge might not be sturdy enough to carry all of us at the same time. Let's go, don't worry about her."

"Okay," she said.

She glanced at Galland and followed Jae. They walked slowly across the bridge. Jae looked in front of them and Bianca stared into the abyss.

"Did I tell you the highest place I've been?" Jae asked.

"Where?" Bianca said finally looking up.

"The moon." He smiled.

Bianca laughed and said mockingly, "Yeah okay. And I've been to Jupiter."

"I have been. It's a really nice place. I think the scariest part wasn't actually being there, it was the trip."

"You aren't joking?" Bianca asked.

"I'm not."

"How old are you?" she said confused. "No one's been on the moon since before the day of ruin."

"I told you I'm 26…in theory," Jae said.

"'In theory?'"

"Mmhmm. I'll explain another time. But back to the moon trip," he said looking back at her. "Space travel still exists on earth. It's died down significantly but there are regions Hellim, and the other god haven't visited in decades. And they've learned to prosper. Their goals are to create an escape for humans."

"So if they're close to the goal," Bianca interrupted. "Then people could escape there, and no one has to die!"

"Precisely." Jae winked. "The spaceship I was in, was very nice compared to the others, but it didn't have any seat belts. Or at least, my seat didn't. So I spent days holding on to a large box that was strapped down. Nothing will be as scary as that. Even if this bridge collapsed beneath us and we fell endlessly, it would be nowhere near as terrifying."

"Gee, thanks for the imagery," Bianca complained. "So what was the moon like? I thought even human colonies on the moon were wiped out?"

"They were. The space station was still in a dome. Remnants of the colonies remained. It was interesting. Even the original base for the gods was rumored to be up there."

"Wow," Bianca exclaimed. "I hope we can go up there one day. Once this is all fixed."

"Yeah, I would love to go there with you." Jae took a large step and touched the gravel on the other side. "See, you made it across. That story helped keep your mind off the pit, right?"

"It did." She smiled. "Did you make it up just so I can feel safer?"

"Maybe," he said. "There's no way to find out."

Bianca scoffed. "I appreciate your help, but you shouldn't get my hopes up about living on the moon."

"Who knows, maybe I was telling the truth about civilizations with space projects." He stopped and turned around. He yelled, "Come Galland."

She neighed and galloped across the bridge. Practically giving Bianca a heart attack with each step and shake of the bridge.

"Atta girl," Jae greeted her with a pet and slowed her down. He bowed to Bianca and said, "Milady, your steed awaits."

Bianca smiled and took Jae's hand as he helped her onto Galland. "Need help getting up?"

"Not right now, we'll walk for a bit. The sun's soon to set, so we should camp near Malarik. Less bandits I assume here."

"Okay."

They walked until the sunset. They were moving fairly slow but had covered more distance than Jae had hoped. He opened his luggage.

There wasn't much he could do. It was too dark to search for firewood. He pulled out some fruit. He handed Bianca an apple, 2 oranges, and a banana. He grabbed for himself, a banana, 2 apples and 3 oranges. He set up the tent and motioned for Bianca to rest inside.

"Are you joining me?" she asked sensually biting her banana. She went inside.

"No," Jae declined and laughed. "I think it's best I stay out here."

"Mm, I don't think so," Bianca said, she poked her upper body out of the tent. "It's enough space for both of us."

"I don't think we should be sleeping that close."

"You didn't have a problem lying with me last night."

"That was different," he said clearing his throat. "We were on an unknown and narrow path. I wouldn't want either of us to get stepped on, nor did I want your head on the dirt. Besides, bandits could show at any moment, I don't want Galland to be kidnapped."

Bianca sighed. "Right, the bandits. Alright, I'll respect your boundaries. Goodnight."

"Goodnight," he said.

Bianca retreated inside the tent. She sat on the other side and crossed her legs.

Why is he so reluctant to sleep me with? she thought. *It's clear as day he wants to. Or is it because of all the men I've slept with? I wouldn't be surprised.*

Bianca rested on the pillow and went under the covers. She could somewhat understand his revolt towards it, but it wasn't like she had a choice. If he loved her, he would look past it. But was it because he loved her, that he was disgusted? What was real love? The men, and sometimes women, would profess their undying love and they didn't care how many people slept with her. But did they truly love her, or was it lust? Infatuation? Bianca didn't know. Seeing only one type of "love" her whole life, her definition of it was warped. But with Jae, she knew it was love. He was the only man that cared about her. Not just her physical appearance. He loved her mind, her intelligence, her personality. If he wanted to never have sex with her, she understood. Their love transcended sexual desires. It was a blow to her ego, but she would get over it.

Outside, Jae leaned on Galland and stared at the stars. He thought, *I hope she's not offended by it. Last thing I want to do is hurt her. I'll talk to her about it in the morning.*

It wasn't that he didn't want to touch her, he just had his reasons. As of then, they had so much on their plate. It wasn't the time nor place. And anything could happen, Jae needed to stay vigilant.

He really did love Bianca. He hadn't loved anyone like her. It had been years since he last had someone special. Thinking about her made him sad. He felt almost guilty. He had broken the vow he promised her when she died. He loved Bianca almost ten times more than he did her. But what could he do? She was gorgeous inside and out. She was insightful, different, kind, and intelligent. What wasn't there to love about her? He loved how curious she was about the world. And all she ever hoped for was seeing it herself. She wanted nothing more than to experience a world outside of that bordello, outside of Lyour. She deserved it. It wasn't her fault the world was the way it was. She was only a victim of an unfair world. A victim of something bigger than she could ever imagine. Something that could make her hate Jae forever. But it could never be undone. And for that, Jae would do anything for her to achieve her dreams. He would never tell her the truth as long as he lived.

The next morning, Bianca emerged from the tent. She looked at Jae who slept peacefully on a distraught horse. Galland whined and moved frantically to knock him off.

"Aww, poor girl." Bianca laughed. She ran in front of Galland and petted her until she calmed down. Galland's innocent large black eyes gazed at Bianca. "You're so beautiful. It's alright. I'll get him off you. It's okay."

She walked around her and tried lifting Jae. She struggled to sit his upper half all the way up. After a while, she managed to push him over and Galland was a free horse.

"Poor gal," Bianca said. She petted Galland again then grabbed the apple from last night and gave it to her. She didn't know where Jae's luggage was to get Galland anything better.

Bianca went back into the tent, changed into her clothes, and placed his folded clothes next to him. She wondered when Jae went to sleep. It was midmorning and time was of the essence. She felt bad waking him but knelt beside him and shook him. Jae stirred and sat up.

He smiled at Bianca. "What time is it?"

"If I had a clock, I could tell you. But we need to continue to Kwtamg."

Jae rolled his eyes and stood up.

"Why do you keep rolling your eyes?" Bianca asked.

"It's nothing."

"It clearly isn't 'nothing,'" she said standing up. "You've been rolling your eyes every time I mention Kwtamg."

Jae rolled his eyes but stopped midroll and looked at her.

"Exactly," Bianca said. "You can tell me what it is. I won't judge you."

"It's nothing, I just hate rainy cities. They're annoying, inconvenient, and ugly."

"Maybe this city will be different."

"I doubt it."

"Well hopefully we won't be there too long."

"I hope so too."

Jae packed up the tent and took out random foods for them. He took out a large bag of grains filled with oat and barely. A little mix of hay was also inside. He poured some on the ground and tied the bag to Galland's saddle. He helped Bianca on Galland and mounted himself. After Galland finished eating, he commanded her to run.

They rode in silence. Jae wondered if she was still upset about last night. He questioned when it would be a good time to talk to her about it. But if he was imagining it, then that would only make matters worse.

They covered even more distance than yesterday. They could see the Malarik wall growing smaller in the distance until it was no longer visible. Kwtamg was a straight shot if the Malarian was telling the truth. The drastic differences between the desert and Kwtamg wouldn't be that hard to notice. Maybe they would see rain clouds in the distance, or a body of water would appear prior to the city.

Jae dreaded going to Kwtamg. He hadn't told Bianca the real reason why he hated the city. Or rather the name of the city. It brought up unpleasant memories. But again, he would never tell Bianca the truth.

By evening, they could see a forest in the distance. Jae decided that where they were was a good time to rest. He stopped Galland and dismounted. He helped Bianca off. He set up the tent. Bianca waited inside while he went into the forest for firewood. When he returned, he plopped the wood on the sand and peeked inside the tent.

"I'm going to start a fire," he said. "What would you like to eat?"

Bianca shook her head. "Nothing. I'm fine with fruit."

"You should at least warm yourself before bed."

Bianca quietly sighed and crawled out of the tent. She sat on the other side of the fire. They sat in silence while Jae roasted vegetables over the flame.

"I want to apologize for last night," Jae said.

"Why?"

"Well, I just wanted to make sure you weren't upset about being rejected."

"No, it's fine. I respect that you don't want to touch me," she said. She didn't look at Jae as she spoke. "I can't force you to have sex with me. I don't blame your reason."

"And what's my reason?"

"The number of guys I've slept with."

Jae shook his head. He walked around the fire to Bianca and wrapped his arms around her. "That's not why I won't. I just don't think right now is appropriate. We have a lot going on, and I need to watch for bandits. I don't want to let my guard down."

"You don't have to keep using the bandit excuse for everything!" Bianca complained. She pushed Jae away. "Not once have we run into one. Just say how you feel."

"I've traveled way more than you," he said sternly. "There are bandits. Yes, we've been fortunate enough to not run into any, but they exist outside Lyour. I've fought them countless times. I'm telling the truth. I've never lied to you Bianca. There's no need to."

"Yeah," Bianca scoffed. She said sarcastically, "Except you know, when you lied yesterday, in Malarik, and back in Lyour, but totally you've never lied to me."

"Somethings aren't worth telling," Jae said. "I understand you have your insecurities but don't take that out on me."

"I wouldn't have these 'insecurities' if you just told me how you really felt. Stop lying and just say it disgusts you!"

"I don't find anything disgusting about you. I told you I don't want to sleep with you because we have a god trying to execute millions of people because you chose not to go."

"I chose not to go?" Bianca repeated offended. "I tried to step out the shed, *you* grabbed me and made me stay. *You* chased after *me*. *You* told me not marry him, *you* convinced me to run away with you. Don't you dare blame this on me!"

"So, if I told you to jump off a cliff, would you do it?" Jae asked. "You can't blame me for you following everything I suggest."

"You're unbelievable." Bianca stood and walked toward the forest.

"Where are you going?!" Jae shouted.

"Away from you!"

"Bianca, there could be bandits! Come back here!"

Bianca turned around and shrugged. "Let them have me then. It would be better than staying with you!"

Bianca continued to walk and Jae tsked. He kicked the sand and sat down. He put his head in his hands and ruffled his hair. He didn't mean to say what he said. It just came out. He knew all of this wasn't her fault. It wasn't either of their faults. It was the actions of the people around them and the fault of that god Hellim. If he hadn't existed, then the earth would never have been destroyed. Bianca wouldn't be the way she was. He may not have been able to meet her if Hellim never existed, but that was better than the horrible life she led.

"Galland," Jae said. "Go after Bianca. If she's in any danger, get her out of there immediately."

Galland neighed and galloped after her. Jae watched Galland make it to Bianca. She petted her and grabbed her reins and walked into the forest.

"Who does he think he is?" Bianca ranted. "I can't believe he tried to blame all of this on me. You weren't there Galland, but he told me to stay in the shed and that he would figure something out. Does that not sound like he's at fault?"

Galland snorted.

"Atta girl." Bianca smiled. She petted her again. "I'm glad you're on my side."

They walked deeper into the forest. Bianca turned around. She couldn't see the sand anymore. She didn't care though. She would return when she was ready. She needed a break from Jae. Even if he was telling the truth about why he wouldn't sleep with her, he still tried to blame their situation on her.

Bianca stopped again. She opened Galland's food bag and poured some into her hand. She dropped it on the ground. Before she could fully close the bag, a hand grabbed her and placed a rag over her mouth.

Bianca screamed and struggled to break free from whoever it was. Whatever was on the cloth, made Bianca lose consciousness. Galland whinnied and tried kicking the person. A man jumped on Galland and grabbed her reins. She fought to get him off, but he knew how to tame a horse.

Soon she was calmed, and the man said, "Put her on here. Grab my horse."

"Yes, sir!" the man who grabbed Bianca said.

"We're gonna make easy money with these two," the man on Galland said. "Let's hurry."

He hyahed and Galland galloped deeper into the forest.

Chapter Five
A Little Detour

~Lyour~

Johnson panicked as he ran through the bordello to accept the package from Malarik shipping services. He checked out the merchandise he ordered. Everything was there. He shuffled through the packages until he picked up the letter from Bianca. He felt nauseous. He opened it.

In the letter read:

Dear Johnson,

I want to thank you for your hospitality over the years. While I don't agree with what you made us do, you still made sure we had a great life growing up. You gave us the best education and let us dream far into the impossible. I even argued with the other ladies that you saw us as your children. You've never touched us, and you protected us from the world. But there are just some things I can never agree with, nor will I settle for. I want my freedom, Johnson. I want to live the rest of my life with someone I love, not forced into a spiteful arranged marriage with a monster. You could never see past your greed and fear of Hellim to understand the unfairness you brought upon me. And maybe even as you read this letter, you still disagree nor care about my happiness.

As of a week from the time you receive this letter, Hellim was made aware of my refusal of the marriage. He claims to be going to Parahae to give me a second chance. If I don't, he will kill indiscriminately. I will not go there. Me and Jae are going to find a way to save everyone and ourselves. I cannot tell you where I'm going, but please take the girls and go to another region before Hellim makes his way to Lyour. That's all I beg of you Johnson. And I'm sorry to be so difficult and a failure compared to the others, but I promise you I will fix this with my freedom and the safety of humanity.

Johnson sighed. Bianca didn't understand why he couldn't refuse Hellim. He didn't do it for the money. It was because the same thing he told her, he told Johnson. Either give Bianca to him, or watch as the world was destroyed. Johnson had given up all hope after reading Bianca's letter. They were doomed.

Johnson handed the letter to a woman beside him and told her to read it to the others. He said to act normal until he thought of something.

Johnson walked into the main room. On the stage, Hellim relaxed on his throne. A few women fed him and two massaged his feet.

Johnson gulped. "Uh Hellim?"

"Can't you see I'm busy?" Hellim roared. The women next to him cowered. "Keep rubbing. This better be important."

"Um, well we received our merchandise from Malarik via their shipping service…" Johnson trailed off. Hellim glared at him. If looks could kill, Johnson would have died a horrible death. "So…Bianca isn't here…. However…I was informed that a letter from her will be arriving soon. I will see what it says. It may have their location on it. So please, give us some time."

Hellim exhaled. He gripped the armrest and broke it off. "Get me a new chair. I will give you time to find her. If you can't find her in two weeks, then you all die."

"Thank you, you are a generous man. I will not let you down."

"Bring the chair, you women leave me at once," he shooed them away.

They bowed and scurried away. Johnson brought him the chair and also left. He called the women into his home. It was packed with 18 out of the 20 women. The other two were entertaining Hellim as a distraction.

"I'm sure everyone's aware of the situation Bianca's put us in," Johnson said. He looked to each nodding woman and continued, "We have to figure something out. I can buy time for you to leave in pairs of 2."

"Are we really that screwed?" Hannah said. "This is the only place Hellim likes, he wouldn't really kill us, right?"

"He's a vicious monster Hannah," Rachel said. "He's killed billions of humans with no remorse. Do you honestly think he cares about a house of whores?"

"I—I don't know," Hannah said. "I just…he's been so kind to me, to us. I spent months by his side, he wouldn't kill someone he spent that much time with. He spent 2 months with you Rachel. He—"

"Oh, cut the 'I'm his favorite' bullshit," Rachel cut her off. "He apparently adored humans, yet he did what Hannah? He killed them and tortures those that remain. He only favors us because of our services."

"I don't think so," Hannah said. "He's a warrior right? He has to be somewhat vicious, but he wouldn't do that to us."

Another woman jumped into the argument. She laughed. "Rachel don't pay her any attention. She falls in love with every man that touches her. I see aliens count too. Maybe while we're all escaping, you can stay with Hellim and keep him busy with your 'love.'"

Half the women laughed.

"Hannah," Serenity said. "Why are you so reluctant to leave?"

"I don't have anywhere else to go. This bordello is all we have. What am I supposed to do afterwards?" Hannah cried.

"We can agree to meet somewhere," Sasha said. "Maybe we could meet in a local city?"

"The point is we need to leave this region, meeting in a town close to here, defeats the purpose," Rachel complained, brushing off Sasha's suggestion.

"But we can go to a region safely if we meet together first. It's safer if we go in a group than a pair, right?" Sasha said. She refused to back down. "I heard Johnson say we were waiting on another letter, right? We could order clothing to disguise ourselves and we could make it…."

"That's just stupid," Rachel complained.

"I agree with Sasha," Serenity said. "If I'm gonna die, I'm gonna die fighting. Johnson you should order outfits for us. If you don't want to fight for your life, then you can stay here and distract Hellim while those of us who actually want to live, can escape."

"Even if we leave, there's nowhere to go," a woman said.

"We can make one," Sasha said. "We could build a shop, not one where we have to sleep with men, but a place where we can showcase our talents. Maybe the rest of the world isn't as bad as the Yulogna region. Think about Jae, he was so helpful—"

"'Helpful?'" Rachel repeated. "If he didn't get that crazy idea in Bianca's head we wouldn't be in this situation!"

"I agree," Hannah said. "We wouldn't be having to fight for our lives if she had just gone with Hellim quietly. All of this is Jae's fault."

"You have to understand Bianca's feelings," Sasha yelled. "All except Hannah, every one of you, has spoken ill of Hellim. Would you be fine if you were in Bianca's shoes? Would you go quietly with him to who knows where, doing who knows what? I know I wouldn't."

The women stayed silent. Sasha was right. It wasn't their place to tell Bianca how to feel, because if the role was reversed, they would have done the same thing as her. Some might have gone as far as killing themselves.

"I say Sasha has the best idea," Serenity said. "All in favor of her plan raise your hand."

All but Hannah and Rachel raised their hands.

"That's that," Johnson said. "You two can pair up and decide what you want to do. I will protect you as much as I can, but my priority will be the women who want to survive. You have a week to decide if you want to be a part of that team. As for the letter, I will try my best to forge one similar to Bianca's handwriting."

"Leave it to me," Sasha said. "Bianca taught me how to write. So, I'm sure my writing looks just like hers."

"Then I leave that to you. Act normal. Once the clothes arrive, you will take what's yours to your room. While Hellim is sleep, you'll escape."

"I don't trust Hannah," a woman said, sheepishly. "I think she should be away from Hellim until we're gone."

"I agree," another woman said.

"He may request her," Johnson said. "And the last thing we need is to piss him off. We'll have Rachel watch her. If she does anything suspicious or says anything to Hellim, stop her."

"Okay." Rachel nodded.

"So on to pairs." Johnson looked around the room. "Sasha and Serenity together, you two seem to want to fight for your lives the hardest. I doubt you will hold the other down."

Serenity and Sasha nodded. Johnson continued to pair the women. He based the pairs on physical abilities and willingness to survive. The two women distracting Hellim would be a pair and would be filled in later.

The women went back to their roles in the bordello. There wasn't much to do except wait for Hellim to call on them. No one was allowed in Lyour. It was officially taken over by Hellim. No one outside the bordello survived his attack. The women took the time to train as much as they could. Running, boxing, anything they thought would help them survive.

~Bianca~

Bianca came to in a cold cell. Her head was aching, and she was weary. Her clothes had been changed. She looked around. The cell floor and walls were stone and the cell door was metal. There was a cot, or rather a sheet on the floor with a flat pillow, and thin blanket. Her cell was dark, but the walkway was lit with torches sparsely placed along the wall.

She stood up and stumbled her way to the door. She peeked as far as she could through the door. There was no one around. Bianca saw a spiral staircase leading up. It was the only part of the assumed basement that was bright.

"Hey!" she shouted. She rattled the cell door. "Let me out of here! You made a big mistake locking me up. Wait until Jae finds me!"

"Shut up you wench!" a man yelled. He sounded like he was in another cell.

"Who do you think you're talking to?!" Bianca sneered shaking the cell door wilder. "If we weren't in these cells, you wouldn't be saying this."

After a minute, she gave up. She sighed and dropped to the floor. "The one time Jae was right."

"What am I gonna do?" She gasped. "Galland!"

She prayed Galland was okay. She wouldn't forgive herself if she was hurt, or worse, killed. She hoped Jae would find them soon and save them.

~Jae~

Jae sat by the fire. He was still pouting over their argument. He wondered how long she would stay there. He wasn't mad at her, he never was. If anything it was everyone else's fault they even had the argument. Her insecurities were a result of what she was forced to do. And he couldn't help that. But he wanted to do everything he could to reassure her. Even if it meant sleeping with her. And boy, did he want to. If she was okay with it, what was he waiting for? They could escape from reality even if it was only for a few minutes. Maybe Bianca was right, maybe there wasn't that big a chance they would run into bandits. He

118

needed to relax and pay attention to the beautiful woman in front of him, that loved him as much as he loved her.

Jae stood up. He wanted to be the first to say sorry to her and that he didn't mean what he said.

He heard Galland's scream and turned towards the forest. He dowsed the fire, and hurriedly packed up the tent and took out Magord. He bolted through the sand to see what happened. Their footprints were just barely in the sand. He followed them into the forest. There was only one clear path to his knowledge, so he continued down the path. He walked for a while until he saw Galland's unfinished food on the ground.

He bent over to examine it when he saw a faint trail of her food sprawled along the path. He unsheathed his sword. He kicked the pile of grains into the dirt and followed the trail.

~Bianca~

Bianca sat in the cell. She didn't know how long she was there. She hoped Jae realized they were missing and was searching for them. The cell door opened and a burly man with a braided mohawk and clothes she had seen in history books, similar to Vikings. She obviously didn't know where she was, but sand covered most of the landscape and it was ridiculously hot. He was covered in fur accessories and a red tunic with no pants. How could he wear so many layers? He carried a sword on his left side and a shield in his left hand.

"Get up woman," he demanded.

"What do you want with me?" she asked.

"I don't answer to you. Either you get up yourself, or I'll make you."

Bianca was conflicted. She didn't want to go with him, but she didn't want that man touching her either. She stood up and followed him out of the cell. A few other men wrapped in chains stood in the walkway. The man grabbed her arms and yanked her to the line. He locked the chains around her wrists and nodded for a man dressed similarly to him, without the fur, and the man pushed the first prisoner in line to move.

They walked slowly in a line, up the stairs and down a long hall. They turned right at a fork in the hall and continued again down a long corridor. The building was larger than Bianca expected. How did a bunch of bandits have a nicer building than the bordello and many buildings in Malarik? They stopped at a large door and the guard opened the door. He closed it behind him and a second later he motioned for them to enter. Bianca peeked around the corner before she fully entered.

About 30 men sat on the ground at different low tables drinking and eating. They watched the prisoners go by and laughed at them. In the back of the room, two low tables with men not eating surrounded a large throne in the middle of the wall. A man sat on the throne. He munched like a slob on a large hunk of meat. He rested his legs on the back of a man who was on all 4. Aside from his table manners, he was dressed elegantly. He wore a sapphire blue colored tunic with matching pants. The blue complimented his ivory skin. He was scrawny. He had black hair tied into a tiny ponytail, the length of an index finger, and bangs that blocked half his vision. He wore sapphire earrings that glistened every time he moved and he wore black boots that went up to his shins.

"Sir." The guard knelt in front of him. "You wanted to see the prisoners?"

"Yes…." The man mumbled and finished the rest of the leg like a pig. He smacked as he said, "I wanted to see the potential money makers. The one with the horse should make us a pretty penny. A simple ransom note and we wouldn't have to live like this anymore. Where is he? Bring him out."

The second guard dressed in fur pushed Bianca out of the line. She screamed as she stumbled and almost fell over. The chains kept her from falling as the other men pulled backwards to catch her. It felt like her arms had been ripped off. Her arms twisted behind her and every muscle in her arms ached. She fixed her footing, and the men relaxed the chains.

The room grew silent, and they stared at her. No one paid close enough attention at the line to notice there was a woman.

The man on the throne shouted, "Hey! What is wrong with you Gunther?! You don't push a lady!"

He stood, kicking the man on his knees down the steps, he walked to Bianca. He was taller than he looked sitting down, the top of Bianca's head reached his armpit. He bent over and smiled. "Are you okay miss? I'm sorry these brutes don't know how to treat a woman. Have they had you in that dungeon this whole time?"

Bianca couldn't look at him. He was trying his best to appear suave, but his face was covered in sauces and his breath smelled like meat. She nodded.

"Do you know how long?" he asked.

She shook her head.

"And you're the owner of that spotted horse, right?" he asked, his face getting closer to Bianca's.

"Yes," she mumbled. "Please don't hurt her."

"Of course not!" he said. "I love animals. She's being taken care of to the best of our ability. My, you have a beautiful voice. So angelic."

Bianca glanced around the room at the 30 men in front of her. Each one gave disgusting gestures like kissy faces, tongue motions, and worse. She looked at the ground.

"Uncuff her," the man said. "That is terrible to have a wonderful lady in these."

Gunther did as he was told and took off the chains.

The man lifted his hand in front of Bianca and said, "Come on. You don't belong among criminals."

Bianca stared at his hand then said, "I'd rather stay in my cell than with you creeps."

The man was appalled. His mouth was wide open as he looked at her. He laughed and said with a forced, gentle tone, "Miss, I would prefer you stay in a nice room than in that dungeon. I am *offering* you a chance to sleep in a room fit for a lady. Take the offer."

"Not unless you give every man here a room 'fit for a lady.'"

The man licked his lips and bit them. He rolled his eyes and said, "As you can see, these are men. Clearly a lady's room would not be suitable for *men*. Besides, there's only one room. Take it."

Bianca didn't say anything. Was it ludicrous for her to refuse what seemed like a good offer? How could a band of shady men who seemed to sell people be trusted? As creepy as they were, who could trust them to not harm her? She was better off in that cell.

The man sighed. "This is what happens when you're nice to females. See this men? This is why females are nothin' but trouble. Their value is so low, they don't even know their own worth."

The men roared in agreeance. This encouraged him more.

"Gunther!" he shouted. "Take her to my chamber."

"Yes sir," Gunther said. He grabbed Bianca and lifted her over his shoulder. She wiggled and fought to make him let go.

"Take the rest of them back to the dungeon," he shouted. "If you'll excuse me, I have something to attend to."

The men cheered as he left the room. The prisoners were pushed to go back as men threw food at them.

~Jae~

Jae followed the trail for hours until it ended abruptly. He looked frantically around the forest floor searching for any indication, a hint of where they went. He looked around him and up in the trees. There had to have been some trace of them. It couldn't have ended cold turkey. He continued down the path until he came to a fork on the path. There were three different paths. He looked to each one. Two of the paths looked undisturbed and unkempt. On the path to the right, the dirt was still, not a footprint or shift in the dirt, and the path ahead of him, was blocked mostly by trees and bushes. It would be impossible to get Galland to go through there. Which hopefully meant no one went down those paths. The path on the left was covered in tall grass up to his knees and the tree branches seemed to have been cut to open the path. Jae took a deep breath and went left.

Over a day and a half had passed since he set out for Bianca. He was tired but he couldn't sleep not knowing Bianca and Galland were safe. He looked for signs of the path being used as he walked. Jae saw some of the grass was pressed down and a thin branch was cut off. The branch looked freshly cut, it was still as soft as the other branches. He could have been wrong but that gave him the motivation to run after them.

Jae ran down the path, he wasn't sure how far they went, but on horse, they clearly covered way more distance than him. He just hoped it wasn't too late.

~Bianca~

"Put me down!" Bianca shouted.

"Hush," Gunther said. "If da boss wans you in his woom, den dat's where you'll be. Be gwateful da boss is a gintle man. Uderwaise you'd be in my woom."

He threw her on the bed and walked out of the room. Bianca composed herself and looked around. The room was spacious and… blue. Every piece of furniture and drapery was blue. His bed was large and cover one half of the room. The bedding was blue, the pillows and sheets were navy blue, and the covers were a tinge lighter. The floor was poorly painted blue, and the walls were white. In the middle of the room against the wall was a brown vanity dresser, etched in gold along each part of it. In the middle of the dresser on top, was an attached wash bin with stale water inside. It was the most extravagant thing in the room. Probably stolen of course. On the other side of the room, was a desk in the corner on the left side, a table in the middle with a couch on both sides, and TV on the right. Three large windows were on the back wall and a window above his bed on the ceiling.

123

Bianca walked to the windows and looked down. She was on the second floor. They were still in the forest, but a large wooden fence encircled their base. On that side of the base, were 4 smaller houses and a stable. Bianca saw black and brown horses. Galland's coat could be seen easily in between theirs. Bianca stared hard for any trace of her. She saw her blonde tail whip from a shadowed corner and sighed in relief. She seemed to be taken care of equally to the other horses. She looked at the edges of the window. She wondered if there was a latch. It was a far drop, but that was better than whatever awaited her.

The door opened and Bianca whipped around.

"Relax," the man said. "I just wanna talk. Please have a seat."

He walked to the vanity mirror and tsked. He mumbled under his breath, "They let me walk around like this? No wonder she didn't respect me."

He grabbed a towel from a drawer and dipped it in the water. He wiped the food and sauce off his face. Surprisingly, he had a handsome physique, it was too bad it was going to waste on a sleazebag. He turned to Bianca. He motioned for her to sit on the couch. "Please sit, I ain't gonna bite."

Bianca cautiously sat on the couch facing him, her eyes never leaving his.

"Thank you," he said. He sat on the couch across from her. He smiled widely at her. Something about his smile was unnerving. "I would like to apologize for my behavior in the dining hall. Gotta keep up appearances, you know? Let's start over. My name is Gian, and your name is?"

"Drop the act," Bianca said. "I know the way you acted in the 'dining hall' was your true personality. You can't trick me."

Gian laughed and dropped his head. He bit his lip and said, "Look…I'm tryin' to be civil. My mother raised me with manners. My *name* is Gian. *Leader* of the Gravalites. P…lease…tell…me your name…."

"That's better. You're still showing a fake smile, but at least you're showing your true colors. I refuse to tell you my name."

"And why's that?" he said. He tried his best to not sound annoyed.

"Because I don't know you. You kidnapped me, along with my horse and the other prisoners with the intention of selling us. Why would I trust you and give you my name?"

"That's the thing miss." He smiled. "I'm giving you the opportunity to be my lady—"

Bianca scoffed and rolled her eyes.

"It's a fine offer. You're safe from being sold, your horse will be safe, and you have the perks of being a powerful man's lady."

"Not interested," she declined.

"Do you know how powerful my gang is? I could wipe out everyone you know and love."

"Precisely why I refuse to tell you my name." Bianca smiled.

Gian smirked and said, "You're acting tough now, but we'll see how you do in a few days. You're staying in this room whether you like it or not."

He left the room, slamming the door behind him. Bianca stared into space for a while before looking out the window. The sun was setting, and she looked down at Galland. She seemed to still be okay. Bianca would be damned if she let that man touch her. She was going to fight, even if it cost her her life. She only wanted Jae and any man touching her, made her nauseous. She rested on the couch and closed her eyes.

She woke up the next day in Gian's bed. He slept on the other side of the bed. She grimaced and slid out of bed. Just the thought of him carrying her to the bed sickened her. Why was he so keen on her? Surely this "powerful" man could easily find a consenting woman to stay by his side. What was he really after? She remembered his discussion prior to finding out she was a woman. He wanted to negotiate the release of the horse owner. So maybe he wanted to use her for her money? Bianca understood she was attractive, but to fight that hard for her. It had to be the money.

She laughed as she looked out the window. Boy was he in for a surprise. She looked for Galland again and she could see her resting in one of the stalls. As long as Galland was okay, Bianca wouldn't act up…or more than necessary.

Arms wrapped around her waist and a head rested on hers. A low and rough voice said, "Good morning."

Bianca instinctively pushed away from him. "What do you think you're doing?"

"Tellin' you good morning. Is that a crime?" Gian asked. His morning voice was jarringly low. Bianca preferred his shrill, immature voice over this and hoped it would return quickly.

"I—It's a crime when I don't give consent," she stuttered.

He grabbed her arm and threw her on the couch. He sat on the other couch and said, "I'm gonna give you one more chance. And your answer better be good, 'cause I ain't a mornin' person. Will you be my lady?"

Bianca shook her head. No amount of intimidation would make her say yes.

He sighed. "Suit yourself."

He stood and Bianca followed his movements with only her eyes. She faced forward as she watched him from the side of her eye. He forcefully opened a dresser drawer and pulled out some clothes. He took off his pajamas and Bianca looked away.

When he was dressed, he said, "Let's go."

"Where?" she asked.

He glared at her and repeated harshly, "Let's go."

Bianca followed him out of the room. Two men waited outside and grabbed both her arms. Gian continued, "Take her to the stables."

"Yes sir," they said in unison.

Gian walked a different direction, and the men carried her outside. She looked to the other side of the stable where a group of men stood. One carried a pot of water, another tended to a fire, and so on. She stared at Galland, and her heart sank. Being out there couldn't be anything good.

Soon Gian made his way to them. A group of men followed behind him. He gave a slight nod to the side and the men holding Bianca followed him into the stable.

"Now let this be a lesson woman," he shouted. He paced around the stable as he spoke. "You don't get to insult me without comsaqwences. I gave you a chance to date me, and you refuse. You seem to not understand your situation. And for that you have to pay."

Gian snapped his fingers and the men on the other side of the stable came over with a branding iron. The men holding Bianca kicked her to her knees and held her face up.

"Idiots," he said. "I ain't ruinin' a pretty face. Bring it out."

The man that carried the water went into Galland's stall and brought her out.

"No!" Bianca shouted. She tried to stand but the men pushed her to the ground. "Please don't harm her. I'm sorry! I'll be your lady! Please!"

The men covered her mouth. She stared at Gian, tears streamed down her face.

"Too late," he said coldly. "You'll be my lady regardless."

"But boss," one of the men spoke up. "Ain't we s'pose ta sell dem? Wouldn't branding it ruin its worth?"

"You can't even spell worth," Gian said. "We ain't sellin' neither of 'em. Now hurry up."

The men held Galland, and another man approached with the iron. Galland saw it and struggled to get away. She grunted as she stepped away. The man hoovered over her skin, the branding iron hadn't touched her, but she felt the heat on her butt. She kicked him and he flew into the stall, the branding iron burning his arm as it fell. He screamed and scurried to his feet.

"You fuckin' horse!" he screamed. He grabbed the branding iron and pressed it deep into her skin.

Galland screamed and kicked him again. She fought to break free from the men. When she was loose, she fought them. She kicked and charged the men. They all screamed as they tried escaping her.

She saw Bianca crying on the ground and charged at the men. Before she could reach them, a shot went off and she fell to the ground.

"A simple bullet to the head is all it takes," Gian laughed. "Can't believe you weaklings lost to a horse."

Bianca stared in shock at Galland. Her lifeless body laid inches in front of her. Blood pooled from her head wound and Bianca screamed. She wiggled to get free from the man's grip, but she couldn't. She dropped her head to the ground and wailed.

It's all my fault, she thought. *If only I had said yes. If only I was stronger. I'm sorry Galland. I'm sorry.*

~Jae~

Jae stood at another crossroad. He had encountered countless in the forest about a mile apart from each other. He wondered if it was a maze. He was able to figure out the path so far, or at least he hoped he had. Now there were two paths. One that went diagonally to the left and one that went diagonally to the right.

Both paths looked the same. There were no obvious differences like the prior crossroads. He wondered if maybe he did take the wrong path. He flipped a coin, heads he went left, tails he went right. The coin landed on heads.

"Heads it is," he shrugged. "Luck don't fail me now."

As he headed left, he heard a gunshot in the other direction. "What the hell was that?"

Jae turned around and took the right path. He continued to run. His luck was better than he thought. It could have been the people that took Bianca and Galland or it could've been locals. Either way, he was glad he didn't take a wrong turn.

Jae breathed heavily. He had gone down three wrong paths and barely escaped death. He wished another gunshot would appear. He walked slowly down the path, his feet were dragging, and he was dizzy. He hadn't slept or eaten in 3 1/2 days and he ran non-stop. He didn't want to give up, but his body wasn't going to let him go further. He dropped to his knees and crawled to the edge of the path. Thankfully that meant no one could see him sleeping, but that also meant, he could get trampled.

He opened his luggage and pulled out the food he cooked the night Bianca disappeared. He scarfed it down then passed out.

~Bianca~

Bianca sniveled on the ground. She stared into Galland's lifeless eyes. It was like her heart had been shattered into a million pieces. Galland was dead and it was all her fault. Her and her stupid mouth. Bianca thought about Jae. She remembered when they first spoke, he talked about Galland being important to him. She had been his companion for years. If he ever found them…Bianca sobbed again thinking about it. She couldn't imagine his hurt finding out she was dead.

Gian laughed and said, "Stop crying like a baby. It was self-defense. Vicious animals deserve to be put down. Its life ain't as important as a human's. Get over it."

Bianca didn't say anything. She continued to gaze into Galland's eyes. As if that would bring her back to life.

Galland blinked and Bianca squinted. Were her eyes playing a trick on her? Galland blinked again and grunted. The stable grew quiet as everyone watched her.

She sat up and stretched. Gian was mortified. He shot multiple rounds at her and Galland screamed falling to the ground again. This time, she stood up quicker than before. The wounds were completely healed, even the brand on her butt was gone.

Gian commanded the men to put her back in the stall. The horse tamer from before moved her into the stall.

Gian grabbed Bianca by the hair and said, "What the fuck is that thing?"

"I don't know," she said.

"Bullshit! It's your horse," Gian shouted.

"I think it's a magical horse," Gunther said.

Gian looked to him and back at Bianca. He pulled her to her feet. "Is he right?"

Bianca had no more an idea of what happened than they did. But if it meant they would stop hurting Galland, she would make something up.

"Uh, you got me," Bianca said awkwardly. "Uh, she's an alien… horse…hybrid…thing… I got her as a gift from my *very* rich daddy."

Gian's facial expressions softened and he laughed. "Ha, Ha ha! You should have said something. What if we had sold her for a third her value?"

"Crazy right?" Bianca said. She thought, *Oh shit! Jae really did go to outer space! There's no way a horse from earth could survive bullet wounds.*

"Well, now we're gonna be rich and I have a pretty lady by my side."

"I'm not going to be your lady," Bianca said, crossing her arms. Now that she knew Galland was pretty much immortal, she wasn't going to walk on eggshells. Galland would be alright, and she could clearly fight. "You tried to kill my horse. If you want to sell her, you have to sell me with her."

Gian bit his lip and nodded. "Fine then, have it your way. I won't beg a woman to be mine, especially not a worthless one. You wanna live a life who knows where, as some slave? By all means go ahead. But I'm not selling you with her. Take her to the dungeon."

Gian called his other men, and they walked the other way. Bianca was carried back to her cell. The men threw her on the floor and locked the door. They talked about Galland as they left the dungeon.

"Decided to be with us huh?" a man said.

"Not quite. But I will never agree to be his woman. Not in a million years."

The men laughed. "They're nothing but a bunch of slobs and savages."

"You got that right," she said. "Now if only my boyfriend finds us, we can get out of here. Hopefully before he sells my horse."

"Yes well," a man said. "We've been down here longer than you, waiting on our leader to save us. Might as well give up."

"No, I know Jae can find me."

~Jae~

When Jae awakened, it was night. He stretched and stood up. He felt energized. He needed all the energy he could, who knew if he would need to fight. Staying vigilant was key.

129

He walked down the path. He took his time to shake off his sleepiness. He reached another crossroad, this time there were 3 paths similar to the first one he encountered. He looked left to right. He smiled. In the distance of the right path, was a faint light. He checked the other paths again. Nothing. He shrugged and went right.

After walking for thirty minutes, he came across a poorly written sign. "No trustpasin'! Dis iz Gravalite taratory u ben worned."

Jae laughed and shook his head. He vaguely remembered a few years ago coming across a group of bandits that idolized the god Gravick. One of the current gods known for terrorizing the Yulogna region. Jae knew there were supposed to be 2 gods left on earth, but he never encountered them, nor heard of them in the news for years. He wondered why the other one disappeared.

Gravick was worse than Hellim. Hellim, to Jae's knowledge changed a few things and was a bit of a tyrant. Gravick on the other hand, made Hellim's actions look peaceful. He was ruthless and despised all humans. Jae didn't know where his hatred stemmed from, but he killed humans indiscriminately since the day of ruin. Though in recent years, about 20 or so years, no one's heard from him again. He too disappeared. There were rumors of him terrorizing a different region but there were no documents about his whereabouts.

The Gravalites were an illiterate group of pesky bandits that believed they were all powerful. They targeted indiscriminately and killed many people solely for not having anything of value. They forced women to wed them and bear their children then killed them after they attempted a coup. They ran amok through a different region until Jae stopped them.

To think some of them survived, Jae thought as he continued past the sign.

10 feet ahead of him was a wooden fence. He crouched and hurried to it. He peeked around the corner and saw 15 men standing guard around the property. Jae thought it was a major improvement to their prior base, though still not enough guards. He unsheathed Magord and brazenly walked into their base.

The men looked at him. They were confused that someone would show themselves in front of so many people. He clearly had a death wish.

"Who da fuck is you?" one of them asked.

"Just a guy…" Jae said pacing back and forth looking from his feet to the men. "Looking for my woman."

"Ain't no woman here," a man shouted. "I suggest you get outta here."

The men shouted in agreeance.

"I suggest *you* take me to your prisoners," Jae said.

The man scoffed. "You're outnummered. Don' act so tuff."

A man to the side of Jae charged him screaming. A dagger raised above his head. Jae swung in his direction, sliced his throat, and the man dropped to the ground. The men were shocked, they looked at their lifeless comrade on the ground and were livid.

"You bastard!" a man shouted.

All 14 men charged Jae at once. Each carrying a sharp weapon. Jae dodged each attack and countered with one slice each, cutting 4 men in the abdomen. He jumped out of the attack of a round man with a sword and landed on top of him. He stabbed him and dodged another attack, leaving Magord stuck in the man. Two men lunged at once, and Jae grabbed both their heads and smashed them into each other. Blood spurted from their faces, and they fell to the ground.

He stretched his wrists and cracked his knuckles. "Man, I'm rusty."

The remaining 7 men hesitated. They clearly weren't going to win, but they couldn't let him just kill them. The man from before looked at another man and gestured with his eyes. He nodded and ran to a large gong and hit it 10 times, on the 11th, Jae threw a dagger and stabbed him. He hit the gong once more as he fell over. The lights in the building turned on and soon 20 men rushed from the house carrying different swords as well as guns.

Jae looked at each one of them and charged the 6 men in front of him. He managed to take down 3 more men, before Gian shot him.

"Take him to the torture room," Gian ordered. He shouted, "He's still alive. Look at this face men, this is the face of the man who killed the previous leader, your fathers and brothers! He will not get off easily with a bullet in the head. Oh no, we'll torture him like he did our fathers!"

The men cheered and followed behind men that carried Jae. Jae was dizzy and could barely keep his eyes open. He looked at the stable. He could see Galland eating and he thought, *Galland.... I need to save you and Bianca...*

Galland's head snapped towards them, and she whinnied as she saw Jae.

"Iz alright," he slurred. "I'll ge yu boh ou her. I promiz."

He lost consciousness.

Bianca lay on the cot facing the wall. She was drained. She didn't know what time of day it was. She just wished that her kidnappers didn't torture Galland.

Her cell door unlocked and opened. She sat up and stared at the man in front of her. He had long silver hair to his back. His ebony skin complimented his hair. He had red eyes and had a scar under his right eye that stretched down to his top lip. He wore a black tunic that outlined his slender but muscular shape, and black pants, and a dagger was equipped to his side. If the circumstances were different, he wasn't a kidnapping loser, and Bianca wasn't in love with Jae, she would have definitely found him attractive.

"Get up," he commanded.

"What do you want with me?" she asked.

"Let's go," he demanded. "I'll tell you when we're out of here."

Bianca uneasily stood up. She slowly walked to the door. Outside her cell, the other prisoners were standing around.

"What's going on?" she asked.

"We're gettin' outta here," a man said. "I don' know 'bout you little lady, but I ceraintly ain't waitin' for dem to sell me."

"Wait so he isn't with those Gravalites?"

"As if," the silver haired man scoffed.

"But there's like 30 people on their side. What chance do we have?"

"I'd rather go down fightin' than ending up wherever," another man said.

The other men nodded in agreement.

"It's up to you," the silver haired man said. "You can wait here and see what happens to a pretty woman like you, or you can go with us where you have a safer chance."

"How do I know you won't do anything?" she asked.

The man shrugged. "Be my guest, I only came for my men. Only woke you out of kindness. It's up to you what you want to do. Let's go."

The silver haired man started to walk away. Bianca panicked and said, "Wait! I'll go with you. Just until I meet my boyfriend."

"Do whatever you want," he said.

One of the men motioned for Bianca to walk in front of him and they exited the dungeon. The silver haired man crouched and crept through the halls, gesturing when it was safe for them to approach.

He kept the lead. Bianca noticed the direction they were going in and she whispered to him.

"Silver hair man," she said. "We're heading to the Gravalites leader's chamber."

He looked back at her. "For one, my name is Ajani. Secondly, I know. We're going to execute him. Why not use this chance?"

"Are you crazy?" she said grabbing his arm. "I've been to his chamber. It's heavily guarded. You're not going to make it out alive."

"Heh," Ajani chuckled. "I'm more capable than you think. My men will protect you. Don't worry about me. If they get the best of me, which I highly doubt, my men will get you out of here."

"Not happening sir," one of the men said. "If you're in trouble, we're backing you up. Sorry lady, but you understand where we're coming from right?"

Bianca nodded. Nothing she said would change their mind. She just hoped she would escape with Galland in the crossfire.

"Ah!" she said. "My horse, she's very special to me. When you kill him, can you help me save her?"

"Yeah whatever," Ajani said. "Now please shut it. You'll blow our cover."

Bianca nodded. She wondered how he even knew where his bedroom was. But she wasn't going to complain anymore, she was happy to be free and yearned to see Jae again.

They arrived by his chamber. Ajani rose a hand to stop them. He peeked around the hall. No one was there. He continued to creep forward, he took his dagger out and slowly opened Gian's door. When he entered, the lights were on and the room was empty.

He turned around to the others and whispered, "He's gone."

"What?" Bianca said. "Where would he go at this time of night?"

Ajani shrugged. It was a disappointing result, but they might as well escape while they had the chance. He wasn't as stealthy as before. He assumed they were all gone, he remembered the lack of security to sneak inside.

He walked boldly through the halls until he heard cheers from around the corner. Ajani stopped everyone and jogged to the end of the hall and peered around the corner. A group of Gravalites gathered around the entryway of a larger room. Their cheers muddled the shouting from inside.

He ran back to the others and said, "Let's go another route. They're all there."

They nodded in unison and followed his lead. They exited the front doors and were welcomed by the stench of blood and 11 corpses sprawled across the yard.

Bianca had a bad feeling and asked Ajani if they could find a way to see in the room the men were in? She knew it was Jae, it just had to be. Ajani rolled his eyes and agreed. They circled the premises until they came across a small window on the second floor. They heard cheers coming from inside the loudest there. Ajani scaled the building and Bianca followed after him. She struggled but managed to make it to the ledge.

Inside were 15 men, they circled around Gian. Gian looked as indignant as always, with the praise from his men.

Bianca whispered, "What are they doing?"

"If I knew," Ajani said. "We wouldn't be hanging on this ledge, right?"

Bianca rolled her eyes and tried to listen to what Gian was saying.

"This man has done nothing but murder us! We did nothing to him, yet he continues to show up everywhere we go! Why? Because his only intent is to wipe us out! I bet he hates our lord Gravick!"

The men roared in anger at the accusation.

"And what do we do to men who disrespect the gods?"

"Kill them!" the men yelled in unison.

"Yeah! But!" Gian paused. "This man gets a little more treatment than non-worshipers."

The men stayed silent. Gian looked awkward after the lack of cheers.

"D-do you want to know why?" Gian stuttered. "Because he killed the last leader as well as our men. He deserves torture and the same death he subjected him to."

This brought up the men's spirits and they cheered again, louder than before. Gian smiled and pulled out his gun. He reloaded it and aimed the revolver at someone who was out of view of Bianca and Ajani. He shot him. Not a peep from the man. Gian smiled. "I guess that tranquilizer was too strong for him. What a weakling."

The men laughed. And Gian shot him again. He shot four more rounds and reloaded. The man grunted as he came to.

"Oh," Gian teased. "Have a nice little nap? You have some balls barging into our turf. Was killing our leader not enough for you?"

The man slurred as he spoke, "You slaughtered innocent people and you're telling me you're upset I killed your boss? Give me what's mine and I won't kill the rest of you."

Gian sneered and looked at him with disgust. "Excuse me? You aren't in any position to make threats."

The man laughed. "Don't act tough 'cause your little flunkies are here. You're much weaker than your leader."

Gian shot him in the stomach, and the man bent over. Blood pooled around the man and under Gian's shoes.

Bianca listened closely, it sounded like Jae. She tapped Ajani repeatedly and said, "That's my boyfriend, you have to help me save him!"

He sighed. "Fine."

He let go of the ledge and dropped to the ground. He spoke with the men, and they all nodded. They grabbed weapons from the corpses and walked back into the building. Bianca turned back to watch what Gian did.

"Do you think I care about whatever I took from you?" Gian laughed. "You took something way more valuable."

"The life of a bandit has less value than the shit on my shoe." Jae spit at Gian.

Gian didn't shoot him. He grabbed a dagger from a man next to him and stabbed Jae in the shoulder. Jae clenched his jaw and closed his eyes.

"Where is she?" he asked.

"Who?" Gian asked.

"Bianca," Jae said. "And my horse. They're all I need, and I'll leave."

Gian scoffed. "First off, I don't know anyone named Bianca, secondly, are you accusing us of stealing from you? I have my own horses. I don't need to steal from a murderer."

"I saw my horse outside," Jae said.

"What proof do you have it's yours? All horses look the same."

"She's mine," Jae said flatly.

"Regardless," Gian said unamused. "Doesn't matter what's yours, you're dying tonight. No amount of groveling is going to save you."

"I'm not begging to leave, I'm giving you a warning." Jae glared at Gian.

A commotion happened in the halls. Men shouted and weapons clanked. The men in the room rushed to the door to see what was happening.

Gunther turned to Gian and said, "Boss! Doez prizners escaped."

Gian tsked. He looked to Jae, then back to the men. "We're in the middle of an execution! Let the men in the halls handle it. We'll join in after we kill him."

The Gravalites looked at each other then closed the doors. They walked around Gian and Jae.

"Now, where were we?" Gian smiled. "Ah yes, killing you. Unfortunately, we'll have to cut this short. Unruly cargo has to be settled. Who knows, maybe your lady friend is in the mix. I'll make sure she joins you."

Jae ripped out of the ropes and grabbed Gian by the throat. "Where is she?"

Gian struggled to breathe but laughed. "Grateli!"

A man jumped on command, and sliced Jae's right arm off. Bianca gasped and looked away.

What is Ajani doing?! she thought. *Please hurry, he's going to die!*

Gian and Jae's arm fell to the ground. Jae groaned and held his wound. He looked at Grateli and lunged. He kicked him in the throat, and he backed into the others. They all charged Jae. He did his best to dodge their attacks. The ground was slippery from his blood, and everyone struggled to keep their footing.

The door busted open and Ajani and his men joined the fight. Ajani and Jae looked at each other with disgust but continued to fight the Gravalites.

Gian ordered them to capture Jae. Two men grabbed him, and Gian scrambled to his feet. He grabbed a sword. The fight wasn't looking good for them, but if he was going to die, he would take Jae down with him.

He sprang at Jae and sliced his head off.

"Jae!" Bianca screamed. She cried as his head rolled on the ground. She climbed down the wall and ran inside.

The two Gravalites let go of his body and it flopped to the floor. Gian cheered.

"Now let's defend our turf!" he shouted.

The free men joined the battle. Ajani tsked at the sight of Jae's head. He wanted to be the person to do it. He kicked the man he fought onto the blade of his subordinate and went after Gian, who stayed back in the corner cheering on his men. His eyes focused on Ajani who walked slowly to him. His eyes widened and he shouted for someone to help him. He raised his hands in the air and backed further in the corner.

"What happened to that bravery of yours when you killed him?" he asked pointing to Jae's body. "Mr. Big and bad when you have 30 men protecting you."

"Look, I don't know what you want, but I won't chase after you. You're free to go, just stop attacking my men."

"Ha! I wasn't captured by you," Ajani said. "You captured my men. I can't let you walk away."

"Who are you?" Gian asked.

"The Amaganys. Ring a bell?"

Gian stiffened. "Uh, I'm sorry. I ain't know who my men brought back. They just found some men by themselves and grabbed them. If we had known…"

"If you had known you would have gone and sold another person?"

"Human trade is the biggest market right now…"

Ajani scoffed. "This is why no one likes the Gravalites. You people think you can just go around selling other human beings. You think you can do whatever you want! You have no class, and your crimes extend past any other group of bandits. It's time someone wiped you out for good."

Gian lowered his hands and tapped his pockets. He looked for his revolver. He looked past Ajani. His gun was on the ground by Jae's head.

"Whatever you're looking for isn't going to help you." Ajani smirked. He could have finished Gian off minutes ago, but like Gian wanted to torture Jae, Ajani wanted to torture him. Not to the same extent, but just enough emotional and psychological torture to make him regret his life choices.

He approached Gian and put the dagger under his chin and Gian lifted his head. Blood dripped from the tiny wound.

"Should I chop you into pieces? Maybe chop off your fingers first?"

Sweat dripped from Gian's forehead and he stammered, "L-look, I made a mistake, I shouldn't die for this!"

"Tell me why I shouldn't dismember you?" Ajani smiled.

"It's part of our regulations. We have no choice but to act the way we do. We're nothin' more than the product of our perdiscissors."

"Hmm," Ajani said. "Well it's part of my upbringing and Amagany rules to kill the misfortunate and misguided."

"Please!" Gian shouted. He looked around the room. All of the Gravalites were dead. "Y-you killed the last of the Gravick worshippers. I'm the last one, I'll change my ways! I won't worship him no more."

"What a coward!" Ajani exclaimed. "The moment you're facing death's door you want to change your ways? Die like a man!"

Bianca ran into the room and looked from Jae's head to Gian and Ajani. Tears streamed down her face.

Gian shouted, "Lady, please. Please tell them not to kill me!"

"You killed her boyfriend. Do you think she's going to ask me to spare your life?" Ajani turned to Bianca. "Woman, get out of here, you don't want to see this."

"What about Jae?"

"I'll bring him out to you. I promise we'll give him a proper burial."

"Lady please! I didn't know he was your man, please forgive me!"

"I—" Bianca wanted to tell Ajani not to kill Gian. She didn't feel right letting him die. But he was Jae's killer, he needed his revenge. And Gian needed punishment. If he were let go then, he would continue to terrorize others. Was it okay to kill someone to protect others?

Before Bianca could finish, Ajani said, "Woman, I have enough class to not make you choose, though your decision will not affect my desire to kill him. I ask you one last time to leave the room."

Gian looked desperately at Bianca. He mouthed, "Please."

"I don't think it's right to kill him," she finally spoke. "As much as I hate him for killing Jae, I don't want his death on my conscious."

"I won't kill him," Ajani said. "Please leave the room. I will punish him thoroughly."

"Promise?" Bianca asked.

Ajani didn't reply. She took his word and left the room. Gian screamed for her to stay there. Bianca closed the doors behind her and ran outside. She wasn't an idiot, she knew Ajani wouldn't listen to her, but it was at least off her mind that she didn't condone violence.

She walked to the stables, when she saw Galland, she broke down. She hugged her and apologized for not saving him. Bianca vowed to take care of Galland.

"Well, that's unfortunate," Ajani said. "Guess your last savior believed me. There are exceptions to when a man goes against his word. I'll make your death quick and painless."

Ajani slit Gian's throat and stabbed him in the chest. It wasn't a guaranteed proclamation that Ajani would make it painless. Gian slumped to the floor. His body jerked as blood poured from his chest and throat. Ajani looked down at him in disgust.

"Grab that tarp and wrap 'Jae' in it. For the woman's sake, keep his head at the top of his body. She can at least think he's in one piece. Don't worry about his arm."

"Yes sir," a man said. He and three other men wrapped Jae up and carried him out of the room.

Ajani continued, "Grab any lit torches, let's burn this place down."

Ajani and the remaining 7 Amaganys ran around the building lighting furniture and bodies on fire.

Bianca was outside untying the horses. She knew the men would need them. She saw the smoke rising from the building and moved the horses out of the stable and beyond the gate. The men carrying the tarp approached first.

"Is that Jae?" she asked.

They nodded their heads.

"Can you help me find a wagon?"

They nodded again. They searched the area for anything to carry him on. They managed to find a cart large enough for at least 5 men, plus Jae. The men helped load him on the cart and attached the cart to Galland's saddle. She asked for them to help take his sword. They struggled to carry it to the cart but with three carrying it, they were just barely able to lift it onto the cart. Bianca didn't want to bury him near the Gravalite base. She hoped to find an area miles away, maybe even in Kwtamg where he could rest peacefully. Ajani and the 7 men regrouped with them.

"So what are you going to do now?" Ajani asked.

"I still need to go to Kwtamg, but I have no idea where it is."

Ajani sighed. "Look, we'll help you get there. After that, you're on your own."

"Thank you," Bianca said. Tears filled her eyes and she looked down.

"Let me ride your horse," he said. "It takes a lot of skill to ride with that attached. Besides, there aren't enough horses and none of us wants to ride with a de—"

He bit his lip. "None of us wants to ride that close with another man. At least it'll be you and one man…if you're comfortable."

Bianca nodded. She wanted to lay with Jae one last time. She climbed in the cart and rested her head next to him. The cart jerked and they were on their way.

Chapter Six
City of Kwtamg

The ride was silent. Bianca felt a little stupid trusting a group of bandits to get her to a city she knew nothing about. But Ajani seemed trustworthy and respectful. She also knew she stood no chance making it on her own. When they left the Gravalite base, the sun was rising. She couldn't sleep with the sun beaming in her face, nor did she have a choice in staying awake. She rode until afternoon lying beside Jae. After that, she sat across from the Amagany named Aamadu. His given name was Chikondi but a rule of the Amaganys, similar to the Gravalites, was to have a name that started with an A. It was a cheesy concept but was adapted by a lot of bandits to show solidarity to their group.

Bianca learned a lot about the Amaganys and Ajani. The Amaganys was founded 5 years ago by Ajani. Ajani struggled during the second fall in the Yulogna region 17 years ago. He was 12 when his family was killed by Hellim, and Gravick. Ajani only survived because his parents had built a small bunker and only Ajani made it in time to hide there. Growing up, Ajani was taken advantage of by crooks and was sold as cargo to a wealthy woman. She took care of him as her son but also had him commit heinous acts against himself and other captives. Ajani couldn't respect her and the situation he was in and escaped when he was 16. After that, he joined a group of bandits called the Notes and changed his name to Norm. The Notes was a group of men and women over 30, their main rule was no kids, but made an exception for Ajani. He didn't agree with their ways, but he enjoyed stealing from the wealthy. They protected him and raised him until he was 21.

The downfall of the Notes happened unexpectedly. They were accused of stealing from one of Hellim's fleets. They caught news of the accusations and knew there was no surviving. They kicked Ajani out of the group and Hellim's soldiers arrested them, they were set for public execution. Ajani disagreed and wanted to die with his comrades, but they only laughed at him. He was too young to throw away his life. He watched the firing squad and saluted before their death.

Ajani grew to hate Hellim more. He had taken away everyone precious in his life and let criminals and the greedy live. From there, he vowed to protect humans from Hellim's army and crooks. He targeted mainly wealthy people but on occasion poorer people. Soon he gained a following and named them the Amaganys.

The Amaganys accepted men and women who didn't have anywhere to go. They weren't required to steal, but if they were to stay on their turf, they had to follow a few simple rules. Pitch in, help your fellow neighbors, and they couldn't show any admiration for the gods.

"You could always join us," Aamadu said.

Bianca shook her head. "Thank you but I can't. I have a mission to complete. Besides, I'm a wanted woman."

"For what?" Ajani joined in.

"I can't talk about it…" Bianca chuckled awkwardly. "The only other person who knows about it now are the people in my hometown."

"Was 'Jae' supposed to help you?"

Bianca nodded. "It was a decision we made that caused all of it. I…I just don't know anymore. Without Jae…I… I should just turn myself in."

Bianca cried.

"So you're going to give up because your little boyfriend isn't here to help you?"

"Ajani…" Aamadu whispered harshly.

He put his hand up to silence him and continued, "You made it this far, I'm sure you would be doing him a disfavor by giving yourself away. Don't you think you should at least finish what he planned for you? He wouldn't be dead right now if he didn't want you to survive."

"I just don't know. I can't do it by myself."

"You aren't," Ajani said. "Wherever we go after death, he's going to be with you through each step."

He was right, what would have been the point of this trip if she turned herself in? Jae died fighting for her freedom. What would be the point of his death, if the end result was going to Hellim?

"We won't reach Kwtamg for another 2 days. You might as well take this time to think," Ajani mumbled. "You're welcome to stay with us until you can assume a new identity."

"I can't get you involved. This is a lot bigger than you think. But I will continue on my own and fight for my freedom."

Ajani smiled. "Next step is to get rid of that body. We're a good distance away from the Gravalite base. This is good soil, easy enough for us to dig."

"If possible, can we go a little further? I was hoping maybe at a cemetery or in Kwtamg."

"Fine, but if his body starts to rot, I'm dumping him," Ajani said. "What's in Kwtamg anyway?"

"I need to see the Rain Prophet."

"Why?"

"She can probably tell me what to do. That's why we were going there."

"Hm. I don't understand how a person who claims to see the future can help you."

"You have to know what we're dealing with to understand why."

"And you're never going to tell us."

"I can't. You're too nice to get involved."

Ajani scoffed. "Whatever. We're stopping here to rest."

The men dismounted the horses and sat on the ground. They motioned for Bianca to join them.

"Come eat," Ajani said. They took the food from the Gravalites. They started eating the perishable items the first few nights, and anything canned or long lasting, was put to the side. "He's not going to run away."

"That's horrible!" Bianca yelled.

The Amaganys laughed. Bianca sat across from Ajani and partook in the food. Afterwards, she went back to the cart to sleep. She didn't want to sleep on the ground, nor did she want to be away from Jae.

"Goodnight," she whispered.

~Lyour~

Johnson and the women sat in his house. The same women were distracting Hellim. With only 3 days left before their time was up, they were going over the plan as well as explaining life outside of Lyour. Some of the women weren't sold by their families. They came willingly to escape the dangers outside. Most of them were homeless or lived in a town more dangerous than Lyour, others simply came because they wouldn't struggle. And their experiences were important for the women like Sasha and Serenity who grew up never leaving Johnson's home or the bordello.

Each woman explained what their hometown was like. Most emphasized human trafficking as the biggest threat. Originally bandits were notorious for stealing, but after realizing the profits of selling humans, that became the biggest business for bandits.

They spoke about defense strategies, Johnson taught them simple but effective techniques to subdue or severely injure their assailant. The women agreed that they wouldn't risk their lives to save someone if they were captured by Hellim's army or bandits. The goal was to survive until they regrouped in Gravick, a small town with not much going on. It was fairly close to Lyour and small enough for them to find each other. Once in Gravick, they would escape to wherever was farthest away from the Yulogna Region. Even if they went to the other side of the region, it was better than staying close to Lyour.

Sasha had finished the letter. She added a sentence, "Jae and I are heading to Jtrepo, please don't look for us." Johnson doubled checked the accuracy. There were tiny errors in it, but Hellim wouldn't have been able to differentiate between their handwriting. Pleased with her work, Johnson moved on to the next matter. Hannah and Rachel.

"Have you decided on what you want to do?" Johnson asked.

"I…want to survive," Rachel said. "I don't want to die. And I know once Hellim finds out you aren't coming back, he's going to slaughter us."

"I still don't think so," Hannah said. "We've been stuck with him for almost two weeks. He hasn't done anything to make us fear him."

"Except wipe out all of Lyour and threaten to kill us daily," Rachel said. "When are you going to understand that you can't trust that monster! He's dangerous and he's going to kill us!"

Rachel turned to Johnson. "I doubt she's going to agree to leave. If I have to go solo, then I'll do it."

"Well, is there anyone willing to go as a trio?" Johnson asked.

The women looked at each other and eventually Serenity spoke up, "She can be with us. Just as long as Sasha agrees and she's serious about the plan."

Sasha nodded.

"I am," Rachel said. "I have a better shot out there than here. If I die, then I want to die to anyone but Hellim."

"Well, there you have it," Johnson said. He turned to Hannah and asked, "This will be your last chance, are you sure you want to stay here? I can't guarantee your survival."

"I…" Hannah looked around the room. She looked into each woman's eyes. She believed with all her heart that Hellim wasn't as bad as people made him out to be. She trusted her life in his hands. But she also didn't want to worry the others nor be a disappointment if she stayed. Their plan seemed foolproof and well put together. She was terrified of being homeless or put into human trafficking, but she wanted nothing more than to fit in with the others and stay with them. "I…I'll go."

The women smiled and clapped. Hannah smiled. She cared deeply for Hellim, but if leaving him made her sisters happy, then that's what she had to do.

They dismissed the meeting and went back to serving Hellim.

~Bianca~

Bianca was jarred awake. It was morning and they were far from their camping spot. They were going across gravel and the cart shook violently. Bianca grabbed Jae so he wouldn't fall of the cart.

"Morning," Aamadu said.

"M-Morning," she said. "Sorry, I don't mean to be weird. I just don't want him sliding off the edge."

"Let's put his sword on him. It's heavy enough."

They pushed his sword up and onto his body. Bianca thanked Aamadu then relaxed again. The shaking cart was actually soothing, and she fell back asleep a minute later.

"AHH!" Aamadu screamed.

Everyone was alert. They stopped their horses and turned to the cart. Bianca was also woken up. Her eyes widened.

Jae was sitting up. His eyes were closed, but he rubbed his forehead then down to his neck with his right hand.

"J-Jae?" Bianca stammered.

Jae looked up at her, then to the men that stared at him, fear in their eyes. He looked around and asked in a low raspy voice, "Where are we and who are they?"

"We're on our way to Kwtamg," Bianca said. She was scared, but elated that Jae was alive. She had so many questions. "These are the Amaganys. They helped me escape the Gravalites. They were going to help me save you but… And when you… They were helping me get to Kwtamg, we were going to bury you…. H-how are you alive?"

"Coulda sworn I saw your head on the ground," Ajani said. "You want to explain why you're alive?"

"I don't answer to you," Jae sneered.

"Then can you tell me?" Bianca asked. "I think I deserve an answer."

"I'll tell you later."

"Why not now?" Bianca exclaimed. "Galland was shot in the head. You *literally* had your head cut off."

"Look, I promise to tell you when we get to Kwtamg," Jae said, his voice becoming clearer with each word. "When we separate, I'll tell you."

"They're good people," Bianca said. "I'm sure they'd—"

"Don't trust trash that easily," Jae said.

"Huh?!" Ajani said. He jumped off Galland and unsheathed his sword. "You want to repeat that?"

Jae grunted and stood up. He unsheathed Magord and jumped off the cart. "Don't get cocky. Want me to beat your ass again?"

"I'll make sure you're dead this time."

"W-wait," Bianca stammered. "Don't fight! Jae, he's trustworthy! Ajani, please, he's still recovering. Jae stop!"

Jae and Ajani stared at each other, then at Bianca. Jae put away his sword and Ajani followed.

"Sorry Bianca," Jae said.

"It's okay. They're bandits but they're not like the others."

"They're all the same," Jae said. "They still commit crimes, whether it's for 'justice' or not."

"You don't know them, how can you judge them?"

Jae scoffed. "I'm well acquainted with 'Ajani.'"

Bianca looked to Ajani, and he nodded. "I got your little boyfriend to thank for scarring my face."

"That's your fault," Jae said, sitting next to Bianca. "Shouldn't have attacked me."

"You slaughtered people!" Ajani shouted.

"I didn't slaughter anyone." Jae waved him off.

"So you're going to continue to deny it?"

"Can't deny something that never happened."

"What is he talking about?" Bianca asked.

"Nothing," Jae said.

"He killed a village of bandits," Ajani said. "He killed innocent people that joined a bandit village to survive. They never committed any crimes."

"First off," Jae started. "I killed the Gravalite village. The worst group in the world. Secondly, the villagers were just as evil as the bandits. The men forced themselves on women, the women abused their children, they forced their beliefs on others. And anyone that worships the gods should be exterminated."

"Do you think those children deserved to die?" Ajani glared.

"I didn't kill them." Jae shrugged. "They were dead when I got there."

"Bullshit!" Ajani shouted.

"I didn't kill them," Jae said.

"Then what happened?"

Jae shrugged. His nonchalant attitude pissed Ajani off. He could never forget how they were brutally killed. No matter how terrible they were, they didn't deserve the death Jae brought upon them.

"They deserve justice," Ajani said. He took out his sword.

"Stop this childish sense of justice." Jae stood up and unsheathed Magord. "I won't let you off easy. Stand down."

"Please stop…" Bianca pleaded. "Ajani, I don't think Jae killed them. He's not that kind of man!"

"Then you don't know him. A murderer will always be a murderer."

"Please don—"

"Bianca," Jae cut her off. "Somethings can't be settled with talking."

"But Jae," Bianca said. "You're still healing!"

"Don't worry about me."

"Are you going to keep talking, or fight me?" Ajani interrupted.

"If you want to speed up your death, be my guest."

"Don't kill him," Bianca demanded. "Neither one of you. If you insist on fighting, settle it and move on."

They ignored Bianca and stared at each other. They slowly stepped sideways away from the group. Ajani attacked first. He charged Jae and swung. Jae blocked and kicked Ajani in the stomach. Ajani slid back and dodged as Jae aimed for his face.

Ajani blocked multiple attacks and countered. He swung and sliced Jae on the cheek, blood seeped down his face. Ajani smiled and continued swinging.

This went on for 10 minutes, neither one of them doing real damage to the other. They stared at each other breathing heavily. Ajani struck again and Jae blocked. Their movements were slower and sloppier, but neither wanted to give up.

Jae lost his footing and Ajani stabbed him in the stomach. Ajani was pleased, he finally landed a lethal wound on him. Jae rolled his eyes and grabbed the blade. Blood oozed from his fist, and he kicked Ajani. Ajani flew backwards letting go of the sword. Jae grunted as he ripped the sword out of his stomach and threw it. Blood splashed the ground.

Jae stomped the ground and roots grew and tied around Ajani's limbs and pulled him to the ground.

"What the hell?!" Ajani wrestled to break from the roots.

Jae walked to Ajani and lifted his sword above his head. He swung.

"Jae no!" Bianca screamed.

Jae stopped mid-swing and sheathed Magord. He took a deep breath and walked to Bianca. "Sorry."

"It's okay," Bianca said hugging him.

"You fucking monster," Ajani shouted, still struggling to break free from the roots. "Let me go!"

"Let yourself out." Jae detached the cart from Galland's saddle and motioned for Bianca to get on. He helped her on then climbed on. He turned to Ajani. "As I said, I didn't kill them. Take it however you want."

The Amaganys hurried to chop off the roots. Ajani glared at Jae as they rode away.

They rode in silence for a while before Bianca spoke, "How's your wound?"

"Already healed…"

"Are you going to explain how you're alive?"

"I don't want to talk about it."

"I deserve to know the truth don't you think?" she paused then asked, "Are you human?"

"Yes…"

"Then how did you survive?"

Jae sighed. "I'll tell you when we're in Kwtamg. Okay? When I'm ready."

Bianca reluctantly gave in. No matter how much she pressured him, he wouldn't tell her. Bianca questioned how much she knew about Jae. He was shrouded in mystery and the more they were together, the more his secrets came to light. Bianca loved him, and no matter what he told her, her feelings wouldn't falter.

"Well, at least," Bianca said. "Can you tell me what happened at the Gravalite village? You didn't kill them did you?"

Jae sighed. "It's a long story. Yes, I killed the villagers, but I did not kill the children. As I told him, they were dead when I arrived. I was hired to kill everyone by a neighboring village they continuously targeted. They were a menace. They did atrocious things like sacrificing non-Gravick worshipers, they were horrible people. And when I arrived in the village, blood was splattered everywhere, no one was outside. I searched the village only to find the children murdered and their parents praying over them. I don't know if they killed them, but it definitely looked like it, and I wouldn't put it past them. So I killed them. Ajani for whatever reason, arrived after I was finished and challenged me. I explained it then, that I didn't kill the kids but he wouldn't listen to reason. He was a kid himself, so I wasn't going to kill him. I won, scarring his face, and never saw him again."

"Wow," Bianca exclaimed. "I knew you weren't that kind of person. I mean, I don't condone violence, but I won't hold it against you, since they terrorized everyone."

Jae smiled and wrapped his arms around Bianca. "Thank you."

He continued, "We have to hurry. There's no telling how many people have died."

"Sorry," Bianca mumbled. "If I hadn't wandered off, none of this would have happened."

"Don't apologize. They shouldn't have kidnapped you."

~Lyour~

The next morning, the Malarik Shipping had arrived. Johnson didn't tell the women right away. He went over the plan one last time with Sasha and Serenity. They were going to hand out their clothing. It was too early to escape, but they would relay to them that tonight was it.

Johnson planned to give Hellim the letter later in the morning. He was still sleep and Johnson didn't want to push anything. There wasn't a guarantee that Hellim would let them live even if he believed the letter. They were taking a huge gamble but that was better than letting him kill them. Even if only some of the women survived, that was better than nothing. Johnson would do whatever it took to save as many of them as possible.

Johnson paced around the main hall, the letter resting on his chin, when Hellim emerged from his room. His heart pounded against his chest.

"He-Sir," Johnson stuttered.

"What?"

"Uh, the letter from Bianca has arrived." Johnson extended the letter to Hellim.

Hellim snatched it from his hand and ripped open the letter. He skimmed it before saying, "It's your lucky day. Smart move to turn her in, cheesy letter or not. Me and my troops will withdraw from Lyour tomorrow."

Johnson bowed, but before he could thank him, Hellim stepped closer and whispered, "There's one more proposition. I won't kill the women or you, *IF* you give me these women too."

"What do you mean?" Johnson asked.

"I have a current mission of mine, and I need women. I'm willing to pay a large amount for your women."

"I think I need a little more information…" Johnson said brashly. "You're going to put me out of business."

"How bold." Hellim smiled devilishly. "I'll let your tone slide. If you must know, I need women to bear my children. They will be taken care of, but as of now, there are life ending flaws with interspecies procreation, but what else are these women for? They'll die at some point."

"Uh give me the day to decide. I will give you my answer in the morning."

"Very well," Hellim said. He stormed onto the stage and sat on the throne. "Fetch me Hannah and someone else."

"Yes sir." Johnson bowed and exited the room.

Johnson sent Hannah and another woman to the main room and called a meeting in his home.

"Good news and bad news," Johnson stated, pacing the living room. "Good news first. Hellim believed the letter and leaves tomorrow."

The women clapped and cheered. One woman spoke up, "So does this mean we don't have to leave?"

"Unfortunately no, the bad news is that Hellim wants to buy you all."

They looked confused. Rachel shouted, "What? Why the hell would he want to 'buy' us?"

"He didn't give me all the details but he wants to sow his seed in all of you."

"He wants us to have his children?" Rachel interrupted.

"Yes, but he said something along the lines of childbirth being life threatening. So if you're fine with that, you're free to back out from the escape."

"If we say no?" Serenity asked.

"Then he'll kill you."

"Great, so we're still in the same situation." Rachel kicked a chair.

"I don't want to," Sasha started. "Can we still continue with the plan?"

"Yes," Johnson said. "Who wants to stay with Hellim?"

Everyone looked around the room. He looked to each woman, and they shook their head.

"Then we'll continue with the plan."

"Can we not tell Hannah?" a woman asked.

"Yeah, I don't trust her," another woman chimed in.

"She's stupid enough to stay, we can't," another said.

Everyone mumbled in agreeance.

"We won't," Johnson said. "Well, we'll go over the plan once more."

He sat down and continued, "From what I gathered, Hellim falls asleep at 10 PM. At about 11-11:30 PM, Hellim's soldiers retire for the night. Meet at the doors at 11:50 PM, come early if you want, latest 11:59 PM. From there, make sure you have your partner, travel light. Pack only necessities in the bags I ordered. Be stealthy."

They nodded.

"Any last questions?" he asked.

"If one of us is captured or injured," a woman started, "do we have to leave her behind? I don't think I can."

"It's up to you," Johnson said. "The goal is to survive. If you want to try and save your partner, by all means, that is your choice. But do not expect others to do the same. Take this time to pack, meeting adjourned."

The women nodded and left.

Hannah and the other woman prepared a meal in the kitchen for Hellim. Hannah stopped breading the chicken and said, "Are you sure we have to do this?"

"Hannah, we can't talk about that here," the woman said, in a hushed tone.

"I know, but I just feel bad deceiving Hellim. He's done so much for us and been so kind. I just don't think—"

"Enough Hannah!" she shouted. "He's not the kind of person you think he is, if we could even call him a person. He's continuously threatened to kill us for 2 weeks, and we may die soon. Please stop being so gullible. We all love you Hannah, we don't want you to die trusting a monster."

"Okay…" Hannah mumbled. She avoided eye contact. "I won't trust him…. I won't be gullible. I'll go with you all, and just do whatever…."

She hugged Hannah and said, "Don't be discouraged. We're going to have an amazing life. We'll get to do everything we want to. Doesn't that seem wonderful?"

"It does." Hannah smiled.

"Chin up, you'll find a *human* man, who will love you unconditionally." Hannah gave a slight smile.

~Bianca & Jae~

They arrived at the outskirts of Kwtamg in the morning. They left Galland to run freely in a field nearby. There was a small town, with houses no taller than 8 feet. The city was gorgeous. Not in the same way as Malarik, but a beautiful gloomy atmosphere. It was too early, the sun hadn't even peeked through the sky. No one was outside, which made the town creepier. They walked slowly through the town until they reached a dock. One small boat with a man resting inside was at the end of it. A pool of water surrounded the city. Kwtamg was small and suspended on wooden boards. In the distance they could see rain clouds that hovered above it, the clouds extended slightly past the edge of the city.

"Well here goes nothing," Jae said, glancing back at Bianca. He walked to the boat and tapped the man with the chape of his sword. "Hey, are you here to take us to the city?"

The middle aged man lifted his hat slightly off his face, only showing one of his baggy eyes and complained, "The sun's barely out."

"Yeah well, we need to get over there regardless of the time, do your job. You aren't getting paid to sleep." Jae sneered.

"Excuse me?" the man said, sitting up.

"Uh, sorry," Bianca butted in. "Jae that's not how you speak to people. Just ask nicely. Do you mind taking us over? I know it's early, but we're extremely late and every second is counting against us. I understand however, if you want to sleep longer."

"Hm," the man said. "Only for you miss. Be lucky she's with you."

"Thank you," Bianca said, stepping into the boat.

Jae didn't respond and sat next to her.

They sat in silence while the man rowed to the city. As they sailed closer, the rain began to pelt them. Jae gave Bianca his cloak and shielded his eyes. He looked absolutely miserable. They arrived as the sun was halfway in the sky. Bianca thanked the man once more as they left the dock.

Kwtamg looked so old timey. The buildings ranged from 10 ft to 15 ft high. They were dull, a dark grey color with little to no windows. The streets were filled with rickshaws, and gas streetlamps covered every corner of the city. The only thing relatively modern about Kwtamg was the cemented streets and sidewalks. There were little to no plant life in the city. There weren't any trees or bushes. But purple and blue flowers lined the bottom of buildings. They weren't a native species. Jae explained to Bianca that they were plants from a planet far in the galaxy. He didn't know what they were called. The flowers were gifted as diplomacy prior to the day of ruin.

As they walked, Bianca spotted a rain shop a bit ahead of them. She pushed Jae into the shop and bought another cloak as well as the last two umbrellas available. They were adorable. One umbrella was pink with strawberries and bunnies on it. The other was mint green with red flowers. Jae went with the mint green one. At least he could have some of his dignity. There were signs pointing in the direction of the Rain Prophet's home. As they walked down the street a "speeding" rickshaw rushed down the street and splashed Jae with water.

"I fucking hate this city!" Jae seethed.

Bianca through labored breath from laughing said, "Aww, it's alright. We're almost there. We'll be in and out. Want me to walk on the curb side?"

"No, I can't let you do that," he grumbled, wiping his face.

"Are you sure?"

Jae nodded. "Let's just pick up the pace."

"Okay," Bianca said. "Seriously though, I didn't even think those cart things could splash that much water."

"I don't want to talk about it…"

"Alright." Bianca giggled.

He wasn't kidding when he said he hated rain cities. Seems like his luck is complete shit since we got here, Bianca thought. She thought it was funny seeing an uncool side of Jae, but she felt bad for him.

After an hour, they reached the edge of the city. At the end of the road was a small red house, eerily contrasting the gloomy city. A field of orange alien flowers surrounded the home. Bianca grew anxious staring at it. She took a step back and Jae placed his arm gently on her lower back.

Jae took Bianca's hand and led her to the house. On closer inspection, the home looked abandoned. The dark brown doors looked rusted, and the windows were poorly patched up with cardboard and duct tape. Who knew how long it had been since they took care of the home? Jae knocked on the door. Nothing. He waited a bit then knocked again. Still no answer. Bianca looked at Jae.

"Maybe it's abandoned?" she said. "Is it a tourist scam?"

"What would they get out of that?"

"I don't know, because we're foreigners, they assume we're going to throw money everywhere we go."

"I don't think so." He shook his head.

Jae twisted the doorknob. It was unlocked, he looked back to Bianca and entered the house.

"I knew you would show up," a feeble voice said.

Jae and Bianca looked to their right and saw an old woman. She was small, no taller than 5'1. She walked slowly past them and into another room.

"Well come on," she said. "We have quite the problem to attend to."

"How did you know we were coming?" Jae asked.

"I see all," she quickly said.

"If you see everything," Bianca said. "Then why didn't you say something about Hellim and what happened?"

"It's not my place. I only interfere with fate when it is deadly."

"You don't think this is?" Jae asked.

"It is," she said. "But when it comes to prophecies, there are multiple ways it can go. A person's decision can have a good turn out or cause havoc."

"So I really did have a choice there?" Bianca asked.

"Yes, and you made a decision that sealed your fate and many others."

"Well, is there anything we can do to change it?" Jae asked.

"Every decision you make will change your destiny. It's your judgement that can give Bianca a better life."

"What about Jae's future?"

"He sealed his fate 135 years ago."

"During the Day of Ruin?" Bianca asked.

The prophet nodded. "I see you haven't told Bianca the truth… godeater."

"'Godeater?'" Bianca repeated, turning to Jae. "What does she mean?"

"I'll…explain it to you later," Jae mumbled avoiding her gaze.

"Another poor decision." The prophet shook her head. "It's now or never. Once you leave here, you will never speak of it again."

Jae sighed. He didn't want to remember what took place 136 years ago. If it had never happened, Bianca wouldn't be in the situation she was in. But at the same time, he was grateful he was able to meet Bianca and fall in love. He didn't care anymore about the repercussions. He just wanted to provide her with the best comfort and her freedom. That was his only goal, even if it meant giving his life.

"Jae," Bianca said, gently touching his arm. "I love you. I will never judge you or hate you for whatever you did. What happened?"

He exhaled and looked down.

"I know you're conflicted with telling me your past, but I did share mine with you. I think it's time you told me yours," Bianca said, sternly.

"Okay," Jae sighed. "Just know, when it started, it wasn't my fault."

Chapter Seven
Jae's Past Pt. 1

"It was 141 years ago. September 3rd, 2035. America discovered an alien pod that crash-landed in what was Kansas. There was a reporter secretly recording what was going on. The American government set up a base surrounding it and evacuated everyone in the city. The pod opened and out came a large creature. It was in a form similar to humans, but its skin was blue, it had long limbs, wore tattered clothing that covered its chest and private area. It looked like a woman and towered over everyone. The agents were stunned. Then it began to speak…

'Lower your weapons,' it said. Its voice was soft. 'Me and my comrades mean no harm.'

'Your "comrades"? There's more of you?' a man stuttered.

'Yes, we have been searching for other forms of life. Our planet was destroyed. We traveled the galaxy until we found "earth." We only seek refuge on an inhabitable planet.'

'And how are we to trust you?' the man asked.

'I assure you we are a peaceful species. Most of us were wiped out. Only 11 remain. We are outnumbered by your kind. We just want to live in peace.'

'And where are they?'

'I do not know,' it said. 'We did not properly calculate our landings accordingly, as well as what kind of terrains earth has. Like "wind."'

The men and women lowered their weapons.

'We will need to discuss it with our president,' he said walking away.

'Is that earth's leader?'

'No, it's America's "leader."'

'Then shall I wait here?'

'Yeah, have a seat.'

Some time passed and the man walked back to the alien. 'Well, fortunately for you, he has given permission for you to stay. But you can't leave this area until we know for sure we can trust you. You will be heavily guarded too.'

'I understand.'

At the same time, in other parts of the world. The other pods were hatched, and locals were dealing with the same issues. But due to the world's obsession with aliens, they were trusted and welcomed.

Over time, the world noticed they had 'powers.' The creatures found out about global warming, and natural disasters. In what seemed like a flick of the wrist, Antarctica's icebergs were restored, and the temperatures fell below -100°F. They were able to stop earthquakes and hurricanes. Volcanoes were dormant, tornados disappeared, and tsunamis were calmed before it reached islands.

To ensure once they were allowed to live on earth, they wouldn't harm nor enslave the human race, the Peace and Ethics code was enacted. It was list of rules the gods agreed upon with the UN and all world leaders. The first 10 rules of the Peace and Ethics Code were:

1. We, the Trwqoyians, will not harm a human or any living beings on earth.
2. We will not use our powers to abuse the human laws of earth nor to abuse humans.
3. We vow to stop any natural disasters before they can occur, and will remove any that do happen.
4. We vow to respect humans and their rules.
5. We vow to each visit a country once a month, to help wherever needed.
6. We vow to use our powers to uphold and improve the betterment of society.
7. We vow to not use our powers for our own purposes, if it shall interfere with or harm humans.
8. We can only use our powers against a human, IF and only if, they are intentionally harming another human. The offending human must remain alive after the encounter.
9. We vow to avoid any conflicts with humans, as we are aware of the differences in our physical abilities. We will escape the situation instead of fighting.
10. We shall uphold the first and second codes of the Peace and Ethics Code, if we do not, we shall be punished by exile from earth or death at the hands of another Trwqoyian.

Humans began to worship them and started calling them 'gods.' Wars ended and almost everyone lived in harmony. The gods introduced advanced technologies like floating cars, spaceships, intergalactic travel, and many more. They were revered."

~Daegu, South Korea~

Jae stared in awe at the god that was triple his size. Something about it scared him. It didn't have the same presence as the others. It didn't make sense. The 10 gods landed everywhere but South Korea. Yet here was one in Daegu. Jae was sure they weren't visiting that day. They visited a country every month, taking turns. He hadn't seen one up close before, but he remembered what color their skins were, blue, black, green, yellow, and red, two to each color. But this one was dark purple. Its grin was menacing. Jae saw its fangs. As it got closer to where he was, he ran behind a pile of boxes in an alley. He hoped because it was night, it wouldn't be able to see him. He was sure the god didn't see him standing there. But what if it did? Chills ran down his spine imagining what would happen to him. He grew nauseous.

A faint purple mist filled the air as it came closer. The mist spread out and filled the alley. Jae covered his mouth, he didn't know what it was, nor if it was safe to inhale. Its large steps rumbled the ground, making Jae stumble. Jae froze, he could hear its breathing. He was terrified, he was sure it was going to find him. As it turned the corner into the alley, a drunk man stumbled along the road yelling incoherently. The god turned around and made its way to the man.

"Huh?" the man slurred. "You one of them gods righ? How 'bout you fix muh wallet?"

Jae had a bad feeling, but he couldn't move his legs. The god bent over and grabbed the man. Blood squirted between its fingers as if it grabbed an orange and squeezed it tightly. It lifted its hand and ate the man. Jae was horrified. He never saw a person get killed before. His arms and legs shook, he wanted to get out of there and fast. The god continued walking down the street, the rumbling got softer and softer until Jae heard and felt nothing. It was pitch silence. All Jae could do was stare at the ground in front of him. The blood splatters covered everything. The walls, the street and stands. The smell of blood hit Jae and he vomited.

"I need to get out of here," he said, standing up. He turned around and walked deeper into the alley, his legs quivering. He could barely move. After a while, Jae finally had the courage to run, and he ran all the way to his hideout.

Jae burst into his hideout. "Jihoon! I just saw one of those gods kill someone!"

"No way." Jihoon laughed. "You must have been imagining things. They don't kill people. They're symbols of peace."

"Not this one," Jae said, getting closer. "It was different than the others. It was purple and evil. And it squished and ate him."

"You must have been imagining it," he said. "You need to rest. You haven't eaten anything have you? Just go lie down."

Jihoon led Jae into their room and laughed as he left.

"I know what I saw," he complained. "He'll see when it's on the news, and people find the blood on their houses."

Jae was so heated he completely forgot his fear and the images of the man dying and fell asleep.

Jae was an orphan. He was placed on the steps of the church when he was 3 months old. As he got older, the church couldn't afford to feed everyone, and many children were left to fend for themselves. The gods could fix everything but specific problems like world hunger. Because of this, Jae decided he would be the person to protect the others. Jae was the oldest. When they left the orphanage, Jae was only 12. Only 3 children went with him. Jae was 16 but took on the responsibility of raising 3 kids. Ji-hoon, the second oldest was 13. Ye-jun was 10, and Dasom was 7. And as the years went by, they grew closer and eventually looked at each other as biological siblings.

He worked as many jobs as he could to provide for them. They bought an abandoned and rundown home for cheap and called it their hideout. Jae cared for them and would do anything to protect them and keep them from starvation even if it meant he didn't eat.

The next morning, Jae woke up ready to say, "I told you so."

"Good morning, guys," Jae said.

"Good morning, are you feeling better now that you got some sleep?" Dasom, the youngest, asked.

"I'm telling you it happened."

"Then why hasn't anyone said anything?" Ye-jun asked rolling over.

"No way," Jae said. "It must have not reached the news yet! I'm going to show you proof. Come on."

Jae led the others to the street where it happened, but there was no blood.

"What?" Jae said in disbelief. He looked the other way to where the pod landed and it was gone, the car it smashed was back to normal. There were no traces that it happened. "It must have cleaned up the mess."

"See, you were imagining things," Jihoon said, placing his hand on Jae's shoulder. "Come on, let's head back."

"It's smart enough to not leave evidence," Jae said shaking off Ji-hoon's hand. He refused to back down. "I know what I saw. Where is it hiding?"

"Come on, let's go," Dasom whined.

"Yeah, it's too early," Ye-jun said. "We all wanna go back to sleep."

Jae didn't say anything. He stared at the space where the pod was. Nothing made sense anymore. He was doubting what he saw. Maybe he really did hallucinate. Jae turned around and followed the others home.

Over the next few weeks, reports of missing people in South Korea grew larger. People assumed there was a serial killer on the loose. Jae stood outside a café watching the news, when an image of the man he saw that night flashed on the screen. Jae jumped and yelled, "That's him! That's the guy I saw that night! I wasn't imagining it."

People stared at him. Jae grew silent and walked away.

If that's true, he thought. *Then it must be killing all those other people. We're not safe.*

Jae ran to a nearby police station. He burst through the doors screaming, "I know what's happening to the missing people!"

The police looked at him unfazed. One finally spoke, "And what is that?"

"It was a god that killed them! I saw it with my own eyes!"

The police looked at each other, then erupted in laughter.

"I'm serious!" Jae slammed the counter. "I saw it myself! I'm not lying!"

"Which god?" a cop managed to ask as he laughed. "The one in Peru or Canada?"

"Neither! It was a purple god! There's an 11th!"

The cops stared at him, then laughed again.

"Kid probably had a nightmare!" The cops laughed harder.

"I watched it kill that guy! I *know* what I saw."

"Go home kid. This isn't a joke."

How stupid can they be? They're going to let it kill us all! Jae thought as he stormed out of the police station. He needed to find something to protect him and everyone at the hideout. But he knew ordinary guns wouldn't be enough. Everyone knew high-tech weapons existed, but they were illegal in most countries, and anyone caught with one was arrested. But Jae was willing to take the risk to save his family and South Korea.

Jae walked to the underground market.

Jae walked into a gun shop that was hidden in the corner of the market. It was barely noticeable unless the sun shined on it. Behind the counter was a scruffy man, his clothes were dirty and sloppy, and his hair was greasy. He looked lazy and like he didn't care.

"Excuse me sir," Jae said.

"What is it," he responded slowly.

"I need a weapon."

"What kind of weapon."

"Something that can kill."

"Kid, that's all of them. You're gonna have to slim it down."

"Strong enough to…" Jae paused and leaned over the counter. He whispered, "Strong enough to kill a god."

"Whoa ho," the man shouted amused. "You really want to try that?"

"Just for protection, all those missing people were killed by one of them."

"No way, they're all in western countries."

"No, there's an 11th. It landed late a few weeks ago and I watched it kill a man. The next day, it cleaned up the blood and its landing spot and I just *know* it's behind these missing cases."

"Hmm, I always wondered about that. They said there were 11 of them, but we only saw 10. I knew not all of them were good. But they just kept proving me wrong."

"Well this one isn't. And it doesn't look the same as them. It's dark purple and looks scary."

"Shit," the clerk said. "Well I can't believe I'm saying this, but I believe you kid. It's too suspicious."

"Do you sell any high-tech guns?" Jae asked.

"Shh, keep your voice down," he said. He lifted the counter and said, "Follow me."

Jae followed him into the back room. The man inputted something into a keypad on the backside of a large TV and a door hidden behind the TV opened. He followed him downstairs, as they walked the clerk said, "Oh by the way, I'm Russell."

"I'm Jae. Nice to meet you."

"Well Jae, as I'm sure you're aware, these guns are illegal in South Korea. But thanks to my connections in the US, I can get these over here easily. There's just one rule, don't touch anything I don't hand you."

"Okay…"

The walk was long, Jae didn't expect that tiny shop to have a huge basement. They continued to walk down a long metal corridor until Russell stopped at a door to the right. He typed something and the pad scanned his eyes. It said, "Welcome Russell," in English and Jae was even more fascinated.

"Come on," Russell said, his voice echoed in the room.

"Wow," Jae said, his mouth agape.

He looked around the room. There were rows and rows of weapons. He looked at a shelf three rows away and saw a large gun. It looked like a regular gun, except it had a blue aura around it. It looked so cool to Jae.

"I want that one," he said, walking to it.

"Noo." Russell quickly stopped him. "That will blow your arm off with the kickback alone."

Russell looked around, his eyes examining every weapon, his eyes widened, and he continued, "How about this one?"

Russell picked up a small pistol. "This guy may be small, but it does close to the same amount of damage as that one, but with less self-injury. Fairly cheap in comparison too."

"Yeah, but I also want something that looks cool."

Russell rolled his eyes and continued to walk. They looked around for an hour. Jae refused the weapons Russell offered, they looked lame. No matter how powerful they were, its appearance mattered to a 16-year-old boy. Russell was getting annoyed. He was about to kick Jae out when Jae spotted a sword on the top shelf.

"What about that one?"

"That? Cost's 1.5 billion Won. It's one of my favorites. I call it, 'Magord,'" he said. "One, because it's a sword and two because it's magical."

"What's so magical about it that it costs ₩1.5 billion?"

"Let me show you," he said taking the sword off the shelf. "It's not too heavy and looks like an ordinary sword."

"Then how is it a high-tech weapon?" Jae interrupted.

"I'm getting there." Russell held his hand out to silence Jae.

Russell drew the sword, the sound as it came out the sheath was mesmerizing. It sounded like a low note on a flute, resonating in Jae's ears. When it was fully drawn, Jae lost his excitement. It was rusted, the blade was jagged, and lined the edge. It was so dated how could that be of any use?

"Doesn't look impressive," Jae said.

"It looks pretty beat up, but this sword can cut through anything. If I had to choose a weapon to kill them with, this would be it. Guaranteed to cut through them. No matter what the material or how thick it is, this will cut through."

"No way," Jae said.

"Follow me," Russell said, walking away.

They left the room and continued down the hall. They passed three more doors, before Russell stopped at a door to the right. He inputted a password and keycard and the door opened. Inside, the room was all metal, there were ten pillars. On the floor and walls were bullet holes, ash, etc.

"This is the trial room," Russell said. "Come in."

They walked into the room and the door slammed behind them. Russell walked to a pillar and said, "Watch."

He swung the sword and in one swift movement, sliced through the metal pillar. Jae was stunned. That dull sword really was able to cut anything. Though he didn't know how hard a god was. Russell was really into it. He stabbed the ground and dragged the sword across the room leaving a jagged line.

"Give it a try." He motioned for Jae to come to him.

Jae grabbed the sword and the tip fell to the ground. It was heavier than Russel made it seem. Jae struggled to pick it up.

"Maybe we should try something else," Russell said, reaching for the sword.

"No, I got it," Jae said, moving away from him. Using all his strength, he lifted the sword off the ground. "See? Not that heavy…"

"Now swing." Russell smiled, his arms crossed.

Jae stared at the sword intensely and shuffled to a pillar. His scrawny arms trembled as he tried to swing the sword. He couldn't build enough momentum and the sword barely nicked the pillar.

Russell burst into laughter. "What the hell was that?"

"A few days of practice and I'll be able to swing it!"

"Tell ya what," Russell said, breathing heavily. "I know you can't afford this. But if you come here every day and practice, I'll let you have the sword… IF you can slice through a pillar in one swing without struggling. Deal?"

"Deal," Jae said, shaking Russell's hand.

"You have two weeks."

Jae stayed behind as Russell went back to the shop. He needed to practice. It was the only option he had. Even though the sword was high-tech, it didn't look like one. He would be able to walk around without getting questioned. Jae spent all afternoon and evening struggling to lift the sword. He had a week to practice lifting it. He planned to come every morning and practice until night.

Jae and Russell became more acquainted and were spending more time together. While Jae practiced lifting the sword, Russell would talk about whatever conspiracy theories he came across in a group called, "Don't trust the gods." He invested himself as the days went by until he believed every theory. Russell began to hate the gods which fueled him to train Jae harder.

Russell gave Jae his own password for the trial room and eye recognition for the weapons room. The other rooms were off-limits. Jae didn't know what was inside and Russell wasn't planning on telling him. But Russell trusted him enough to show him how to lock up his shop, including a secret metal door he pulled above the stairs. It was done so to make sure no one found his stash of high-tech weapons, cops or any bold robbers.

Every day more and more Koreans were disappearing. The police issued a curfew to protect everyone. No one was allowed out after 10 PM. The only exemption from the rules were if people were returning from work and had proof or if they were accompanied by 1 or more people for protection. Anyone caught outside would be investigated and given a fine.

On the nights Jae stayed late, Russell would escort him home. He had a fake pass he used to prove his identity for work. The police let them go on numerous occasions. Russell made sure to bring regular looking weapons small enough to hide in his pants. But they were still strong enough to kill a god. Or at least Russell believed they could.

The issue was reported to the gods, but the matter was beyond them. They all agreed that the S. Korean police could handle a killer. There was no need for them to get involved. They did not believe in violence and if they were to help, they felt that would go against what they stood for. Their stance angered many S. Koreans. And soon it spread throughout the country that the gods were useless. They were only there to look go and help minor issues with humans. What good were they if they didn't fix every problem?

Russell was even more suspicious after their response. Jae knew they weren't responsible for the killings in S. Korea, but the blogs had a point, why didn't they want to help? Russell on the other hand, believed they were in on it. They were all-powerful. They could find the killer with a snap of a finger, yet they refused. Russell spoke his theories to Jae. At first Jae thought he had gone crazy, but as they spent day in and day out together, his ideals seemed more logical. They didn't mention the eleventh alien, they hadn't mentioned anything about the "destruction" of their planet. As Russell put it, "Who knew if their planet was even destroyed?" They didn't act like a species whose home and people were extinct.

Jae spent his time at the hideout trying to convince his siblings they were no good. But no matter how much he tried, they still laughed at him. Dasom loved them, Ye-jun admired them, and Jihoon trusted them. There was nothing Jae could do to convince them otherwise. He could only stand guard and when the time came, defend them no matter what. Even if it cost him his life.

A week went by, and Jae was able to hold the sword. Swinging was another thing. Russell took away the "Magord" and had Jae practice swinging a normal sword. He wanted Jae to learn the techniques before learning any unhealthy habits from a sword he could barely hold.

With only two days left of their bet, Jae understood the basics of how to handle a sword and switched back to the Magord. After spending 5 days away, it felt like he was back to square one. He struggled to hold the sword. But after 2 hours of practicing lifting it, he was able to hold it comfortably again. He spent the next 2 days trying to swing it.

By the final day, Jae could swing better than his first try, but was nowhere near able to slice through the metal pillar. Russell already knew he couldn't do it, but he liked Jae and his ambition to kill a god. Russell still gave the Magord to him. Except, the only stipulation was that Jae kept the sword at his store and practiced until he could cut through a pillar. Jae was impatient but he knew Russell was right. No matter how much he practiced holding it, if, and when the purple god came after him, he wouldn't be able to protect himself or his siblings. Jae spent less time at the shop but still came 5 days a week to practice.

As Jae practiced, Russell cleaned one of his personal guns. He had gone on another conspiracy spiel.

"And you wanna know what's even crazier?" Russell said, excitement in his eyes.

"What?" Jae asked. He was used to his theories, but sometimes Russell scared him.

"I heard that if you eat one of them, you'll gain powers."

"Ew, who would want to?"

"You never know. What's the worst that could happen? Bad taste? An upset stomach?" Russell aimed his gun at a pillar far from Jae and pulled the trigger, shattering it into millions of metal shards. "If that thing comes after me, I'm blasting it to smithereens and roasting it."

"Eh, I don't know about that," Jae said uneasy. "Wouldn't it be better to give its body to the police? That way we have proof that there was a bad god. We could see how the gods respond to it."

"Do you trust them?" Russell's tone grew serious. "Do you think, you killing one of their kind, would go easy with them?"

Jae tried to answer but Russell cut him off. "No. They said they were almost extinct. What would one death, vicious or not, cause them to do? They're all evil, Jae. You need to wake up. They know about that god. I just know it. Why haven't they visited our country? Why haven't they investigated the missing people? Symbol of peace and ethics? They didn't care about that when they stopped the wars."

Jae listened. He stopped practicing and stared at Russell.

"All I'm saying kid, is we can't trust them. A few years on our planet doesn't make them trustworthy. This could all be a ploy. They could be brainwashing us right now. I don't trust them, and I never will."

Is he right? Jae thought. *Could they really be dangerous? How could we trust them*?

Jae didn't know what to do. He hoped the police found out about the god before they did. Russell would never give up its body, nor would he forgive Jae if he went against him. He just prayed that the god would go elsewhere and leave him and S. Korea alone for good. He would've wasted his time training, but that was worth his siblings' safety.

After a month, the murders were still happening and at that point, Koreans worried about their dwindling population. The streets grew emptier and emptier. They were too scared to leave their homes. Who would be next? Stores had limited purchases due to the onslaught of citizens across the country buying as much as possible to bunker down. Anyone seen walking in the streets were looked at as crazy. Because who would be sane enough to hang outside with a murderer still at large?

Jae was finally able to swing the Magord with ease. He had built up strength and his arms were no longer twigs. He wasn't muscular but there was a slight bump. He sliced through the metal pillars as if he were slicing bread, smooth and steady. There was nothing else Russell could teach him. Anything more, he would have to learn on his own.

"Well, this is it," Russell said, as they emerged from the basement. "Good luck out there. Don't die after all that work."

"I won't." Jae smiled. He gripped Magord and stared proudly at it. Finally Magord was his. He would treasure it forever. He looked at the clock. It was well past 11 PM and if he were caught, he would be arrested. "Uh, Russell? Can you walk me home? Or give me like a fake work pass?"

"I only have one," he said.

"I see, you need it to get home." Jae nodded.

"Nope, not for that."

"Then how do you get home?"

"This is my home. I have a nice little bunker two doors from the trial room. You're welcome to stay the night."

"I can't. I need to check on my siblings."

Russell sighed and grumbled, "Putting me at risk helping you."

Russell went down to the basement, Jae followed behind him. Russell went into the weapon's room and grabbed the small pistol he offered Jae. "Let's go."

"Is that for you?"

"Obviously. Once I take you home, I have to get back here in one piece."

They walked down the streets with caution. "Be on guard kid. Less people out means a bigger chance it'll come for us."

"Let's just hope it's in another city…" Jae checked around him.

They quickened their pace. The hideout wasn't far from the underground market. Russell started running and Jae followed. The air seemed creepy. The streets were empty. Not even the police were guarding outside. Something was off, Jae could feel it. The stench of blood grew stronger as they reached his home. Jae felt sick, he knew that smell all too well.

"Hurry Russell," he said, speeding up.

"Wait kid," Russell shouted. "Don't just charge in, we need to assess— Jae!"

Jae didn't care what he said. It was close to his home. He wasn't going to risk his siblings' being in danger to "assess the situation." Russell couldn't keep up with Jae and soon they were blocks apart.

Jae turned the corner and his eyes widened. The street was covered in blood. Multiple body parts strewn about. Gaping holes through buildings and houses were crumbling. Cars were embedded into homes. In the distance he saw the purple god.

On the ground was Ji-hoon's head. His eyes were opened, and a horrified look was frozen to his face. The rest of his body had been eaten. In its hand was Dasom, she was unconscious, blood oozed between its fingers. The god opened its mouth and lifted up Dasom. Rage engulfed Jae and he screamed. He charged the god and sliced off the arm that held Dasom. The god shrieked and shrunk back a little. He ran to her. He pulled its fingers apart and his heart sank. Dasom had been squished to death. Her body was as thin as paper. He held back his vomit. He couldn't look anymore. He erupted into tears. If only he had been there on time. He opened his eyes quickly and searched around.

Where's Ye-jun, he thought.

In the corner he saw Ye-jun, his eyes widened, tears fell from his eyes, and he trembled, his legs were shaking intensely. In his quivering hands he held a small piece of plywood aimed at the god. His eyes not leaving it.

"Ye-jun," Jae shouted. "Get out of here!"

Ye-jun snapped out of it and turned to Jae. His expression softened and he cried, "Hyung!"

Before Jae could run to him, the god screeched and swung towards Jae. Jae didn't have good reflexes, there wasn't enough time to block with Magord. He closed his eyes and was smashed into a wall. Blood spurted out of his mouth, and he fell to the ground. He writhed in pain. It was difficult to stand. The impact alone was enough to make him lose consciousness. His eyes slowly closed.

"Hyung," Ye-jun screamed. "Get up! Hyung!"

Hearing Ye-jun's cries, snapped Jae out of it and he used Magord as a cane. He was kneeling.

"Run away Ye-j—" before he could finish, more blood gushed from his mouth.

"I'm not leaving you," Ye-jun cried.

"Don't…worry about…me." Jae could hardly breathe. He managed a smiled and said, "I won't di—"

The purple god kicked him, and he flew across the street smashing into a car.

"Hyung!" Ye-jun gathered the courage and charged at the god. He hit its leg.

The god looked down and fear washed over Ye-jun again. Its teeth barred and it turned to him.

"Ye-j—" Jae coughed. "Run."

He was too weak to speak, and he struggled to stand again. The god raised its arm and swung down to smash Ye-jun. Ye-jun couldn't run, his legs wouldn't let him. Ye-jun closed his eyes. Bracing for death.

"Ye-jun!" Jae used all of his might to stand.

A shot went off and a bright light blinded everyone. When the light faded, the god's other arm had been blown off. The god's arm crashed into a building. Jae and Ye-jun stared wondering what just happened.

"All that training and you still can't beat it," Russell yelled in the distance. Everyone looked at him. "That's the only time I'm saving you kid. You better stand up and focus on killing that thing."

"Thanks," Jae said. "Ye-jun, I need you to calm down and listen to me. Don't try to save me, I can beat it. Run to that man over there. He'll protect you."

"But Hyung," Ye-jun protested.

"No buts, get out of here."

Ye-jun nodded and forced himself to run out of range of the god.

Russell shouted, "With two arms gone, it's at a disadvantage. You better not lose to that thing!"

Russell motioned for Ye-jun to get behind him. He continued, "Don't worry kiddo. Jae's not going to lose that easily."

Jae felt heavy and dizzy, but he needed to avenge Ji-hoon and Dasom. He knew if things got too intense, Russell would jump in to save him again… maybe. He lifted up Magord and raised it to his shoulder. The god wasn't looking at him anymore. It stared at Russell. It hadn't moved a muscle. Jae wondered if it was at its limit or if it had given up. Either way, he wasn't giving it another chance. He ran at the god, stabbed its leg, and sliced it open. The god dropped to one knee, still not moving. Jae lifted Magord again and swung to cut it in half.

Before the blade hit the god, its arms shot out of its body, and it swung back at Jae. Even though he had been taken off guard again, this time Jae was able to dodge.

"What the hell?!" Jae stumbled backwards. "It can heal?!"

He looked at the spots where its arms landed. All that was there was a pool of purple liquid.

"Oh ho." Russell smiled amused. He shouted to Jae, "So that's another theory proved!"

"Will you forget about your theories and help me?" he yelled back. He jumped and rolled out of the way of the god's attacks. Barely keeping his footing.

He timed his swing with the god's and its right arm was cut off. But its leg had grown back.

Russell whistled and looked at his watch. "Buy me some time kid. I need to see something."

"I'll try. Hope I don't die waiting."

Jae swung twice and cut off its other arm and left leg. Without a moment's hesitation, he twisted around and sliced off its right leg. The god stood on its nubs and grimaced at Jae.

"This is for my siblings," he said as he swung the sword and cut off its head.

Its head rolled a few feet away. The god's mouth still moved, and its eyes blinked wildly. Jae stared at it for a while as its blinking stopped.

"I did it Russell. It's dead." He breathed heavily.

Russell didn't pay him any mind and stared at his watch. As he looked up, the right arm grew back. "Just as I thought. Its regeneration is 5 minutes! Its other limbs should be popping out soon!"

Just as he said that, the other limbs grew back, and it stood up. Jae backed away quickly. "How is it not dead?! I cut off its head!"

"Might not be enough," Russell said. "Maybe try stabbing its heart. These things can't be immortal. You need to figure out how to kill it."

"How about you help me?" Jae complained. He looked back at the god's body. It picked up its head and positioned it back on its neck. The nerves and skin reattached itself to where Jae had cut it and the god moved its head back and forth to check if its head was on properly. When it was done, it turned back to Jae and smiled, nothing but its large teeth showed. "You've got to be kidding me."

It rushed Jae and he was back to ducking and dodging. He knew it wouldn't be easy to kill a god, but that fight was just unreasonable. Why was it so hard to kill? He tried to think of a way to kill it, but he couldn't focus like Russell could. Jae wondered if he hadn't been careless at the beginning, he wouldn't have had such a difficult time. He sliced off its limbs again but also cut it in half. Jae decapitated it again. He stabbed it in its chest multiple times. He could see Dasom's lifeless body in his peripheral and his rage took over. He stabbed it again and again in different spots. Each stab more forceful than the other. When he stopped to take a breath, the body was full of holes. Looking at it for the first time, someone wouldn't know what they were looking at.

Was that enough? Jae thought. He looked at Russell and Russell lifted 5 fingers. Jae looked down and its limbs burst out again. Jae jumped back, but before it could get up, he sliced off its legs and then its arms. He wasn't giving it a chance to reattach itself.

He looked at the god's head. It looked angry. Even though its body was separated, it moved its mouth and tongue as if it were breathing.

"We have to be missing something," Jae shouted to Russell.

"No shit! Keep dicing it up!"

Jae continued to stab, the holes in its chest kept closing. He stabbed and cut again. But it kept regenerating. Jae was confused. Did it have a heart? Clearly it wasn't human, so maybe it didn't have all the same organs? Jae looked at its head, still struggling to get back to its body. He walked up to it and raised his arm to stab it.

The god scowled and opened its mouth, purple fumes poured out of its mouth and from the holes in its body. Jae backed away. He remembered the purple mist from the night he first saw it. He knew there was something dangerous about it. He covered his mouth with his shirt. Jae looked at Russell who motioned 5. And its limbs grew back. This time, its upper and lower half, a meter apart, both shot out vessels and muscles and reattached to each other. Its neck reattached its head and the god stood.

The mist filled the street and Russell carried Ye-jun who stood stiff far away to a neighboring street. "Stay here."

Ye-jun nodded.

Russell ran back to the street and squinted to see through the mist. Jae dodged its attacks, but his movement grew slower. He struggled to hold his breath and fight. And his wounds from earlier didn't help anything.

"Think," Russell demanded to himself. He thought, *I could shoot another bullet, but that could probably screw the kid over. What can I do?*

Jae swung cutting its legs off and his shirt fell from his face. He paused to pull it back up and lost his footing. Jae tripped and fell. He scrambled to get up as the god punched. Its punch sent Jae down the street. Though the mist hadn't reached that far, Jae inhaled a lot from the impact of its punch.

He lay there. He tried his best to stand, but he couldn't move. It was like his body wouldn't listen to him. The god crawled slowly to him. Jae was confused then it hit him. It was paralyzing gas. That explained why he couldn't move in that alley way and why he was stuck then. He tried to force his mouth to move and warn Russell, but it wouldn't work.

Think, he thought. *What did you do last time?*

He couldn't remember what he did. Had he done anything back then to remove the paralysis? Nothing. He stood in the alley for who knows how long and over time he was able to move. Even after he walked, it was hard to move his legs. If only he could speak. He needed Russell to buy him time for the gas effects to wear off.

The god's legs grew back, and it stood. Its pace quickened as it made its way to Jae.

Shit, he thought. His eyes were the first to move and he watched as it ran towards him.

A blinding light filled the street, and the god was sent flying past Jae and into a building. Its legs yet again lost.

"You okay kid?" Russell yelled walking closer. He had his shirt wrapped around his mouth and nose. He kept his eyes on the god who struggled to climb out of the house. "What's wrong, you're not dead right?"

Jae looked at Russell trying to speak.

"Can you blink? Blink once if you're not dead."

Jae managed to blink with one eye.

"That's a wink, but I'll take it. Blink if you're paralyzed."

Jae winked again.

"Was it that mist? Blink once yes, twice no."

Jae blinked once.

"Shit," Russell said. He looked back at the god. It made its way out of the building and lifted itself over the metal gate. "Ye-jun is hiding, so you don't need to worry about him. I need to get you somewhere safe and finish this thing myself. Damn you might be paralyzed forever."

Jae grunted and blinked twice.

"How do you know? Blink twice if you've dealt with this before."

Jae blinked twice.

"Do you know how long it takes? Once yes, twice no."

Jae blinked twice.

"Fuck." Russell looked at his watch. "5 minutes."

The god's legs grew back, and it charged at them.

"Close your eyes," Russell shouted. He shot three blasts, two shots hit its legs and the third blew a hole in half its torso. The blasts sent the god back. Sending it into another building.

If he can do this much damage, Jae thought. *Why can't he just kill him and take care of me later?*

The god spewed more mist, but it was too far to reach Jae and Russell. Russell grabbed Jae's legs and lugged him farther down the street. He grabbed Magord and set it next to Jae.

"If you get your movement back, feel free to join in." Russell stood up. He pulled out a light blue vial and poured it into the gun. "This is the last of my ammo. You better move again before I run out of bullets. That's if it's still alive."

The alien stood. It was extremely angry. Its teeth barred and it ran to Russell, it was faster than before. It dodged two of Russell's shots and swung at him. Russell dodged and shot off its arm. He shot multiple rounds, hitting it in its torso and chest.

"Why won't you die?" Russell shouted. He shot again missing it as he dodged another attack.

Three shots left, he thought. *Can't miss any more.*

He shot twice again, knocking off its leg. It fell to the ground. Russell aimed at its head and said, "This is the end for you. Not so tough now huh? Think we're just going to let you kill us off?"

Russell looked at his watch. 2 minutes until its limbs grew back. Russell smiled. He knew he won, so why not waste some time?

Russell kicked it as it struggled to get up. It stared at him with such hatred, it sent chills down his spine, and he smiled. "Look at me with that hate. Just remember this face when you burn in hell."

He looked at his watch, 30 seconds remained. "This is it."

He raised the gun to its head and pulled the trigger.

Click* *Click* *Click

A cold sweat dropped down his back. He was out of bullets. Somewhere in his blaze of bullets, he had lost count of his ammo.

"Fuck."

The purple god's arm grew back and it smashed Russell into a building.

"Russell," Jae shouted. He paused. He was able to move again. He picked up Magord and rushed the god. Just as the god was about to crush Russell, Jae sliced off its arm. Throwing it off balance. Jae sliced again, cutting off its arm then its leg. It fell over and Jae cut off its other leg. He sliced it in half and cut off its head.

He stabbed its head multiple times and it stopped moving. He stabbed its body and chopped it into chunks of flesh. He looked at Russell who struggled to stand up. He looked at Jae and put up 5 fingers. Jae looked at its body and the limbs hadn't grown back.

Jae collapsed to the ground. His energy escaped him. Russell ran over. "Did you kill it?"

Jae nodded.

"Right on," Russell cheered. He turned towards where Ye-jun was hiding and said, "See he didn't die."

Ye-jun ran over to Jae and hugged him.

"It's gonna be alright," Jae said, holding him. He glanced at Dasom then Ji-hoon and squeezed his eyes shut. He cried hard and held Ye-jun tighter.

Russell rummaged through the wrecked buildings and found any large boxes that he could. He carefully lifted Ji-hoon's head into a small box and Dasom's into a crate. He handed them to Jae and said softly, "Here. Let's clean up the alien remains and find a place to bury them."

Jae looked up and asked Ye-jun to carry Ji-hoon. They chopped up the purple god and put it into numerous boxes. They hid it in their hideout and limped to the church that sheltered the orphanage. They walked into the cemetery and in an abandoned corner, Jae and Russell dug one hole. Dasom and Ji-hoon's boxes were small enough to put together.

Jae and Ye-jun prayed and Russell refilled the grave. Jae and Russell carried over a rock and with a marker they found in the shed, wrote "*In loving memory of Ji-hoon and Dasom. Their lives were taken from them, but they will live on in their siblings.*"

No one spoke on the way back to their hideout. Ye-jun was still scared and didn't want to stay there. He knew the god was dead but memories of it smashing through the wall and ripping out Ji-hoon scared him most.

They searched the broken homes for keys and drove the only workable car to their hideout. They loaded the car with the boxes of the alien parts and memorabilia and headed to Russell's shop.

When they arrived, they put the boxes into a room at the far end of the basement. The room wasn't metal like the others. It was a kitchen. The floors and walls were tiled and a fridge, oven, sink and part of a counter were inside. There was a mat on the floor and a rotten table that looked on the verge of collapsing any minute. They stacked the boxes on the counter and the floor in front of it. Russell pulled out a first aid kit from one of the cabinets and handed it to Jae.

Russell led them to another room. In that room the walls were metal and only one flat bed was inside.

"This is the only other bedroom I have," Russell mumbled. "You're free to stay here as long as you want. If you're up for it in the morning Jae, let's talk about what we discussed a month ago."

Jae nodded and said, "Okay thanks. Goodnight."

"Night." Russell left the room and the door swiveled closed.

Ye-jun sat on the bed and looked at his blood-covered shoes. "Is this where we're going to stay?"

"For now," Jae said, walking over. He knelt in front of Ye-jun and asked, "Did you get hurt?"

Ye-jun shook his head. Tears filled his eyes. "We should've listened. They wouldn't be dead."

Jae hugged him. "That's not why. If I had come home earlier, I could have saved them."

"Are they all like this?" Ye-jun asked.

"I don't know..." Jae let go of Ye-jun and sat on the floor. He faced away from Ye-jun and lifted his torn shirt. He looked at his wounds. His body was blue and purple, swollen, and his wounds hadn't healed, blood still leaked out. It might have been the adrenaline. He hadn't felt pain since the beginning of their fight. He opened a bottle of *revive*, a newly formed medication introduced by the gods. It healed most wounds on the exception of deadly ones. It couldn't cure every ailment, but it did its work. Jae hated the taste of it. He squeezed his eyes shut and chugged it until it was empty. He winced as the medicine took effect. His body burned as the wounds sealed and his broken limbs snapped back in place. After 10 minutes, his body was back to normal. That was the only thing Jae was grateful to the gods for.

Russell came back with clothing for them. He gave Jae and Ye-jun the code to the door and the bathroom, then headed to his own room. Jae and Ye-jun took showers and Jae tucked Ye-jun into bed. He rested on the floor beside the bed.

Neither Jae nor Ye-jun could sleep but they didn't utter a word to not wake the other.

The next morning, Jae met Russell in the kitchen. Ye-jun had finally fallen asleep around 4 am.

Russell was taking the alien parts out of the refrigerator. He placed the boxes on the table and the counter and opened them. He and Jae stared at the purple flesh. Jae looked disgusted and Russell looked excited.

"How are we even supposed to eat this?" Jae asked.

"Let me check the forums." Russell took out his phone and searched online. He swiped furiously through the pages. "I...don't know. Some say eat it raw, others say cooked..."

"Do...you think we should try both?"

"I guess. We have no other choice." Russell grabbed a box and threw it in a pot. "I'll take the cooked, you eat it raw."

"Hell no!"

"Look kid, I'm older and I have a bad stomach, I can't be eating raw foods. You're gonna have to take one for the team. Don't forget I saved your ass last night."

"The debt was paid when I saved you."

"No. I saved you multiple times. You eat its head. If one of us feels a certain way, we tell each other. If nothing happens, we just finish it off and never speak of it again. Deal?"

Jae nodded. He waited until Russell was done cooking and cut into a piece of the alien's head. They made eye contact and nodded.

Before they took a bite, Ye-jun knocked on the door. "Hyung, Mr. Russell, can I come in? What are you guys making?"

Jae put his fork down and opened the door. "We're testing something out. This isn't the time."

"Can I at least watch? I don't want to be alone."

Jae's heart sank and he nodded. "Don't touch anything."

Russell went into the fridge and made Ye-jun a sandwich.

Ye-jun watched them pick up their forks and asked, "What are you doing?"

"Nothin—"

"We're testing to see if eating that god will grant us special powers," Russell interrupted. "If we do gain powers, we can fight off the other gods."

"Whoa," Ye-jun exclaimed. "Can I taste some?"

"Absolutely not," Jae yelled.

Ye-jun flinched. Jae had never yelled at him. He sat down on the mat and looked at his sandwich.

"I'm sorry I yelled," Jae said. He bent down to Ye-jun's level. "This could be very dangerous. We don't know what will happen. I couldn't bear to lose you too. If nothing happens to us, you can have some. But not during our trial."

Ye-jun nodded. "I understand."

Jae smiled and patted his head. He stood up and grabbed his fork again. He nodded to Russell and said, "3…2…1…"

They both gulped down a chunk of flesh. They waited 5 minutes, but nothing happened. They felt no difference.

"Anything?" Russell desperately asked Jae.

Jae shook his head.

"What a waste of time." Russell threw his fork on the ground and stomped on it.

"What does it taste like?" Ye-jun asked.

"Here," Russell said, grabbing a new fork and handing him a piece of cooked meat.

Ye-jun took a bite. "It doesn't taste bad. We've had worse."

"We did." Jae laughed awkwardly. He remembered two years ago when he stole old meat from a butcher. He didn't know it was spoiled and brought it home. Jihoon was pissed and Dasom pretended to like it.

Thinking about it made Jae want to cry. He bit his lip and said, "If it's not that bad, guess we can finish off the rest over the week."

"Guess so," Russell said. He put the meat back into the fridge. "But I want you to finish off the head like that."

"Why? It won't do anything."

"Who knows, it could have effects later. That is the heart of the god."

"Then shouldn't Ye-jun not eat anymore?"

"I'll be fine," Ye-jun said. "I don't feel anything wrong."

"But…"

"You heard him," Russell said. "Just let the kid eat an alien delicacy."

They continued to finish off the purple god's body. For the first three days, nothing was wrong. Russell and Ye-jun grew accustomed to the taste and ate it for all three meals. Jae on the other hand, took his time eating the head. Russell refused to let him eat the body. Not until the head was completely gone.

Russell called Jae into the weapons room. He handed him a black and red ring that matched Magord's sheath.

"I'd been meaning to give this to you a while ago. If you're separated from Magord, a twist of this ring on your finger and it will fly back to you."

"This would've been useful with that god fight."

"Yeah well, not my fault you…" Russell paused. "That's beside the point. You have it now. If you're ever in a predicament, this will save you."

"Thanks." Jae put the ring on his right middle finger.

Jae grabbed Magord from his room and put it at the far end of the hall. He used his thumb to twist the ring counterclockwise and Magord shot towards him with extreme force. He was grateful he didn't unsheathe it.

On the fourth day, Ye-jun developed a stomachache. They assumed it was from eating too much and told him to stop. By the fifth day, Jae had finished the head, its brain and eyes included. He felt sick after feeling the texture of the eyes POP in his mouth. Similar to eating a fish's eye. He didn't want the body anymore. If he looked at another piece of alien, he would throw up.

"How are you feeling?" Jae asked, walking into their room.

"I'm okay," Ye-jun said. He rested in bed. His stomach hurt too much to move.

"Seriously," Jae said, sitting on the bed. "If you feel worse, let me know. I'll take you to the hospital."

Ye-jun nodded and fell asleep.

Jae left the room. He went to Russell who was working in the store. Russell leaned over the glass case. He wore a pained expression and sweat trickled from his forehead.

"Are you feeling okay?"

"Yeah, but I think I caught whatever Ye-jun has." Russell held his stomach. He stood up straight and said, "Don't worry about it. But if you can, man the store while I grab a revive."

"The revive didn't work on Ye-jun," Jae said. "But I can watch the store anyways."

"Thanks. It doesn't hurt to try." Russell went into the back.

Jae stood behind the glass case and looked inside. It was full of ammo. He didn't know what went where, but it was still cool. Not as cool as the blasts from the pistol Russell carried. He looked around the store, he didn't want to touch anything, but he never got the chance to examine the guns. Russell always yelled at him when he did.

"Jae," Russell shouted from the back.

Jae flinched and said, "I didn't touch anything!"

"What are yo—" Russell started. "That's not the point. Hurry it's Ye-jun!"

Jae ran to the basement and followed Russell to his room. Ye-jun convulsed in the bed. Blood gushed from every hole in his body.

"Ye-jun!" Jae rushed to his side and held him. "Is he having a seizure?!"

"I don't know," Russell said, running in with the first aid kit. He opened the revive and tried to get him to swallow, but too much blood poured out of his mouth.

"Damnit!" Jae cried. "Not you too."

"It's going to be alright, we can save him," Russell said. He was also panicking but he didn't want Jae to become worse.

"I need to get him to the hospital," Jae said lifting Ye-jun. His small body flailed around, and Russell grabbed his legs.

They hurried to the hospital. On the way Russell said, "Don't tell them about the god."

"Then how do we explain this?" Jae asked. Jae sat in the back holding Ye-jun.

"We'll tell them we ate something off the ground. We don't know what it is. They'll pump his stomach of whatever is causing this."

"'Whatever is causing this,'" Jae repeated angerly. "What do you mean whatever. This is clearly because we ate that god! You said nothing would happen. You said you didn't feel sick and for us to continue eating it!"

"You said that kid," Russell shouted back. "You suggested we continue to eat the meat. Yeah, I suggested it the first time, but it was your decision to let him try it! Don't get angry at me for your bad decisions. Yes, I fucked up suggesting this to begin with, I share the blame, but I left him eating it up to you. I understand you're frustrated but taking it out on me won't change anything."

Jae hugged Ye-jun tightly as his lower half thrashed around. He knew Russell was right. It was all his fault. From the very beginning, if he had done things differently, none of his siblings would have died. Ye-jun wouldn't be suffering if he had turned the body in to the police. None of this would have happened if that purple god hadn't landed in S. Korea.

When they reached the hospital, they handed him to the doctors. Onlookers were horrified seeing him. The doctors had no idea what to do. They had never seen anything like what was happening to him. They tried pumping his stomach, replacing blood, they gave him an IV. After a long period of time, they gave him sleeping pills and he stopped thrashing around. Even though he was unconscious, blood still poured out of him. They had numerous blood packs on hand to keep him from losing all his blood. They put a tube into his mouth to suction up the blood and clear his airways.

Jae sat in the waiting area. He didn't speak a word to Russell and stared at the ground. He prayed for Ye-jun to make it.

The doctors came out and explained what they did. But they questioned them further. Their story didn't make sense. They didn't know what they ate, they suspected poison, but neither one of them was like Ye-jun.

They asked to monitor Russell since he had eaten the same thing as Ye-jun. He agreed if it would benefit his recovery. Jae was left alone in the waiting room again. He was the only one there. The secretaries and security guard had also gone to help Ye-jun.

The silence angered him more.

Why is it so quiet? he thought. *I can't take it!*

Russell returned to Jae after a few hours. He shook his head. They couldn't figure anything out. Jae had a bad feeling and demanded to see Ye-jun. After causing a scene, they agreed to let him into the room. Jae erupted into tears when he saw Ye-jun hooked up to the machine, blood spilled on the floor, he was attached to an oxygen machine, and he was unconscious. Jae held his hand and mumbled to him. His words were unintelligible. The heart monitor flatlined. Ye-jun's heart stopped.

Russell and Jae drove home in silence. Both felt guilty for his death. Jae had lost everything he cared for in only a week. His world had shattered in front of his eyes. It was all his fault. If he had thought of another way to deal with the alien, if he had gone home early that night instead of talking with Russell, if he had done the right thing, none of them would have died. He was angry at Russell for suggesting the alien flesh but was angrier at himself for agreeing to let Ye-jun eat it. He knew what was going to happen next. They had all eaten the alien and soon he would join them.

What am I thinking? Jae thought, and chuckled slightly. *They're going to a place I don't belong.*

When they arrived at the shop, Russell and Jae sat quietly in the trial room, waiting for their demise. After a few hours, nothing happened.

Confused Jae asked, "Why haven't we died?"

"I don't know…" Russell responded. "Maybe it'll take longer. He was a third our size."

Jae laughed. "What a cruel thing. Making us wait to die."

Russell didn't respond. He couldn't think of anything to say. He wasn't interested in his conspiracy theories anymore. That's what got him into that mess. If he hadn't been so gung-ho, they wouldn't be facing death's door.

Days passed and they still sat in the trial room. Russell's stomach pain had intensified but he didn't say anything to Jae. He just continued to ask if he felt any different.

"Maybe we aren't going to die," Russell said. He stood up. "It makes sense for me and Ye-jun, but maybe, you won't. If I die, and you don't then you know the answer."

"What do you mean?" Jae asked.

"Sorry, you'll have to figure that out yourself." Russell smiled wearily. "Well, I'm not going to sit around forever until I die. I'm gonna have a cold one before I go. Wanna join me?"

"I'm a minor."

"What does that matter if you're going to die?"

Jae stood up. "You're right."

They went into the kitchen and opened a few bottles of soju. They sat on the dirty mat and cheered to their deaths. Jae couldn't handle a sip of the soju and spit it out. Russell laughed and called him a lightweight.

Jae reminisced about his siblings while Russell got hammered and gloated about how he acquired his guns. They moved the party to the trial room. Jae sliced pillars with Magord, and Russell sat in the corner and watched. He was getting weaker, and his stomach hurt to hell. Russell leaned forward. He had the urge to throw up. He began to dry heave and blood dribbled from his mouth.

Jae noticed and ran over. "Russell? Are you okay? Did you drink too much alcohol?"

Russell shook his head and his body jerked. Blood gushed from his ears, then poured from his eyes. Soon blood erupted from his mouth, and he started choking.

Jae's eyes widened and he said, "We gotta get you to the hospital!"

As he stood to open the door, Russell grabbed his arm and pulled him down.

Through a blood-filled mouth, Russell managed to say, "No point."

He fell onto his back and his body violently convulsed like Ye-jun's did. His hand still gripped Jae's. Blood slowly filled the trial room floor.

"I won't let you go," Jae cried. His pants soaked from his blood. Reality sank in. First, he lost Dasom and Jihoon, then he lost Ye-jun, and now Russell was dying. Soon he would be next. "I'm here."

Russell kept eye contact with Jae, not blinking. Jae didn't know if he could hear anymore. But the light was still in his eyes. Soon Russell's eyes rolled behind his head. His convulsions continued, but Jae wondered if he was still conscious. Russell held Jae's hand tightly.

After an hour, Russell's body stopped, and his grip loosened. Jae lay to his side in Russell's blood, his head next to Russell's. He didn't let go of his hand. What was he going to do? He was going to die alone. He knew he deserved it, but he was afraid. He didn't want to suffer with no one to hold his hand.

He stood and made his way to Magord. If he was going to die, he would do it himself. He wasn't going to convulse on the floor or wait days until it happened. Russell had recently died, so he wouldn't have been dying alone. He took a deep breath, lifted Magord over his head and stabbed himself through the gut. He screamed from the pain but pushed the sword deeper into his abdomen. Tears fell from his eyes, but his face was fierce. He took deep breaths and moved the sword from one side of his stomach to the other, then ripped the sword out of his body. The pain was unbearable, and he lost consciousness. Blood spilled across the floor filling the other half of the trial room.

Chapter Eight
Jae's Past Pt. 2

Jae opened his eyes. His head hurt as he sat up. He looked to the corner where Russell's body laid, the blood around him dry. He gasped and looked down at where he stabbed himself. The wound had healed. Not a scar in sight. Confused, he grabbed Magord and slit his throat. He couldn't breathe and shut his eyes. The pain was intense. After 5 minutes, his breath returned, and his throat sealed.

He sat up again. Why hadn't he died? He sat there staring into space when he remembered what Russell told him. If he didn't die, it was because he ate the head. The conspiracy theory was actually a fact. He gained the god's ability to heal. Did that mean he was immortal?

Jae laughed, he laughed for minutes and soon he was laughing manically.

What a cruel fate, he thought, he stopped laughing and cried. *Am I forced to suffer through my mistakes for eternity? Why didn't I give the head to Ye-jun?*

"This is all my fault," he mumbled. "I shouldn't have done it. I shouldn't have stayed longer. I shouldn't have given Ye-jun the alien. I shouldn't have listened to Russell. It's all my fault. It's all my fault."

He paused. "Not my fault. If the purple god never came, none of this would have happened. If the gods had come to S. Korea, they could have stopped it. If they told us about the purple god, *we* could have stopped it. If the gods never came here, they would still be alive."

Jae repeated those words over and over again. He didn't eat, he sat in the corner for days. Mumbling to himself. After a while, he crawled over to Russell and took out his phone. "Where are the gods now?"

Jae swiped through the apps and found a conspiracy blog based in S. Korea. It gave news of a god arriving. The writer complained about the god showing up earlier than scheduled after the accident in Daegu. They were talking about the area by his hideout.

"The gods refused to help catch the serial killer. For over a month we asked for assistance. But now that the slaughter happened here one comes to 'investigate.' He's only here to

take credit for whatever he figures out. Don't trust them.
They're only about the glory. Look how that one is dressed…"

A video was attached. In the video, the towering god was green. It was covered in gold. Even though the value of gold had lessened to less than a few cents, in some places it was considered high value. It wore a long red and white mantle, it wore golden chains, and black sunglasses. Jae's mouth dropped. For a peace-loving species, it sure was materialistic. He continued to watch as it examined the blood on the ground. It lifted its sunglasses. It touched the purple blood that was mostly dried. Its face went from smiling to confusion to anger. It stood and looked around. It snapped its finger and the mess around the street disappeared and the homes restored. They looked brand-new, the cars were clean, and the holes in the street were filled.

The green god waved at the cameras, a smiled returned to its face and it started to walk away. The reporters shouted to it things like, "Did you figure out how this happened? How did you clean up this mess? What are your plans now? Do you know who's responsible?"

The god turned around and said, "I do not know what happened here. It appears to be some kind of explosion. This matter may be related to the missing cases, but I do not think it is. This could be caused by what you call 'gas leaks.' I will discuss it with my fellow gods and go from there. Do not worry, I will be here to catch the killer in the act."

The crowd erupted into cheers and its grin grew even wider. It walked down the street and around the corner.

"I can't be the only one to notice his face when he looked at that purple fluid," the blog continued. "He knows something. I wouldn't doubt it if one of his 'fellow gods' created that mess. Be wary of them! Avoid the area by Sampilbong. The god built a 'temporary' fortress. He promised to remove it after his investigation, but who knows, he could be trying to take over Daegu!"

Jae exited the blog. The writer was right, the god knew what happened. The look on its face was enough for Jae to know it knew the purple god was dead and maybe it knew what Jae looked like. He wasn't safe. It could find him in an instant if it wanted to.

Are the gods really hiding something? Jae thought. *Did they know about what the purple god did? They did nothing to stop it. Now that it's dead, they're going to investigate. They're going to come after me.*

Jae trembled. *I will not die to them. They knew about this. They're the reason why everyone I cared about is dead. It's their fault. I knew it. It's their fault. All their fault. They have to die. They need to die. They WILL die.*

Jae stood. He walked to the door but paused and looked at Russell. He dragged his body out of the trial room and up to the store. He didn't know what to do with him. The hospital never contacted him about Ye-jun's body. Maybe they were performing an autopsy? Jae called the hospital and told them Russell had died as well. He told them to meet him at the neighboring street to the underground market. He dragged his corpse through the street, his clothes dyed with blood. Many looked at him in horror, others were used to it. It *was* the underground market. The EMTs arrived to retrieve his body. Jae asked them when they were done with the autopsy to take care of their funeral. In agreeance to letting them research what happened to them, they could cover their funeral costs including cremation. Even if they denied, it wasn't like they would be able to find him after that anyways.

Jae went to the weapons room and searched for the weapon Russell used as well as any others that looked powerful. He loved Magord, but he needed more security. He found the gun but didn't know how to use it…. He couldn't use any of the weapons in the basement. Why couldn't Russell train him on one?

He went back into the trial room and grabbed Magord and its sheath. He opened Russell's room and went through his closet for clean clothes. Jae found his khakis, a black shirt that barely fit, and a green jacket. He also grabbed a hat, belt, and a messenger bag. He filled the bag with food and drinks. He looked through his room and grabbed some of his siblings' belongings and put them in for good luck. He took Russell's cellphone. He searched Russell's wallet for money. He tsked. Russell had all cards. In cash he had about ₩50,000. Jae stuffed it in his pocket and put his wallet back in his dresser drawer. He kept Russell's room as pristine as he had left it. Not like it mattered anyways.

He stood at the bottom of the stairs and turned around. He sighed. This might have been the last time he would be there. He wasn't sure how long he'd survive. He grabbed the store's keys and locked up behind him.

Goodbye, he thought, as he turned around and walked deeper into the underground market.

Jae walked for hours before he reached Sampilbong. It was the middle of the night. He looked up from the entrance. He could partially see at the top of the hill, the mountain peak behind it, was a large building modeled after a western castle. He rolled his eyes and hiked up the hill. He took his time, hiding behind trees and in bushes. He didn't know what ability this god had, nor if it could see him from so far away.

He reached the castle after an hour of climbing. It looked medieval. From the way the god dressed, something this outdated didn't match its style. There was a drawbridge that attached Sampilbong to the next mountain. At the other end, was a gate. The outside was built out of stone and the gate was metal. In front of the gate on both sides, were huge flames. The castle was slightly larger than the gate. There were 4 square towers on all sides of the building. At the top, the crenellation was strangely designed. The merlon was shaped like the god's face. Each one had a different expression. Most were of it smiling, and the others were one of each emotion. The crenel was shaped like its hands. Each section together looked like they could be holding hands, but individually like it shrugged. Green torches lined the circumference of the towers.

Jae cautiously crossed the bridge. His hand ready and gripping Magord's hilt. He arrived at the gate and slowly pressed it. The gate was unlocked. He pushed the gate open and went inside. The mountainous greenery filled the castle courtyard. It was beautiful. The trees covered most of the courtyard. Flowers lined the path leading to the castle door. Butterflies and fireflies flew around the courtyard. The way the fireflies danced around, created a magical ambiance. In the corner to the left of the entrance was a fountain shaped like the god. It was dimly lit, and water spouted serenely from its hand.

Jae walked slowly until he reached the main door. He cracked it and peered inside. Objects moved around the main hall. Tables with plates of food hopped across the hall, silverware following close behind.

Is its ability animation? Jae thought. He had to hold himself back from admiring such a cool power. To be able to turn any object to life, that would be so convenient. He cleared his throat and entered inside. He followed behind the silverware. Hiding ever so often just in case the god emerged from a corner.

A door opened at the end of the hall to the right and the table and silverware went inside. The door slammed shut behind it. Jae cautiously approached the door. He put his ear against it and listened closely. He could hear humming and metal scraping plates. He grabbed the doorknob and slowly twisted it. He cracked the door as quietly as he could and looked inside.

Inside was a large room. It was vacuous. There was no furniture, to the left of the room. He scanned to the right. There still wasn't anything there. He opened a little more and stuck his head in. In the corner of the room the god floated on a red throne. It was padded with red pillows and was made of stone. It reclined its legs onto the arm of the throne and hummed as food floated into its mouth. A goblet raised above its head, and it opened its mouth again as wine poured in.

Jae was confused. What was up with that god? It was alone in an empty room making living objects feed it. He knew it was materialistic but to go this far. Jae wondered if their ethics hadn't gotten in the way, would it have humans there surviving it?

Jae felt something press against his back and he jumped. He turned around as a pitcher of wine tried to come in.

"I know you're there," the god said. "Move aside so I can get my refill."

The door swung open, and Jae grabbed Magord's hilt.

"Relax," it said. It hadn't looked at him once. "I'm not going to harm you. Here, come have something to eat."

A plate with grapes, pineapple, strawberries, honeydew, and pitted cherries hovered to Jae.

"I know you humans prefer meat. However I cannot stomach eating another being…" It continued, glancing at Jae.

"Well, that's one of the ways we survive," Jae said. He shooed away the plate. "I'm not hungry."

The god snickered. "You certainly were hungry when you ate a comrade of mine."

"It had it coming," Jae sneered. He thought, *So they were aware of what it was doing.*

"Not quite," the god said. "We did not know what was going on. We genuinely believed that he was lost in space. Don't forget, your people were the ones to tell us about a serial killer. Matters that small aren't worth our time."

Jae wondered how it knew what he thought. "But if you had come when you were asked, it would have never gone this far."

"Would it?" the god inquired. "Don't get the wrong idea boy. We are not your servants. If we decide to help, then it is of our own volition. As for Muragrak, he was a lost cause. Even if we had found out he landed here, we would not resort to violence to stop him."

"So you're saying *IT* would have been free to kill us regardless of your knowledge? Us being slaughtered by your kind isn't a big enough problem for you things?"

"No matter what we did, *HE* would not be stopped. Once you reach that level of insanity, there's nothing we can do. And do not refer to us as 'things.' My name is Hrayrp. I am a man. Do not call me an 'it,' I am sentient. Don't forget how the state of your world would've been if not for us."

"A thing is a thing." Jae scowled. "Whether you like it or not, you are a creature beneath us. Our planet would have been fine without your help. We lived through it before you, we could have afterwards."

"'Beneath you?'" Hrayrp sat up amused. "Us beneath you? Please."

"Yes, you're nothing more than savages, creatures who only seek to kill us. But you want us to worship you."

Hrayrp laughed. "You humans are the savages. You kill your own, yet are enraged when another species does it? Humans were destroying this planet and the other species on it. You, *things* walk on this earth as if you rule it. Before we came, you humans were in the stone ages, behind other planets and galaxies. You should be groveling at our feet for what we have done to advance your kind. You humans lack knowledge. Do not act as if we were the ones to push your people to worship us. As I've read from your history books. Humans attach themselves to whatever is most powerful. Another foolish thing. Don't think you can look down on us when you can't even think for yourselves."

"I'm not thinking, I know I am above you. All you can use as an excuse for gratitude is one thing you did years ago. Don't forget you live here too," Jae said, mockingly. "We allowed you to stay here and seek refuge and the way you repay us is by calling us savages? Savages wouldn't have let you stay. You things didn't even fix every issue. Just the ones that affect you."

And for that, you all must die. Jae withdrew Magord. *He seems weak. What can living objects do to me?*

The god grinned. "How foolish. To think I'm weaker than Muragrak. That man is far weak in comparison. You must be as crazy as him if you think you can beat me."

"Actually," he continued, his grin widened. "You are as crazy as him. You gained his temperament in addition to his powers. Ha! You don't even know how to use his ability. The only thing you can do is sit in a corner and cry it's not your fault."

Hrayrp stared at Jae and a sharp pang sensation hit him. Jae's head hurt and he dropped to one knee holding his head.

"If only you hadn't given Ye-jun Muragrak's body. He would still be alive, if you had convinced the authorities about the god, those runts slaughtered by him would be alive." the god laughed hysterically. "What makes it funnier, is if you had a brain, you could have saved Ye-jun and Russell. A taste of Muragrak's head could have helped their body adjust to the poisons. But no. You were possessed by greed and power. You kept his head for yourself. You let them die, didn't you?!"

"No, it wasn't my fault. It's your fault." Jae crawled away. His body trembled as he remembered each death. Images of Dasom and Jihoon's final moments flashed in his head. The fear spread across their face, the screams as they were brutally murdered.

"It's all your fault! Do not blame us gods for your actions. You killed them! You think lashing out on superior beings will bring them back? Do you think killing me will help you atone for your crimes? They're never going to forgive you."

"Shut up," Jae cried. "It's not my fault! It's not…."

"It is your fault. If you had done things the right way, they would be alive. You wasted your entire life taking care of things you later killed. Is that the work of humans? Of savages?"

You're wrong, Jae thought.

"I'm not wrong. I can see right through you. I know what you did. You can't hide your inner thoughts from me!" Hrayrp laughed.

"Why?" Jae asked. "Tell me why I'm at fault and not that purple thing!"

"Do you want to know what happened to Muragrak?"

Jae nodded. *I need to buy time to think.*

"Buying time won't save you. But I will oblige you with knowledge before your death." Hrayrp opened his mouth, and a grape flew in. "Muragrak took the fall of our people the hardest. As we searched the galaxy for a place to live, his mentality couldn't handle any more. And soon he had gone Yurtpo, what you humans call…unhinged. His skin turned purple and his ability to speak diminished. He parted from us, and we never saw him again. Muragrak was not sane, what he did was not of his own choice but because of what happened to our people. You, on the other hand, killed him with ease. Not even checking to see why he did it."

"You think I should have checked on him?" Jae stood up and walked closer. "Do you think it would have stopped killing my siblings if I stopped and asked it if it was okay? You said it yourself that it was impossible to take down. But you expect me to put an end to its terror without violence? Or do you think I should have let it kill me too?"

"Precisely. It is your crimes that caused them to die. If you had reported him to us, we could have done something. Instead, you chose to kill him in the most violent way possible and devoured him. And to top it off, you couldn't leave it at that. You decide to come to *my* castle and attack me? What good will that do you?"

"You 'gods' have to die. Without you, humans can live peacefully again."

The god smirked. "Is that so? You continue to accuse us of your crimes. You killed your siblings, you killed Russell. If not for you, humans and my kind could live in harmony. And for that, you die."

A table tore across the room and smashed into Jae. Jae slammed into the wall. Dazed and confused from what just happened, Jae stumbled to his feet. He looked at the wood pieces from the broken table and then at Hrayrp, who still sat in the throne.

What the hell was that? Jae thought. *Did the table attack me? How in the hell would it even think to do that?*

Hrayrp smiled. The wooden pieces rose from the ground and aimed at Jae. As the pieces launched his way, he swung Magord, slicing them into smaller pieces. More objects in the room hurled his way and he cut through every item.

Breathing heavily, Jae asked, "Is that all you got? I can dodge all day."

Hrayrp kept smiling, not a glance Jae's way. A rumbling sound came from outside and a tree burst through the wall and smacked Jae across the room.

Its ability isn't animation, Jae thought. *What is this called? I've seen it before.*

He lifted to one knee, waiting for the effects of the impact to wear off. He stood and a branch crashed into him. He fell over again. The silverware he followed smacked his face, each cheek, back and forth. Alternating. It wasn't as painful as the larger items, but it was humiliating.

"Enough," he yelled. He grabbed the spoons and threw them. "Why don't you fight me like the man you claim to be?"

"I am fighting you," the god said, amused.

"You're having objects do it."

"A fight's a fight. I cannot hurt you with my own hands. That is the code upon which I agreed to. But that doesn't mean I can't do this." A stone from the wall flew out and smashed into Jae's face knocking him down. The stone wall collapsed on top of him. Blood oozed from the pile.

"Hmph." Hrayrp lowered the throne and stood. "What a waste of time. Muragrak must have really let himself go to die to such a weakling."

He left the room. Jae struggled to get up. His body had been crushed under the stone. Thankfully the way three stones fell, it left a gap large enough for his head to not get smashed. After a while, his body tried rejoining his bones. He grunted and did his best to slide from under. From his neck down was a flat pancake. How he managed to maneuver from beneath was unknown. He lay there, until his body fixed itself. He stood up and stumbled to the door.

Where did it go? he thought, walking down the corridor. He remembered that it had psychic abilities and could hear his thoughts. He said out loud, "He better not have super hearing or some shit."

He reached the front door again and looked both ways. "If I were an evil creature, which way would I go?"

He turned left and continued to an open room. Loud rap music filled the room. Hrayrp had his back turned to Jae. Jae crept forward, lifting Magord up to his shoulder. His mind was silent. Halfway there, a chair launched at him. He sliced it in half, splinters cutting his face.

"You can't sneak up on me."

"Fight me without your telekinesis."

Hrayrp snorted. "You have a better chance with spoons than if I fought you."

"Try me. No cheap tricks."

The god turned around. "This time, I'll make sure to crush your skull."

Jae blinked and the god was in front of him. He grabbed Jae's head and smashed it into the ground. They slid across the floor until the collected rubble stopped them. Hrayrp slammed his head repeatedly, each force stronger than the last.

Jae couldn't think, the pain made him dizzy. What could he do? Was he gonna die there? Jae had dropped Magord. There was no way he could get him off. He gripped Hrayrp's arm. The cold pressure on his middle finger made him remember the ring. He loosened his grip on Hrayrp's arm, slid his hand down Hrayrp's arm and turned the ring counterclockwise.

Magord bolted towards them at lightning speed. Hrayrp sensed it and reached his hand out to catch it. The blade sliced off his right hand and he jumped out of the way. He grimaced at Jae who struggled to stand.

"Hmph." He turned his nose up. "'No cheap tricks' yet you did that."

"That wasn't a trick," Jae said, staggering to his feet. The wounds on his head healed. He picked Magord up and aimed it at him. "You were in the way of my sword."

Hrayrp's face scrunched, and he said bitterly, "Regardless, I can kill you with one hand."

He lunged at Jae. His left fist raised, Jae moved Magord in front of him and Hrayrp ducked low and kicked him in the side. The force sent Jae flying into a pillar. He groaned as he stood on his hands and feet. From the corner of his eye, he saw Hrayrp jump towards him. He rolled out of the way and Hrayrp crushed the pillar.

Shit, Jae thought. *Maybe the objects would've been better.*

Hrayrp smiled. "See your mistake now? Do you regret challenging me? Do you wish to end this fight? Too bad. You'll die here. You will atone for your crimes."

Hrayrp charged again, Jae scrambled to block with his arms. The impact from the punch cracked Jae's bone and he was flying yet again. But before landing, Hrayrp jumped behind him, and kicked him forward. Hrayrp ran behind him again and kicked him diagonally towards the main hall.

"I've never played tennis with a human ball." Hrayrp laughed. "Maybe I should make it a sport."

He grabbed Jae by the collar before he landed into the wall. He threw Jae behind him and backhanded him. It wasn't as strong as the other hits and Jae caught himself before falling. He looked up as Hrayrp's fist smashed into his face. He hit again using the nub on his right arm, green blood smudged across Jae's cheek. Then his left hand uppercut Jae, his right elbow knocked his head down. A fury of kicks and punches came upon Jae. There was nothing he could do. Hrayrp left no time to do anything. He twisted his ring again and Magord flew towards him. Hrayrp stopped and let Jae catch it. Jae swung Magord and Hrayrp ducked and knocked it out of his hand.

The fury of blows continued, and Jae was losing consciousness. Hrayrp kicked him and he fell onto his back. Hrayrp lifted Magord with ease. His face serious and disgusted, he approached Jae and stood over him. He raised the blade above his head.

"This is where you die."

Jae was freaking out. He didn't want to die there. Not to that creature. His energy left his body. Time had slowed for Jae. Hrayrp stabbed downwards at Jae. Aiming for his head. He stared at Magord as it slowly came down to him. His heartrate quickened and his breath heavier, he closed his eyes.

I'm not going to die like this, he thought.

A hissing sound came from his body, and he opened his eyes. Purple mist came out of his body with an alarming amount.

That thing's paralyzing mist, Jae thought. Boy was he happy to see it.

Recognition hit Hrayrp's eyes, and he jumped back. But it was too late. He had already breathed in a large amount. He staggered back before falling onto his knees. He froze in place. He glared at Jae as he struggled to get up.

He stumbled as he walked to Hrayrp

"You said no dirty tricks," a voice said, in Jae's head.

He looked confused at Hrayrp. There was no way he was strong enough to speak and he knew the gas wouldn't have run out that quickly. Especially the large dose Hrayrp had gotten. "Did you just speak in my head?"

"Are you really that stupid," Hrayrp said. "Are all humans as dense as you? Have you yet to figure out what my powers are?"

"I know telekinesis."

"You humans are dirty. You ask me to fight fairly, yet you resort to this."

"What was fair about our fight?" Jae took Magord from Hrayrp's hands. "I didn't plan on using that. Didn't know I had it."

"I know you didn't know. You don't know anything about us gods."

"You aren't gods. You're aliens that don't belong on this planet. Sorry you couldn't kill me like you hoped."

"If you care about an honest fight like you begged me, wait until this wears off."

Jae laughed, the gaps in his teeth showed his tongue. "One thing you should know about humans is that we don't fight fair. If you're beating my ass, I'm pulling out a gun. Why would I wait until the gas wears off for you to kill me? Maybe you shouldn't have been so smug to fight me one on one."

"As you human's say, 'Fuck you.'" Hrayrp gained enough movement back to sneer.

Jae shrugged and sliced off his head. His head rolled a bit before stopping face up. Hrayrp's eyes stiffened, and blood oozed from his neck. Judging from his fight, and the fact his hand hadn't grown back, Jae knew that regeneration was a trait specific to Muragrak.

To be safe, Jae thought. He raised Magord over his head. As he stabbed into his head he said, "Maybe I should play alien tennis with you."

Jae looked at his head. He contemplated eating him to gain his ability. He wasn't sure how strong the other 9 were. If they were stronger than Hrayrp, he wouldn't survive. He knelt. His stomach lurched as he remembered the way the other god tasted.

"Come on, you can do this. Psychic abilities are worth it…whether I can use it at will or not…"

He lifted Hrayrp's head and carried it into the other room. There was one table still intact and silverware across the floor. He set his head on a plate and started eating it. Each bite churned his stomach, but he needed to do it for humanity's sake. He finished his head in a few hours. He wasn't sure what to do with his body. If at some point another god came to visit, all hell would break loose if his decapitated body was decomposing in that room.

He dragged his body outside and to a corner of the courtyard. He dug as deep as he could with Magord and rolled Hrayrp's body inside. He stopped and looked back at the loose dirt. He walked to a flower garden and plucked a bunch of flowers.

Even though you beat the shit out of me, it was a good fight, Jae thought. He dug small holes and planted flowers along the grave. *There's some humanity left in me.*

Jae went inside the castle and cleaned up the blood as best he could. His and Hrayrp's. He wondered if it was a good idea to spend the night there. But he didn't know where else to go. He vowed to not return to the weapons shop until after his mission was complete. He barely had enough cash to eat food at the convenience store let alone get a hotel. He needed to charge his…Russell's phone and figure out what to do next. There was no going back. He needed to find the next god's location and strike before Hrayrp was determined missing.

Jae was grateful for Hrayrp's materialistic nature. Even though he stayed in a medieval castle, he still had the latest technology in one of the rooms. Jae plugged Russell's phone into one of the charging ports and scrolled for news on the other gods.

He found an article based in Chad. A yellow god had arrived that day and in 3 hours, had already stopped 4 major accidents, saved a child from falling off an 8-story building, and was soon to depart to Faya. Jae smiled. It looked weak in comparison to Hrayrp. He read in the article, the god practiced the Peace and Ethics Code the most. It refused to harm the wildlife in Africa and found different ways to stop them. It tried to stop robberies and hostage situations without harming the criminals.

Jae scoffed. "What a coward."

He didn't know what ability it had, but from how it acted, he knew it must have been weak. Not worth taking seriously. But it needed to die regardless of their codes.

Just so he wouldn't get roughed up, Jae spent two weeks, one week in the castle and the second on Taebaek mountain, training. It was a quick run through of moves. Learning how to dodge, practicing his swings, etc. He wasn't worried about the yellow god. But this was the only chance he had to get some training. Who knew how fast he would encounter the others? He knew this one would be a quick kill.

He booked a flight for N'Djamena, Chad. Due to the increase of advanced technology, other more convenient and safer methods of travel became the preferred way of travel. Airplanes were used less and eventually the gods decided to pay airlines to provide free travel to those who couldn't afford advanced travel. Jae just needed a passport, and he would be allowed to travel wherever.

The next morning, Jae went to the Ministry of Foreign Affairs and requested a passport. He lied about his reason for needing one short notice. But since it was by airplane, they didn't really care. He received his passport the same day. He packed his sword in a suitcase he found in the trash and went to Daegu international airport. It was barren and kind of broken down, but free travel was free travel. He waited in the gate and when his flight arrived, he boarded for Chad.

He arrived 14 hours later at N'Djamena airport. He didn't understand a word they said but he followed their gestures until he made it out of the airport.

He walked along the streets. The air was stifling. He wondered why it was so hot and struggled to move. He was hungry and he didn't think to exchange his Won for XAF, or rather, he didn't know how. He sat on the side of the road. He held a newspaper over his head to block the sun. His stomach growled. He'd gone days without eating growing up, but how would he survive in that climate?

A burlap sack lowered down to him. "Tienne, mange ça."

Jae looked up to see a woman smiling. He didn't know what she said, but he took the sack. He opened it. Inside was full of fruits. Oranges, dates, guava, and mangos. He thought for a bit before saying, "Merci."

"Je vous en prie." She smiled. She squatted next to him. She could see the confusion on his face. She figured he didn't know any French. She decided to speak in one-word responses to help him understand. "Où allez-vous?"

Jae looked at her.

She repeated it again slowly. She gestured with her hands, "where," and Jae understood.

He took out his phone and typed Faya.

"Vous avez besoin d'aide pour vous y rendre?" She gestured as she spoke. She waited for a response then said, "Help?"

Jae still stared confused. She gasped and she took out her phone. She went to Digital Translation App. She originally put in English, then Jae changed it to Korean.

She spoke and it translated as she went. "Do you need help getting to Faya?"

Jae nodded.

"I have friends who can drop you off as they go to Sudan. I'm sure they won't mind a small detour."

"Merci," Jae said.

"Follow me." She stood and motioned for Jae to follow.

He opened the bag and ate guava as they walked.

"What is your name?" she asked.

"Jae," he responded. He pointed at her and said, "What's your name?"

She placed her hand on her chest. She didn't use the translator and said, "Je suis Amara."

They walked a few blocks before arriving at a large building. Jae was wowed. It was one of the major tech-car companies. Who did Amara know that would have time to help him? They went inside. The lobby was crowded. They weaved through the crowd to a secluded private elevator. She tapped Jae's shoulder.

"We go up from here. My brothers need to transport cars. I'm sure they will help you."

"Are you sure?" Jae asked.

Amara held her phone to him, and he repeated it.

"Yes, they will help me, and that means helping you. I will say you are my friend, and you need to get there asap."

"Merci," Jae said. He sounded like a broken record, and she laughed.

They reached the top floor and she exited first. She spoke with the secretary then motioned for Jae to follow her. They walked past the desk and into a waiting area.

"Sit wherever," Amara said. "I will be back."

She peeked into one of the offices and went in. Jae looked around the room. It was small. It had space for 20 chairs, 5 against each wall. There were 3 people sitting, 2 next to each other on the left and a woman in a seat by the back wall. On both sides of the back wall were two doors. Jae didn't know what the signs above the doors said. In the middle was a coffee table stacked with holographic magazines. Another thing Jae had never seen before. He picked one up. He wondered why they would be left out? Anyone could steal them. The base was a light grey rectangle. It was very thin, it felt as fragile as glass, but they were extremely durable. The base was small and could fit easily in a hand. On the front side, there were settings on how translucent a user wanted the hologram.

He pressed the power button and a screen, the size was 9x8, popped up. He lowered the translucent feature so the woman sitting across from him couldn't see what he looked at. He looked at the back as the settings configurated. The back darkened gradually until it looked like something solid was there. He poked his finger through it and wowed. He composed himself and turned it back around. Holographic magazines had unlimited content. Anything a user wanted to see was accessible on them. They were extremely expensive and way better than a smartphone. He changed the language to Korean. He flipped through the pages. He pulled down the search bar and looked up what the god in Chad was doing. It warned the citizens in Faya that there was a sandstorm soon to come and they should stay inside until it confirmed their safety.

Jae scoffed. *Look at it trying to act heroic. They won't praise you for stopping it. Just do your job and die.*

He saw a related article and his stomach sank. The headline was, **The Gods go to South Korea in search of Hrayrp.** He gulped and clicked it. In the article read:

> The recent god, Hrayrp, last seen on video investigating the
> serial killings in S. Korea has gone missing. He did not
> respond to the messages from the South Korean police for
> weeks. They reported to the other gods for answers.
> Hyrogliphic has yet to receive a comment from the gods on
> what is going on.

The serial killings in S. Korea have halted. Maybe because
of the appearance of Hrayrp. Thank you for your help,
wherever you are! We here at Hyrogliphic wish for your
safe return and continued guidance on our planet....

UPDATE: We thankfully received a response from
Yulogna. "Please do not be alarmed. We are sure Hrayrp is
alright. He may have taken a breather in space. He does this
from time to time. When we receive confirmation of his
whereabouts, we will let you all know."
As she stated, we should not worry. He is powerful and
nothing can happen to him. They will be okay. The Gods
have done a lot for us. And in their time of need, we should
respect their wishes and stay calm. Do not panic, do not ask
for too much. Please give them time to find him.

Jae tsked. *Guess it was only a matter of time. Damn police. I don't have
much time. I need to at least kill this one before they're on to me.*
The door opened and Amara stuck her head out. "Come in."
Jae stood up. He stuffed the magazine in his pocket as he walked to
the door. The people groaned and complained quietly about his jump to
the front of the line. He peered around the corner before fully entering.
3 men in black business suits looked at Jae. 2 men sat at a meeting table,
and the third sat at a desk. The room was bare, the carpet was tan. The
third man stood up and moved to the table. He was bald and wore thin
framed glasses.
"Asseyez-vous š'il vous plaît," he said. He pointed at a chair on the
other side of the table.
"Il ne parle pas française," Amara said. She slid her phone to her
brother and said, "J'ai utilisé ça."
He rolled his eyes and leaned over the phone. "Sit down there."
Jae did as he was told.
The man continued, "What do you need to do in Faya? Haven't you
heard the god? No one should be out right now. We're putting our own
business on hold as well. I suggest you wait until we're given the
greenlight."
Jae spoke but the man stopped him. "Don't you have a phone? Open
the Digital Translator App."
Jae took out Russell's phone and opened the app store. He searched
for the app but couldn't find it. He looked up and shook his head.

"Let me see," the first man said. He was the first person Jae saw when he entered. He was the tallest out of the three, his hair was short, and he had a small beard. Jae slid Russell's phone to him. He typed for a bit then shook his head. "It's region locked."

"Amara use your phone for him." the third man said. He slid Amara's phone down to Jae and pulled out his own phone.

Jae reversed the translation and said, "I don't have time. I need to get to Faya as soon as possible. I… have to meet my father there. He isn't going to wait for me."

The second man tsked. He had an afro, recently cut, and no facial hair. "We aren't going to risk our safety for you. Your father isn't going to just leave you."

"He really will," Jae insisted. "He's done it before. That's why I'm alone in N'Djamena now."

The first man turned off the translator. He spoke to the men. His tone quiet. They went back and forth, and Amara glanced at Jae. Finally the men stopped and turned the translator back on.

"We're willing to give you a cheap model of our hoover scooter," the second man said. "But we want you to try a product of ours. If you're willing to test it, the hoover scooter is yours to keep."

Jae perked up. Another awesome thing he never got to use. "Yes. I will try it."

"Wait," the third man said. "You should hear what it is first. Don't just agree."

Jae nodded.

The third man continued, "I don't know if you're aware, but Digital Translator is another invention of ours. Unfortunately, it still has problems, especially its availability. We invented a sort of device implanted in your head, that will allow you to understand what anyone is saying and speak whatever language they speak without a pesky app. Do you still want to try it? The price for the hoover scooter we're offering you is 100,000 XAF."

"I do not have time for surgery."

"No surgery required." The second man went behind the desk and opened a case. He held up a tiny chip that Jae could barely see. "It is very tiny. There are two pieces to this device. The first one attaches itself to the front left side of your brain. The chip… how do I say this so you understand? The chip basically digs through your skin and skull and attaches itself to your Broca's area. The second piece does a similar thing but attaches to your Wernicke's area. Both play a crucial role in your speech production and language comprehension. I would explain more, but it looks like even this is confusing…."

He was right, Jae could barely process what he said. Jae asked, "Does it hurt?"

"Uh…maybe. We have yet to try it on humans. In theory this will work. However, we are unsure of what problems it may have. It is up to you. We will not force you to take this. But we won't take you to Faya until after the sandstorm."

Jae thought about it. The concept, whether he understood it or not, was cool. To be able to understand other races without learning their language, who wouldn't do it? Besides, he had the healing abilities. If anything happened, he wouldn't die from it… or at least, he hoped not. It was going in his brain, his new "weak spot."

"Well?" the second man asked.

"I'll do it. But I want a scooter that's fast."

The third man sighed. "Alright. We'll give you our second cheapest hoover scooter. Deal?"

"Deal."

They printed a contract stating he agreed to do the trial and would not sue if anything happens. Jae signed it, not understanding a thing it said, and was handed the first piece.

He placed it on his temple. He felt it latch to his skin before feeling a sharp pain. He winced as it burrowed into his skin. His eyes teared and he did his best to not show how much it hurt. After he calmed down, they handed him the second piece. This one he put above his ear and a few centimeters to the right. By that point, his adrenaline kicked in and he no longer felt pain.

The third man turned off the translator and asked, "Well, does it work? Do you know what I'm saying?"

"Yeah," Jae said.

Their faces lit up. Though Jae thought he was speaking Korean, what he said was in French.

"It works!" The first man hugged his brothers then walked over and hugged Jae. "You don't feel anything. Nothing wrong?"

"No, it hurt really bad in the beginning, but I don't feel any pain now."

"Wow," the third man said. "I can't believe it actually works. Do you know what this means?"

"Yeah, we've changed the game," the second man said.

"Do I have to give this back?" Jae asked.

"No. That's not sanitary. We have multiple prototypes," the first man said. "I think we should give him a better scooter."

"I agree. We'll make millions off this." The second man shook Jae's hand. "We're gonna give you our latest model. It's fast and…"

The men and Amara stared horrified at Jae. His nose and left eye were bleeding. He touched his cheek and looked at the blood.

"We need to get you to a hospital," Amara said.

"No, I'm fine. This will heal on its own," Jae said.

"That is not fine, it is not normal. Just let us take you. Your father can come get you later."

"No, I really need to go. Please don't worry about it. Just give me the scooter and I will make it to Faya. I will stop at a hospital there if the bleeding continues."

They looked at each other and wrote down, *Trial participant refuses treatment.* Jae signed the bottom, and they called a secretary to bring out a scooter for him.

Jae thanked them and Amara for all their help and left the building. He was handed the keys and title registration. He climbed on the scooter and started it. The scooter lifted into the air, just above the curb. The scooter was amazing. It was black with a red light underneath. Most hoover vehicles were a light blue or white light. Amara's brothers really were ahead of the game. The scooter wasn't loud. Very few hoover vehicles had a soundless engine or whatever was used to make them. Jae was nervous. He hoped no one would ask him for a driver's license.

How hard can it be? Jae thought. He waited, searching for how to get it to move.

The woman at the front desk who handed him his title info ran out and said, "First time using one? Press that green button to start moving, and the red one to stop. You can control your speed right here. Turn the dial clockwise to speed up, counterclockwise to slow down. Please be mindful of the speed limit. And don't forget to put your helmet on."

"Thank you. I will." Jae put on his helmet and pressed the green button and moved slowly. He looked down at the speed dial. It was set to 5 mph. He rolled his eyes. He looked around the street for a sign. The speed limit was 35 mph for normal cars and hoover vehicles on the street, 45 for hoover vehicles above the minimum height limit and the max sky limit. No one was allowed to go under 20 feet high or over 30 feet high. The minimum limit was obvious. So drivers couldn't hit pedestrians or cars. And the 30 feet limit was for the driver's safety. Most public high-tech transportation was above the city. To stop horrific accidents, the limit was placed to keep cities and corporations from being sued.

Jae was too scared to go above ground. He stuck to the streets until he was on the highway where the speed limit increased to 55 mph. To protect drivers from harsh elements and intense wind, an auto-setting was placed on hoover vehicles. A small shield activated and covered the surroundings of the vehicle once the speed hit 45 mph and off under 30 mph.

Jae wondered why they were so afraid of a sandstorm. The hoover scooter had a shield. He wouldn't be hit by sand and if push came to shove, he would use the navigation system.

Soon he was in the desert. He went off the road so he could go as fast as he wanted without getting caught for breaking laws or almost hitting other cars. In the distance, Jae could see the sandstorm. The sky was dark. It was a deep orange and yellow puffs covered everything.

Jae whistled. He pulled over and turned on his shield. He looked at the user manual. He was amazed. The chip in his head, even translated text. He looked through the book until he found the weather section. He lifted a cover to the side of the scooter. There was a hologram with a cloud picture. He clicked on it and swiped through the settings. He found the sandstorm setting and selected it. The shield enclosed around him. It was airtight. An oxygen meter popped up in front of the scooter. It was lime green and at 100%.

He started to move again and the scooter beeped then stopped. A warning popped up on the weather screen. *Sandstorm ahead. Please pull over and wait until the storm clears.* Underneath were two options. *Okay, Ignore.* Jae selected ignore. Another warning popped up. *Are you sure you want to ignore message? Yes. Please select a reminder time. No reminder.*

The safety settings were pissing him off. He moved again and continued into the storm. He couldn't see anything the farther he drove. He saw silhouettes sparsely, but his vision was filled with orange. He set the navigation to Faya and leaned forward. He wasn't going to reach Faya for another 2 hours.

Jae pinched his nose. It was strange. His nose hadn't stopped bleeding. It was well over the regeneration time. He wondered if even small knicks like the one from the chips could cause issues with his head. It wasn't possible. Jae figured it was because he overworked himself. He took out the sack of fruits and ate an orange. He was low on energy and that could be the cause for his healing ability to be slower.

He took out the holographic magazine and searched for any information on their search for Hrayrp. Nothing. If they had the same ability as Hrayrp, once they found his body, they would know it was him. He couldn't let that happen. It took an hour for his nosebleed to stop.

He reached Faya and the streets were empty. He knew the yellow god was over there somewhere. He saw the sand moving in one direction. Pulling inwards to a center just outside of the city.

That must be it, Jae thought. He turned around and exited the city gate.

The wind was strong. It pushed his scooter with intense force towards the center of the sandstorm. Jae struggled to gain control. The speed increased. Soon he saw the god in the distance. It moved its hands in a large swirling motion. A pile of sand accumulated behind it. Jae let the wind take him towards the god. He turned around and opened his luggage. He took Magord out and quickly fastened the belt around his waist. He made eye contact with the god, and it panicked.

What is it worried about? Jae thought. *I wouldn't be surprised if it's the one causing the sandstorm.*

The god moved one of its hands towards Jae and built a wall of sand between them. Jae crashed into the sand.

"What are you doing out here?" the god shouted, its soft voice barely heard. "I specifically said it wasn't safe to travel right now. Please hurry back to Faya!"

"No," Jae said. He stumbled off the scooter but didn't dare to remove the shield. "It's time for you to die!"

The god looked mortified. "I—I don't have time to play fight with you. Please I need to stop the sandstorm."

"I don't care about that. It'll fix on its own. It's done it in the past and people survived. They can survive now."

"Why risk that when I have the power to stop it from happening?" The god fidgeted trying to focus on the sand and persuade Jae to leave. "Please, if you really want to challenge me, please wait and do so after I'm finished. We can discuss why later."

Jae didn't respond. He sat on the scooter and leaned forward. He glared at the god. The god averted eye contact and moved further from Jae. "Don't try running!"

"I won't. I don't want you to get caught in the sand."

They stood in the sandstorm for hours. The sand thinned and the pile behind the god towered above even him.

The god sighed.

As he walked away, Jae got off the scooter and shouted, "Hey! Where do you think you're going?"

The god turned around and said, "I really do not wish to fight you. I have a lot of work to do. Please find another human to fight."

Now that the wind had calmed down, his voice was easier to hear. It was low but soft. He sounded like a man. He turned around to continue walking and Jae threw Magord at him. Sand rose and the sword impaled it.

"Please, I have a lot of work to do in Chad. I do not believe in fighting and wish not to fight you."

"Too bad."

The god stopped walking and turned to Jae. "What is your name?"

"Jae."

"I am Lyour. I believe in peace and harmony. I follow our Peace and Ethics Code more than anyone else. Please, if you wish to try your luck with a god. There are 9 others you can challenge."

"8," Jae corrected him. "There are 8 gods left to challenge."

Lyour facial expression stiffened, and he asked, "What do you mean 8 left?"

"Exactly what I'm saying. I killed Hrayrp, I killed Muragrak. And I'm killing you next."

"I…know that humans have a 'dark humor' but please do not joke about Hrayrp. He is in space right now…"

"If that's what you want to believe." Jae smirked. "If, I was lying, how would I know about Muragrak? I know that thing's name because after I killed it, Hrayrp wanted revenge. I sliced off both their heads and ate them. I know exactly where Hrayrp is buried. As for Muragrak, his body was fully consumed."

"If you are telling the truth, why did you do it?"

"Because you *things* refused to help. You knew Muragrak was on earth, you knew it was killing my people, yet you did nothing to stop it. And because of that, I lost everyone I loved. It's all your fault."

"I am sorry for your loss, but rest assured, we did not know about Muragrak landing on earth. He was lost in space. If you explain yourself to the rest of the gods, you can be excused of your crimes…maybe you will face a few years in prison, but there is no need to continue as you are."

"Bullshit," Jae yelled. "You think I'm going to fall for your lies? You knew it was here! You knew it was killing us! But you didn't care. You probably agreed with Hrayrp that because it was in Uropo or whatever the hell you call it, that we should have let it kill us! You things don't belong on this planet! Do you think I can trust you disgusting creatures won't kill me for killing your people?"

"You are not wrong that some will be upset, however we will still follow our Peace and Ethics cod—"

"Fuck your code. That means absolute shit! You don't think I know about all the loopholes?"

"Please calm down. As I said, I will not fight you. As for your confession on murder, I…will not tell them it was you. But please stop attacking us."

"Why would I trust you? You know what I look like, what I did. Ha! I have even more reason to kill you. You 'gods' must be erased from our planet. I will take it back."

Lyour looked uneasy. He turned around and started running.

"You coward," Jae shouted. He turned on the hoover scooter and chased after him.

Lyour was fast. His long legs alone furthered the distance. But Jae was right behind him. Lyour swiped his hand inwards and the sand beneath his feet rose. The wind around them increased and Lyour was riding the sand.

Jae again admired a god's ability. To control sand was cool, but to be able to ride on it, Jae had to have his power. He increased his speed.

Lyour looked behind him as the distance between him and Jae decreased. He swung his arm and walls of sand came between them.

Jae gasped and swerved dodging the sand walls. He shouted, "You refuse to harm humans, but you put up walls at this speed?"

Lyour couldn't hear him. He continued to put up walls. Jae's patience dwindled and he grew angrier with each wall. *If only I had a tech-gun!*

Soon they were in Ennedi Plateau. The scenery was beautiful. The moonlight shined through the arcs. The stars were visible, illuminating the sky. The sky was different shades of blue, white, and a small drop of purple. Some clouds floated over the stars.

Lyour turned around. "Are you not tired? Please call off your chase and get some rest!"

"Don't pretend like you care about me. Stop running and fight me! You things want to play pretend you're humans, calling yourself men and women, yet you're just a coward. How about you stand tall and act like a human MAN."

"It is not pretending if that is what we are," Lyour said, uncomfortably. "Humans are not the only ones to create the concept of difference in sex. I do believe what we say our gender is should not matter to you.”

“It does when you refuse to fight!” Jae lowered the shield and almost flew off the scooter. He held on tightly and gained his composure. It was hard to keep his eyes open. He unsheathed Magord and threw it at Lyour.

Lyour rose another wall to block. Though the sword would never hit him, he didn’t want to take the risk. Jae grabbed Magord and activated his shield. Lyour jumped down the cliff into Guelta d’Archei Lake. He ran along the stream hoping to lose Jae in the rocks. Jae ducked and swerved. Thanks to the chase, he had gotten better at driving. Lyour looked back to see Jae still behind him. He tsked and ran up the canyon. He didn’t know what to do. Why was Jae so adamant about fighting him? What did he do to deserve such resentment? He still couldn’t believe Jae killed Muragrak and Hrayrp, but no one mentioned Muragrak. So how did he know his name?

“Tell me,” he said, not looking back. “Are you telling the truth about killing them?”

Jae laughed. “Ha! Finally taking some interest? Stop running and I’ll tell you.”

“Unfortunately, I cannot.”

“Yes, everything I said is true. I killed them both and ate them.” Jae tsked.

“Is the lust for power the reason you’re killing us?” he asked.

“No it’s revenge. You’re the cause of my siblings dying. If acquiring your powers will help me slaughter you all, then that’s how it’ll be.”

“I cannot condone such a thought. But please understand we are not at fault for your kin dying. If we did not land on Earth, who is to say Muragrak wouldn’t have still come? Without the advancement of technology, your planet would have been doomed.” Lyour swiped up sand and rode it. He turned to Jae and sat down. “I am sorry for what happened, but to think it logical to wipe out the rest of my kind is absurd. We did not know. We only wish a place to stay in peace. We only want to repay human kindness with helping your climate. Please listen and think wisely on your actions.”

“My actions are wise. If you don’t want to die, then you should leave this planet. But you refuse to do so.”

“You have not asked.”

“…Well it doesn’t matter, you shouldn’t have come here to begin with. I lost everything, and you all should lose everything.”

“Please reconsider.” Lyour stood up.

Jae smiled. Was Lyour finally tired of running and ready to fight? He gripped Magord.

Lyour continued, "I refuse to fight. And soon I will lose you. I warn you. Though I am peaceful, there are warriors among us that will gladly fight you. Hrayrp was one. Though I am sure they will continue to follow our code, there are people more ruthless than him."

"Are you threatening me?"

"I am not. I only wish to tell you to cease your hatred and hunt of my kind. I care about you, even if you don't me. Your body is small, taking on so many abilities will only hurt you in the end."

"Ha! I have a healing ability. I won't be hurt."

"That healing does not make you invincible. Otherwise Muragrak would still be alive."

"You're only saying that because you want to trick me."

"Please child, open your eyes. Look past your hatred of me and heed my warning."

"I'll keep my eyes closed for the rest of my life than to stop hating you things."

Lyour's expression changed to sadness. "I wish you well Jae. But I will not raise a hand towards you."

Lyour turned around and increased the sand beneath him. His speed quickened. A large wall of sand rose in front of Jae. It was too wide for him to dodge. He hit the brakes. The impact would kill him. Not even the shield could protect him from it. He turned sideways as the scooter lowered to the ground. The scooter jumped and screeched as it slowed. Jae was still too fast and smashed into the wall.

The shield on the scooter shattered as he crashed through it. He lost his grip on the handles and fell to the ground sliding as the sand beneath him helped him stop.

Lyour watched. He looked mortified as Jae lay there motionless. He wondered what he had done. He never meant to kill him. He slowly walked towards him. Jae lifted himself up and Lyour stopped. He sighed relieved that he hadn't broken his agreement. Jae fell back to the ground unconscious. Lyour turned around and ran away.

He took out a communication device. It was different than a phone. It was shaped like a watch. In the middle was a small light and buttons. He wrapped it around his wrist. When he was a safe distance away from Jae, he stopped and composed himself. He entered his code and soon 4 of the gods answered.

"What is it Lyour?" A woman asked.

"Yeah, I'm kind of busy right now make it quick," another voice, a man, said. In the background was a loud thunderous sound and the wind was loud.

"I…have grave news…" he started. He paused as two more entered the call. "Hrayrp was killed, as well as Muragrak."

"Impossible," a third man said.

"I thought so too. However there is a human child who is hunting us down. He is angry over Muragrak landing on earth and killing his kin. He is blaming us for their deaths."

"Lyour, I think you're letting human jokes take over too far," a woman said.

"I am not joking Kwtamg," his voice was stern as he replied. "I just escaped him myself. He chased me for hours stating he was going to wipe us out. I…in the heat of the chase, I raised a wall and accidentally knocked him out."

A voice laughed. "You knocked him out with sand and you're telling me he killed Hrayrp?"

"He claims that he has. He states he knows where his body is buried. I…believe him. If I hadn't been unfortunate enough to be chased across Chad, I wouldn't believe it as well."

"So where are they?" A soft-spoken woman asked. She entered the call as Lyour spoke.

"I do not know. But he said he ate Muragrak completely and just the head of Hrayrp."

"So he's after our powers?!" A man roared.

"He stated he only wants our abilities to wipe up out. As revenge for his kin's death."

"And have you seen his abilities?" Kwtamg asked.

"I have not. I refused to fight him."

"Then he doesn't have it. If he did have Hrayrp's powers, he could stop you instantly." Kwtamg sighed.

"He may not know how," another voice chimed in.

"How foolish. To think he can wipe us out. And over something that had nothing to do with us," a woman said.

"Remember, Muragrak went Yurtpo. He may have adopted his insanity," the soft voice replied.

"Then we should put him out of his misery."

"You know we cannot harm a human."

"But he can harm us?"

Multiple voices in the call argued amongst each other. Speaking about the Peace and Ethics Code, the unjust he's doing, and much more.

A strong voice hushed everyone. He spoke, "We should discuss this in person. Meet at our headquarters. Lyour, it may not be safe for you there. As you refuse to harm them, I worry about your safety."

"I am fine. He was unconscious when I left. I am miles away from him."

"Still," Kwtamg said. "I am in Sudan. Let's meet at Lake Katam. If he shows up, I am willing to break the code and face whatever punishment you all throw at me."

"Kwtamg," Lyour said, awkwardly. "You are a fine warrior and way stronger than I. However, I…do not want a woman to fight for me. You, Yulogna, and Myetorp are crucial to our species' survival. You all must survive."

"Do not insult me," Kwtamg yelled. "I am a warrior first and a mother second. When we mate, then I may be treated delicately, but until then, treat me as the glorious warrior I was on Trwqoy!"

"I apologize." Lyour bowed as if she could see him. "I will meet you at Lake Katam. Then, I will leave the call first. Ex—"

As he spoke, a sword stabbed him in his abdomen. Blood spurted from his mouth and everyone on the call heard him. They shouted what was wrong.

"Got you," Jae said, his breath heavy.

"What a coward," a man shouted. "To sneak from behind. Lyour, where are you?!"

The voices called out to him. He weakly took the watch off. Kwtamg shouted, "Lyour where are you?!"

"You said you weren't going to tell," Jae said, bitterly. "Going against your word, you deserve to die."

Lyour hung up and put the watch in his pocket. He stepped forward to remove Magord. He threw sand up and Jae dodged backwards. He hopped on his sand and rode away.

Jae yelled angrily, "Running away again you coward? Just roll over and die!"

He ran to his scooter that was parked a long way away and chased after him. Lyour held his wound and covered it with sand. He couldn't heal like Muragrak, and the sand definitely wasn't going to heal him. But he packed his wound anyways. It was all he could think to do.

How could I have let my guard down? I've gotten weak, he thought. He continued towards Lake Katam, but he remembered the risks for Kwtamg and changed course. *Sorry. You'll have to find another mate.*

He didn't quite know what direction he was going in. His wound threw off his senses. But he knew to go whatever way was away from the direction he originally stood.

Jae thought about Hrayrp's ability. He still didn't know how to use it. But that was a moment where he needed to stop him. He had already alerted the others. Who knew when they would come? He stood a chance against an injured weakling like Lyour but who would come to his rescue if not all of the gods?

Jae focused on the boulder in front of Lyour. He thought continuously, *Fall.*

But nothing happened, they passed by, and he exhaled furiously. He still couldn't control the abilities. How much longer would it take for him to use them? Was he that stupid and incompetent he couldn't figure out how to use his own body?

Jae lowered his shield again and threw Magord. Lyour didn't bother raising a wall. He let it fall onto the ground and Jae picked it up as he rode past. He raised the shield again.

"Tell me," Jae shouted. Lyour barely heard him and looked back. "Why do you fight so desperately to live? You know sooner or later you're going to die. Why bother extending it?"

"The same question could be asked back. Why do you avenge your kin when they would have died anyways?"

His response angered Jae. He cried, "What do you know! They were children! You've lived for who cares how long, the oldest didn't even make it to fourteen! Do you think they deserved it or that they were less deserving to live than you?"

"All death is sad. And we must all face it without a say when. It is sad that they lost their lives at the hands of one of my own, mentally ill, or not. But don't forget we have lost way more than you. Yet we continue to live and thrive to keep our species alive." Lyour turned to Jae completely. "Do you think only adults lived on my planet? Children younger than your kin died horrible deaths, I assume worse than your kin. Were we sad and angry? Yes, but we did not seek out to kill every creature in this galaxy that was related to the ones who invaded our planet."

"That's your fault! Just because you were stupid enough to not seek revenge, doesn't mean I have to follow suit."

Lyour sighed. "You think as a child does. You refuse to listen to logic. Even if you do manage to catch and kill me, then what? You anger my kind, and they kill you. It is nothing but an endless cycle of death. You must stop this. You've killed the equivalent of your kin. Let it be at that. Please tell me where you buried Hrayrp."

"Never. And I will continue to kill you all. The equivalent? How so? The lives of my kin and my friend are way more valuable than you *things*. Don't lower their lives to such lowly trash."

"I do not mean to speak 'lowly' of your kin. But just as valuable as they meant to you, the ones you killed mean very much to me. End this cycle of hatred. I am sure they would not want you to kill indiscriminately and end your life on their behalf. Live for them."

"Ha! You don't know them. You don't know what they would want. If you want the cycle to end, you all should kill yourselves and save me the trouble."

Lyour shook his head. He turned around. There was nothing he could say to Jae that would satiate his anger and lust for blood. He needed to find a way to apprehend him without harming him and without the others catching him first. But that meant going against his sword. Lyour wondered how he could even possess a high-tech weapon. He was sure that most nations banned them, so how did he get one? The bleeding from his wound had stopped, and the pain was gone. He was still dazed but rational enough to not slip up. Or at least he hoped he was.

They continued for 2 hours. Lyour had no idea where he was going, and his mental capacity was slowly recovering. His morale weakened and he thought about letting Jae kill him. He wouldn't stop until he did so.

A burst of water shot through the desert and struck Jae. It cracked his shield and sent him flying. The force from the ground shattered the shield and he snapped his neck on impact. Multiple bones broke as he slid, caught in the scooter until it finally stopped.

Lyour was stunned. He looked from the unconscious Jae to the direction of the water. In the distance he saw Kwtamg. She walked slowly towards him. Her hair and clothes blew wildly from the wind. Her blue skin blended in with the night sky. He asked, "What are you doing here?"

"What do you mean, 'What am I doing here?'" she asked, frustrated. "I told you to meet me at Katam hours ago!"

Lyour averted eye contact. "Sorry."

"Do you still look down on me?" she asked, sadly. "Am I not the best warrior amongst us?"

"Only between you and I…. I…wanted to protect you in my own way. What is the point of us both dying here to this child?" his voice was low as spoke, still refusing to look her in the eye. "I do not look down on you. I never have. My only goal in life is to protect you. And see to it that you carry on our species."

"I get that," she said. "But I told you I will only mate with you. I do not want those brutes near me. If you die, then I will not conceive."

"You can't do that!" Lyour looked at her. "Don't be foolish and waste your life on me!"

"I'm not wasting anything! Do you really think this child can kill us?"

Lyour nodded. He looked down again. "He killed Hrayrp. He may not have been as strong as us, but this kid's resolve has kept him alive. And with the five abilities combined, he may be difficult to handle."

"And that's why we kill him now."

"He's only a child Kwtamg. He is angry for Muragrak killing his young kin. What justice is there in us harming him? As I told him, this cycle of killing needs to end."

"Someone as blind with fury as him will never stop. Killing Muragrak wasn't enough, killing Hrayrp wasn't enough, if he kills you, it will never be enough. He wants to erase us all. Do you think his life is above mine?"

"Not in the slightest," Lyour quickly answered. "I love you more than rtmghu did ashwyet in the ceremony of tyrnop. But I still can't kill a child."

"That is a sweet analogy Lyour, but very 'old school' as the humans say." Kwtamg smiled. "Then what do we do with him?"

"I do not know. I want to turn him in to the others, but who knows what they will want to do."

"Kill him like I want to. You and maybe Yulogna are the only ones who wish to spare him."

"Yes, who knows what kind of problems will arise if we were to kill him. The other humans may hate us or fear us."

"I think it is a price to pay. It will teach them not to try this. Who knows who he will tell next? If he has not already told humans about our abilities."

Jae stirred. He sat up in pain. His neck hurt and each bone snapping back in place sent shockwaves through his body, each tremor of pain helped him regain consciousness.

"Kwtamg, please go to headquarters and tell them what is happening, I will catch up soon."

"Not happening," she said. "You are the one who is injured. Leave him to me."

"I cannot do that," he complained.

"Lyour, for once, please stop treating me as if I am weak. Go. I promise you I will not let this child kill me. If he proves difficult, I will inform the others and escape as soon as I can."

Jae staggered forward. He stumbled as he walked closer. "If you want to die…wait your turn."

"Ha?" She laughed. "Child I am not as docile as Lyour. You are not going to kill either of us."

She raised her hands in front of her and slid one foot back to sturdy herself. She whispered to Lyour, "Hurry and get backup. I will hold him off."

Lyour nodded. He started to run before stopping. "I love you."

Kwtamg smiled. "I love you too."

Lyour hopped on his sand. He shouted as he left, "I will be right back!"

Jae yelled to him, "How much of a coward are you? You're letting a woman fight your battles?"

"This 'woman' is one of the best warriors alive. Do not let appearances deceive you."

Jae scoffed. "We'll see about that."

She waved at Lyour then focused on Jae. "Tell me boy, why are you so adamant on killing Lyour?"

"Because he's a weakling and a coward."

"Hardly. He was one of the strongest on our planet. He just refuses to fight. He's always been that way. Do not confuse kindness with weakness."

"If he's the strongest, then why isn't he fighting instead of you?"

She sighed. That child was thick skulled and listened to nothing. "I do not have time to chat with you. Let us hurry this up. Be grateful. Lyour is the reason I will not kill you."

"Hmph," Jae sneered. "If that's how you want to die then so be it."

Sorry Lyour, the way this child speaks, I do not know if I can keep my word, she thought, as Jae lunged forward.

Jae swung Magord and she flipped backwards to dodge it. She ran backwards, her eyes not leaving Jae.

"Don't tell me you're running away too?" he complained.

"Never." She smiled. They reached Lake Katam. She smiled again and said, "Now we can fight."

Jae looked confused and positioned Magord over his shoulder. Kwtamg lifted both her hands and a large amount of water rose from the lake.

"Now that's just unfair," Jae complained.

She thrusted the water at him. He ran to the side but wasn't fast enough. The water hit him with immense force and slammed him into the sand. The sand thickened and sloshed like mud, and he struggled to get up. Kwtamg gripped her hand tightly and yanked her hand back. Jae lifted into the air and was thrown in the water. He gasped for air as he swam back to the top.

"Don't tell me you have telekinesis too?!"

She smiled. "Warriors do not speak on the battlefield. Nor do they reveal their techniques."

The water bubbled under him as he swam to shore and a gush of water pushed him into the air. More water came from the side and smacked him down on land. He lay there writhing in pain. How could he fight something like water? He could slice through it, but what could that do besides drown him?

He wished he could use Hrayrp's ability. That was the only way he stood a chance. He couldn't get near her without water striking him. She looked amused, almost deranged in her attacks. She smashed more and more water onto him. He couldn't stand. Each time he made it to his knees, she threw more water.

He gasped for air. "Don't you think it's cruel to use one of the only sources of water in the desert?"

He was hoping to buy time. Even just enough for him to catch his breath.

"The water is not running out. Besides, we can bring a god who controls weather to fill this with more water."

"But what do you think about the fish who are dying when you take the water out?"

"I intentionally grab water away from them. Enough talking." She clenched her fists and a ball of water formed behind her.

"But what do you think about when the water runs out? Do you think a god can arrive by the time you run out? How many lives will be lost for you to be satisfied killing me? Are you that cruel to even torture creatures who can't defend themselves?"

She glanced back at the water. It was significantly lower than when they first arrived, but it was still deep enough for them to swim freely. Was Jae right? While she did not mind torturing Jae until help arrived, she didn't want the fish to lose their lives. If she continued at the rate she did, how much longer until their demise?

"You are lucky. I will give them a break. I will lessen the amount I use."

She ripped two strips of her clothing off and wrapped it around her hands. She positioned her stance as Jae stumbled to his feet. He was soaking wet. The night breeze chilled him to the bone. Jae walked over to Magord, not taking his eyes off her. He rose Magord over his shoulder and charged.

Before he could make contact with his sword, Kwtamg roundhouse kicked him in the face. She had broken his nose with one swift kick. Jae winced and steadied himself. He swung again and she dodged, sending him a right hook. Before he could steady himself again, she sent a left hook, then a jab. As she punched again, a small amount of water followed smacking him in the face. She uppercut him, then another gush of water. Then a cross punch. She sent a series of punches mixed with water attacks to Jae. Her technique was more refined than Hrayrp's brute strength. She wasn't as strong but her eloquent attacks were more than effective.

She kicked him to the ground and put one foot on his chest. "See boy, this 'woman' can do more than just throw water. Hrayrp is not the only one with efficient hand to hand combat."

"You're just not as strong. Hrayrp did way more damage in less time," he said, trying to not show his pain.

Kwtamg shook her head and moved away from Jae. "Such a stubborn child. Please, for your own sake, do not get up. I cannot guarantee what will happen before the others arrive."

"Shut up you ugly hag." Jae stumbled to his feet. "Don't pretend like you care."

"I do not care about you. Only the promise I made Lyour. You could burn on the sun, and I would not shed a tear."

"That's how evil you things are."

"We are not things. You are inhuman and psychotic. A child should not have as much hatred as you. Do not be foolish and continue as you are. You will meet your end sooner than you think."

Jae laughed. "Don't be too sure of that. After I kill you, I'm making sure to dice Lyour into millions of pieces and put him in a salad."

Kwtamg was furious. She charged Jae and crescent kicked him. Her force was stronger than before, knocking Jae to the ground again. She kicked him repeatedly in the gut. Jae struggled to keep consciousness.

There was no way he was going to die. Especially not to a woman. Didn't matter how strong she was, he couldn't think of a death more humiliating.

Think! There has to be a way to use their abilities, he thought. He tried to remember how he activated the paralyzing mist, but he couldn't. He was just on the brink of death, and it happened. Did that need to happen for him to use his abilities? The gods weren't on the brink of death beating the shit out of him. So that wouldn't be fair nor logical. He was activating it subconsciously. But how could he do it?

She was well advanced in combat than him. There was no way to win against her fair and square. She lifted Jae by his collar and kicked him in the water. He didn't swim up. He held his breath. He needed time to think. He regretted not taking more time to train. But he would never have had the chance to confront Lyour. Whether this little hurdle was in the way or not. If he had taken time to figure out his ability, he wouldn't have fought her. He would have killed Lyour without alerting everyone.

He looked at a rock wedged in the sand and focused on it. He thought, *Lift.*

Nothing. He tried again and again. He tried releasing the mist. Nothing. Jae felt an invisible force around his body. Kwtamg lifted him out of the water.

"Cannot have you die yet. Not until we find the right punishment."

She threw him on the ground and left him there. She walked a bit away and sat down. Jae coughed madly and panted for air. He wondered why she wasn't continuing her assault. Was it yet again because of her promise to Lyour? Jae, although he hated the idea, took the chance to think. He lay on his side away from her gazing in the distance, staring at nothing in particular. A small pebble appeared in the corner of his eye, just inches in front of him. He focused on it and thought, *Lift.*

The pebble shifted a bit and Jae perked up. Had he actually done it? He focused all his might, his nose bled, and the pebble lifted inches above the ground. Some movement was better than no movement.

He looked again at a large rock in the distance, he thought *lift*, but nothing happened. Was he only capable of lifting small objects? Jae sighed. What good would that do him but to piss her off more?

Jae smiled. Just like Hrayrp, she was proud. Her cockiness would take over and ruin her skills. He couldn't use the same method as Hrayrp...nor did he want to. Without agitating her, he had already seen the extent of her skills. Water and martial arts. She had the advantage either way.

He heard her complaining behind him. Who knew what those gods were capable of? Who's to say she didn't lose him in the desert. Who would question her if he did die? Lyour would have been upset, but Jae wasn't *that* stupid. He would side with Kwtamg no matter what. And if he did act like a good boy and wait, all that awaited him was death. Those vicious creatures wanted him dead just as much as he wanted them lifeless. He heard them speaking before he stabbed Lyour. They weren't to be trusted. She even said herself, she wouldn't feel an ounce of remorse if he died.

Jae wasn't going to let them have the satisfaction of an easy kill. He would take down as many with him as possible. Starting with the "bitch" behind him. He kind of understood the grasp of his skills. He couldn't lift too much…not because he was weak of course, but because he didn't know the technique for larger objects.

Kwtamg rested her head on her arm and swirled the water from the shore. She was lost in thought worrying about Lyour's safety, when a fish flew out of the water and smacked her in the face.

Jae burst into laughter. "Did you see the way it hit you? What a loser!"

She did her best to ignore him as she hurried the fish back into the water. "You complained about me killing fish, yet you do that?"

"I don't care about their lives. I'm not the one who has to honor a code. Or do you get to pick and choose who falls under it? You certainly had no qualms hurting me."

"Because you deserve it." She moved into a fighting stance. "I am sure there is an exception to the rule."

"Again with the exceptions. You pick and choose who you protect and who you harm. Shows how little you should be trusted."

"Do not overstep boy. We are the ones who have saved your planet from your ruin. We work every day protecting people."

"As you should," Jae interrupted. "It's a price to pay just like every other being on this planet. It's called rent. Do as you're told and shut up."

"Child, your disrespect will not be tolerated."

"'Disrespect?'" Jae scoffed. "You disrespected me by living."

Kwtamg grimaced then lunged at Jae. Her skills of course, excelled his and he was back to getting his ass beat. But instead of backing down or falling, he kept his balance. He needed to use the paralyzing mist. That was his only hope. He thought hard like he did the pebble and a small bit of purple gas puffed out his mouth. Kwtamg inhaled an even smaller amount and fell stiff.

He laughed. His bumptiousness, no matter how small the mist was, prevailed and he mocked Kwtamg. "Not so tough now."

Kwtamg didn't say anything. Due to the small amount she inhaled, she was able to move her eyes. She closed them and focused.

"Giving up already?" Jae teased. "Oh, don't think you're getting off that easy. I'm chopping off each limb, stabbing you in as many places as possible, and smashing your head in. You'll die a horrible death just like you wished on me."

He turned his ring and Magord flew into his hand. He sliced off her left arm then her right. "Doesn't feel so good does it? Don't pretend like you don't feel it. Suffer like you wanted me to suffer."

He stabbed her in the gut and blue blood darker than the night sky, gushed from her stomach. Jae smiled. Something about stabbing her, excited him. It was a kind of satisfying aesthetic he could enjoy forever. Maybe all their stomachs sounded that way?

He stabbed again laughing. "You can try all you want to seem composed, but I know you're in pain. You can't hide it."

She smiled. Her arms grew back instantaneously, and she lunged for Jae's neck. She gripped his neck with immense strength. If she tightened her grip even just a little, his neck would snap.

"How?" he managed to ask. He grabbed her arm to pull it away.

She laughed. "Not so arrogant are you. Muragrak was not the only one with regeneration."

"Fuck you."

"Where is your arrogance? You were going to torture me? Ha! You give us women little credit. I do not think someone like you deserves a council. You should be executed on the spot."

Jae dropped his hands. He looked down to her abdomen. The wounds hadn't healed. Blood stained her clothes and leaked from the holes.

She sighed. "Giving up so easily. After chopping off my arms and stabbing me with pleasure, I cannot give you another chance boy. I will atone for breaking my promise with Lyour another way."

Jae twisted his ring and Magord bolted into his hand. He swung as best he could and almost sliced her in half. The angle he held, kept just a sliver of skin, muscles, and nerves attached to her lower half. Her grip loosened and she fell to the ground. Jae fell after her. She breathed heavily as blood oozed from her lower half.

Jae, still unable to breathe said, "You… you don't have… the same regeneration as him…. Your stomach hasn't healed. And I doubt you'll heal from this."

She thrusted her arm to her side and attempted to grab water. Jae sliced off her arms. "I may be weaker, but I still manage to survive. You should have killed me when you had the chance."

He was going to stab her head, but rage filled him with her words over the duration of the fight. He wanted her to suffer a gruesome death. One like she wished upon him. He focused intensely, and lifted a heavier rock from the lake. Blood oozed profusely from his nose as he struggled to bring it to shore.

Kwtamg grew her arms back and tried again, Jae dropped the rock and sliced them off.

"Just die. No reason to keep trying." He bent in front of her and thought again, a little puff of mist escaped his mouth and she inhaled it. "I'm sorry, but you don't deserve to live with the hatred you hold for me."

He refocused on the rock. He leveled it over her head and dropped it. It smashed against her skull, knocking her out. That was most likely the best thing for her. Jae knelt and grabbed the rock. He lifted it above his head and smashed her head, again, and again. Each strike full of rage. He hit her until her head was flat on the ground.

In the corner of his eyes, he saw Lyour staring at them. His face mortified as he watched Jae strike her. He had called for help, but didn't return to their base, he couldn't wrap his mind around leaving Kwtamg to fight Jae. No matter how much she argued she was strong enough, he just couldn't do it. He turned around and headed back to Lake Katam. He rushed at impossible speeds to get back to her, reopening his wounds as he pushed himself to the limit. But it was too late.

Jae smiled. He stood up and kicked her dead body. "This could have all been avoided if you hadn't run away. If you hadn't had her fight your battle, she would still be alive! But you chose to run, and this is the result!"

Jae laughed as he continued, "What, will you raise your hand against me now? Will you break your peace and ethic's code to avenge your woman? She had to go like this! She tortured me first, it's only fair that I did the same!"

Lyour heard Jae, but his eyes were only on what remained of Kwtamg. It was like he had inhaled Jae's mist and could do nothing.

"You should've let her kill me. She had multiple opportunities to, but she didn't want to break her promise to you. Look at what your peace brought you. A dead lover. So loyal to keep her word, even if it meant dying. And you know why? Because of you!"

Jae's words struck Lyour harder than any blade could. Harder than any boulder could. Lyour, instead of attacking Jae, burst into tears. He fell to his knees and wailed. It was the worst sound Jae had ever heard. His pain and sadness enveloped his cries.

"Kwtamg," Lyour screamed. He buried his face into the sand. "I'm so sorry. I shouldn't have left you!"

"Ha! Do you wish you had told her to kill me?" Jae said, uneasy. Something about his pain and his cries made Jae uncomfortable.

Lyour ignored him. Even though he hated Jae for what he did, he wanted the cycle of hatred and killing to end. What would that have done, but prove that child right? As he lay in his final moments of life if Lyour had fought, his thoughts, Lyour's words for peace, would have all been in vain.

Lyour was too stricken with grief to even stand, let alone fight him. His mind was full of the if onlys, and that he should have stayed while she got help. His life meant nothing without her. His wails grew louder and harsher. Tears poured down his face. A pain worse than the harshest death ripped through his chest. Gripping his heart and crushing it to pieces.

Jae felt a little bad for him. Lyour, even though Jae antagonized him, did not attack him. He stuck to his word about not seeking revenge. Lyour had felt pain almost as bad as he had. Even though he did not regret killing Kwtamg, he regretted killing her so harshly… in front of Lyour.

"Look," Jae said, slowly approaching him. Lyour still remained tucked into the ground, crying. "I—I will end your life quickly. Please just join her in the afterlife and live together for all of eternity."

Lyour still didn't budge. His cries grew harsher until they sounded like roars. He lifted his sword above Lyour's head and said, "Thank you for standing true to your code."

As he swung down, sand attacked him from the side, and he landed a distance away. He sat up confused. Was Lyour faking his sadness? Or did he finally have the resolve to kill him? He looked at Lyour who still screamed in agony. His skin darkened, like a banana rotting at an alarming rate. His skin turned purple and he grew long, white hair.

Lyour had gone into Yurtpo.

Jae was frozen. He knew by the color of his skin that that was not a good thing. He remembered his fight with Muragrak and how difficult it was. His thirst for blood. He stopped at nothing to kill him. Lyour and

Kwtamg both mentioned how much stronger they were than the other two. Was this where he was going to die?

But why? he thought. *What could have made him go...*

He remembered what Hrayrp told him. That Muragrak had gone through intense despair at the death of their people, the loss of his home, and changed. Jae caused Lyour so much agony, that he changed too. He still needed to fight. The Lyour he knew and now somewhat respected, was long gone. As Hrayrp explained, Yurtpo caused extreme mental illness. He was no longer conscious and whatever force controlled this Yurtpo, was inside of him.

Jae sighed relieved. He was happy that Lyour's resolve for peace had not been corrupted. Jae stood and faced Lyour who still cried on the ground. He was a danger to society and needed to be stopped. He reminded himself continuously that he was not the Lyour he spoke with. It was nothing more than a thing that needed to be eradicated.

He cautiously walked up to Lyour and tried to attack. Another force of sand blocked and struck him. This time, Lyour didn't stay down. He rose to his feet and turned to Jae. Fear washed over Jae like nothing before. Lyour did not look the same. He looked evil and ready to kill. His anger when he saw Jae intensified and he lunged at him. Jae tried slicing his arm off like he did Muragrak, but it wasn't enough. Sand covered his arm and Magord embedded in it. It engulfed the sword leaving Jae defenseless. He struggled to remove his arm from the sand. Lyour lifted the sand and smashed Jae to the ground. Up and down until he slipped his hand free. He hurried to his feet and looked at Lyour.

He stumbled backwards. Without his sword, he stood no chance of survival. Though even with it, he stood zero chances. He turned around and ran to his scooter. Lyour chased after him. Before he could reach it, the sand beneath him thrusted upwards, and sent him flying. He smashed into the ground and scrambled to stand. He tried for his scooter, but Lyour hit him with sand. Jae fell over, and Lyour pierced his stomach with hardened sand.

Jae screamed in agony. Lyour smiled. He stabbed him multiple times. Jae dodged the last strike by rolling over. He rushed to his feet, holding his wound. He managed to get to his scooter and drove off. Lyour shrieked with fury and chased him. Piles of sand launched at him, the sand beneath him propelled him into the air, and sand and wind from above knocked him back down. He released a large amount of paralyzing mist, but Lyour increased the wind and blew it away.

He was terrified of Lyour. There was nothing he could do to escape him. He looked at the horizon as dawn slowly appeared. He was thankful to be able to see clearly, but what good would that do him since he was going to die? Jae moved his scooter higher in the sky, as far above as it would take him. He sighed as he looked down at Lyour. He wasn't going to be able to attack from that low. Jae focused in front of him and figured he wouldn't come down until Lyour gave up.

A sand claw launched from the ground and grabbed Jae. Lyour swung his arm downwards and threw Jae down. He fell off the scooter. He got up and bolted to his scooter again, he had no idea where he was going but anywhere away from Lyour was fine by him.

Lyour roared in rage. He hadn't ridden the sand like he did previously. He ran almost as fast by foot. There was no escaping that monster. He was beyond reason and Jae stared death in the face. He regretted sending him into this state, but nothing could change the past. The best he could do was maybe lead him to the other gods. But he had no idea where their base was. It was strictly hidden from human eyes.

In the distance, Jae noticed they had rounded back to Lake Katam. His stomach sank. If he saw Kwtamg, he would really go crazy. Before he could turn, another sand attack sent him soaring off the scooter. He skidded across the sand until he was inches from Kwtamg. Lyour approached, his eyes on nothing but Jae.

He growled as he stared at him. He lifted his hand and sand formed into a spear and hardened. It was as sharp as a dagger. Maybe as sharp as Magord. Lyour took his time forming the perfect weapon. Jae was too exhausted to keep running. His stomach wounds hadn't healed, and he was losing consciousness from blood loss.

The sand spear thrusted into Jae's chest. Jae screamed, the pain jarring him awake. The spear exited his chest and rose to his head. Lyour drew the spear back ready to impale him. As he swung, Jae closed his eyes.

He sat there for a long time. A loud gushing sound pierced the silence. Jae opened his eyes. Lyour was spewing purple blood and the wound on his stomach seeped endlessly. Every hole in his body drained blood. It was like Ye-jun and Russell's deaths. His body didn't convulse but blood gushed from his mouth. He vomited the blood in droves. As he grasped for air, and blood spilled from his eyes, he continued to glare at Jae with pure revulsion.

The sand next to him dropped and soon Lyour fell over too, his head just inches from Jae. Jae sat frightened. He should have died but there he was alive and kicking. Was he really that hard to kill? Blood oozed from Lyour's body. The purple blood touched Jae's foot and his shoe began to melt.

Jae didn't speak. He didn't celebrate or talk shit about Lyour. He should have died there. He yet again escaped death. He sat quietly next to both their bodies as the sun rose over the horizon.

He looked from Lyour to what remained of Kwtamg, and closed his eyes. He turned his ring and Magord returned to him. He pulled their bodies away from the shore. He used Magord as a shovel and dug two graves next to each other. He rolled their bodies into the graves and filled it with sand again. He didn't want their abilities. Kwtamg's head was smashed to almost nothing, he would not have had all the parts. And Lyour, he just didn't feel right nor safe eating. Who knew if he could be affected by the poison?

He turned on his busted scooter and went to the nearest town. Everything was still closed. He saw a bouquet of carnations outside and took them. He went back to Lake Katam and placed the flowers on their graves.

He felt bad about Lyour and maybe some of his words did seep into his mind. But him, the most docile man going Yurtpo, anything would be possible of the others. He remembered Lyour's wish of ending the cycle and Jae for the shortest second, thought he might have been right. However, Jae justified his hatred even more with their Yurtpo. They were a danger to society and needed to be eradicated. Who knew when and what would cause them to go Yurtpo? His resolve was unwavering.

But he knew he wasn't ready as he was. He needed to train. Where, he had no idea, but he would follow wherever he was destined to go.

Jae didn't feel just celebrating the death of those two. Though he was not sad for Kwtamg, Lyour's pain was enough to make him mourn.

He jumped back onto his scooter and drove away to a destination unknown to even himself.

Chapter Nine
Jae's Past Pt. 3

The Gods
~Headquarters - navigation room~

"Has anyone heard from Lyour or Kwtamg?" a red god asked.

"Not yet Hellim," a red goddess said. "Parahae and Jtrepo are in Chad searching for them."

"We will await their return to discuss what to do with this killer," Hellim said. He turned around and sat in a large chair. He rested his head in his hands and sighed.

"Don't worry," the soft-spoken goddess said. She was a black goddess. "I'm sure they're fine."

"Last we heard of them was when Lyour turned back to help Kwtamg," a black god said. "He promised to give word when they apprehended that child. It's been hours."

"They are both skilled warriors," the black goddess said. "I doubt a child could kill them both."

"Yet we haven't heard anything," a blue god said, entering the room. "If this child managed to kill Muragrak and Hrayrp, then he's more trouble than we're acknowledging."

"We do not know if they are dead. The child could be lying," Hellim said.

"Don't be so sure," the red goddess said. "You are too trusting."

"It is not that I am trusting this child, I am trusting the skills and determination of Lyour and Kwtamg."

"Yet it's been hours," the blue god said. "Let's face it, this boy is more trouble than we imagined."

"Please," the black goddess said. "Have faith in our comrades. Let us wait until we hear from Parahae and Jtrepo."

"Yulogna, you're also too trusting," the red goddess complained. "But I guess that's why the two peacekeepers are a couple."

"Myetorp," Yulogna said. Her voice was still soft but stern. "Our union has nothing to do with our decision in this matter. We simply believe in them."

"Then let's wait until we hear word," the blue god said. He turned around and left the room.

The red and black gods left as well.

Hellim sighed. Yulogna sat beside him on the arm of the chair.

"Don't worry, they will be alright. Have patience with the others and we will see who is right."

"I know Yulogna. I just…I have the feeling they did not make it out. But I want to keep just a little hope in case they do return."

Yulogna smiled and kissed Hellim's forehead. "I will keep faith for the both of us. Please inform me when you hear from Parahae and Jtrepo."

"I will. Please rest for now."

Yulogna kissed Hellim once more and left.

~Lake Katam, Chad~

"Any sign?" the yellow god asked.

"Not yet," the green one replied. "They shouldn't be too far. We should see a battle."

"Kwtamg, wouldn't leave the area," the yellow god said. "She is out of her element. Check Lake Yoa, I will search here."

"Got it," the green god said running away. "Jtrepo!"

Jtrepo looked back. "What?"

"Let's stay positive."

Jtrepo nodded. He ran along the shore as Parahae ran as fast as he could to Lake Yoa. He ran around looking as best he could for any sign of Kwtamg. Jtrepo ran searching left and right. He could tell by the water level she was in fact there at some point. He ran until he made it to the other side. He looked to his right, a few feet from the shore, were carnations.

As he walked closer, he saw the trail of purple and blue blood dried by the water and his heart sank. He pulled up his watch and dialed Parahae. When he answered, Jtrepo said solemnly, "Found them."

Parahae rushed as fast as he could to where Jtrepo pinged his location. He looked at the mess of blood. Blue, red, and purple all along the path from the water to the spot with the carnations.

"Forgive me," Parahae said, digging up the sand under the carnations to the left. His and Jtrepo's hearts sank even lower. Such a gruesome way to kill Kwtamg. She was barely recognizable. They looked at each other and Parahae continued, "Guess this means Lyour was the one to go Yurtpo."

Jtrepo nodded sadly. He dug up Lyour's grave and lifted him on his shoulder. "Grab Kwtamg."

"I…" Parahae paused. "I don't think it's a good idea to show them her."

"She needs a proper burial. It's sad, but without physical proof they will deny that she's dead."

Parahae lifted Kwtamg and carried her gently in his arms. Afraid that even the slightest mishandle would tear the rest of her body apart. He looked down, pain in his eyes. He ran behind Jtrepo, refusing to look at her again.

Jtrepo called Hellim and informed him of their findings. He asked for Hellim to wait until their arrival with their bodies before he told the others. Hellim agreed. They boarded their hoover car and went to headquarters.

The gods gasped in horror at the bodies lain across the table. Blood still dripped from Lyour's body. A blanket was placed over Kwtamg.

"What kind of sick human is this?" Malarik, the black god said. "I get it was a battle but to do something so horrible to Kwtamg…I…"

"It's twisted. And mind you this is the same child that Lyour tried to convince us needed a small punishment. Look what he did to her and what resulted of Lyour." Gravick, the blue god sneered.

"We need to find him and kill him. He is a danger to us. These humans may hear about our powers," Myetorp, the red goddess shouted. "He should not be allowed to live freely. He deserves a death as grim as Kwtamg's!"

"He is still just a child," Yulogna pleaded. "As I said before, he is not there mentally. He inherited Muragrak's mentality. He needs to be given psychiatric help."

"Yulogna, do not be as imprudent as Lyour. He is a threat and should be wiped out. How about you take him on and experience what he did to Kwtamg," Gravick said.

"Watch your tongue," Hellim yelled. "Yulogna is right. Lyour was right. Where we went wrong was in underestimating him. We need to bring him back here. He is lusting for power. If given the right psychiatric help, once he is cured, he should join our ranks and help this planet. No sense losing the abilities he's acquired."

"I apologize for how I spoke to you Yulogna," Gravick said. "But Hellim, do not forget your silly ideals for peace and negotiation is what caused our planet to be destroyed! Do not fool yourself that this *beast* is any different than them!"

The other gods nodded in agreement.

"I..." Hellim said, mournfully, "I made that mistake and I have to atone for it for the rest of my life. This is nothing more than a mere human. He can be easily swayed into the ranks of gods."

"I can't believe you're still this gullible," Myetorp said. "You and Yulogna are the only ones left who think this child should be spared. I do not care why he is on this tirade. He needs to face punishment equal to the execution of Muragrak, Hrayrp, Kwtamg, and Lyour!"

"But is that what Lyour would want?" Parahae interjected. "I disagree wholeheartedly that this child should join our ranks. I cannot stomach to even look at him. However, I know Lyour fought desperately to keep him alive. Kwtamg, I am sure followed his wishes and it turned on her. I say we find him and get him help. Afterwards, he will face punishment. Not death, but imprisonment on an insufferable planet. Is that agreeable Hellim?"

Hellim nodded.

"I—" Myetorp stuttered. "I can't believe you're not siding with me on this!"

"It isn't a matter of siding with anyone but finding a solution in-between and just." Parahae avoided eye contact.

"He's right," Jtrepo said. "We must keep our emotions in check. Calm yourself Myetorp."

Myetorp tsked and looked away.

Jtrepo continued, "Do you agree Malarik, Gravick, Yulogna?"

They nodded. Gravick was pissed but he knew a unanimous vote was final. And no matter how much he complained, nothing would change the decision.

"The next matter is how we find him," Hellim spoke. "We cannot mention the issue to other humans lest they discover what eating us will do."

"There's no way to find him," Gravick said.

"The only way to catch him is when he goes after one of us," Parahae said.

"Which could be fatal," Jtrepo added.

Myetorp tsked. "I don't know about you, but this child will not harm me. And if he does come after me, I will not guarantee I will bring him alive."

"And that is fine," Gravick said. "If he proves too difficult, we should be allowed to defend ourselves. Even if it means him dying."

"Yes, but the ultimate goal is to get him help. If you can avoid killing him, even if it means severing his limbs do so," Parahae said.

"Then for now, our meeting is adjourned," Hellim said.

He didn't wait for the others to leave first. He stormed out of the room and into his own. Gravick would never forgive him for what happened on Trwqoy. Nor did Hellim have the right to ask for forgiveness. He was doomed to live in the regret of his actions for all of eternity, with no hope of alleviation.

On Trwqoy, they lived in a lustrous land. Full of bright colors and the happiest of people. They had vast riches and was one of the wealthiest planets in the galaxy.

Their lives weren't always peaceful. At least 3 times a year, a neighboring planet would wage war. Everyone was after their money and their abilities. After a planet of beasts kidnapped a fleet of Trwqoyians soldiers, they boiled them alive and developed powers. News spread and planets in the galaxy, especially the planet, best written in English as "Bkptud" and the planet of beasts were constantly after their power.

Trwqoyians were the strongest. Even with hundreds of fleets against them they managed to win every battle. Women and men, civilians and warriors alike fought hard for their planet. And prevailed every time. They eradicated the planet of beasts, leaving them on the edge of extinction. Other planets seeing this brutal desecration of the beasts withdrew. All but the planet of Bkptud remained at war.

Hellim was the son of the ruler of Trwqoy, Xltwey. At 17, his father was struck down in battle and Hellim was named the new ruler. He was their only son, and his mother was too weak to take over after Xltwey's death. He had no idea what to do. He didn't even want the throne. To constantly fight in wars and decide what cruel fate to give prisoners of war. He wanted nothing of it. He wanted nothing more than to live a peaceful life with Yulogna, a peasant his parents forbade him to marry. He begrudgingly married a woman his mother chose and ruled for a year. To his luck, all but one war happened. And with the guidance of Gravick, he didn't have to do anything. The citizens did not like how Hellim was ruling. He was nothing like the success of his father. Hellim agreed with them, but there was nothing he could do but ask his wife to bear a son as soon as possible. The sooner the child grew up, the sooner he could have him take the throne.

Years went by and it seemed like peace had finally come to Trwqoy. The citizens all believed Hellim had some hand in this and praised him. Hellim was confused but gladly took credit.

One day, 20 spaceships filled with Bkptudites landed on Trwqoy. The leader of the Bkptudites, begged Hellim to let them seek refuge on his planet. Their planet had gone to waste and was not habitable. They couldn't turn to the planet of beasts because it was too cold, and the next planet was too far.

Hellim and the council of elders discussed seriously about the sudden change of heart and desperation. Hellim persuaded them to let them live in the countryside. It was similar to their land and far enough away from Trwqoyian villages. They agreed and the Bkptudites moved to the countryside.

Gravick told Hellim something was off. But Hellim ignored him. He told him reassuring things like, "Maybe they realized they're no match for us."

As the months went by, the citizens grew uneasy. The Bkptudites were peaceful, but they would do weird things that made the Trwqoyians uncomfortable. They couldn't be trusted. Gravick as well as Hellim's newly appointed guards, Hrayrp, Jtrepo, Lyour, Malarik, Kwtamg, and Muragrak expressed concerns among the people.

But Hellim assured them that nothing would happen. They were peaceful and had changed. It had been months since they arrived and nothing bad happened. They were just not accustomed to their weird practices. He told them every day, "They can be trusted."

However, one day a Bkptudite "accidentally" killed a Trwqoyian child. He not only ran him over with a cart, but he also stomped him to death for screaming, and devoured his head. This enraged the Trwqoyians, and riots broke out into the streets. Hellim did his best to calm both sides to no avail.

He met with the leader of the Bkptudites to discuss the matter. He pushed for punishment on the Bkptudite who killed the child. But their leader expressed his grievances. Gravick who was in the room spoke up.

"We gave you a home, we ignored your weird practices and your disgusting habits of looking at us like livestock! The least you can do is shut up when your people do something as horrible as what he did to that child!" He looked at Hellim who was unsure of himself. "You should be lucky Hellim is kind enough to not execute him. He has the right to do so. He is the ruler of this land, not you. I suggest you get off your high horse and thank him for an easy punishment."

"You!" the Bkptudite leader stood up.

Hellim held his hand up. "Both of you stop. Gravick is right, I do hold the power to do so. However I will not. If you disagree that imprisonment is not a good idea, then you must deal with it. I will not show favoritism to the people who once slaughtered my nation and the man who killed my father. He is to suffer life in prison. We will strip him of his powers, and he can repent the death of that child."

The Bkptudite glared at him. He didn't utter a word and left the palace.

"I told you," Gravick said. "We all told you. They are not to be trusted. Whether some of them are peaceful or not, they will continue to kill us. They do not see us as beings, only livestock. I suggest you have them leave as soon as possible. I am sure even you are willing to give them fuel to make it to another planet."

Hellim rested his face in his hands. "Not now Gravick. I do not think they are untrustworthy. They just need to adjust to our customs and undo the hatred and evil that was once their society."

"If I may be so frank your highness," Gravick said, his tones clipped. "You are too unreasonable. As king, you need to be cutthroat. Not this peacemaker. You cannot reason with creatures like them. What they did in the past, is still who they are. It has not been that long since they were invading our planet. It has not been long since that leader cut down your father. If not for Malarik, he would have gained his powers. They come to our planet and believe they own it. They still look at us as if *we* are beneath *them*!"

"I know…" Hellim said. "I get it, I'm not meant to be king! If I could change that, I would. If our laws allowed women to take over, then I would step down and Myetorp could lead. She's the better fit, but there is nothing I can do!"

"You can change your ways and see the universe as it is!" Gravick approached Hellim and grabbed him by the collar. "You need to wake up to reality. Not everyone is as peaceful as you and Lyour. You cannot find a peaceful solution to everything. War is required. War is what has kept our people alive."

He let go of Hellim. "I am sorry for touching you. But I cannot sit by and watch you lead our people to ruin."

They stood in silence before Hellim spoke, "Then what do you plan to do about it?"

"Nothing, I cannot do anything without your permission. If, I had the option, I would slaughter them all."

Hellim sighed. "I will do as you suggest. Send word to the Bkptudites, they are to leave at once. They will restock whatever food they need and are free to take as much fuel as they want and depart no later than tomorrow night. Anyone left without express permission from myself, will be imprisoned and deported."

"Right away sir." Gravick bowed and turned to leave. "You're making the right decision."

Gravick left the room, the door slamming behind him.

"Am I?" Hellim said. He looked out the window at the royal city. It was the only place that wasn't ruined in the riots. He watched as the Trwqoyians bustled along the streets. Working, and performing. He couldn't help but feel bad for the Bkptudites. He was taking away their security and who knew if their next destination would let them stay. But the more they stayed there, the bigger their problems grew and the more the citizens were unrest. He would be looked down upon forever and Gravick would lose the little respect that remained for him. "I hope I'm doing the right thing."

It was the last night the Bkptudites were to remain on Trwqoy. Hellim had retired to bed. He slept in a separate room from his wife and son. Though as the years went by, he did grow to love her, just not as much as he did Yulogna. And his son, he loved him unconditionally. Whether he was the product of an unhappy union or not. He just didn't feel right lying with her when he knew his heart would always belong to Yulogna.

As he rested, Lyour burst into his room. "Your highness, wake up!"

Hellim was jarred awake. "What is it?"

"The Bkptudites are attacking Trwqoy!" Lyour looked devastated. "It seems, from my guess, their planet wasn't actually destroyed. Thousands of fleets…thousands…"

Hellim jumped out of bed. He dressed as he asked, "Is everyone stationed for battle?"

"Yes, we are awaiting your orders."

"Do not wait for me. Fight and defend Trwqoy!"

Lyour nodded and ran as fast as he could.

Hellim ran into his wife's room and woke her. He ordered her to take their son and hide in the underground passage. She insisted on fighting, but he told her their son was more important and needed protection. She reluctantly agreed and ran to retrieve him. Hellim put on his warrior's garb and headed to battle.

They were obviously unprepared, and most of their citizens outside the royal city were massacred in their sleep. They were outnumbered. How many forces did the Bkptudites have? Their population was nowhere near as many ships as there were.

Then it occurred to Hellim, it wasn't just the Bkptudites, but many planets were using this time to invade. How long had they planned this? Was that the reason so many planets stopped attacking at once?

He along with the warriors fought their hardest to save their planet. But as the streets filled with lifeless corpses, it was inevitable. All who remained were a group of warriors and some civilians. 30 survivors including Muragrak, Hrayrp, Gravick, Yulogna, Malarik, Lyour, Kwtamg, Parahae, Jtrepo, and Myetorp. Hellim ordered them to the last intact ships while he got his wife and son.

He ran killing everyone in his path until he reached the palace. He ran to the underground passage, and they were nowhere to be found. His heart sank and he felt nauseous. He searched the palace grounds for them but could not find them. A trail of blood led from the main hall into his son's room. Hellim ran into his room. Blood was splattered on the walls and floor. He looked to his son's bed, where his son laid lifeless. His wife had just fallen over when he arrived and standing above her body was the leader of the Bkptudites.

Hellim yelled in rage. He charged the Bkptudite, and they clashed. Hellim unleashed all his rage and hatred and killed the leader.

Gravick went after Hellim to aid in his rescue. When he arrived, Hellim gasped in pain. His grief was taking over him and he was going into Yurtpo. Gravick ran to him and grabbed his shoulders. He mumbled, his eyes closed, and a dim light shined. Hellim had calmed down. Gravick had the ability to cancel Yurtpo in the early stages. It was a technique only passed down to the family that guarded the king.

It took some time for Hellim to gain his conscious again. He took his son and Gravick carried his wife, and they went to the underground passage. They didn't know what was in store for their planet, but Hellim didn't want them eating his wife and child. He buried them deep in the ground and headed to the last ship with Gravick. They parted Trwqoy. They looked back at their planet one last time, a hole in their hearts.

Hellim spent most of the time on the aircraft apologizing. He knew it was his fault. No matter how much they denied it. Even if he could not control the number of species that attacked, maybe they would have had a better chance of survival had the enemy not been on their land.

But they couldn't dwell on it forever, they needed to find a safe place to live. But who could they trust? They couldn't discern what planets partook in their genocide. They went to the farthest part of the galaxy and decided to go to earth. They knew the inhabitants weren't as advanced and could not possibly have abetted in their erasure.

On the way, they were attacked by an enemy ship that trailed behind them. Two ships of warriors were destroyed and theirs was close to breaking. They made it into their escape pods and left before their ship exploded. In the confusion of the blast, the enemy ship didn't see them escape. They focused on the charred bodies that floated through space.

They were even more distraught. All hope seemed lost. Who knew if these monsters would soon take over earth? Muragrak took the loss of their planet the hardest. But seeing even more people die when they thought they were in the clear broke him. He cried to Hrayrp whose ship was the closest to him. But he hid his ailments. Soon he went into Yurtpo. Gravick couldn't help him and Muragrak changed course to the unknown.

Hrayrp was hurt the most by this development. He and Muragrak were childhood friends and they confided everything to each other. Gravick kept watch over Hrayrp, and they made it to earth. Separated from each other. They continued to seek approval to stay, and they did their best to help the humans save their world and advance to almost the same level as Trwqoy.

~Headquarters - Hellim's room~

Hellim woke up. He wondered why he had to dream about the past. There was nothing he could do to change that. But the people on earth did not deserve such malice. The child was no different than how they were at the loss of family. He understood what the boy was going through. Did he agree with it? Not in the slightest. But to punish him to death at such a young age? Hellim had committed far worse crimes and a death toll over thousands. Did they think he deserved to die for his gullible beliefs? He wasn't going to make the same mistake again. But the child should live even if it meant years of imprisonment. It was a better outcome than death.

He needed to think of a way to get the child on their side. Surely, he still ranked higher than their unanimous decision. They still treated him like royalty even though they were equals on earth. He didn't know how he would respond when he saw the child in person, but he hated the idea of loathing him. He was still wet behind the ears like he was years ago. He agreed with Lyour and wanted to fulfil his wishes. But if the child showed no signs of change, he should be imprisoned. But not on an insufferable planet. He was the product of violence that led to his hatred of them.

And as much as Hellim wanted to believe, he had the blood of Hrayrp and Muragrak coursing through his veins. It would be like killing his own.

~Headquarters~

"I swear they are going to be the downfall of our species," Gravick ranted. He stormed down the hall.

"I couldn't agree more," Malarik said, following after him. "But you have to admit that it's nice not everyone has changed. Even if it's causing problems, at least they're still themselves."

"The loss of our home is affecting us all differently," Jtrepo said. "If they want to keep the peace there's no harm in that. We simply have to make sure this boy doesn't kill anyone else."

"And I can't guarantee to do that without killing him," Gravick said. "I will not standby idly like I did with Hellim. We are equals and I will stop at nothing to ensure our people survive."

"And how do you plan on doing that?" Malarik said. "We have no idea what the kid looks like."

"If we can't figure out who he is," Gravick said, stopping. He turned to them and said quietly, "We destroy the earth."

"Are you crazy?" Jtrepo asked. "You're going to kill innocent lives over one child?"

"There are billions of them, even if I killed half their population, they would still be the majority. Think about Trwqoy. How many people died over that one Bkptudite?"

Malarik joined in, "He's right. It wouldn't cause them to go extinct. I'm willing to take that risk if it guarantees his death."

"War is required," Gravick said. "We can't stop whatever happens. We may have stopped their petty wars. But this child is causing one he cannot win."

"And what are you to do if this angers the humans and they wage war?"

"Then we kill the rest of them. Simple as that." Gravick continued to walk. "I will raise the issue at the next meeting. If anyone else dies, then I'm pushing for their erasure."

235

Jtrepo stayed quiet. There was no point trying to persuade him. He and now Malarik had made up their minds. Once they were determined to do something, there were no other options they would settle for. He just hoped this kid didn't continue.

~Myetorp's living quarters~

"How long are you going to stay mad at me?" Parahae complained.

"You didn't stand by me. You promised you would always have my back and you didn't," Myetorp said.

"I'm sorry. But I know you don't really mean to kill that child."

"I do. Once you resort to murder, you are no longer a child."

"I disagree." Parahae shook his head. "Do take into account that he only became this way because Muragrak slaughtered hundreds of people in South Korea. And I'm sure Hrayrp's biased nature didn't help the situation."

"So you're saying they deserved to die?"

"No one deserves death. But you and the others are doing the same thing as him. I agree with Lyour, to end this cycle of death. And to carry forth his wish, is to protect this child and change his mind. He has Yurtpo blood coursing through him. He's not sane."

"He is sane," Myetorp yelled. "He ate Hrayrp. His mentality should have adapted to his too! He is choosing to kill."

"Yurtpo blood is stronger than ours. And do not act as if Hrayrp's ego had not grown since we arrived here. Consider that he may have inherited Hrayrp's ego and not his logical side."

"I can't believe you're speaking ill of our dead comrades. You're the worst!"

"I am not speaking ill of anyone. My point is that the kid is gone in the head. We cannot blame him for his actions when reason is not an option. Trust me, I despise that child. Seeing Kwtamg's body angered me. But I listen to reason. And reason said he is not mentally stable. He is a child that has done a terrible act."

"An act that cannot be undone." Myetorp slammed her hands on a table. "Tell me Parahae, if he were a man and he committed the same atrocities, would you still fight this hard to save his life? Even if he was mentally ill?"

"I…" Parahae didn't know what to say. Would he have done the same for an adult? He was a demented child that was grieving and taking his

236

hatred out on innocent beings. Leaving in his path, more bodies than that of what he lost.

Myetorp smirked. "You know I'm right. If he were an adult, none of you…maybe on the exception of Hellim and Yulogna… would be standing up for him. You would be the first to suggest executing him on sight. But because he's a child, you think he deserves a second chance? Do not kid yourself. He is a monster and should be treated as such."

Parahae didn't respond. He stared at the ceiling.

"So what? Are you going to ignore me?"

"That is not why." Parahae sat up. "You are right that I would not stand up for an adult. An adult would have common sense and know right from wrong. We don't know how old this child is. But I can guarantee he is at an age where he doesn't understand the effects of his actions. That is why I stand for him. Do I think he should be punished? Yes, but death is too harsh a punishment. A few years in prison and he will learn his lesson."

"You're letting Hellim's gullibility rub off on you."

"I am not letting anything rub on me. I am speaking from a place of compassion. That is where we never stood eye to eye. I always disagreed with you. But because I love you, I never spoke my mind. You are as ruthless and coldhearted as your father was!"

"Do not speak about him that way. He was a ruler. If not for him, we would have been wiped out long before. His death is proof of that." Myetorp sat beside Parahae. "I love you as well, but we will never agree on this. And if more of my comrades die, it will be your fault as well as my stupid brother's. I…do not wish to have children with you."

Parahae sighed. He nodded and walked out of the room. To think that child would come between their relationship. Parahae wished he wasn't wrong. More was at stake than he imagined. He walked until he bumped into Yulogna.

"Why are you so glum?" she asked.

"The death of our comrades…" he paused. "As well as the end of my relationship with Myetorp."

"Oh no," she gasped. "Was it because you agreed with us?"

"Partly. She wants that child dead, and I cannot let it happen. If she wants to find another mate, then so be it. I cannot force her to stay with me." Parahae walked away.

Yulogna sighed then went to Myetorp's room. She tapped on the door. "It's me."

"What is it," Myetorp asked, opening the door.

"May I come in?"

Myetorp moved to the side and Yulogna walked in. Yulogna continued, "I heard your decision to find another mate."

"News travels fast, doesn't it?" Myetorp shook her head.

"Not at all. I just ran into Parahae and he told me." Yulogna sat at their table. "Are you really willing to ruin your relationship with him over this child?"

"It's not just a child," Myetorp shouted. "It is a monster that is killing us off. How much longer are we to take this abuse? Parahae doesn't agree with me, he looked down on me and my father."

"I do not think he looks down on you. Yes, he doesn't agree with your beliefs, but he loves you dearly. And I know you love him too. Do not force yourself to mate with someone you do not love. I know you are like me in the sense that we do not want another male to touch us. Are you willing to suffer through the mating process with Gravick?"

Myetorp shuddered at the thought and they laughed.

"That is the first time I have seen you smile since the news developed. Myetorp, please reconsider and tell Parahae you want only him."

"I will tell him in time. But for now, I want him to think it's over. Unless he comes back begging, I will wait."

"I see the humans are influencing you," Yulogna said, amused.

Myetorp grew serious. "Yulogna, do you really think this child deserves to live?"

"I do. I understand more than all of you, what Yurtpo is and what it does to your mentality. If we cannot handle it, this child 3 or 4 times smaller than us, will smother in it."

"But he ingested Hrayrp."

"That is not enough. If it were that simple, do you think it wouldn't be a serious disease among us?"

"I just can't forgive him for what he did."

"Forgiveness is crucial to growth. I do not condone what he did. And it is painful to remember what Kwtamg and Lyour looked like. And it hurts to image how we will find Hrayrp, but Lyour's words are absolute. End the cycle of violence. This child will learn to stop his hate and our people will coexist peacefully with the humans."

"And if he doesn't?"

"He will. There is no way he does not hold an ounce of remorse for his actions. If it takes him years to see the problem, then imprisonment and time to think without outside influences is what he needs."

Myetorp nodded. She didn't agree fully with Yulogna, but she explained things in a way that made sense.

Yulogna continued, "You and the others are not alone in your resentment. Even I hated this child. But after long consideration, I realized he was not of mind. He is also young. And children do not think the same as adults, especially human children. They are slower developers than most species. We have to be patient with them and understand them. His experience is no different than ours."

"While you make sense," Myetorp said. "I disagree on our experience. He experienced a few deaths, we experienced thousands and a lost home. Yet we remain calm and collected. But how long do we have to be the ones to take the high ground? At some point, these humans may turn on us, are we to not defend ourselves then?"

"We can defend ourselves when the time comes, but we cannot kill based off anger. I cannot answer your question about high ground. I do not know what the right answer is. But there's no harm in it."

Myetorp looked dissatisfied with her answer but gave up. She changed the subject, and they spent the rest of the afternoon talking about nothing of importance.

Hellim and Parahae set off to search for Hrayrp's body. Since he had buried Lyour and Kwtamg, they figured he might have done the same for him. They searched where his castle was and found his body buried in the courtyard. Only his head was missing. They were relieved his body wasn't as mutilated as Kwtamg's, but it made her death all the sadder. Why just her? After retrieving his body, they removed his castle and gave him a proper burial.

The gods made an announcement to the public. They explained that Hrayrp, Lyour, and Kwtamg had stepped down from their obligations and wanted to relax in a far-off galaxy. They also mentioned that they were taking a break from their commitments for two months. If anything serious were to happen, they would step in, but for the meantime, they were off duty. This was of course, not because they were tired but because they needed time to plan a defense against Jae.

Jae didn't mind. He was taking time off to study martials arts. He heard the announcement while he trained at a dojo in Japan. He planned a map of the different countries he would learn a fighting style from. He needed to build up strength. His body wasn't healing as fast as it used to. The injuries sustained from Lyour had healed, but that night caused him a huge disadvantage in his regeneration. He learned he had super strength, most likely Hrayrp's other ability, and worked to improve it. He still couldn't use telekinesis without drawbacks. And he could only puff out paralyzing mist. He kept his powers a secret from people and never used it unless to train.

Jae skipped past his training arc. He knew Bianca wouldn't be interested in his journey to learn how to fight, nor did he want to tell it.

~Jae~

Five months had passed. The gods went back to work months ago. They apologized to the societies that depended on them the most. Jae knew the break was for him. He wondered what they had up their sleeve. There was no way he would be let off the hook for killing 3 gods. He continued to train for additional months as he lay low to avoid any attacks from them.

Logically, he knew they had no idea what he looked like, but fear crept in, and he was paranoid. His last training session was in America. He learned boxing as well as MMA. He was still new, but he was considerably good for only learning these techniques in 5 months.

He still carried the holographic magazine. He searched the web for any news on their whereabouts. The green god, Parahae, was in Brazil. He along with 4 other gods were sent there to help with a bush fire. Jae knew not to underestimate them, but out of the 5, he looked the weakest and easiest to take on by himself.

He didn't know what ability he had, but Jae wanted more power. He wanted to be the only being on earth with power. Power to destroy them once and for all.

He hopped on a flight to Brazil. Thankfully throughout his training he was able to make money, starting with selling his hoover scooter. Busted and falling apart, it was still worth a lot of money. He booked a room at a cheap hotel. He needed to rest. He didn't know what was ahead of him. He was confident he wouldn't die, he escaped death on numerous occasions and was cocky.

The gods finally made it to the Amazon. The fire had spread covering more acres than they originally heard. Gravick was in command. He brought along Jtrepo and Parahae. Their abilities proved useful in this situation. Jtrepo could control weather, and his rain was crucial to extinguishing the flames, Parahae controlled earth, Gravick didn't know

240

what exactly he could do to help, but out of the remaining 3, he was more useful, and Gravick was a water wielder. Malarik and Myetorp were brought for added defense. They knew Jae would use this opportunity to attack one of them. With Malarik's cloning, Gravick hoped Jae went after one of them. If it was destroyed, they would know he was there. If Jae went after the real Malarik or the other gods, they would ping their location.

The trip to the Amazon was awkward. Myetorp was still giving Parahae the silent treatment, but they were back to sharing a bed. She still hadn't told him she wanted to continue dating him, but she would tell him eventually.

Originally, they were to work in pairs, but with the spread of the fire, it was no longer possible. Jtrepo, Gravick, and Parahae needed to split up to cover more ground. Malarik and Myetorp would run around the forest watching for any strange movement or people.

They began working upon arrival. Myetorp with her super speed ran around the forest checking everyone who passed and shooed animals to safer regions of the forest.

The next morning Jae set off for the Amazon. It took him hours to get there. By the time he reached the area the fire was in, it was already night. He looked at the orange glow that illuminated the sky, the smoke rising. He didn't care about the fire. There were 4 other gods that could take care of it. He put on a mask and black goggles. For two reasons, one, to protect himself from the smoke, and two, to hide his identity from the other gods.

He jumped down into the forest. He was stealthy and made sure no one saw him. He searched the forest for Parahae. He was green, he could blend in with his surroundings, so Jae had to look carefully.

He saw Parahae and a black god run into each other, discuss something then separate. He trailed after Parahae. He followed him to a secluded area. The fire spread quickly, surrounding them. Parahae turned around to escape the blaze and saw Jae approaching him.

He sighed. "Do you really need to do this right now?"

"Best time to do it. The others can handle the fire."

"No, only 3 of us can. You're just making this more difficult," Parahae complained. "Why can't you wait until we're finished to fight me?"

"Because the others will jump in."

"I don't have time nor the will to fight you child. Just go." Parahae smashed the ground with his palm. Dirt rose and smothered the flames.

"What's your ability?" Jae asked.

"None of your business. Go to a safe place, challenge me another time." Parahae turned around to run.

Jae threw a throwing knife at Parahae, and he blocked using a dirt wall. Jae thought, *What is his ability? Earth? That's not bad.*

Parahae sighed again. "Do you really want to do this? Why not join our side and help your planet?"

"Not interested," Jae denied harshly.

"I figured as much," Parahae said, scratching his head. "You only want to murder us indiscriminately."

"I'm not attacking you for no reason."

"In theory no, Lyour explained it to us. You're blaming us for the death of your siblings, right? It's still killing us for no reason. We didn't kill them. Kwtamg and Lyour didn't kill them, Hrayrp didn't, I haven't even been to South Korea yet."

"That's not the reason. It's because I've seen your Yurtpo. If someone like Lyour can do it, then you things are even more dangerous. You aren't safe for humans. You can kill us if the slightest discomfort causes Yurtpo. You're better off dead."

"You think so?" Parahae moved both his hands behind his back. He was going to ping his location but didn't. He thought about the risks if Myetorp were to come. She was the fastest and would get there before backup arrived. Images of Kwtamg flashed in his mind. He would deal with him by himself. If that failed, then he would lead him to another god. "You're just as guilty for your murderous ways. Doesn't that mean you're better off dead as well?"

"It's different."

"How so?" Parahae scoffed. "Because you don't see us as beings? Because you hate us over something we had no control over?"

"You did have control," Jae sneered. "If you had come when we reported missing people, you could have stopped all of this from happening. But you thought you were above us. None of this would have happened if you never came to earth!"

"Well, it would have happened either way, whether we were there or not. You seem to know more about that situation than you're letting on."

"I saw Muragrak kill someone, but no one believed me."

"So you knew about him but chose not to tell us? You're at fault for your siblings' deaths. Maybe if you had said something they would be alive. You're just taking out your regrets on us. Maybe you need to sit down and apologize to the dead. Their deaths are on you."

"Shut up," Jae shouted. "You don't know what you're talking about!"

"I think I do," Parahae said. "You're in pain over the loss of your people and you're lashing out at us. But that will never bring them back. Killing more innocent people won't change that."

"You aren't *people*, you're not human! You don't know what pain is!"

"I don't?" Parahae stepped closer to Jae. "Trust me child, *you* do not know what pain is. Pain is the destruction of your planet and the genocide of your people. Being one of the only to survive with the burden of saving your species from extinction, only to have a *child* throwing a fit kill the last of us. You have no idea what pain really is. Yes, you lost someone but guess what, every person in this galaxy has lost a loved one."

Parahae was a few feet from Jae. He continued, "I am not erasing your pain and your sadness but do not act as if you're the only person in pain. Every second there is a person dying. No one but you has gone to the extreme of killing innocent people just because they're not of the same species. Cease your anger and find help. You're only hurting more people and continuing a cycle of hate. You've done horrible things to my comrades. The way you killed Kwtamg was brutal! By your logic, I have every right to kill you, but I won't! See how an adult deals with pain and grow up."

"She deserved it. She wanted to torture me to death."

"Do you not comprehend how cruel it was? Actions speak louder than words. She would have never done something as horrid as what you did. Don't you feel any sympathy about her death?"

"I don't feel an ounce of remorse. She deserved it. Do you think it was okay for her to torture me while she waited for back up? She wished the worst death on me. So I gave a slightly less terrible death."

"You're a demented child. You need help."

"You don't understand. You're heartless."

"I'm not the heartless one. You are the one who doesn't understand. No matter what excuse you give, your actions are not justified. And they never will be."

"As Kwtamg told me, 'Shut up. Warriors do not speak on the battlefield.'" Jae moved into a fighting stance. "It's time to atone for your sins."

"What sins?" Parahae asked.

"Your sin for living." Jae lunged at Parahae.

Parahae dodged and slammed the ground. Roots shot from the ground and formed a circle around Jae. Before it could tighten, Jae swung Magord and cut them into pieces.

Yeah, I figured it wouldn't be easy... Parahae thought. He jumped above Jae and ran away.

"What is with you monsters running away? What cowards!"

"If we're such cowards, yield your sword!"

"Never!" Jae said. His nose started to bleed. He rose 8 throwing knives in the air. He threw one at Parahae. Parahae dodged and jumped into the trees.

He swung from the branches. He looked at his communication watch and searched for the nearest god... minus Myetorp. The closest was Malarik, but he was still miles away.

Jae continued to throw more knives. "What are you a monkey?!"

"Gotta adapt to your environment!"

As they ran through the forest, Parahae suppressed the fire with dirt. "You might as well give up child! You can't keep up with me. Not even in a hundred years would you be on my level."

"Shut up and just fight me!"

"Not happening. You're powerful, I will not underestimate you. Go home to your family...oh wait, you killed them." Parahae laughed. He knew it wasn't a good idea to provoke Jae, but if that was enough to catch him, he would continue. He smiled and waited for Jae's reaction.

Jae didn't respond. He glared at Parahae. His steps didn't falter. Parahae knew he was hiding it. His eyes told him just how furious he was.

Parahae continued, "This is your last chance child. Cease this fight. You will not win."

"Come down here and try me."

"How about you come up here? Can't get everything you want in life."

Jae didn't respond. He looked down at the ground. Jae's nose bled again.

Is he giving up? Parahae smiled. Parahae looked down, the rocks in front of him had risen. He looked back at Jae.

Jae jumped right, in one swift motion onto the trunk of a tree, then one of the rocks. He jumped to a tree on the left then another rock higher than the previous one, then another tree. He kept jumping until he was as high as Parahae. He jumped on the branches.

Parahae was impressed. The kid had more skill than he thought. But it was one thing to get into a tree and another to stay in the trees. He moved his arm swiftly and the branch in front of Jae bent downwards.

Jae gasped and fell back onto the ground. He tucked and rolled back into a sprint.

He needed a break from telekinesis. He didn't know how much his body could handle. How was he going to get him down?

"You know what?" Jae shouted. Parahae glanced back at him. "I think I'm going to go after a different god. You're just going to keep running."

"Ha! Good luck," Parahae said, calling his bluff. "I'm the only god in the area that doesn't want to kill you on sight."

Jae scooped up a rock and threw it at Parahae.

"You talk about my methods, but isn't that primitive? What, can't use your… excuse me, Hrayrp's psychokinesis?"

Jae still didn't respond. He continued to throw sticks and stones at Parahae. Parahae didn't block. They didn't hurt nor did he need to waste his abilities. Jae picked up a boulder and threw it. Parahae gasped and let go of the branch. He pulled two trees forward above his head and the boulder fell to the ground.

So he figured out Hrayrp's super strength. Damn, he thought. He landed on the ground but didn't stop running. When he regained his footing, he jumped back into the trees. This time he didn't swing. He stretched the branches to make a path, pulling each branch across to the other, and ran along the branches.

Jae admired his use of his skills. He wanted to take note for when it became his. So far Jae only saw the one ability. He wondered what his second could be. Regardless, he would take it.

Parahae dialed Malarik's number. "I'm on my way to you. The child is after me. Please do not tell Myetorp."

"Got it, what direction are you running from?"

"I'm north of you. Please head this way."

"I'm surrounded by flames, I will send a clone in my stead," Malarik said. "Please hold on until I get out."

"Alright, I will meet you there."

Jae saw his communication watch flicker and Jae panicked. He thought, *He's already calling for backup? What a weakling!*

Jae thought for a bit. He needed to get him down. Could his body handle just a little more of his psychic abilities? It was worth the risk. Soon Parahae would reach another god. Jae lifted the rocks again and jumped into the trees. He unsheathed Magord. Before Parahae could drop him, Jae lunged forward, Magord leading the way. Parahae turned around and dirt flew into the air. It incased his arms and he blocked Magord.

Jae was stunned. *How could he block Magord?*

Parahae lost his footing and they fell to the ground. Jae stabbed him multiple times, but Magord couldn't impale him. Metal reverberated through the air and sparks flew.

Parahae kicked Jae in the stomach sending him flying to the ground.

"What is that?" he asked, standing up. "Is that your second ability? Some shield?"

Parahae didn't respond. He moved into a fighting stance. Dirt climbed Parahae's legs and incased his body.

Jae wanted that ability. Needed it. With it, he wouldn't get as fucked up by the gods as he had previously. Jae gripped Magord with his hand and swung it downwards diagonally. They waited for a bit, before Jae attacked. He charged Parahae and swung his sword sideways. Parahae used his right arm to knock Jae's sword down. He grabbed Jae's right arm with his left and punched him with his right. Jae reached for Parahae's face with his left arm and Parahae let go of his arm as he dodged backwards.

Jae lunged again and swung his sword diagonally. Parahae blocked again. Jae and Parahae went back and forth, Jae constantly on the offensive. Parahae blocked again, but this time he knocked Magord out of Jae's hand. He hardened his fists and punched Jae. He punched Jae again and again. Jae gained his composure and blocked his next swing. He did a back sweep kick and Parahae fell on his back. Jae twisted his ring and Magord shot into his hand. He stabbed down at Parahae, but his shield was too strong. And each time Jae made a crack in his shield, more dirt would accompany it.

Jae blew paralyzing mist at Parahae. He froze and stared at Jae. Jae smiled. That was the first time since his fight with Lyour that he produced a decent puff of gas, and not on the brink of death at that. He swung down at Parahae, but dirt encased his head and Magord deflected off it. Jae tsked. *The one god that can use its ability without its hands. Just lovely. There has to be some weak spot.*

Jae continued to swing blindly. He hit Parahae's chest, his abdomen, his arms, his legs. Jae was wondering if his ability was that overpowered.

The paralyzing mist wore off and Parahae swiftly grabbed Jae's arm. He broke the dirt mold over his head and kicked Jae off. He stood up and attacked Jae. He couldn't afford to continue the fight. He didn't want Myetorp to run past and he didn't know how long Malarik would be. He slammed the ground and tree roots sprouted from the ground. They encircled Jae. They attacked Jae one at a time and he cut them. It was like fighting a Hydra, every time he cut one root, three more sprouted.

Parahae sat down and watched as Jae struggled. Jae saw him and it angered him. He wanted to slice his head off. He cut another root and threw a throwing knife at Parahae. Parahae didn't move. A dirt wall lifted and blocked the knife. Jae looked around as he swung. There had to be some way to stop the roots or make Parahae stop them. He saw the fire that was covered by Parahae's dirt. He slowly made his way over, pretending to move out of the way of the roots. He reached the spot of dirt and kicked the dirt.

The embers were bright red. Jae cut the roots and they landed on the fire. The cut roots smoked and soon another fire spread.

"Are you crazy?" Parahae shouted. He stopped the root attack and threw more dirt on the fire, smothering it. "We're trying to stop the fires. You can fight without destroying nature."

"Then stop fighting me with wood in a forest fire." Jae shrugged.

This child really is psychotic, Parahae thought. He covered himself with more dirt. He ran at Jae and punched him. He dropped the sword.

Jae staggered backwards but countered with a kick in Parahae's shin. Parahae's knee buckled, and Jae punched him in the face. He used his MMA training and used a takedown move on Parahae. He mounted on top of Parahae and tried punching him. Parahae wrapped his arms around Jae and hugged him tight.

"What are you doing?!" Jae struggled to get out of his hold.

Parahae smiled. Roots grew from the ground and bounded them to the ground.

"Well great, we're both stuck like this. Genius plan," Jae complained.

Parahae didn't respond. He laughed and closed his eyes. Jae felt a jerk and Parahae sunk into the ground. The roots tightened even more around Jae.

Damnit, Jae thought. He tried wriggling his way out, but each move, tightened the roots.

Parahae emerged from the ground in front of Jae and pulled out his watch. He typed something into the watch. He dialed Malarik again. "How far away are you?"

"I'm still a ways away. What happened? Are you still running?" Malarik replied.

"Don't worry. I managed to catch him. I just need a clone to help me get him to the others."

"Are you sure?" Malarik asked. "I can still provide back up."

"No just look for Gravick or Jtrepo and tell them I caught him."

"You really are something," Malarik praised him.

"Yeah well, he wasn't much of a challenge," Parahae teased, glancing at Jae.

Jae glared at him.

He looked back ahead and said, "Send one as quick as you can."

"Gotcha."

Parahae hung up and sighed. "You must have used some dirty trick to kill the others. No way they lost to someone like you. Wait here, I need to extinguish the fires."

Jae didn't respond. He tried moving but the roots tightened again. He needed to get out of there quickly. He knew those things would kill him when they took him back. He wiggled and the roots tightened again. This time, it felt like one of his bones broke. He looked around the ground. Then he remembered Magord. He used his thumb to twist his ring. Magord slid at an intense speed and cut the root around his right hand and into his leg. He grimaced at the pain but with his wrist, slid Magord diagonally away. He twisted his ring again and the blade sliced down his arm.

His right hand was free below the elbow, and he awkwardly whacked at the roots until he was free. He sat up and stretched. Whatever bone broke, hadn't healed, it sent a jolt of pain through his side. He followed the direction Parahae went. Parahae was focused on smothering the fires. Jae snuck slowly to him and stabbed him in the abdomen. Parahae swung backwards and Jae dodged.

"You call us cowards but you attack while our backs are turned."

Jae shrugged. "No such thing as fighting fair when it comes to your life."

Parahae covered himself in dirt. Jae watched where the dirt covered. There had to be a missing spot. He noticed the dirt stopped at his collarbone. Jae remembered the shield around his head. He smiled and thought, *So it's his neck that's his weak spot.*

He lunged at Parahae who held his stomach wound. He regretted telling Malarik to send only a clone. They could do basic things but were extremely weak in comparison to the real god. He tried slamming the ground again, but Jae kicked him backwards. He waited until Parahae was leaning back up and charged him again. He swung quickly and sliced his neck.

Parahae's head rolled along the ground to the feet of Malarik's clone. It stared at the head then back at Jae. Jae's stomach sank. He wasn't ready to fight another one. He threw a knife at it, and it dispersed into a grey translucent goo.

Jae was confused. *What in the hell was that? No way it was that weak.*

Jae wasn't going to wait to find out. He stabbed Parahae's head, grabbed it and ran. He stopped for a second and grabbed a flower that survived the fire and put it on top of Parahae's body. If the black god hadn't seen him, he would have buried him.

He ran as fast as he could through the forest. He didn't care what god saw him, his cover was already blown and if he had to fight, he would do so.

Malarik stood in sheer terror. Whatever his clone saw, he saw as well. And the image of Parahae's head being chopped off haunted him. He quickly dialed the other gods.

"The child killed Parahae," he screamed. He entered the coordinates Parahae sent him and continued, "I knew I shouldn't have listened to him. I should have gone anyways!"

"Slow down," Gravick said. "Is the child here?"

"I don't know if he's still in the area, but he killed Parahae. Anyone who's close should search for the child. I'll retrieve Parahae."

"Myetorp," Jtrepo said. "Do not go to Parahae. You're the fastest. Find the child and send us the location…. Myetorp!"

Myetorp didn't respond. The moment Malarik sent the coordinates, she ran there. She stared at Parahae's lifeless body and cried. She dropped to her knees and rested her head on his chest.

"I'm so sorry," she cried. She buried her face in his chest and hugged him. "I'm sorry."

Regret filled her mind. If only she had spent more time with him. If only she had told him she still loved him. But it was too late. She could never change her actions and she would never feel his warmth again.

She screamed so loud and horrid as she held him, her cries could be heard through the forest. And they all turned in the direction of the cry.

"Not good," Gravick said. He was the farthest away, but he needed to get to her before she went Yurtpo. He ran as fast as he could. He dialed the group again. "Whatever you do, do not go to Myetorp! Malarik, send one of your clones to watch her from afar. I'm hurrying there as fast as I can."

"Got it," Malarik said. He worried about losing another comrade. He hoped Myetorp would be strong enough to fight it. He split two more clones and sent one to search for Jae and the other to watch Myetorp.

She growled and her breathing was heavy. She tried her best to fight it, but her grief was too strong. Her skin turned purple and she grew twice in size. Malarik called Gravick again and said it was too late.

Gravick called the group and said, "We need to apprehend her. It's better we stop her than for her to die painfully. Jtrepo, you continue to stop the flames. Malarik and I will deal with Myetorp."

"Understood," Jtrepo said, solemnly. He was grateful he wouldn't have to deal with the pain of striking her down. He focused on the fires as he cried.

"Malarik," Gravick said. "I will call you personally. Keep your eyes on her whereabouts."

"Right," he said. "I will arrive before you. Just try to get here as soon as possible."

Malarik took a deep breath as he approached the location his clones were in. The last one squished to goo. Myetorp turned around and growled at him.

"If only you saw what the boy looked like. Could've gotten your revenge then." Malarik went to a fighting stance and said, "I'm sorry."

He created 6 clones and they circled her. None of his clones nor himself attacked. He just didn't have the heart to. She inhaled and Malarik flinched. He ran to the side as fire blew from her mouth. She ignored the clones and chased after the real Malarik, spewing fire everywhere.

"I think you have another task," Malarik said, in the call. "She's spreading the fire."

"Of course she is," Gravick complained. They caught up with each other and Gravick threw water at Myetorp. He continued, "Don't run away! All you're doing is spreading it."

"Sorry, I just…"

"I know, but we need to do this for her and for ourselves."

Myetorp swung at Gravick and knocked him into a tree. He fell to his knees and stood up. He sighed and closed his eyes. He gathered his will to kill her.

20 water droplets formed and grew to the size of baseballs. He slowly opened his eyes and launched the balls at her. While they hit her, he formed more water to dowse the flames.

Myetorp shrieked as the water hit her. She blew more flames and Gravick used a water shield to extinguish it. While Myetorp attacked Gravick, Malarik snuck and attacked her from behind. He split 3 clones and they jumped on her. He detached his butterfly sword from his belt and pointed it at Myetorp. She struggled to get the clones off her back while dodging Gravick's water. He took a deep breath and charged. He stabbed her back and she flung him and his clones off. She glared at him, and flames covered her body.

"Not good," Gravick yelled. "She's reaching her limit. We have to hurry!"

"I'm trying!" Malarik cried. He charged her again. He aimed only at her chest. He couldn't fathom stabbing her in the head. But he knew, he couldn't let her go on like that. She would die a painful death if her Yurtpo ended.

He swung and she dodged, Gravick countered and threw water at her. She flew forward back to Malarik, and he swiped. Myetorp blew fire and Malarik jumped to the side. Gravick doused her more.

"Keep this going," Gravick ordered. "I'll keep her fire down, on the next burst you have to stab her!"

Malarik didn't say anything. He nodded and focused on Myetorp's movements. She covered her body in flames and Gravick threw water. Her body sizzled and smoke rose from her skin.

"Now!" Gravick launched more water.

Malarik winced and closed his eyes as he charged her. He opened them and jumped in the air. Myetorp saw him and swung to knock him down. Gravick moved in front of her and blocked her attack. Malarik closed his eyes and stabbed her in the head. Myetorp stopped moving. She stood still before falling to the ground. Blood slowly flowed from her head.

Malarik and Gravick walked until they were standing above Myetorp's body. They said a Trwqoyian prayer, or rather a chant for forgiveness. It was a ritual performed when a warrior went Yurtpo and was struck down by a comrade. It was a way of wishing them a safe travel to the afterlife. As well as making sure the deceased understood there was no other way. It was a hope the deceased warrior didn't curse them a horrible death.

When they finished, Gravick mumbled, "I need to put out the rest of the fires. Carry their bodies to the car and report to Hellim."

Malarik gave a slight nod and did as told. Hellim said after their mission was done, they were to report back to headquarters right away. They would discuss the matters of the killer and what they could do to capture him. When the call was over, Malarik looked down at his once favorite sword and tossed it to the ground. He could no longer look at it without remembering Myetorp's final moments. He cloned 2 of himself and sent them to carry Parahae. He lifted Myetorp and cried sorry to her repeatedly until he placed her in the car. His clone gently laid Parahae next to her. One picked up the flower Jae placed on him. It reached to put it on Parahae, and Malarik slapped the flower out of its hand.

"We're not using that," he said. "What kind of act is this? Who murders someone then does this? I don't care what the others say, I'm killing him no matter what."

Malarik dispersed his clones and sat in the car. He exhaled and closed his eyes. Jtrepo had cleared most of the fire while they fought. Not much remained besides the areas Myetorp reignited and the 2 acres Parahae covered. When Jtrepo and Gravick finished, they met up with Malarik.

Gravick put the ship in autopilot and sat in the back with the others. He said, "When we get back, I'm pushing for what we talked about. The boy's still in the area. If we target this continent, there's no way for him to escape."

Malarik nodded, tears streamed from his eyes.

Jtrepo looked uneasy. He didn't say anything. He was on the fence of agreeing with them, but he couldn't fathom killing hundreds of millions of innocent people. But in that moment, he couldn't voice his disagreeance. They needed to express their hatred and emotions. Who was he to tell them after cutting down a loved one, to silence their anger? What right did he have? Though he was also grieving, he was saved of the heartache of killing her.

~Jae~

Jae ran as fast as he could out of the forest. He didn't know how many of them were on his trail, and he wasn't stopping to check. He put Parahae's head in his bag and ran to his hotel. He couldn't waste any time eating him. Who knew when they would find him? Parahae's shield ability was needed as soon as possible. He scarfed down his head. Even though Jae had only eaten 2 heads, he had gotten used to the taste. Or rather, his tastebuds had gone numb to it.

He waited a day before going to an open field. He sat on the ground and tried to manipulate the dirt. He tried everything he could think of. From swinging his arms like a madman to using his mind. But each time he did, the dirt would lift. He wondered if he could use two abilities that required brain power at the same time? There had to be some trick to it.

Jae gave up. There wasn't enough time to sit and ponder how to use it. Jae wasn't sure of where to go, but he needed to get out of Brazil. He randomly picked Luanda, Angola. He booked a flight and hurried to the airport. He wanted to go back to South Korea, but the gods probably assumed he would, so that was out of the question.

Luanda was one of the world's best space travel cities. It had the biggest space station. It was the most advanced city in the world. A lot happened in Luanda. Jae could easily lose himself in the crowds. Everything in Luanda was expensive. Jae could barely afford a capsule hotel. He only needed to stay there for a few days until the gods lost any traces of him. He worried about the black god seeing him. But there was no way to distinguish who he was. His face was covered. They could search every man with black hair, tall, or skinny and they wouldn't have proof as to who it was nor could they even search millions of people before Jae slipped away again.

In a few days, he would go back to training. The new abilities he had, were crucial to his life. Jae believed he was invincible… if he learned how to use it.

~the gods~
~Headquarters~

Gravick slammed his hands on the navigation table. "I don't care about this boy's mental illness. He's killed half of us! He needs to die!"

"Gravick," Yulogna said. "I understand your pain, but this isn't the way to vent your anger. A life for a life is wrong."

"With all due respect," Malarik interrupted. "Yulogna, you aren't a warrior, you don't understand the ways of this life. Please let us speak amongst ourselves."

"Whether I've fought on the battlefield or not, does not make my opinion any less valid. This child is in Yurtpo, the only reason he hasn't died yet is because of Muragrak's regenerative capabilities."

"Then it's all the more reason to kill him," Malarik said. He looked at his hands. Holding back his tears, he said, "I…I had to kill Myetorp because of Yurtpo, I should be allowed to do the same to him! If he hadn't killed Parahae, she wouldn't be dead!"

"I understand your pain," Yulogna said. She reached over to touch his shoulder.

Malarik smacked her hand away. "Don't erase my anger! I'm entitled to feel this way. Taking away my emotions just because you don't agree, is wrong!"

"I don't want you going Yurtpo," she said.

253

Hellim jumped in and said, "Watch it Malarik. Do not put your hands on her."

"Why?" Malarik responded. "Because she's your mate? Ha! How wonderful for you to not lose her. You don't care about any of us. You never did. You thought only about yourself and what made you look good. None of this would have happened if you hadn't been as stupid and naïve as you are now!"

Hellim didn't respond. He looked down and clenched his fist. What did he say that was wrong? No matter how much it hurt Hellim, at the end of the day, his actions killed his species.

"Malarik," Jtrepo said, touching his shoulder. He shook his head.

"Why do I need to silence myself? I'm not the only one who thinks this way. He needs to hear the truth. Why should I suffer to not hurt his feelings? I'm hurting too. We've lost everything. We lost our home because of him. And now, he wants to save some child because Yulogna thinks it's best. We've lost half our comrades. If anything happens to her, we're doomed." Malarik dropped to his knees and cried. "None of you understand what it was like to kill her. None of you…"

Yulogna kneeled in front of Malarik and hugged him. "I'm not going to erase your pain. Just let me hold you. You're right, I don't understand. I know how much you loved her, and I'm sorry you had to go through it."

Malarik wrapped his arms around her and cried on her shoulder. No one spoke.

After some time, Gravick said quietly, "I want to propose an idea."

Jtrepo's stomach sank. He knew what he was going to say.

"Do you two understand the gravity of our pain? Look at him. It is only right that we exact some kind of vengeance," Gravick continued. "As of right now, the boy is in South America. I say we destroy the continent."

"What?" Yulogna shouted. She let go of Malarik and stood.

Before she could speak, Gravick silenced her. Continuing he said, "It's unfortunate that so many people have to die, but this is our best chance at dealing with him."

"I don't agree," Yulogna shouted.

"Of course you don't," Malarik said, wiping his face and fixing his composure. "A civilian would never understand."

"They'll fear us!"

"Good," Gravick said. "Then we will never have a situation like this again."

"I disagree as well," Hellim finally spoke. "We would only be committing the same crimes as him, but on a larger scale. We would be no different than the species that killed ours."

"You don't have a right to speak on that," Gravick said, through gritted teeth.

"I have some right." Hellim stood. "Yes, I am mostly at fault, but that attack would have happened either way. I cannot discern if we would have survived if we had everyone to fight. But the fact of the matter is that you are attempting the same thing."

"We'll put it to a vote," Gravick said. "You are not in charge of us. You are the king of a planet you failed to protect."

Gravick turned to Jtrepo and Malarik. "All in favor of destroying South America raise your hand."

Malarik raised his hand immediately. Gravick and Malarik looked at Jtrepo. He looked down. He slowly raised his hand.

"Wait Jtrepo," Hellim said. "You know as well as I do that this is wrong. Those innocent people do not deserve to die. They are not at fault for this boy's actions. We can find another way to apprehend him. Do not choose the path of violence."

Jtrepo looked to both sides of the room. Hellim and Yulogna stared at him with worry, and Gravick and Malarik glared at him.

"I—" he finally said. "I disagree."

"You fool," Gravick shouted. "How could you choose them? You were there! You saw what happened!"

"The people of South America don't deserve to die. Whether we're upset or not. Don't believe that I care about this kid's life. Not in the slightest. I want him dead as much as you all. But I don't think it's fair."

"Then what do you suggest we do?" Malarik grimaced.

"I have a method," Hellim said. "We give one warning. We make an announcement across the world for him to turn himself in. We will threaten severe consequences if he does not show up. Intimidation and responsibility will have this child come."

"Great idea," Gravick said, sarcastically. "Why don't we say outright that he's killing us and see how these humans react."

"We don't have to tell them," Yulogna spoke up. "They do not know his crimes. We don't have to specify what he did."

"And what if he speaks up about them?" Jtrepo asked.

"He will not," Hellim said. "That would be confessing to his crimes. And I doubt there will be a human who hides him."

"All in favor of an announcement raise your hand," Yulogna said.

"Wait," Gravick said. "And what happens if he doesn't show? You clearly don't want to take drastic measures."

No one responded.

"Exactly," Gravick said. "This is nothing more than a bluff."

"Well, you have no other choice," Hellim said. "Your notion was denied. All in favor?"

Yulogna and Jtrepo raised their hands. Malarik looked to Gravick then raised his hand.

Malarik shrugged. "I just want to kill him. I don't care what punishment you may throw at me, but the moment I see him, I will kill him."

Gravick sighed. "This better work."

"It will," Hellim said. "On to the next issue. Should we continue our duties?"

"You think now is the time to ask that?" Gravick glared.

"Yes. We still made a promise to better their land. And we need to act as if everything is fine."

"I say we continue," Yulogna said.

"Unfortunately, you need to stay here. You will no longer perform any duties," Hellim said.

"I will continue to help these beings," Yulogna protested.

"No," Hellim shouted. "You are our last hope. You're almost at Lyaniung. We cannot have anything happen to you."

"I agree," Malarik said. "Just stay here. Our survival is more important than their trivial needs."

"It is temporary," Hellim said, placing a hand on her lower back. "Once we catch the child, you are welcome to continue helping."

Yulogna nodded. The loss of the only women left added more stress to her life. But Hellim was right, whether she wanted this or not, it was reality and she needed to save her species. Her Lyaniung was nearing, and she needed to protect the offspring. Lyaniung was when female Trwqoyians laid eggs, the amount ranged based on the woman's health, the poorest health could lay 1, and the healthiest could lay 30. It happened every 4-7 years and stopped when she was towards the end of her life. She had already mated with Hellim, all that was left was safely laying them.

Prior eggs from Myetorp and Kwtamg did not survive on earth. The environment was too harsh. Gravity didn't help either. When they understood the cause was earth, they moved their headquarters to a space city on the moon. The area was heavily trapped, and no one was allowed within 50 feet of the premises. The traps were for any alien species that may have landed. They weren't threatened by the humans.

But to be safe, no one was allowed. Yulogna didn't like staying at the headquarters. The silence on the moon was discomforting.

~Jae~
~Luanda, Angola~

Jae walked around Luanda. He didn't plan on leaving just yet. He enjoyed how different it was from other parts of the world. Aliens were present. This was one of the only cities they were allowed in. Jae loved looking at them. Especially when they would react angrily at him. He enjoyed the space delicacies like fried space squid, nuloiy—a Martian flower roasted with chicken and skewered, and drunghun—he didn't know what it was, it had a horrid smell but a weirdly satisfying taste. He wondered how many delicious foods were in space. He wanted to take a trip to outer space. If he saved up, he could go to a cheap planet like Mars. But…he needed to finish his mission on earth before he took a vacation. Once they were dead, he could move to another planet and restart his life.

As he walked along Main St. eating nuloiy, a news broadcaster switched to every screen on the road. "We have an urgent message from the god Hellim."

The screen switched over to a room that was all white. In the back, he saw different devices and computer screens, and buttons that alternately lit up every 5 seconds. Hellim stepped in front of the camera.

"Attention humans, we are looking for the godeater," Hellim spoke. "He has committed serious crimes on earth. Those crimes cannot be spoken out loud, due to the people he has offended. We ask that the godeater turns himself in or there will be grave consequences. If anyone sees or hears anything suspicious, where a god is located on earth, we ask that you inform us immediately."

The people in Luanda murmured amongst themselves. Who was the godeater? Why was he called that? And what crimes did he commit? Jae didn't listen to the rest of the announcement. He turned around and walked away.

What does it mean by grave consequences? Jae thought. *Does it think with a threat like that, I'll turn myself in? Not happening.*

Hellim's bluff did nothing but justify Jae's actions even more. A threat? Jae wasn't going to sit by and let them threaten him. He needed to kill them and quickly. He didn't know how strong the red one was, but he wasn't going to attack him. Not yet, he needed stronger abilities. He

258

pulled out his holographic magazine. He searched for a picture of the gods. He took a screenshot and opened it in another tab. He crossed off Hrayrp, Lyour, Kwtamg, and Parahae. He looked at the remaining 6. The men looked strong. He wondered if he should target a female next, but after his fight with Kwtamg, he had to be cautious with them as well.

After a while, he couldn't figure out who to kill. He settled for, whichever god was the closest to him. On the exception of the red god and the black god. If he had to rank their strength, it would be the red god as the strongest, then the black god, it always had weapons on it and with the ability Jae saw in Brazil, it looked like trouble. Next would be the blue god, it always wore a frown on its face, then the yellow, and the two women on the bottom, Jae didn't care who was above whom. They were both significantly weaker than the men.

As Jae walked back to his capsule, he overheard two aliens speaking. One was long, slimy, almost like goo, and orange. The other was short, transparent, and green. They both looked like stereotypical nerds. The orange one was wearing broken glasses taped together, and a backpack. The green one also had glasses, he wore a hat, he had large braces, and carried the latest gphhc handheld console.

"But how would the godeater turn himself in?" the orange one asked, in a nasally voice. "No one's allowed by their base."

"Maybe they'll let him go," the green one said. He had a lisp and spit flew out of his mouth with each word. "That would be so cool. He would be the first to enter their base!"

Jae paused and turned to them. "Wait, you know where their base is?"

Four eyes scoffed. "How do you not know? It's common knowledge."

"It's on the moon," metal mouth said. "They try to keep it secret, but everyone knows."

"Wait," four eyes said. "How did you know what we said?"

"You're right," metal mouth exclaimed. Saliva flew out his mouth and Jae flinched backwards.

"I uh," Jae said. "I speak your language."

"Oh yeah," four eyes said. "Then what is it?"

"I don't know," Jae said. "I just learned a language I heard. I don't know what it's called."

"That's impossible," metal mouth said. "You would need to know the name of a language to find study material."

"Well, I didn't have to," Jae said.

"I bet he's wearing fake skin," four eyes said.

"Probably," metal mouth agreed. "Whatever, it doesn't matter what he does. It's way better to look like we do than a human."

Four eyes nodded. "Let's go. He's clearly inferior, he couldn't understand our conversation even if he tried."

"And that skin looks so fake," metal mouth said. "What a waste of money."

They both turned up their noses and walked away. Jae rolled his eyes and continued to his capsule.

As he rested, he thought about their base. The moon was an expensive place to live, let alone get a pass for. If he made enough money, he could attack there. He thought about what kind of attack would work. He couldn't afford any high-tech weapons, at least nothing strong enough to take them on. Jae turned over and went to sleep.

The next morning, he checked out of the Capsule hotel. If he was going to buy a moon ticket, he couldn't afford anything else. He went to the space station.

It was gigantic. It stretched for miles. Spaceships were seen high above the building. To reach them, there were elevators that carried 18 passengers. Inside, the station was all light grey, the building was made of metal, the inside reflected the outside, except it was overcrowded. Passengers could barely walk past without bumping into each other. The rows of clerks had 10 people in each line. In the express lane, passengers scanned their retinas and a ticket printed out.

Jae checked out the flight prices. His mouth dropped when he saw the prices. The cheapest flight, which included terrible shock, no seatbelts, and slower travel, was 40 million KZ. There was no way he could make that much in a short time. He couldn't afford to waste any more time. Who knew what those gods would do? They needed to be eliminated as soon as possible. He looked around the station. He wondered if he could sneak on a flight. But how could he do it? He could hide in the cargo bay, but he didn't know where it was.

Jae tsked and walked away. He would have to fight them on earth. He would save up just in case they escaped to the moon permanently.

As he left the station, a man dressed in a cloak, his face covered, called him. "Psst! Hey kid, come here."

Jae looked at him. He was going to ignore him, but the man continued to call him. Jae rolled his eyes and approached him.

"I saw you looking at ticket prices. I can help you get to where you need to go," the man said.

"How?" Jae asked.

"I know someone that can get you on the flight."

"How much?"

"For you, how about 12,000 kwanza?"

"I don't have that much," Jae declined.

"Wait, wait." The man grabbed Jae's arm. "I can go lower. How about 2,000 KZ? If you're willing to deliver something, we can go cheaper."

"What would I need to deliver?"

"I can't disclose that. I just need you to deliver a few packages. If you do that, I can get you on a flight."

"So it's something illegal?" Jae asked. The fact that the man was so desperate and secretive, it was easy to tell. Jae wasn't willing to commit a crime. He was an upstanding citizen. But he needed to finish his mission. He sighed. "Alright. When do I leave?"

"Come back tomorrow at 3 PM," the man said. "Thank you. Thank you."

Jae ignored him and walked away. He thought, *That takes care of travel expenses. Now if only I could find some weapons.*

He searched the streets for an underground market. Every city had them and there was no way, a city as large as Luanda, didn't have at least one or two. He thought about asking around, but he didn't need any traces of himself nor did he want to alert the police.

After a few hours of searching, Jae found a market. He searched the stalls for high tech items. None of them carried anything. But there were old-school weapons. Like C4, dynamite, pistols, a musket, and other useless items. Even old-school weapons were expensive. They were deemed collectables even though they could be bought for half the price in a neighboring country. Jae didn't have the patience nor the funds to travel that far. He gave up and booked a capsule room for the night.

The next day, he arrived at the space station an hour early. The shady man from the day before still lingered outside of the station.

"Yo," Jae said.

The man turned around. A sliver of his eye peeked from beneath the cloak and he smiled. "You actually showed up! Ha HAH! You're early but come on, I'll lead you to him."

Jae readied his luggage in case he needed to defend himself. They arrived at the back of the space station. It seemed like many employees were in on their scam. They let them sneak into the back door of the station. Inside was a large warehouse. It was filled almost to the ceiling with packages.

"Alright," the man said. "I had them put everything on board. Since you're flying for free, you unfortunately have to ride in the cargo bay. You'll see 8 green packages labelled 'To Kruagyna' taped to the side, here are your directions. Please, make sure nothing is damaged. Once you hold your end of the deal, stay on the moon as long as you want. When you're ready to leave, show the attendants this badge and they will send you back to the cargo bay."

The man handed Jae an envelope. It was written in an alien language. Jae could read it thanks to the chip in his head. The man continued, "If you double cross me, you'll regret it."

As if. Jae laughed. Out loud, he said, "Got it. How will they know I'm the one delivering it?"

"You'll have some of my employees guiding you. Everything they need is in that envelope," the man said. "Just give it to them, they will give you your badge and you'll be on your way."

"No money to deliver back to you?"

"Ha, as if I'd let a stranger hold my money." He laughed. "Get on your flight. They'll take you. You don't have much time. Oh, and if you get caught, you don't know what's inside and that some random alien gave them to you. Don't tell them any unnecessary information. Proceed to the drop off location with the crew and inform them of what happened."

Jae nodded and followed the staff. He looked in awe at the spaceship he was riding it. It was a luxury one, which thankfully meant cargo wouldn't be as rough as it would have been on the cheap flights. The outside of the ship was black, it was one of the largest ships and carried 30 passengers. Jae walked into the cargo bay, 3 other men and 1 woman joined him. They looked busted and desperate.

Jae turned to one of the staff and asked, "Are they coming with?"

"No," a woman responded. "They can actually afford a flight."

Jae rolled his eyes. He searched the cargo for the green boxes. When he found them, he sat across from them. He sat on a divot in the floor and held onto the metal handle beside it. He assumed that meant it wasn't going to be an easy ride after all. He looked out the small window on the other side of him. The ship jerked and angled itself upwards. Jae held the handle tighter and took a deep breath. The ship lifted into the air.

This isn't so bad, Jae thought. He smiled as he watched the ground get farther away.

When the ship was a safe distance from the ground, it jerked again. It whipped around, and Jae slammed his face into a box next to him. The ship blasted off at full speed sending Jae falling over again. The ship rumbled and Jae was getting nauseous from the motion.

He looked at the other stowaways and the staff. They remained in place. Eventually they grabbed an oxygen mask from above their divots and put them on. Jae looked above his head. His mask was covered in dirt and mysterious fluids. He cringed and put it over his face.

Soon they were out of the earth's atmosphere. He lifted from the floor and grabbed onto the handle again. He looked at the other passengers and saw they were holding onto two handles and had seatbelts. He looked down for his, but saw it was cut off. He rolled his eyes. To make matters worse, the other handle was blocked by the box he smacked into. He rose higher and soon his legs were in the air. The other passengers watched him and laughed. He pulled himself down and grabbed onto the box next to him. He hugged it tightly. How was he going to deal with this for 48 hours?

Chapter Ten
Jae's Past Pt. 4

When they approached the moon, the captain announced the soon to be landing. Jae managed to look outside and his eyes widened in awe. There was a glass dome that covered 75% of the moon, on different parts of the moon, inside, were cities and colonies, separated by aliens and humans. Giant brown aliens lived in a densely forested area, then a bustling city past the wall, leading to the space station, and just to the side of Jae's vision, was a large building, large in length, but seemed to be only one or two stories high. With how unnecessarily tall the gods were, there was no way to tell how many floors there were. It was metal, with a lavender flag, Jae couldn't make out what was on it, but it had to be the gods' base. It was surrounded by an open field, then a large gate.

How gaudy, Jae thought.

There were 10 gods…previously…why did they need so much space? Jae scowled, how materialistic were they? Hrayrp wasn't the only one to think it needed a large living space.

The ship jerked, and Jae fell against the box beside him. He held on tightly until the ship docked. His legs quivered as he stood up.

"Ready to go bumblebee?" an employee asked, laughing at Jae.

"Shut up." Jae didn't understand what the bumblebee reference pertained to, but he knew it was an insult.

They grabbed the boxes and loaded them onto the cargo bed of a pickup truck. Jae had to sit in the cargo bed as well, him along with three others. Jae wondered how they were able to get that on the moon. While they drove, they offered 4 masks for Jae to choose from. It was currently the festival of the gods. A festival thrown every 6 months for a week, as a thank you and full worship for the gods, though the gods never attended, except on the occasion of Hrayrp wanting worshippers bowing at his feet. Everyone was required to wear a mask, if not, they were forced to stay inside until it was over.

Jae grimaced at the masks. They were masks of Kwtamg, Hellim, Malarik, and Jtrepo. The sight of Kwtamg, built up a lot of rage in Jae, and he had to repress it. She was already dealt with. He took Hellim's mask. He tied it on his head and leaned on the side of the truck. He watched as they drove through the streets, the bright colors, crowded streets, live music, food vendors and gaming stalls. The faces of the gods were everywhere. Jae held back his emotions as much as he could. Thankfully the mask hid his frown.

They arrived at an alley, it was dimly lit and covered in lunar regolith. Jae watched the spaceport employees leave the truck and hopped out himself. They walked around the corner and pointed at a warehouse. They instructed him to carry all 8 boxes by himself. He stacked 3 boxes on top of each other, and carried them inside the warehouse. When he was done unloading the truck, he joined them inside. When he entered, he was greeted with a thunderous roar.

"Who the hell is this?" the voice yelled. He was speaking in Lunese, the official language of the moon.

Jae looked around the warehouse, until he saw a grey skinned man approaching him. He was small, his eyes were as large as two lemons, and blacker than space, he wore a black business suit, his jacket hung over his shoulder, and a cigar in his mouth.

"Uh this is…." the employee said in Lunese, then looked at Jae. In Kimbundu he asked, "What is your name?"

"Jae."

"'Jae,' he was sent to deliver the packages, since Butor was busy on earth."

"But did I give him permission to be here?"

"No sir," the employee said.

"And what are we to do if he rats us out?"

"Uh…I don't think he would, he's here illegally," the employee responded sheepishly.

"Well we can't trust him regardless," the gangster said. He turned around and sat on a stack of boxes. "Get everything I need from him, and exterminate him by the giants."

"Y-yes sir." The employee bowed then turned to Jae and said, "Is there anything else from Butor?"

Jae opened the letter and took out his badge. He handed it to the employee whose face stiffened. He tried his best to reseal it before handing it to the grey man. The gangster read over the letter while puffing out smoke. He looked at Jae, then tossed the letter on the ground.

"Take him out."

"Right away," the spaceport employees said.

They led Jae back to the truck, they didn't look at Jae once. They spoke amongst themselves about how to get Jae in the field with the giant monsters he saw while landing.

"I know what you're planning," Jae said, glaring at them. "I wouldn't do it if I were you. Just let me out close to the gods' base and pretend like you did it."

"We can't deny orders…."

"It's up to you if you want to die," Jae said, shrugging. "Let me out by the base and I'll meet you back at the spaceport."

The employees looked nervously at each other before nodding. One spoke up, "Fine, but don't come back to this area. Do what you need to do, and get back to the spaceport. No touring."

"Smart move," Jae said. He jumped out of the moving truck once they were a ways away from the alley. "I'll go there myself!"

The employees sped off not looking back at him.

Jae looked around the street at each stall. He spotted another mask stand. It was giving away free god masks. The quality was worse than the ones the spaceport employees gave him, but this one had a cloth that covered the rest of his head. Jae approached and asked if he could switch his. He grabbed Lyour's, he was the only god Jae somewhat respected enough to wear on his face, and put it on his head. He didn't feel safe in his clothes either. He walked along the street, looking for a clothing stand. He came across a cape stall and looked through the inventory.

"12 lunes," the vendor said.

"What?" Jae asked.

"Everything is 12 lunes and up."

"You're not free like all the others?"

"I got a business to run boy."

"That's not very 'honoring the gods,' is it?" Jae smirked. "And to think these cheap capes are worth that much?"

Jae shook his head, he didn't know the conversion of 12 lunes, but he didn't have enough anyways.

"These are made of the finest materials from earth," the vendor said. "It's worth more than your life."

"What earth materials?" Jae asked.

"Cotton and silk."

Jae laughed. "My clothes are made of the same things. I don't know how valuable they are here, but they're worthless on earth."

"What does that matter? What I'm selling is valuable on *this* planet."

"How about this," Jae said, digging through his bag. "I'll give you this earth phone. It's vintage and worth a lot."

"Hmm." The vendor tapped her chin. "Fine, and your clothes."

"Why?"

"Because that looks valuable too."

Jae tsked. "Okay, but in exchange for those jogging pants and that black shirt."

They exchanged items and Jae continued on his way. The moon base was large and could be seen from every corner of the moon, that or the buildings were so low, that it was seen. He walked through the alleys. He didn't plan what direction to go, but knew he would eventually make his way through.

~the gods~
~Earth, Brazil~

"Stay vigilant," Hellim said.

The other 3 gods grunted in agreement. They were in South America for any clues as to who the godeater might be. They checked surveillance footage at almost every transportation port, on the exception of the airports, because who would be that crazy to travel on the most dangerous travelling method? They checked hotel cameras. They even went the extra mile to leave for other locations to see similarities. But nothing, there was no way to decern who could be a suspect. By Gravick's standpoint, everyone seen more than once leaving and entering the transportation ports, was a suspect. Hellim and Jtrepo believed the opposite. There was no way the godeater would be so open about his murders. He snuck up numerous times on the gods, he was a sly person, why would he be careless to not wear something over his face, or appear in the same port twice.

Malarik was the only person to see him and survive, and though he was wearing a mask, Malarik was certain he would remember him the moment he saw him. And no one at those ports were vaguely familiar.

"This is pointless," Gravick yelled. He threw his arms in the air as he left the hover-station.

The others followed after him. They entered their ship and Gravick continued once he was out of earshot of humans, "We aren't going to find the bastard. I say we resort to my method. Let's head back to the moon at once and destroy South America!"

"No," Hellim said. "These humans do not deserve to die because of a problem with us and a child."

"He's no longer a child once he's murdered someone," Malarik chimed in bitterly.

"Nonetheless," Jtrepo said. "We aren't going back to the base, we aren't killing humans, we're going to search to the ends of the earth to find him."

"Then what do you suggest we do?" Malarik asked.

"How about we devise a trap?" Hellim asked.

"Like what?" Gravick said.

"As if anything else we've tried has worked," Malarik mumbled.

"How about we announce where one of us will be, when the boy arrives, we catch him. He is cowardice enough to only attack when we are alone," Hellim said.

"Then who do we use as bait?" Jtrepo asked.

"You."

"Why me?" Jtrepo chuckled nervously.

"Because Malarik carries too many weapons, Gravick looks mean all the time, and I am the largest out of all of us. You are uh…you look weak in comparison to us…"

"…"

Gravick and Malarik burst into laughter and Hellim joined in. Jtrepo, after being offended wore off, followed after. They laughed until their stomachs hurt. They couldn't remember the last time they laughed. The past several years had been nothing but stress. And soon, hopefully everything would go back to their new normal. A life with humans respecting them, and the betterment and survival of their species.

They announced publicly that Jtrepo would be in Gabon at Kongou Falls for a week on a break. They asked natives and tourists to avoid Camp Kongou and the waterfall for Jtrepo's privacy. Once they were sure the news was spread, they set off for Ivindo National Park.

~Jae~

Jae walked through the alley. He heard bloodcurdling screams coming from a direction opposite of the base. He sighed, it sounded like it came from a woman, Jae felt he had to do something. He took out his suitcase, brought it to regular size, and took out his sword. He walked in the direction of the screams.

When he arrived, he saw a young navy blue woman crouched over as two grey men kicked her down, and a third went through her bag. Jae hated thieves, and he especially hated those who harmed people weaker than them. It didn't help that they wore masks of Hrayrp, Kwtamg, and Gravick.

His nose scrunched as rage filled his mind. "Hey!"

The men and the woman looked over at him. One of the men asked, "Who are you?"

"What the *hell* do you think you're doing?!" he asked, approaching them. He unsheathed Magord and said, "You have 5 seconds to return everything you stole from her, and leave all the money you have on the ground, or I'll dice you into little moon cubes."

The men did as they were told, and ran away with their tails between their legs.

"What cowards." Jae tsked. He walked over and collected their money. He counted it then stuffed it in his bag. "You alright?"

"Huh?" she responded.

"Aareee yoooou al.r..i..gh..t?" Jae repeated.

"I don't know what you're saying," she said, awkwardly. Her eyes were larger than the gangster's. They were unnervingly stunning to Jae. Her nose was small, and her lips were full. She was short and looked frail.

Jae sighed, maybe the chip stopped working? He repeated once more.

"Ah," she exclaimed. "I'm alright! Thank you so much!"

"No problem, it's my duty as a man to help." He nodded and walked away.

"Wait," she said, running after him. "What language was that?"

"What do you mean?"

"What you spoke originally. I've never heard it before."

"Well..." Jae thought about it. He felt like he was speaking Korean most of the time, but he knew the chip changed it to whatever language was spoken to him. Was he speaking Korean when he talked to her? "Korean?"

"Where does it come from?"

"South Korea, a country on earth."

"You're an earthling?!" she exclaimed, excitement in her eyes. "What's it like? I've never seen a human before!"

"Surely there're other humans on the moon..." Jae said. He quickened his pace.

"None I've seen." She ran to catch up. "They don't come to this side of the moon. What's your name? I'm Maki, short for Makianpe."

"Jae..."

"Jae. Wanna go to the festival with me?"

"Can't, I'm busy."

"Please, I don't have anyone to go with!"

"Why not go alone?"

"Because in two days, they're having the asteroidworks."

"What's that?"

"When they destroy asteroids. The meteoroids for some time, are red and it's really pretty."

"Huh, didn't think that was possible in space…"

"It is, and you should come with me. No one wants to go alone. It's said if you attend the asteroidworks alone, you will suffer forever."

"No one else to go with?"

"Not really," she chuckled. Sadly, she said, "I don't have friends, and most of my family is on earth. The family I do live with, don't like me as is. I just wait for the day my mom and dad come back for me."

Jae sighed. "Alright, *if* I have time, I will meet you. But for now, please, I have business to attend to. And I don't need you following me."

"Oh…" she said, disappointed. She slowed to a stop and Jae looked back. "Can I at least see your face?"

Jae turned back to her and lifted his mask. She studied his face. Her 4 fingers caressed his skin. She traced the outline of his eyes, then his nose, and his lips. A little flustered, Jae cleared his throat and pulled down his mask.

"I gotta go."

"Okay," she said, solemnly. "I will see you by the vroytesas section in two days."

Jae didn't respond. He waved as he continued down the alley. He pulled the cloak's hood over his head. It wouldn't be long until he reached their base. There was no guarantee anyone was there, but even then, he could still vandalize it. Who could they blame but punks from the moon colony?

~the gods~

Jtrepo shivered on the edge of the rocks on the waterfall. The rain was pouring hard and the night air was chilling to the bone. He trembled and whispered, "How long do I need to stay here?"

"Until someone arrives," Hellim whispered back from a bush.

"But it's so wet…and cold…" he complained. He crouched and hugged himself.

Gravick and Malarik felt the idea was stupid. They leaned against trees a little bit away from Hellim's bush, bored out of their minds. It was the 3rd day without any sign of the godeater. Jtrepo stayed in the same spot most of the time, venturing out to the other side of the falls and back. They brooded about how much of their time had been wasted on this poorly strategized trap.

"Jtrepo," Malarik said. "You literally control the weather."

"And?" Jtrepo replied. "You know I don't like tampering with what earth wants the weather to be."

"Then stop whining," Malarik said. "You have the power to change the situation, but you don't want to."

"In more situations than this," Gravick grumbled.

Hellim rose to his feet. Ignoring his remark, Hellim grabbed twigs from around the area and walked to the middle of the clearing. He inhaled and blew out a light flame. The twigs caught on fire and Hellim motioned for Gravick and Malarik to sit with him.

"Come Jtrepo," Hellim called. "I doubt he will be here any time soon. Come join us for the night."

Jtrepo hopped over the bushes. He pulled off his soaked clothes with each step. He broke off a few small branches and threw them on the ground. "Hellim, do you mind?"

Hellim blew flames at the branches and Jtrepo continued, "Malarik, let me borrow your sword."

Malarik unsheathed his longsword and threw it into the trunk of the tree next to Jtrepo's fire. Jtrepo thanked him and hung his clothes on the sword. He sat next to Gravick.

"See?" Hellim said, smiling. "Solved the problem without losing Jtrepo's conviction. We do not always have to resort to one method to solve our problems. Sometimes, it is as simple as lighting a fire to warm up."

"Somethings aren't that simple," Gravick said. "Do you think I want to murder innocent people? No. But it's a necessary evil that will save *us* in the long run. You've always tried that method of running away and taking the easy way out. Look where that's gotten us, genocide on our nation, half our surviving comrades dead, and us sitting in a shitty bush huddled up by a fire. When are you going to accept that not everything can be settled with peace?"

"I do not deny that some situations do not require violence," Hellim said firmly. "I believe that it should be a last resort. If I can stop something without a life lost, then I will do that."

"5 lives were lost..." Malarik said.

"And we are working to find the assailant. We are together and Yulogna is safe at our base. Everything will be fine. All that is left, is waiting on the godeater to arrive. There is no way he will not take this opportunity to slaughter Jtrepo."

Jtrepo chuckled awkwardly at Hellim's choice of wording. "Look, we will give this a try. One more night. If he doesn't show, then we go back to the moon and discuss other actions…. *Except* murdering the humans."

Hellim nodded in agreement and the others shrugged simultaneously.

~Jae~

Jae arrived at the side of the gods' base. The fence was tall. Jae would have to climb a long way. The way the moon colony buildings were positioned, he needed to walk along the fence to get out of the view of the citizens.

Once in a spot he believed was safe, he scaled the fence and hoped over. When he landed, a bear trap set off just inches behind him. He looked back and sighed. *What kind of trap is that*?

He looked along the edge of the fence and it seemed that was the only bear trap. To be safe, Jae walked cautiously through the yard. He used Magord to swipe the lunar regolith to the side, making sure no more traps were hidden.

He reached the building and looked around for an entrance. There were two large doors on both sides of the building. They were 3 times his size. He didn't want to risk one of the gods coming out as he entered, so he walked along the side of the building looking for a window. He found a small one just under a ledge on the first floor. The window seemed to belong to a room in their basement. Jae didn't necessarily want to start down there, but it was the only window he found low enough for him. The base was built out of metal, the texture was slippery and unclimbable, and although Magord could easily slice through it, he didn't want to climb again.

Jae broke the window and dropped into the basement, cutting his leg on the broken window. He shivered. The room was significantly cooler than outside. It was so cold, that his blood froze to his body within minutes. He trembled as he walked through the dark room. He took out his lighter and tried to ignite a flame. No good. There was no way he could use the lighter he had. Flames weren't possible on the moon, even in the bubble. While they were able to create gravity, there still wasn't enough atmosphere to be able to start and keep a fire. Jae didn't know all of the science behind it, nor how they kept the colonies at a relatively warm temperature without fire, but he didn't care enough to study it. He used his hand and his sword to feel around the room. He traced the wall until he found a doorknob. He opened it and the light blinded him for a split second. When he got his bearings, he turned around and looked in the room. He was in the freezer. He stepped partially out of the room. It was warmer than the freezer of course, but still not as warm as outside.

He glanced around the hall. It was eerily white. He saw that the ground was metal, but the bright white walls and ceiling reflected off it, making it appear white as well. He continued to gaze across the hallway, at the end of it, to Jae's left, was a stairway that led upwards. He slowly crept out of the freezer. Unbeknownst to Jae, a red light flashed above the freezer door. A whirling sound slowly built in strength and at the other end of the hallway, the wall turned to show spikes. Jae looked back at it, and his stomach dropped. He ran down the hall as the wall picked up speed. He kept his hand on the wall hoping to disengage it somehow. Jae stopped at the bottom of the stairs and looked up to make sure there wasn't another trap. He ran up the stairs as the wall crashed into the bottom of it, the spikes thrusted outwards, just barely missing Jae's ankles. He smirked and thought, *Ha! What kind of trap was that? "Advanced species" but they can't even make a trap that can stop me.*

He turned around, another white hallway. But this time, there were two doors each on both sides of the hallway and farther down, the hall branched off in three directions. He walked slowly, being careful not to set off another trap. He didn't hear a peep, he wondered if anyone was there? If not, he might as well vandalize their base. He needed to check every room to verify no one was there.

He approached the first door on the left. A large sign in bold red letter read, **Keep out! You've been warned.**

Jae scoffed. *What is the thing hiding? A porn collection?*

He laughed at the thought. If it did have some in there, he would release it to the public. The gods were nothing more than perverts. He kicked the door in, and a large blade with immense speed shot out of the room, Jae dodged, but his left arm flew across the hall. Jae dropped to his knees and winced in pain. He grabbed a chunk of his cloak and stuff his mouth. He held back his scream. He couldn't risk alerting them.

Who the hell booby-traps their own room?! Jae thought, tears in his eyes. He bit hard into the cloth. He held his arm…or where his arm was… and rocked back and forth to soothe his pain. *Great, didn't expect to lose a fucking arm!*

After ten minutes of crying at the side of the door, he felt a nub on his shoulder. His arm slowly grew back. He watched as it sprouted little fingers. It felt weird, something he couldn't explain. When it was completely grown, he clenched his fist. All of the feeling in his arm returned. He felt invincible now. Jae scoffed. *Guess I really did get all of Muragrak's abilities.*

He stood up and looked at the blade. It was still retracted. He crouched beneath it and entered the room. His mouth dropped. The room was full of weapons, covering every wall, desk, table. Jae assumed it was the black god's room. He was the only one he knew to carry weapons. He was tempted to steal some, but he didn't trust if it was trackable, nor if touching them setoff traps. He exited the room and picked up his severed arm. He tossed it on Malarik's bed, "as a gift" and walked away.

He approached the room on the opposite side of the hall, just a few feet down from Malarik's. He was cautious to open that door. He twisted the knob and pushed it open as he stepped to the side of the door. Nothing. It really was only Malarik's room that was trapped. Jae thought he was a psycho. He peered in the room. The furniture was suspended on the walls. He went inside. The floor was covered with sand. It was Lyour's room. The wallpaper he had was a rainforest. When he reached the middle of the room, his foot sunk. He looked down to see his foot sinking into the floor, the hole in the floor widened and the sand started pouring in. It was quicksand. Jae panicked and grabbed onto Lyour's bed and pulled himself on it. He watched as the floor became a bottomless pit. He climbed across the furniture until he reached the door. He was standing on a dresser. He stepped as far back as he could, and ran forward, he jumped and landed on the edge of the doorway. He wobbled and fell forward. He didn't expect Lyour of all things to set a deadly trap.

He was nervous. Were all the rooms booby-trapped? He thought it was pointless to continue. But what if someone was in their room? He didn't want to feel like he wasted his time. He would check each room quickly until he found someone, that or he used Magord to shred their walls.

He went to the room next to Lyour's. The floor was full of water. Little alien fish swam about. It seemed like Kwtamg's room. He didn't utter a word. He slammed the door shut and went to the last room in that part of the hall. The room was full of trees and a hammock hung from the branches. Parahae's room. His room was cool, almost as cool as Malarik's, but Jae had to suppress his admiration. He closed the door. He was fine not knowing what trap awaited him. He reached the fork in the hall and looked around. The path to the left, was just a door leading outside, the path to the right, was short and ended just after 2 doors, and the path straight ahead was long and stretched around the corner. He checked the two rooms to the right. It was the kitchen and a living room area. Neither, to his knowledge, were booby-trapped. He walked down the long hall, checking each door. He found a room with all gold furniture, floors and walls, assumably Hrayrp's room, he experienced temperature changes in one room, the door almost locking him in before freezing shut, he couldn't tell whose ability that was, he dodged a room that was scorching hot, how when nothing on the moon could be on fire, he didn't know. He sat down in the middle of the hall exhausted, he needed a break, he had walked for what seemed like hours.

~Yulogna~

Yulogna grunted as she pushed to get the last egg out. She was in terrible pain. Sweat dripped from her head and she leaned against the wall, gripping her dresser handle. She was in Lyaniung for 12 hours. She didn't have time to notify Hellim and the others. The moment it happened, she needed to get to her incubator in time. She laid 14 eggs and could feel the last egg was almost out. She pushed again and the egg slipped out onto a large pillow. She gasped for air, the relief after it was out, rushed her body and she dropped to her knees. She lifted the last egg and smiled. It was red, which meant the baby would hatch that color. It wasn't a guarantee as they grew up that they'd still be the color they were born as. Their skin color could lighten or darken. There were so many colors her babies could be. She gathered her strength and carried it to the incubator. She looked at her 15 eggs. The eggs were translucent, but full of a thick fluid, only the silhouette of the baby could be seen floating around. She had 3 red eggs, 4 black, 2 green, 1 yellow, 1 blue, 2 brown, and 2 pink. She was excited. Pink babies were rare, and considered beautiful when they grew up. Of course, she believed all of her babies would be beautiful, but to lay a pink egg, which happened once every century and two of them, she felt special.

She wondered what abilities they were going to develop. She hoped many of them inherited her sensibility ability and her power of emotions. While they did need powers to protect themselves, she felt having understanding and reasoning were something they were better off with. How abilities for Trwqoyians worked, was not something passed down from their parents. While some could inherit their parents'

275

abilities, it was not that common. Take Hellim and Myetorp for example. They both had fire from their father, but after that, their abilities branched off. Their skin color did decide what their abilities were, but only for their main power. They developed one to four abilities. And she hoped as they grew up their colors coordinated with peaceful abilities. She knew the four black eggs, if they stayed black, would have a higher chance of peace abilities but also powerful ones. She just wished it was the former and not the latter.

She heard the alarm go off and her head whipped to the door. Her heart sank. She was too weak to protect her babies and it would take forever for the men to reach the moon. She sluggishly made her way to the door, using her incubator as a crutch. Her room wasn't as "nicely" trapped as the others, she didn't have the heart to harm any invaders. Jtrepo and Hellim's rooms, as well as the navigation room were the closest to her. She thought about putting her babies in their father's room, but she didn't know how Hellim would respond if she died. Jtrepo was the only one she believed would be mentally stable enough to handle her death. She wheeled the incubator to his door and tapped on the side. A part of the wall jerked and lowered to reveal a number pad. She typed in her code, a light above his door flashed green, the number pad was shut, and his door opened.

She closed the door behind her. She looked around his room for a safe spot to hide them. Jtrepo's room was unusually large. He had four beds, one in each corner of his room, his furniture was spaced apart and in between each wall. She used all of her strength to move his bed in the far right corner as far as possible and pushed the incubator in the corner. She closed her eyes, and flowers and leaves bloomed along the incubator and the top of his bedframe, until the incubator was no longer visible. She added more layers of plants to protect it from any damage. Jtrepo was the only one that could move her flowers without damaging them or himself. She walked backwards to see how visible the eggs were, it was like they weren't there, on the exception of one flower that rested on the top of the bedframe.

She couldn't stand any longer. She dropped to her knees and crawled to his desk. She lifted herself onto his office chair and grabbed his notebook. She wrote a letter and used the chair to wheel herself back to the incubator. She folded the note and used another blossom to cradle the letter. She wheeled herself to the door and typed in another number pad and the door opened. She quickly closed it and rolled to the navigation room at the end of the hall. She opened the door, and hurried inside forgetting to fully close it. She went to the security cameras and switched them on. She watched Jae open each door, dodging traps.

"Oh no!" she exclaimed. "The godeater!"

She stood up, her legs trembling, and ran, as best she could, stumbling to the navigation table. She typed in Hellim's number.

~the gods~

Another day passed, and still no sign of the godeater. It rained nonstop in Gabon and at that point, Malarik was pissed. Jtrepo refused to stop the rain and Malarik suspected he was the one making it rain.

"This is straight bullshit," Malarik complained. "I *know* you're making it rain. There's no way this place would rain two days in a row."

"Why would I make it rain? I'm the one who has to stand in it," Jtrepo said.

"Ain't no way it's raining this hard!" Malarik approached Jtrepo and grabbed him by the collar. "Stop the rain."

"No," he said, his hands in the air defensively. "I don't tamper with what mother earth wants. This is human's mother."

"You do realize that they just call the earth that," Gravick said. "It's not actually a living, cognizant being."

"You have no proof of that," Jtrepo said. "They wouldn't just make up something like that. That's why everyone says, 'protect mother earth.'"

"They also made us into gods," Malarik said. "They just worship things that are unexplainable and different. Change the weather!"

"No!" Jtrepo shouted.

"Guys," Hellim said. "Keep it down. He could be near."

"He's not—" Gravick shouted.

Suddenly, they heard rustling west of them and Malarik instinctively threw 3 daggers in that direction. The daggers flew through the air and into a person. They screamed in agony, and the gods ran towards them.

Hellim arrived first and looked at the young man. He was an African man, no older than 25. He trembled in fear and pain as he looked to Hellim. One of the daggers stabbed him in the leg. Hellim saw another person a little behind him. She stared at her friend's stab wound. Hellim's stomach sank. He knew this wasn't the godeater based off of Malarik's description.

"Oh my Trwqoyian god," Hellim said. He crouched beside the young man and placed his hand on the dagger. "I'm sorry, this is going to hurt."

277

He pulled the dagger out as quickly as possible and the young man screamed in agony. The other gods caught up to them and looked from the young woman to the young man.

Gravick sighed and approached them. "Didn't we tell you not to come here?"

"W-we just wanted a picture of Jtrepo," the young woman stuttered.

"Shit," Malarik said. "I'm sorry for stabbing you… but when we say stay away, stay away!"

Gravick held up his hand to silence Malarik. He crouched on the other side of the man and put his hand on his wound. A bright light shined and the wound closed up.

"Let them take a picture with him and send them on their way," Gravick said quietly. "We're done here. He's never going to show up."

Malarik's watch flashed and an alert popped up. "Someone set off the trap in my room."

They looked at each other then ran towards the ship. Once Jtrepo caught up after giving the young adults a photo, they shot into the sky, ignoring the speed limit.

"This is why I said we should return days ago!" Gravick shouted in panic.

"Do you guys think it's the godeater?" Jtrepo asked.

"Has to be," Malarik said. "Who else would be bold enough to attack our base? Ugh! This is why he didn't take the bait!"

Hellim ignored their bickering. He focused on getting them to the moon on time. His only thought was getting back before the godeater reached Yulogna. It would normally take 2 days to get there, but at the speed he was going, it would take 14 hours. He panicked. Praying that she would fight and survive until they got there. His watch rang, he looked at it quickly. Gravick pressed the answer button for him.

"Are you alright?" he shouted.

"I am for now," Yulogna said.

"Where are you?" Gravick asked.

"Navigation."

"Navi—" Hellim composed himself. "Get to my or Jtrepo's room fast!"

"I don't think I can make it in time," she said sadly. "I'm trapped here. He's in the hall."

"Yulogna, there is a gun under my station," Malarik said, leaning over the passenger seat. "Defend yourself until we get there."

"I… I don't know if I can do it."

"Yulogna," Hellim said softly. "I believe in you. You have to survive…even if it means killing him. You have to do it for the survival of our species and to save your life."

"I have to go!" she shouted. "I'll look for the gun."

She hung up.

Hellim floored the ship's boosters. He was going at an insane speed. They could probably reach it in 6 hours. It had been years since they used any of their hyper-speed equipment, they didn't know if the ship could handle it, but they were willing to take the risk. Maybe they would even arrive in a couple of hours, if it worked.

~Jae~

Jae made it to the last hallway. There were four doors, two on the left, one on the right, and a door in the middle. Jae was approaching the first door on the right when he noticed the last door was slightly ajar.

He smiled. Someone was surely in there. He hoped no more than one, but if there were more, he could still take one out before his demise. He crept to the door as quiet as possible. He slowly pushed it open, just slightly to peek inside. He saw the black goddess sitting on the other side of a large high-tech table. He approached her slowly, he looked around the room, looking at the cameras and back to her. She sat cross-legged, her arms rested on her knees, like she was meditating, and her eyes were closed.

"So you knew I was here?" he asked. "How come you didn't greet me like a decent being? How tacky."

Her eyes still closed, she said, "It's not that I did not greet you, but rather I was preoccupied. I wasn't aware of your presence until you tripped the alarms. Besides child, it's not *tacky* to not greet a person that's on a killing spree, and invading my home."

"I'm not on a killing spree…." Jae said. His manner of speech was off. "You *things* killed my siblings and my friend. I'm only seeking revenge."

"You already achieved your revenge by killing my comrade Muragrak."

"Still…" Jae clasped his mouth. Why was he agreeing with her? "N-no, I didn't achieve it. I won't achieve it until you all are dead."

"What will you achieve?" she asked.

"Uh, the s-safety of mankind."

"Do you truly believe you are saving mankind from a species that has advanced it?"

"No." Jae bit his lip. What was he doing? Of course he was saving them! What tricks was this woman pulling? "I will save them. You are a danger to our kind. You should have never come."

"If we leave now, would that stop your rage?" she asked. "Will you believe humans are safe?"

"Never…." Why couldn't he stop answering her? "You will always be in this universe. Who's to say you don't seek vengeance?"

"Why would we do so?"

"Because I killed your kind."

"And do you think that was wrong?"

"Y-NO!" Jae's willpower was bending. But he wasn't going to let her brainwash him. That's what it was, brainwashing. He didn't feel that way, she made him think he was. "No! No, no, no! It wasn't wrong. If you had stopped that purple monster from killing so many of my people, none of this would have happened."

"We were not aware of his return."

"Stop lying! Hrayrp already confessed to knowing! That is why he was punished!"

"He did not confess, but rather tormented you prior to what he believed was going to kill you. He wasn't telling the truth. We did not know."

"I'm inclined to believe the man in his final moments than a conniving bitch like you!"

"Am I not in my final moments of life myself?"

"Y-no," he said unnervingly. "Because you'll attack me just like the others."

"And will that justify you killing an unarmed woman?" she interrupted.

"Yes," he said. His answer wasn't forced that time.

"I cannot fight you," she said. "I'm not a warrior like my brethren. Does that mean you murdered me unjustly?"

"Y-no. Because you'll fight me. You're tricking me, I know it. You'll attack when you think your life is in danger."

"I already believe it is," she said.

"Grab a weapon!" he demanded.

"I will not. If I must die here, then so be it. It is up to you to end this. I won't tell them of your whereabouts, if you lower your sword."

"Not until all of you are dead." An unusual feeling washed over Jae's body. He felt dizzy for a second and stumbled into the navigation table. "What did you do?"

"How terrible," she said, her voice quivered.

Jae peered around to see her face. Tears rushed down her cheeks, and Jae felt the same uncomfortable feeling when Lyour cried. *Maybe it's a trick of theirs*, he thought.

Yulogna's cries increased as she continued, "You're so far gone, nothing will appease your rage."

"What…did…you…do!" Jae screamed.

"Even if you spent time in solitude, your Yurtpo is too strong for your body. It has slowly eaten away at your sanity. Almost nothing remains." Yulogna at that moment realized, that it was for the better to sacrifice herself. Their species was saved, so long as they properly raised her children. She knew it would break Hellim's heart, but Jae could not be stopped. She also accepted they wouldn't make it in time, her death was certain. There was no point in prolonging it. If he chose to eat her, her sense abilities would hopefully stabilize his mentality. It was the only way to truly end this cycle.

"Tell me! What did you do?!" he asked. "What is your ability?"

"I will not tell you." There were many reasons why she denied it. One, because if he knew her ability would end his tirade, he wouldn't eat her head, two, she just didn't want to give into his rant.

"Suit yourself, you're going to die anyways," Jae said. He unsheathed Magord and raised it above his head. "This is your last chance to stop me."

Yulogna didn't respond. Her tears flowed endlessly. Each tear expressed her final emotions. The sympathy from the sadness and pain in Jae's heart, knowing Hellim's heart would break, and not seeing her children grow up. She just prayed that her eggs would go unnoticed by Jae.

"Glad you're like Lyour," Jae said. "Keep to your ways in the afterlife."

He swung sideways, slicing her head off in one quick sweep.

Chapter Eleven
~~Jae's Past Pt. 5~~

Yulogna's head rolled on the ground, and Jae looked at it. Tears stained her face and her eyes never opened. Jae felt somewhat guilty, but it was a necessary evil. For the survival of humans, so no one had to deal with what he went through. He stabbed her head, and picked it up. He didn't know how far away the other gods were, so he decided to eat her head back on earth.

He tucked it into a plastic bag he had in his messenger bag. He moved his cloak above the bag so the bulge wasn't seen. There wasn't anywhere to bury her body. He just pushed her body under the navigation table, and drew a flower with a marker he found on one of the desks. He wrote sloppily underneath the poorly drawn flower, **Sorry, I can't bury her.** He looked in the spot where she sat. There was a gun hidden just by the navigation table.

That lying bitch, Jae thought. *She really was going to kill me!*

The sympathy or whatever it was called for her was washed away and he felt justified in her death.

He hurried out of the room. He stopped in front of the door to the left of the navigation room. He was tempted to see what was inside the other rooms, but realized he didn't have much time. His presence was already known and he didn't want to die to those things.

He burst out of the building, running straight for the fence ahead of him. He didn't care who saw him leave, his identity was hidden anyways. He was running in the direction of the spaceport when he remembered the things he gave to the vendor. He turned in that direction and headed there. He saw Russell's phone lying on a back table and his clothes folded just beside it. They were being sold for 200 lunes. He snatched it while she wasn't looking and ran to the spaceport. Laughing about his wonderful scam.

~the gods~

They reached the spaceport at record time. The ship they used was badly damaged, but Yulogna's safety was top priority. The moment they entered the glass dome, the ship dropped to the ground and they ran out of the ship. Employees approached them asking where they wanted it parked, but Hellim declined, telling them to not drive it, it was dangerous and could explode when next turned on.

When they exited the terminal, the crowded spaceport erupted in cheers. Everyone welcomed them home and they put on their fake smiles. They left through the main doors of the spaceport. More fans greeted them, dropping to their knees and bowing.

As they weaved through the crowd, Malarik noticed, to what he believed a native Luna, walking with their head down towards the back of the spaceport. Although Malarik wasn't one for attention, he thought it was suspicious for one to not stop and praise them. Under normal circumstances, he would have confronted a suspicious person, but his main focus was saving Yulogna.

~Jae~

Jae walked through the spaceport sidewalk when the gods appeared from inside. Everyone around him cheered and 3/4 of the crowd dropped to their knees and bowed. They did some weird chant Jae had never seen. He contemplated blending into the crowd, but he couldn't lower his pride. Not even if the world ended would Jae bow down to them. He kept his eyes on them as he walked towards the back of the warehouse. He made eye contact with the black god and quickly looked away.

Jae panicked as he ran to the warehouse. He was sure one of the gods was looking at him. The employees from his trip there were gone. He flashed an employee the badge "Butor" forged for him and they let him on a ship. This time he was more prepared. He made sure his seat had a seatbelt, clean mask, and handles. The ride was 100 times better than before.

~the gods~

They arrived at their base and busted the door down. They ran to the navigation room and found her body under the table. Hellim, too stunned to speak, stared at Yulogna's body. It was like his planet being destroyed all over again. His world once again snatched from him, leaving only a gaping hole in his heart. He dropped to his knees and cried.

Rage possessed Gravick. "This is what your method has done! You've doomed our species to extinction! You failed us on Trwqoy and

284

you've failed us here. You were never meant to rule. You're at fault for your wife's, your son's and now Yulogna's death!"

Hearing Gravick's words, cut deep into his heart. He tried so hard to keep the peace and protect this child, but at what cost? The cost of his comrades and the woman he had loved since childhood? He desperately wanted to follow Yulogna's and Lyour's words for peace, but look where it led them. Gravick was right, their deaths were on his hands. His cries intensified until they became roars of rage. Hellim's body turned purple in some spots and Jtrepo's stomach sank.

Hellim's breathing was heavy and glared at Yulogna's body. He saw the poorly drawn flower and note and his fury intensified, foam spewed from his mouth. Gravick watched as Hellim was going Yurtpo, disgust in his eyes.

"Help him!" Jtrepo yelled.

Gravick ignored him.

"For Trwqoy's sake, stop him from going Yurtpo!" Jtrepo screamed. His heart was breaking more and more. "We don't need to lose another comrade!"

"He's the only one that deserves to die," Gravick said.

"Just help him!" Jtrepo cried. "Punish him later, I don't care, but don't do him like this!"

Gravick stared at Jtrepo then back to Hellim. He crouched and placed his arm on Hellim's back. His skin turned red again and his breathing calmed.

"This is your fault," Gravick said. "I want you to live knowing that for the rest of your life. Let's search the premises. He could still be here."

"Right," they said.

Hellim didn't move. He stayed still staring at Yulogna. Was murder and violence really the only path? It seemed like every notion for peace, backfired, like someone spat in his face. Maybe Gravick was right, necessary evils were needed and he needed it to extract his revenge.

They checked the halls until they made it to Malarik's room. The hall in the basement did not retract, it could only be done manually. Malarik noticed the bloody arm on his bed and tsked.

"Savage bastard." He sneered. He grabbed the arm and brought it back to the navigation room. Gravick and Jtrepo didn't want to look at it.

Gravick approached the navigation table and said, "I'm calling a meeting. All in favor of destroying the earth raise your hand."

Malarik who stared emotionless at nothing, nodded and raised his hand.

"We have an even number," Jtrepo said, sweat accumulated on his forehead. "We won't be able to cast—"

Jtrepo's eyes focused on the hand that was in the air. Hellim's head still hung low, but his hand was high in the air.

"What are you doing?" Jtrepo asked. "What about all that you and Yulogna fought for? Don't do this!"

"Somethings can't be settled simply," Hellim said, emotionless. His eyes never left Yulogna's body

Gravick smiled at his words. "He's right. Now we destroy earth."

"You can't be serious!" Jtrepo yelled. "Why do we need to do this?"

"Because we're condemned to extinction, they will too. This is the only surefire way to kill the godeater!" Gravick retorted.

Hellim stood up. "Let's do it."

"Wait!" Jtrepo said. "C-can we give him one more warning to turn himself in. If he doesn't, then I'll do what you guys say."

Hellim finally looked away from her. "We will do that. He has one chance and that's it. All humans are dying."

Malarik showed Hellim Jae's arm, complaining about his bloodstained bed.

Hellim snatched it and closed his eyes. He copied Malarik's curse ability. He said, "You will lose everyone you ever loved. You will suffer the way I do, until you die the gruesome death that awaits you. May every person you love die. Suffer like you caused us to."

He slammed Jae's arm on the floor and stepped on it. Hellim walked in front of his broadcasting station and issued an urgent message. The cameras turned on every TV in the surrounding universe, one as well in the cargo bay of Jae's ship.

"Godeater, you have done something unforgivable. This is your final chance to turn yourself in." He glared at the lens. "You have one week, if you do not show up, there will be grave consequences to a greater scale than you could ever imagine. If you care about the future of humanity, turn yourself in."

The cameras switched off and he stepped away from the broadcasting station. He lifted Yulogna's body and hugged it tightly. He whispered, "Let's do the burial ceremony. After that, let's review the footage from the cameras."

The others nodded. They left the navigation room and walked to the basement. Malarik and Jtrepo pushed the trap wall back in place and they turned to the left. Gravick tapped the wall and the outline of a door appeared as it opened.

Inside was a large room that covered most of the basement area. It was a room Yulogna built with everyone's help, to resemble a popular field on Trwqoy. The walls were one large screen that stretched across each wall, displayed on it was a video of a blue sky with purple colored trees swaying in the wind, beneath the trees was a field of burnt orange flowers, a national flower named Ruotawl, only livable on their planet, it had 6 petals and a small lime-green stem, from the wall, the Ruotawl blossomed along the floor. Yulogna found the Lunar Regolith had similar properties to their planet's soil, she had to add certain chemicals to make up the same compound, of course. From old videos they still had, they took the sound, so the room sounded like the cities in their hometowns. Since the godeater's appearance, they had to use this area as a sacred burial for their comrades. It was the closest thing to returning to their homeland.

Jtrepo, Malarik, and Gravick dug a spot next to Myetorp's grave while Hellim held Yulogna's body. He couldn't let her go. When Jtrepo asked for her body, Hellim shook his head, tears poured from his eyes and he squeezed her tighter.

"Control your emotions," Gravick whispered. He crouched beside Hellim and grasped his arm. He pulled his arm away from Yulogna. "We can't let her be seen like this. Let her go."

Jtrepo took Yulogna and gently laid her in the grave. Malarik sat at the end of her grave. His hands were positioned for each finger to touch the other and his palms apart and mumbled their Trwqoyian Warrior prayer. When he finished, they pounded their chest once with their right arms.

In unison, they said in the Trwqoyian language, "May you rest in peace."

~Jae~

Jae tsked. He thought to himself, *Why the hell would I turn myself in? They're bluffing. What consequences? They said that last time, and nothing happened. Besides, why would I sacrifice myself for people I don't know? Dumbasses.*

Jae considered himself a hero of humanity but there was only so far he would go for them. Giving up his life without a fight, was not one of them. He laughed. He was going to count down the days, he would refrigerate Yulogna's head until the final few days they warned, and enjoy his imagination of their faces when he calls their bluff. He sighed after he finished laughing. He missed being home. He didn't know where Ye-jun and Russell's bodies were nor if they were still being researched. But he could still visit where he buried Dasom and Ji-hoon.

When he arrived at the Luanda Spaceport, he bought a flight. There wasn't one that went straight to Daegu International airport, so he had to go to Seoul then Daegu. The flight was 39 hours from Luanda to Seoul then 2.5 hours from Seoul to Daegu. He regretted not using the last of his money to buy a cheaper but better travel method. He wasted 4 days since the gods' announcement. He wanted to hurry to their grave then eat Yulogna. He planned on his flight to prepare for their called bluff like a New Year's countdown.

~the gods~

They reviewed the cameras from the night of the invasion. They watched the masked godeater running through the halls. "How *dare* he wear Lyour's mask!" Gravick sneered.

"Damnit!" Malarik shouted, slamming his fist on his desk. "I *saw* him. I let him get away again!"

"It's not your fault," Jtrepo said. "Everyone was wearing a mask. Who you saw, might not have been him."

"I know it was," Malarik said. "I remember those disgusting eyes of his. I should've stopped him."

He dropped his head into his hands. "I'm such a failure."

Hellim walked over to Malarik and gently rested his hand on his back. "It's not your fault. No one is to blame but the godeater."

"You're right," Gravick said. "This is none of our fault, and because of this inhumane thing, so many lives will be lost."

"*If* he doesn't show up," Jtrepo corrected him. "I have faith he'll show up. Wasn't he doing this for humanities sake? He wouldn't let them die."

"That was nothing more than an excuse to slaughter us," Gravick said. "He doesn't care about these humans no more than he cares about the proverbial gum on his shoes."

Hellim walked to the broadcasting station. He issued another announcement. "If you see a boy dressed like this, report his location immediately. Do not hide him, do not stay silent. Everything is riding on you making his whereabout known."

A photo of Jae in the mask and cloak appeared on the screen. It was an unusual outfit to begin with, for earth anyways, Hellim believed there was no way they wouldn't remember something as suspicious as that.

"Time is running out," Hellim said. "You have 3 days left godeater."

He stepped away from the cameras and said, "I agree Gravick, he doesn't care. Do any of you, besides Jtrepo, think he's going to turn himself in?"

Gravick and Malarik shook their heads.

"There's no point prolonging this then," Hellim said. "It's time."

~Jae~

He arrived at where he and Russell buried them. The rock remained untouched but the note was gone, most likely washed off with the rain. He sat beside them and prayed. Wishing them well and hoping Ye-jun found his way to them. He told them about his adventure and his new powers. He promised when he finished the rest of the monsters off, he would use his powers for good and rule over humans in place of them. Of course, he wouldn't do as much as the gods were willing to, but he would still help.

He said his goodbyes and went to Russell's gun shop. He was surprised it was still intact. Nothing inside seemed to be stolen. Dust covered the guns and display cases. It had a nostalgic smell. He opened the back room, memories of him and Russell made his heart hurt. He continued to the bunker, closing the metal door above the stairs Russell showed him to do whenever the store doors were unlocked. He wasn't afraid of any robbers, he did so out of muscle memories. His eyes watered as he walked down the hall. Memories of his, believed, final moments, Russell's death and in his room, where Ye-jun suffered, crushed him. He vowed to avenge them, soon he would kill all of them. He spent the day reminiscing about his training, his siblings and what could have been his normal life.

The 4th day, Jae walked around the trial room. He kept his eyes focused only on the weapons. He picked up each one. He desperately believed he needed to use them. He searched each weapon for the trigger and how to turn off the safety. Nothing. He was frustrated, he slammed a gun back on the shelf, when Russell's phone pinged. Jae took the phone out of his pocket, a notice popped up stating there was another urgent message from the gods. Hellim appeared on the screen issuing a warning, his picture showed up and Jae laughed collapsing to the ground.

"What kind of idiots are they?" he said, out of breath. "That does nothing to prove where I am. Who's going to remember that?"

He laughed until his stomach hurt. Jae grew serious when the last warning was done. *Who the hell does he think he is threatening me?*

Jae stood up, left the room to grab Magord and a marker and returned to the trial room. He drew ugly drawings of the remaining 5 gods on the pillars. He unsheathed it, and started attacking the pillars. *When these three days are over, I'm making sure to kill that one.*

On the 5th evening, Jae took Yulogna out of the fridge and pulled out Russell's phone. He turned on a news channel hoping for another broadcast. This time, them apologizing for scaring their followers. He considered the possible time difference in space and wanted to make sure he didn't miss anything. He watched all of the boring events while he ate her head. When he gulped the last chunk, a chill ran through his body and sadness washed over his body.

"What have I done?" He sobbed, resting his head on the table. The memories of Hrayrp, Parahae, Muragrak and Yulogna flooded his mind and he grabbed his head. He felt like his heart was going to explode. Pain and regret from each of them and their lives before moving to earth was too much for him. He thought about the eggs she laid, taking away their mother, how could he? Jae was finally seeing their humanity. What was his reason for fighting them? He knew it was about his siblings, but his urge to kill the gods was gone. He questioned what possessed himself to do it? "I'm so sorry. Please forgive me."

Nothing could ever change what he did. He still believed the gods were bluffing. But if he could get there in time, he would still take whatever punishment they deemed fit. If they were the kind people he knew through their memories, they wouldn't harm him. And if they denied any form of punishment, he would take it upon himself to dole one out.

He stood up and headed for the door. Before he could press the open button, the room shook violently and he tumbled to the floor as everything around him fell over, the table shook, the cabinets opened and items dropped to the floor breaking glasses. The shaking went on for what felt like an hour. When everything settled, he looked around the room in confusion. *Was that an earthquake?*

~the gods~

"You can't do this!" Jtrepo shouted, following behind Gravick and Hellim, Malarik walked alongside Jtrepo. "You said a week!"

"5 days is enough," Gravick said, smirking. "If he wanted to turn himself in, he would have done so days ago."

"He could be on his way," Jtrepo said. "Please Hellim, you have to give him more time."

He stopped and turned to Jtrepo. "I gave him months…"

"That…that doesn't count. There weren't any conditions or warnings."

"Like Gravick said, if he wanted to do so, he would have been here," Hellim said, he continued to walk. "He's too selfish."

"Please!" Jtrepo cried. "What was the point of you, Lyour, and Yulogna trying to find a peaceful solution, if you're going to make it all in vain?"

"If we had fought him, none of them would be dead," Gravick said. "That is why Lyour died, and his views in turn led to Kwtamg's fall. If we let ourselves die to this boy, *that* would mean everything was in vain."

"Hellim," Jtrepo said, ignoring Gravick. "Did you *not* just give a speech about finding a solution without losing your conviction? Why are you doing this?"

"Do you really need to ask why?" Hellim asked. "I've lost almost everything now, and I'll be damned if I lose any of you too. He killed Yulogna, her life meant way more than any of those measly humans. It's time I took away everything from him. And in his final moments of life, he'll see that their deaths are on him."

"You can't be serious," Jtrepo said, faltering in his step. "What about you Malarik? Didn't you love the humans?"

"Not really," he said, shrugging. "I loved their cute little inventions."

"And you can justify slaughtering them how?"

"Any one of them could be the godeater, so long as I remember that I can kill'em all day."

"What has happened to you all?"

"The godeater happened," Gravick said, glancing back at Jtrepo. "Get with the changes, we've given up on the peaceful route. If we can't continue our bloodlines, neither can they."

"And what if some survive?" Jtrepo asked.

"We won't let that happen," Hellim replied. "After we fire the lasers, we're going to earth to finish the job."

Jtrepo's stomach lurched. "You can't be serious…"

"Very," Hellim said.

"If they still manage to survive after that," Malarik said, he unsheathed his katana, twirled it around his hand, and pointed at Jtrepo. "We'll rule over them. Right guys?"

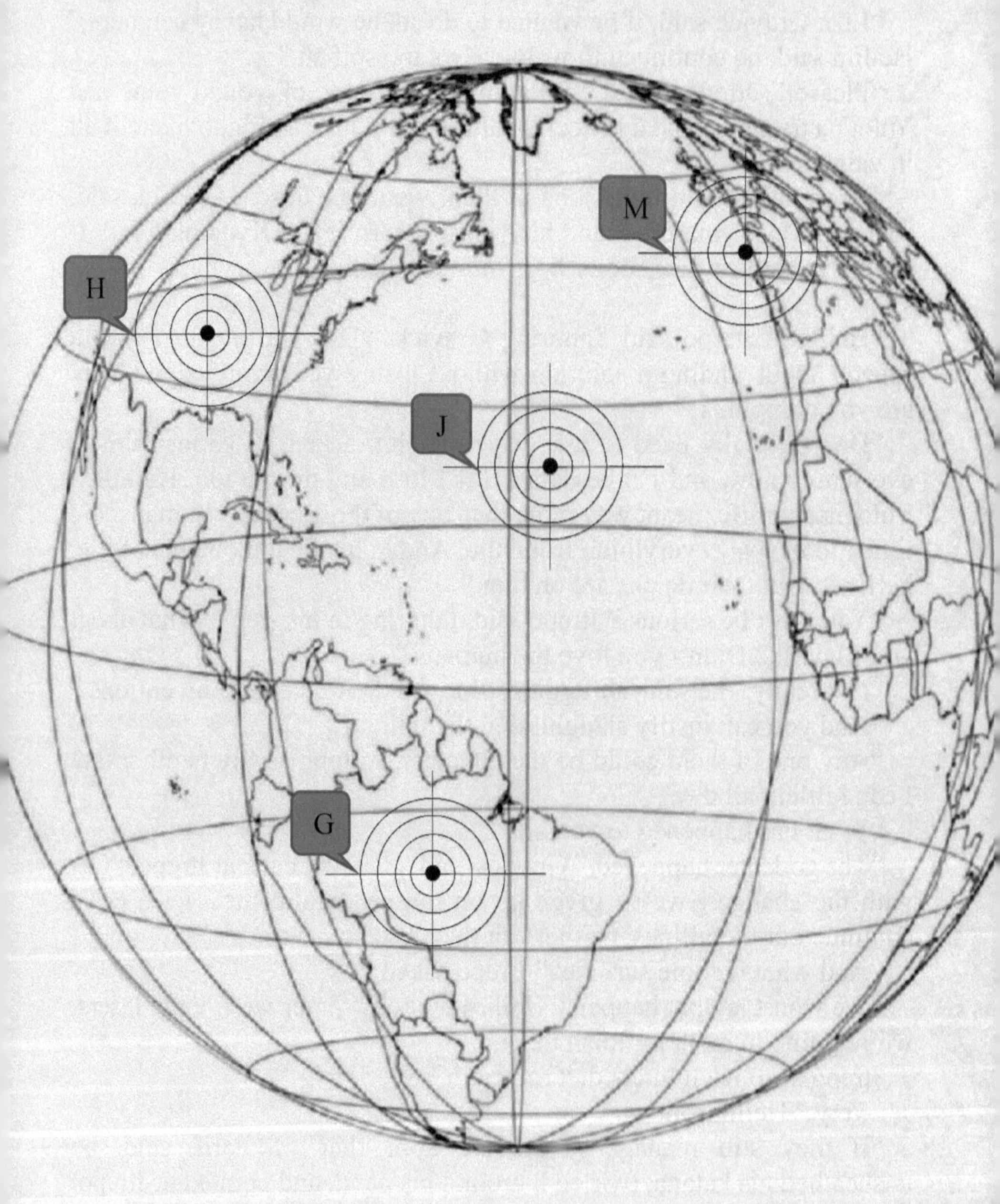

H
M
J
G

"I don't think it's a bad idea," Gravick said. They reached the navigation room and positioned themselves in their stations. "Hellim, you take the Americas, I'll take Europe, Malarik can have Asia, and Jtrepo, if you get off your high-horse of morals, you can take Africa. We all get a continent."

"Whatever you want to do," Hellim said. "Jtrepo, I expect you to go all out, it was your agreement that you would take part if he never showed."

"I know I said that…" Jtrepo murmured. "I just can't—"

"You're a warrior," Hellim interrupted him. "You've slain millions of our enemies, whether it was defending Trwqoy or when my father invaded other planets. Your hands aren't clean from bloodshed. So go all out like you did before."

Jtrepo looked down. His resolve was gone. Nothing he did, no matter how much he pleaded, they would never listen. His once kindhearted friends were gone. "Yes sir."

Hellim walked to his seat and everyone followed going to their stations. Hellim nodded and pushed a button. On their desks, a holographic screen popped up and a handle rose out of the desks. Jtrepo hesitantly grabbed the handle and looked at the screen. Outside of their base, a loud sound pierced the air and the Lunas looked towards the gods' base. A large weapon rose from the front of the base, it had 4 cannons attached. The cannons turned towards the earth. The Lunas glanced at each other wondering what the gods were doing. It didn't look good, so many of them sought shelter in their basements. Their basements were used only as a last resort if the moon were ever invaded, but they knew something was up, and they weren't sticking around to find out.

"Aim for the Americas first," Gravick said. They waited for the earth to spin around. "Let's cleanse the soil and our memories of what happened."

"I couldn't agree more," Malarik said, smiling. "Jtrepo? Where the hell are you aiming at?"

"Hellim and Gravick already took both continents," he replied. "Besides, it's good to go after the sea, they need water to survive right?"

Malarik scoffed. "You just don't want to hit them directly. I'll go for Europe then."

Hellim rose his arm in the air. The others glanced back waiting for his signal. He clenched his fist and Gravick and Malarik, both smiling ear to ear, started firing the lasers. It was a refreshing feeling. It had been so long since they had any wars. They missed their old warrior lives. It brought back a rejuvenation they could never express. The tiny, *very* tiny, reserve of disgust Malarik had for killing them was gone. Jtrepo hesitated then joined in.

The earth emitted red lights as the lasers made contact. From the moon, they could see large red circles spreading over the continents. One blast was enough to cover most of the countries. Even Jtrepo's hit to the Atlantic Ocean spread across hitting parts of the Americas, Western Europe, and parts of North and West African countries. The heat alone, dried the water and created a massive crater. As the earth turned, Jtrepo aimed only for the seas of water, taking nearby islands and the ends of continents out with it, while the others continued to shoot lasers until each continent was hit once. They of course, wanted to save some humans for their combat and takeover.

They exited their base and Hellim shouted loud enough for many to hear, even in their bunkers. "Listen Luna Natives, if you see any humans on the moon, imprison them until our return. If anyone is caught harboring humans, you will be executed. Do I make myself clear?"

The Lunas shouted, "Yes sir."

They grabbed any humans they saw and escorted them to nearby police stations. Maki looked around at the chaos that surrounded her. With the assumed permission of the gods, some Lunas even took it upon themselves to commit atrocious attacks on humans. They shot them, sliced off limbs, and more vicious actions.

Maki ran to her home. Her extended family had blended families with humans. She worried what would happen to them? Would her family take the risk? Or would they turn their backs on them for the sake of their own survival?

The gods made their way to the spaceport and took out a brand new ship. Gravick gave an order to the spaceport employees, let all non-humans off the ship, any humans onboard were to be sent back to earth or transported to jail. He told them to pass the message on to all spaceports in the nearby galaxy, and the ones on earth to not let any humans on the ships. The gods were tempted to shoot the ships they passed, but they didn't want to kill any innocent aliens.

Before landing in Russia, or what remained of it, they used the guns on the ship to shoot down any buildings still intact. They dropped Gravick off, he was to take over Europe on his own, he was free to do anything he wanted to achieve it. Malarik was dropped off in Asia, again the same directions as Gravick. Soon it was only Jtrepo and Hellim. They rode in silence as they drove for Africa.

Breaking the silence, Hellim said, "I know this seems cruel but humans are no more special than any other species in the universe. This can all be blamed on the godeater, whatever you want to feel justified in completing the mission. But think of it no more than you did any aliens you'd slain."

"I can't," Jtrepo said. He was holding back his tears the entire trip, and he couldn't do it anymore. He felt more comfortable crying in front of Hellim, he felt there was still some inkling of empathy left in him. "They aren't like other aliens! They don't have any powers, they are weaklings. It feels like we're harming babies."

"We aren't," Hellim said. He pulled the ship over, turned off the engine and turned to Jtrepo. "Do you remember what humans were like prior to us helping them?"

Jtrepo nodded.

"That is not the work of babies. They had continuous wars, they killed each other on a massive scale, what does it matter if we do the same? They were never good, no matter how much we bettered their society, they are still the same evil beings, no different than any other species. They may not have powers, but they found other ways to kill each other."

Hellim continued, "And that is why I have no qualms killing them. If any of us kills the godeater, all of their lives will not be in vain. It's, as Gravick always said, 'a necessary evil,' to get vengeance for our comrades. We've lost everything, they may lose many, but the gravity, will never be the same as ours. They will still have a planet to live on, they will still have a species to thrive on, while we die ending everything we worked hard to build. I know you don't agree with this, and I'm happy at least one of us is still…I'm glad you still have your heart. Keep going, you are free to do with Africa how you like. If you want to rule over them as a good god, then do so. But I expect you to kill many of them and lay down the law. After that, be who you are. Close your eyes and plug your ears to drown out their cries. You've done it before."

Hellim gave a weary smile and started the engine again. Hellim wished he could still be the loveable person Yulogna wanted him to be. But it was too late to turn back. If only things had been different. He wished they had never arrived on earth. Why didn't they move to the moon or some other habitable planet? If they had been patient enough to look for different life, would they be thriving? Would there be no heartache?

They were approaching Africa, Hellim knew Jtrepo wouldn't be able to kill them. He put the ship in autopilot and shot the land they passed. Jtrepo was in more disbelief than he thought possible.

"I know you wouldn't be able to, but you have a quota to fill," Hellim said, sitting back in the driver's seat. "Now you don't have to kill as many people."

When they reached Central Africa, Hellim landed bombs destroying a lot of cities, and released Jtrepo. Hellim flew to the Americas and slaughtered as many as he could.

~Jtrepo~

Jtrepo landed on the ground. It was still warm from the bombs. His heart ached from the sight of the land. He dropped to his knees and said, "I'm sorry mother earth, I'm sorry humans."

He cried for what felt like hours, before standing up. He made his way across the landscape. He couldn't find any humans. He wondered if Hellim had killed most of the ones in the area. He came across a village that was somewhat still holding up. People held their children and their dead family members, crying horrible sounds Jtrepo couldn't handle. He did his best to drown out their screams. Storm clouds brewed in the distance and thunder rumbled the ground. He held his hands in the air as the lightning accumulated on his hands.

"I can't do it," Jtrepo cried. He dropped his hands and the thunder stopped. He mustered as much strength as he could to create a large raincloud. The rain fell on central Africa and neighboring countries surrounding it. He couldn't do anything to save them, but for the ones that survived, and had horrible burns, even a cool rain shower was a blissful thing. He kept the rain going for 30 minutes, the relief on many faces as the rain hit their skin, made Jtrepo feel like he was doing something. He, of course couldn't fight his brethren nor did he want to, but they couldn't tell him what to do anymore. He wanted nothing to do with the atrocities they brought upon humans.

He ran through Africa, the raincloud following after him, cooling off the land from the space attacks, until he reached the Luanda spaceport. He took a ship and headed back to the moon base. He arrived in his room and started to pack. He wanted to get away as far as possible. After what he saw, there was no way he could look at them the same. He would always love them, but what they did was far worse than any wars they fought.

He walked to the back of his room. He never went that far back. He only had the two far beds for when the others spent the night in his room. It had been months since he last slept there. He opened the dresser next to the bed and looked inside. In the corner of his eye, he saw his bed pushed too far forward, something he hated seeing. He walked to his bed to make sure the godeater didn't leave any traps when he saw the plant cocoon and the letter Yulogna left. He took it from the flower and opened it.

The letter read:

Dear Jtrepo,

I cannot express the happiness and sorrow I have right now. I have laid 15 eggs, but as you'll soon be aware of, there is an intruder at the base, I do not know who, but to be safe, I am leaving the incubator in your care. If everything is okay, you might not see this letter and I'll steal the incubator back before you know it haha. If not, then I assume you're reading it now.

I am scared of what is going on, and what is happening to our brethren. We have lost many, and with each death, they become more and more unstable, each refusing to let me erase their pain. I...cannot guarantee their reaction to my death, nor how their mentality will hold up. I wanted to leave our babies with Hellim, but you know as well as I do what happened after his wife and child died. If he goes Yurtpo, then no one will know about these eggs. I couldn't leave them with the others. Malarik is too immature and he wears his heart on his sleeve, he cannot control his emotions. Gravick is too cold-hearted at times, and with his push for humans to be killed, I don't want him raising our next generation with his views. You are obviously the best match to look after them. If Hellim is still there, and he is handling my death well, please give him the eggs if you do not want to care for them.

Please do me this favor, if you feel like they are not handling my death well, I want you to take the eggs and move to another planet. There are many peaceful, habitable planets similar to earth where you can take them, like Veuyteo or Nyatrem, both located past earth. Decide if you

want to tell them about my eggs. I know it is a lot to handle
by yourself, but the fate of our species is up to you.

   Wishing you love and success,
   Yulogna.

P.S. I laid pink eggs!

Also the next sheet is a list of the foods you need to feed
them once they hatch.
1. Do not open the incubator unless absolutely necessary....

When Jtrepo finished reading the letter, he collapsed to the ground and cried. *It's all my fault. If only I had checked here days ago. I'm sorry Yulogna, I failed.*

But no matter how much Jtrepo wanted things to be different, there was no guarantee they would have handled the situation better. Once he was calm, he lifted the plant cocoon and carried it along with the few items he could carry and food, and boarded his ship. He vowed to raise the children to be the best Trwqoyians they could be. Though after them, their species would be extinct, the least he could do, was keep Yulogna's bloodline and her love for her children going until the day he died.

Chapter Twelve

"When I came out of Russell's bunker, everything was gone. Nothing remained but a wasteland of rubble, dead bodies, and an orange sky," Jae said. "I couldn't believe it. They had actually done it. I never thought they would, or rather, they could do something to that magnitude. After that, I went back into his bunker and packed everything I could. There was nothing left of the world, and I thought I was the only one alive. I didn't have a motivation to kill them anymore, nor did I have a right to. I wandered around aimlessly until I found Galland starving on the side of a road. We—"

"I'm going to stop you right there," the prophet interrupted. "You've gotten the most important part out. We have a lot to cover before you need to leave. You can tell Bianca the rest of your past later, and Bianca, make sure he does."

Bianca nodded. "Wow…that is a lot to uncover. I'm still trying to process everything. But I do need to hear the rest later."

"Now that you know the truth and the *real* reason why the day of ruin happened," the prophet said. "Do you still wish to continue this journey with the godeater?"

"Yes," Bianca said. "While this is Jae's fault—"

"I said it wasn't my fault," Jae said.

Bianca gave him a weird look. "We'll discuss how, very much so, you are at fault later, but let me continue…. I think Jae is at fault for everything that happened and the result of Hellim being the way he is. But I'll stick by him no matter what."

The prophet sighed. "So you're willing to accept his mission?"

"I am," Bianca responded. "I vowed for us to live happily ever after. He saved me from an unbearable future, I won't turn my back on him. There has to be some way to get the old Hellim back. The memories of Hellim that I guess are from the gods he ate, showed a completely different side to him. If we can get that back, maybe he can come to terms with his heartbreak and join his children, right?"

"It's not that simple," Jae said. "He's a ruthless monster that can't be stopped with reason. He's not the same being, it's been 135 years. He's had time to cope with it. Now he's just killing to kill."

"And whose fault is that?" Bianca rolled her eyes. "What happened? I thought you saw their humanity. Why do you still call him a monster?"

"Because he is," Jae said.

"Bianca there's a lot more to the story that Jae hasn't finished," the prophet joined in. "For now, I can only do so much. I don't want to be in the Yulogna region. Let's hurry this along."

The prophet walked to a bookshelf and pulled out a book. She walked to a table and motioned for them to join her. She opened it and studied its contents before saying, "I come from a bloodline of prophets. My mother told me the story of the godeater and her survival. She explained what I would need to know, should you arrive during my lifetime. And over the years, visions have come to me. Each pertaining to the different people you came in contact with. I do not know if each person was a different path, but I took note of them in this book."

She flipped through the pages as she continued, "I cannot find anything different. Every path leads back to the same conclusion…"

"And what is that?" Jae interrupted.

"I'm getting there," she said. "There is no good future for the godeater. You have curses on you that will only lead to your demise. However, as I say, there are many choices you can make, and there may be a path along the way that will change the outcome. I know you two want to be together, but as of what's written, Jae doesn't have a happy ending. I suggest you think only of the worst case scenario to save yourself the heartache."

"What is the worst case?" Bianca asked.

"That, I cannot tell you." The prophet shook her head. "Interfering in your future can lead to a quicker downfall. It is best to make your decisions on your own. I've already said more than I wanted to."

"Then what was the point of us coming here?" Jae asked, annoyed.

"So you could tell Bianca the truth. I cannot do more. If I told you what would happen, another possible future would pop up, far worse than the other. I can only give you advice."

"And that is?" Jae motioned for her to spit it out.

She sighed. "Your manners are still terrible and you're the oldest human in the world."

"Frank Johnson is actually," Jae said, smirking. "I'm the second oldest…"

"Anyways," she said, smacking her lips. "Once Jae explains the rest of his past, you two need to figure out what to do from there. Follow what you think is best and, as hard as I know this is for the godeater, take the most selfless path. Consider all of your options and think twice about it."

She turned to Bianca and asked, "What do you think the best option is?"

"Uh," Bianca said. "I think we should go to Hellim."

"Do you know what would happen if you went to Hellim?" Jae asked.

"What other choice is there? He doesn't care about me, but I'm not trying to be the fault of millions of people dying. We need to see him and confront the situation head on."

"You want me to go fight a huge army, kill Hellim, and be done with this?"

"I don't know," Bianca said. "I'm being put on the spot right now. I'm still trying to process not only the fact that you're like 150 some years old, but also that all of this was the result of something between you being mentally ill and killing innocent beings, and Hellim and some gods choosing to ruin all of our lives for your actions. This is a problem between him and you. If you can squash whatever problems you have, and leave the rest of us out of it, then that's the best choice. Who's to say he would want to fight? Besides, you've survived every other fight right?"

"I don't know Bianca…"

"I mean it doesn't seem like a bad idea, the prophet hasn't said anything disapproving it, so has to be correct right?"

"I can't give you the answers," she said. "Whether it's right or wrong."

Jae rolled his eyes and stood up. "If there's nothing else, then let's go Bianca."

"Where?" Bianca asked.

"To Parahae, that's where he's at right?" he asked, extending a hand to help Bianca up.

"Are you sure you want to do this?" she asked, taking his hand.

"Yeah, I mean before meeting you, that's why I came to this region." Jae smiled and said, "You were an unplanned…distraction."

Bianca smiled. But before she could respond, the prophet interrupted.

"Wait," she said, standing from her chair. "It's up to you if you want to rush things and not plan with me, however, I must speak to Bianca alone. Can you wait outside?"

"Anything you need to say to her, you can say in front of me," Jae said.

"Jae…" Bianca looked him in the eyes and raised an eyebrow.

"Fine," he said. He turned around and exited. Instant anger possessed him once he left the home. He remembered where they were.

"What is it?" Bianca asked.

The prophet took her hands and led her back to the table. She squeezed her hands and said, "You are going to face many challenges if you continue with the godeater. Are you sure you want to do this?"

Bianca paused, she was going to answer an undoubted yes but hearing how he was in his past warped the image of the romantic kind Jae that promised to run away with her and show her a beautiful world. How could he, after causing so much pain in the world, still see the beauty in it? He spoke about justice and hating how people were, but he was the reason they became that way. This was something she needed to discuss with him.

"I…" she started. She looked down and said, "I love Jae, there's no doubt about it, but I feel like there are things I still don't know, and I'm afraid if I find out, it'll ruin everything I have with him. What would be the point of everything we're going through, risking our lives and everyone around us, if I lost these feelings?"

"You're young darling. You have time, even if you decide you don't want to be with him, that won't be the end of the world. You're sure you love him now, but if that ever falters, you didn't waste anything."

Bianca smiled. "I just, he opened up the possibility of a new world, and I want that. That's what's keeping me going, imagining a future with him and my freedom."

"And keep thinking that, you aren't wrong to want what everyone else has. But I need to warn you," the prophet said. "There will be hardship and pain ahead of you. When it happens, you have to think of yourself, and think rationally. Do not act upon emotion and understand that Jae does not get a happy ending."

"You said fate can be changed right?" Bianca asked. "I'll work to change his fate. I won't let anything bad happen to him, and we'll have our happy ending."

The prophet sighed. "If that's what you want. But heed my warning, when the time comes, do not act on emotions. You are soon to face great heartache. One more thing before I let you go and escape myself, do not listen to Jae. Take time to think about his suggestions and do not ask for his advice."

"How come?"

"I cannot tell you why," she said. "Just don't listen to him."

Bianca left the house and sighed. The gravity of the situation was heavier than she thought. She looked over to see Jae squatting in the field of flowers. She smiled wearily and approached him. "Do you like these flowers?"

Jae glanced back at her, and plucked a flower. "This is that Trwqoyian flower I mentioned. I guess earth soil can grow them."

"It's beautiful," she said. Jae handed her the flower and she studied it extensively. "I wonder which god planted them. Do you know?"

"None of the ones I fought." Jae shook his head. Thinking back on it, Jae remembered seeing them tucked in a corner outside of Lyour's gates and in the forest area of Malarik. It had to have been one of the 2 remaining gods.

"Hm." Bianca nodded, then started walking to the main road. "Come on, we better hurry before Hellim destroys anymore cities."

"That's assuming he waited another week for us," Jae said, catching up to her.

As they walked, Bianca, trying to make light of the situation, laughed awkwardly and said, "I guess I know why you really hate this city."

Jae scoffed and grinned widely. "Yeah, she's the only one that still irks me after all these years."

"Good." Bianca nudged him playfully. "You owe her the biggest apology."

"Hmm, no…. While I think the way I killed her was overboard, I don't feel remorse for killing her."

Hearing his coldhearted comment made her heart sink, she couldn't bear listening to that side of him any longer. Changing the subject, Bianca asked, "Are you going to tell me the rest of your past?"

"Yeah… After we get out of this city."

"You can't dodge my questions anymore, you do know that right?"

"I know." Jae smiled. "But I don't want others to overhear."

"Fine. But the moment we grab Galland, you're talking. You've told me so much and your actions affected more than you wish to acknowledge. You have to promise me you'll tell me."

Jae hesitated at her last word but reluctantly said, "I promise."

~Lyour~

The time was 11:30 PM. Hellim's soldiers had just went to sleep 30 minutes before. The women crowded the halls, the silence added an eerie atmosphere to their intense fear.

Johnson in a loud whisper said, "Alright, is everyone clear on what y'all are supposed to do?"

Most of the women nodded, but Johnson wanted to make sure everyone understood. He went over the plan again. "You're leaving here in pairs starting with Sasha and Serenity, head to the side gate. Walk quickly but silently. Do not let your fear cause any noise. Once you're out of the town, go west, meaning make a right at the gate, and continue all the way until you reach Gravick. It's a straight shot. If you meet up with each other prior to Gravick that is fine as well. Make sure you count all 20 women, before setting out. Do not trust anyone besides yourselves. I'm going to do one more headcount, and once Sash and Seren are ready, you're free to go."

Johnson stood on the 6th step of the stairs and counted. Only 19 were there. "Who are we missing?"

"Hannah," a soft spoken woman replied. "She was still packing when I left our room. She was scared and needed some time. She asked me to tell you to wait just a little longer for her."

Johnson sighed. "That woman. We can't wait. Rachel, I'm sorry but you will have to be the last person to leave. If Hannah isn't here by midnight, leave without her. You can catch up to another pair, if need be."

Rachel nodded. She prayed she didn't have to go alone. What the hell was Hannah doing?

Johnson wasted no time telling the women to set out. Sasha and Serenity ran off first. It was a ways away to the town's gates, it would take at least 20 minutes at the pace they were going. They had to be stealthy in their steps not to awake any of Hellim's soldiers sleeping outside. The women poured out, 2 by 2 until only Rachel and Johnson were left.

"Come on Hannah," Rachel said, tapping her foot.

"I'm going outside to make sure there aren't any problems," Johnson whispered. He grabbed the light machine gun he had leaning against the door. "Don't waste any more time when she shows, I need you two to run. If any guards wake up, I'll handle them."

"Are you really going to stay here?" Rachel asked.

"Only until I know y'all are out." Johnson smiled. "Then I'm getting the hell out of here myself. He ain't gone catch me slippin'."

Rachel stifled her laugh and turned back to the main hall. Johnson watched as the women walked quickly through the streets. He looked at his watch it was almost midnight.

Hannah snuck through the halls, and into the attic. There was a laundry chute that led to the backstage room. She crawled into the chute and covered her mouth as she fell 5 floors down. She landed in a laundry hamper and sighed, grateful to be unharmed. She exited onto the stage and into Hellim's room. She crept quietly to his bed, switched on his lamp, and sat beside him.

"Hellim?" she whispered.

He continued to sleep.

"Hellim," she said louder.

Hellim opened his eyes and looked at her. "What is it? This better be important."

"It is," she said, bashfully. "Right now, the others are escaping."

"What?" he said, sitting up.

"Everything up until now was a ploy to distract you. If you don't believe me, check out the letter Johnson gave you and this one." She handed him the original letter Bianca sent. "You can see the difference in the handwriting, right? It looks like the same letter but you can see where Sasha messed up. See?"

Hellim studied the note, seeing every mistake Sasha made. He ripped the letters to shred. "How dare they!"

"It's because they're scared!" Hannah said. "They don't know what to do."

"And why are you telling me this?" Hellim asked, glaring at her.

"Because I love you, and I don't think it's fair to lie to you." Tears flowed from her eyes. "I couldn't leave without saying goodbye, and I didn't want you to think I betrayed you."

"I appreciate you telling me this," he said. He got out of bed and headed to the door.

"Where are you going?' she asked.

"To deal with liars," he grimaced.

"Wait!" she shouted. "You're not going to harm them, are you?"

Hellim turned to her and said, "I don't like liars, and I especially don't like people who think they can pull a fast one on me. Hannah, you're the only one that will survive tonight, thanks to your honesty. However, the others cannot be forgiven."

Hannah felt nauseous. "But!"

Before she could protest longer, Hellim slammed the door shut. Hannah ran after him, she was too frightened to speak, she hoped the others were long gone.

Rachel tapped her foot impatiently. She glanced at the clock on the wall, 12:10. "Hannah, come on. I don't want to leave you."

Johnson told Rachel to leave 10 minutes ago, but she believed Hannah was coming. She didn't want to risk her being alone, nor having to travel alone herself. She looked out the door. Sasha and Serenity still hadn't made it to the gate. If she didn't come in 5 minutes, she would run to catch up with them, or at least the slowest pair. Rachel heard a door slam behind her and she looked inside. She felt like her heart had stopped. Hellim emerged from the main room, Hannah trailing behind him with her hands clasped in front of her, fear in her eyes.

Rachel exhaled. "Hannah… you didn't…"

She spun to the door as fast as she could and yelled, "Helli—"

Before Rachel could finish his name, Hellim shot water from his hand, formed like a gun. The water was powerful and pierced Rachel in the head. She fell to the ground as everyone turned around.

Johnson's eyes widened as he saw her lifeless body on the ground. He turned to the stunned women and shouted, "Run!!"

Hellim pulled out a high-tech whistle, it was metal with a blue light on the tips. He blew it and his soldiers sprang to action. They came from the buildings in droves, shooting everyone in sight. The women ran franticly, covering their heads as they ran through the remnant alleys and streets.

Johnson opened his mouth as the barrel of a gun came out. A large laser shot through the street taking out 20 soldiers. He retracted it, and grabbed the light machine gun. He shot as many soldiers as he could. Each one shrieking as they fell to the ground. Johnson was focused on gunning them down when he heard a creak behind him. Hellim swung at him and Johnson blocked, flying into a building.

He stepped out of the broken wall, the skin on the right side of his face was ripped off revealing his mechanical face. He knew he didn't stand a chance against Hellim, but he was going to do his best to save time and the women. He glared at Hellim. Out of the corner of his vision, he saw Hannah peek around the corner of the door.

Rage possessed Johnson and he shouted, "How could you Hannah! Their deaths are on your hands. Never forget that you're the reason the women you considered your sisters are dead!"

"She isn't at fault for anything," Hellim said. "You should have agreed to my offer. Their deaths are your fault."

Johnson didn't respond, he knew Hannah enough to know she would continue to think about this night forever, his words were enough to make sure of it.

Hellim and Johnson stared at each other. Hellim made the first move, attempting to use his water pistol again. Johnson brought up his left arm and a shield materialized from his arm. The force of the water slid him back 2 feet. Before Johnson could counter, Hellim lunged at him, and punched the shield over and over with immense strength.

"Come on Johnson," he shouted. "This all you got?! You've been nothing but a coward! I've wanted to kill your ass for years."

"Yeah?" Johnson responded, wincing with each strike. "What a coincidence."

"You don't stand a chance against me," Hellim said. "Just give up and die."

Johnson clicked a button on his left arm with his right and a p-90 came out of his back and aimed at Hellim. Hellim dodged backwards as the gun shot at him. He hardened himself with Parahae's full body shield and crossed his arms over his face. The bullets hit his arms, torso, and nicked his face. When Johnson ran out of bullets and was reloading his p-90, Hellim lowered his arms. Blood spilled from two cuts on his face.

"That'll be the only scratches you'll get," Hellim snarled.

He attacked Johnson full force. Johnson tried to raise his shield, but Hellim grabbed his left arm and ripped it off. The p-90 reloaded itself and rose to the top of Johnson's head. Hellim snatched it off the rod attached to Johnson and threw it. Johnson swung with his right arm, punching Hellim in the gut. He stomped Hellim's foot and punched him again, uppercutting him. Hellim reached down to grab Johnson's head and he ducked, hopped backwards, and gained himself distance.

Johnson knew the fight wouldn't go his way, but to think it was that unfair. Johnson gazed around the town, staring at the women's dead bodies. His heart sank, he'd failed his promise.

Catching on to his heartbreak, Hellim smiled. "You did all this only for them to die! Just accept the loss and face your death like a man."

There was no point in continuing to fight. There was no one left to protect. Johnson closed his eyes. He would be damned to let Hellim finish him off.

"Not one woman survived," Hellim gloated. He raised his arms as he approached Johnson slowly. "You can die knowing you're a failure."

Johnson chuckled. "That's where you're wrong. I may not've saved these women, but two of my employees did survive. You'll never have Bianca you clown."

Hellim scowled and ran towards Johnson. "Die you piece of trash!"

Johnson smirked as he initiated his self-destruct. His eyes and mouth lit up a blue light, and a high pitched sound whirled from inside him. *I'm sorry I couldn't be more supportive of you. Good luck Bianca, I hope you enjoy your freedom. Protect her with your life Jae.*

Johnson's body exploded, catching Hellim off guard. He dove towards Hannah to protect her from the explosion. He created a cocoon and hugged Hannah, using Parahae's body shield again.

After a few minutes, the cocoon collapsed. Hellim let go of Hannah and looked around. The blast had only taken out a small part of Lyour, including the bordello. His soldiers at the end of the town advanced towards them.

Hellim scoffed. "He couldn't even take out one person with that weak explosion. Let's move out."

Hellim and his soldiers marched away. Hellim's anger intensified as he thought about where Bianca was. He wasn't going to let her get away. If he had to destroy everything in his path to find her, he would do it. And the prick who let her escape would be tortured and hung for the rest of humanity to remember to never cross him again.

"W-wait!" Hannah shouted, running after Hellim. "What am I supposed to do now? I have nowhere to go."

Hellim glanced back at her. "Come, I might have some use for you."

Hannah slowly walked behind Hellim. She tried her best not to look at her fallen friends. She closed her eyes and grabbed onto the back of Hellim's clothes so she wouldn't separate from him.

They boarded his ship and left Lyour.

The gods' Powers

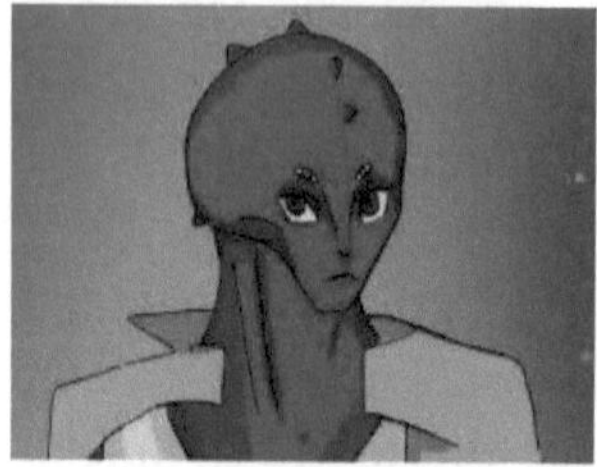

Hellim
Copycat: Unknown

Yulogna
| Sensibility: Blossom: Emotion |

Jtrepo
Weather

Gravick
Water: Healer: Unknown |

Hrayrp
Psychokinesis: Super Strength |

Malarik
Fragmentation: Curse:
Unknown

Kwtamg
Water Wielder |

Myetorp
Fire: Super Speed |

Parahae
Earth: Shield

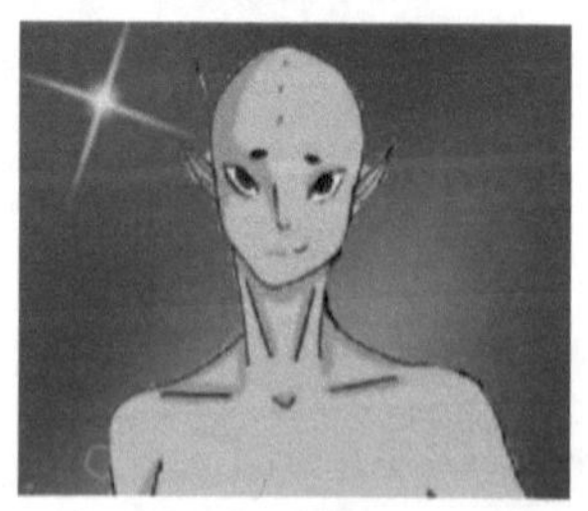

Lyour
Sand Wielder: Wind: Unknown

Afterwards

Oh man, I'm so happy I finished this story! This is another book I started in 2018, just a few months after I began writing *A Life: Worth Living*.

Would you believe it if I told you the inspiration from this story came from two completely random things? A BTS album and a video game called *Kingdom Hearts II.8: Dream Drop Distance*. If you know who BTS is and/or you know the video game series, you're probably confused about how this story could even relate to it…. Me too. Haha.

BTS had just released *Love Yourself: Tear* and I was in love with that album. I played the songs on repeat for hours, especially the song *The Truth Untold*. I had also just recently gotten *K.H. HD II.8* and was playing that on my PS4. It's a little embarrassing, but while I was playing in the final world, *The Truth Untold* playing in the background on repeat, my imagination went wild. I can't go into full details, because I imagined the final scene of this story. While I played the game, I kept replaying the scene in my head and decided I wanted to make a story out of it. (I'll explain more about that in the final book…. Maybe…) The end of the story was the first thing I wrote, while listening to The Truth Untold on repeat. Whenever I needed to get into the mindset or mood to write this book, I always listened to the *Love Yourself: Tear* album on repeat. So thanks to BTS and Square Enix (and all of the developers of K.H) for existing and being awesome!

Everlasting, Us developed into something way more than I originally planned, and way more complex. I hope you liked it. I'm genuinely curious as to who you think is at fault for the world being destroyed. Is it Jae's fault? Considering he was in Yurtpo (a disease among Trwqoyians that caused insanity then death) would he really be at fault? Or was it Hellim, Gravick and Malarik's fault? But then again, they were grieving and acting on their emotions. Or both? Was it right for the gods to kill humans because they were going extinct? Did Jae force them to kill 6.3 billion people? Or is it never justifiable?

Let me know what you think!

See you in Book Two!

About the Author

A.J. Hughes is the author of *Walk on the Other Side, A Day of Rain,* and *A Life: Worth Living.*

A.J. Hughes lives in Madison, WI. with her adorable cats Fatty, Oreo, and Anakin. She loves to read Manga. Her passions are music, writing, learning languages, and art. Her hope is to create amazing novels for readers all over the world to enjoy.

Follow her twitter @AJHughesAuthor, Instagram and Facebook Page A.J.HughesAuthor, and TikTok @a.j.hughesauthor for updates on her other books and novels to come.